NOTHING BUT THE TRUTH

Charles Holborne Legal Thrillers Book Eight

Simon Michael

SAPERE
BOOKS

NOTHING BUT
THE TRUTH

Published by Sapere Books.

24 Trafalgar Road, Ilkley, England, LS29 8HH

saperebooks.com

ISBN: 978-1-80055-805-2

ACKNOWLEDGEMENTS

I continue to owe a great debt to John Pearson for his two books, *The Profession of Violence: The Rise and Fall of the Kray Twins* and *Notorious: The Immortal Legend of the Kray Twins*. I recommend both to readers keen to learn more of the Krays' story, and I thank Mr Pearson for his painstaking research, from which I have shamelessly borrowed. Similarly, I have relied on *Nipper Read: The Man Who Nicked the Krays*, written by Leonard "Nipper" Read himself, with James Morton.

I must also thank Sir Ivan Lawrence QC for his kindness and the details contained in his very readable memoir *My Life of Crime*. As stated above, he was junior counsel for Ronnie Kray, and the details in the relevant chapters were very helpful to this fictionalised account of the trial.

I owe a particular debt to Elaine Ibbotson in respect of this book, for it was she who suggested the key plot device (no spoilers here in case you have opened the wrong end of the book first!). My thanks also go to Mike Gratton, formerly a criminal solicitor at Morgan and Lamplugh in Hastings and who, incidentally, sent me my first murder case, for his knowledge of the town in the 1960s.

As always I have to thank my beta readers for their thoughts, corrections and eagle-eyed attention to detail, including Neil Cameron, Debbie Jacobs, Carly Jordan, Steve Witt and Karen Crawford. The opinion of these last two, both Americans, on the very English matters related herein, was particularly useful.

Finally, a thank you to all at Sapere Books who have been on this journey with me for the last eight books.

PART ONE

CHAPTER ONE

Charles Holborne weaves his way up the steps of the court building, dodging accused men (and a few women), witnesses, police officers, solicitors and a few bewigged and gowned barristers. He thoroughly dislikes the seventeenth-century garb he and his learned friends are required to wear. It makes them look like a waddle of stuffed penguins. In the fashion battle between the 1960s and the 1660s, Charles knows which he prefers, but he is in the minority; most of his colleagues love the black gowns, horsehair wigs, bands and starched winged collars.

He pushes his way into the cramped entrance hall of Thameside Assizes.

The crumbling building is always busy, but Charles has never seen anything like this. All the usual multitude is crammed into less than half the usual space. Several of the courts opening off the central hall are closed, their doors taped shut. Charles sees the cause immediately. A pond has formed on the marble floor in one corner of the hall and is being augmented by a steady film of dirty water that ripples down the green Victorian wall tiles from somewhere above. Scaffolding is being erected, and men in hard hats splash urgently through the water, elbowing groups of barristers out of their way. A man wearing a suit and Wellington boots unfurls a blueprint and shouts to make his voice heard to a tight circle of construction workers.

'What on earth's going on?' asks Charles of a black-gowned usher.

The usher turns.

'Oh, hello Mr Holborne, sir. Haven't seen you in a while. It's the roof. It's been leaking for years, but last night's storms ripped off a load of the lead and now the whole river side of the building's inundated. We're down to two courts.'

'You can't work like this, surely?' says Charles, looking around.

The usher shrugs. 'It was too late to cancel today's lists. The Old Bailey's using us as an overflow court, till we close for renovations later this year. What can I do you for?'

Charles leans over the man's shoulder to examine the court list clipped to his board. 'There,' he says, pointing at an entry. 'First on. The Queen versus Gandapur. I'm for the Defence. Is it going ahead, bearing in mind all this?'

'Far as I know,' says the usher, writing Charles's name above that of the defendant. 'I've not seen anyone else in your case yet, but it's such a scrum in here, they could be anywhere.'

'Thanks. I'll scout round.'

Charles moves off, shouldering his way through the tightly packed hall, and feeling his toes becoming wet as water seeps into his expensive leather shoes. He casts about for someone who might be his client but, seeing no likely suspects, he comes to a halt, draws a deep breath and calls loudly.

'Mr Gandapur? Bazir Gandapur?'

The noise levels drop suddenly as everyone looks for the source of the stentorian voice but no answer comes. The clamour resumes almost immediately and Charles heads back outside to the court steps.

A young Asian man in a suit is just reaching the top of the staircase. He is followed by someone who might be his mother, an older woman dressed traditionally in Peshawari shalwar that descends to her ankles.

'Were you calling me?' asks the young man.

'Mr Gandapur?'

The young man gives a nod. He is in his late teens and has large, attractive dark eyes surrounded by thick lashes, a flop of Brylcreemed hair and an anxious expression.

'I'm the barrister Mr Dewar has instructed to represent you. My name's Holborne.'

'You're a brief?' asks Gandapur, surprised.

Charles smiles gingerly.

Even at his best he looks more like the criminals he represents than a refined member of the Bar. Charles is built like an ox, with wayward dark curls, an olive complexion and a trace of a Cockney accent, especially when riled. To many East End criminals he remains "Charlie Horowitz", a name he has tried to avoid for two decades. To others, members of the boxing fraternity, he is still the *"Yiddisher brick shithouse"* — an ex-boxer with a past sufficiently chequered to make him one of their own.

Today, however, he looks even more of a blackguard than usual, sporting a split lower lip, a healing cut on his eyebrow and a black eye.

'Despite appearances to the contrary,' he says, 'I am indeed a member of the Honourable Society of the Middle Temple.'

The young man looks puzzled.

'A barrister,' explains Charles. 'Don't worry about this,' he says pointing to his own face. 'I had an accident.'

'Accident?'

'I was careless and ran into a surprisingly good combination from a former heavyweight who rejoices in the name "Masher Murray". Should've moved faster. Anyway, have you seen anything of Mr Dewar?'

Gandapur shakes his head. 'He said 'e was gonna be late.' Although Gandapur obviously has east Asian heritage he speaks like an East Ender. 'Apparently, 'e's got another case on.'

'Did he mention a handwriting expert?' asks Charles.

Gandapur shakes his head.

'I see,' says Charles, pursing his lips in frustration. 'And this lady is … your mother?'

'Yeah. But she don't speak no English.'

Charles nods politely at the woman and looks round for somewhere quieter to speak. The staircase is almost as packed as the court building itself.

'Follow me,' he says, descending the stairs and crossing the road to the quieter pavement outside St Paul's Church. Gandapur and his mother follow.

Charles pulls the bow of the pink ribbon on his brief and juggles until he finds the document he's looking for. He shows it to Gandapur.

'You've seen this letter?' The young man looks briefly and nods. 'My instructions say you didn't write it. Is that right?' He nods again. 'Any idea who did?'

'I dunno.'

Charles leafs through his papers again and locates another document. 'It says here that you and the complainant, Mr Rosenberg, are friends.'

'We were. I've worked next to that *mamzer* since I was nine.'

'You speak Yiddish?' asks Charles in surprise.

'We've a stall in Petticoat Lane. Leather goods. They sell *schmutter* right next to us. There they are,' he says, pointing across the road.

A slim and well-dressed young man in his late teens or early twenties is walking up the steps to the court building accompanied by an older couple. They enter the building.

'His parents?' asks Charles.

'Yes.'

'As a matter of interest, where's your father?'

Gandapur looks at his feet. 'He wouldn't come. He's ... ashamed of me.'

'I see. Look, I have to ask you this, Mr Gandapur: are you ... is there... *was* there anything more than friendship between you and Mr Rosenberg?'

Gandapur doesn't look up as he answers. 'No.'

'Because you do understand the meaning of this letter, don't you?' says Charles, waving the document in his hand.

'I didn't write it.'

'Yes, you said. But I'm still asking if there's anything more to your friendship.' Gandapur doesn't answer. 'Do you have a girlfriend?'

'No. Me parents are arranging a marriage to a girl from back home.'

'It says here you've no witnesses to call on your behalf.'

'No.'

'Not even a member of your family? Someone who could tell the jury that you're not ... the sort of person to have written such a letter?'

Gandapur shrugs but makes no answer.

'Listen,' insists Charles. 'This is serious. If the jury believe Mr Rosenberg and decide you *did* write it, you're going to prison. Two years I'd guess. It's called attempting to procure an act of gross indecency.'

Gandapur lifts his eyes to look into Charles's. 'I didn't write that letter. And I don't feel ... like that about him. About any man.'

Something about the lad's emphasis strikes Charles.

'What about him?' No answer. 'You've been friends since you were kids. Has he ever said anything, done anything, to suggest he's homosexual?'

Gandapur shrugs again, evasive.

'What does that mean?' asks Charles, frustrated. 'Mr Gandapur — Bazir — you need to help me here! We're first on; the case'll be called any second. Without handwriting evidence, by lunchtime you'll be on your way to prison! I don't understand you; is this loyalty? Even now?'

Charles looks up to see the usher waving at him urgently from across the road.

'Shit,' he mutters, 'we're out of time. Come on.'

He leads the way back across the road into the court building.

By the time Charles has robed and he and his client have found their way into the courtroom, everyone else is waiting for them.

It is an imposing space, tall, wood panelled, with the judge sitting high above the fray under a wooden pediment and the royal arms, but it's shabby and badly in need of repair. Charles's eyes are drawn to the once brightly coloured figures making up the coat of arms; both the lion rampant and the Scottish unicorn are mildewed and the gilded inscription underneath, *Dieu et mon droit*, seems to have lost its attachment and hangs at an odd angle. The room smells of damp and decay.

English justice looks unimpressively tatty today, thinks Charles.

Charles delivers his client into the custody of the dock officer and sidles into the barristers' bench, nodding at his opponent, an elderly prosecution barrister named Adams whom he knows slightly.

'How nice of you to join us Mr Holborne,' says the judge dryly.

Charles doesn't know the judge and treads carefully in his response.

'I apologise if I've delayed the court, your Honour. It was so busy outside we went across the road to have a conference and I didn't hear the case being called.'

'Well, let's get on. The list is heavy, as you've probably seen. Are you ready for your client to be arraigned?'

Charles looks around the court, seeking his instructing solicitor.

'Yes, your Honour.'

Charles only gives half of his attention to his client being formally identified and pleading not guilty. He examines the members of the jury in waiting, deciding if he should object to any of them, but is happy enough when the first twelve called include six men and six women, at least half of them his age or younger. Neither he nor the prosecution barrister exercise any of their challenges. Charles is still looking behind him in vain for the arrival of his instructing solicitor when, after a mere fifteen minutes, the prosecutor completes his opening speech and the court clerk calls the first witness.

'Benjamin Rosenberg!'

The door opens and the young man whom Charles spotted outside enters court. He is escorted to the witness box where an usher awaits him, a Bible in one hand and some laminated cards in the other.

'Silence in Court,' shouts the usher. She addresses Rosenberg. 'Will you swear or affirm?'

'I'll swear,' says the young man in a soft voice.

'Jewish?' asks the usher.

He nods. She hands Rosenberg the Old Testament. Voices can be heard from the back of the court and the usher looks up.

'Silence in Court!' she repeats.

She hands a laminated card to Rosenberg. 'Take the Bible in your right hand and read the words on the card.'

'I swear, by Almighty God, that the evidence I shall give shall be the truth, the whole truth and nothing but the truth.'

Charles studies Rosenberg intently. The oath finished, the usher takes the Bible and the card and replaces them on her desk. Charles's eyes follow the usher's actions, and widen in surprise. He frowns, thinks for a moment, and then turns slowly, scanning the court for Rosenberg's parents. They sit at the back of the public gallery, overdressed, looking slightly daunted by their surroundings, but Charles notes that from under hooded lids, Mrs Rosenberg's eyes are riveted on Bazir Gandapur with startling vindictiveness.

'Mr Holborne!'

Charles stands hurriedly and switches his attention forward. 'Yes, your Honour?'

'I was addressing you. Does the Defence concede that the actions described in the letter referred to by Mr Adams in opening would, if committed, constitute an act of gross indecency with another man?'

'Yes, your Honour.'

'So the only issue for this jury is whether or not the accused sent the letter to the complainant?'

'Yes.'

'In the circumstances I do not intend putting the letter, and the disgusting actions described in it, before the jury. Are you content with that course?'

'I am, your Honour.'

'Then you can proceed, Mr Adams.'

Charles resumes his seat. Adams stands, shifts his gown back onto his shoulders and adjusts his *pince-nez* over which he peers at the witness.

'You are Mr Benjamin Rosenberg of two hundred and thirty-four Mile End Road, East London, is that right?'

'Yes,' replies the witness quietly, looking down at the bench before him.

'Keep your voice up please, Mr Rosenberg. Do you know the man standing in the dock?'

'Yes.'

'How?'

'We were friends. We worked next to each other at the Lane. Petticoat Lane Market.'

'And have you ever seen this document before?' says the old barrister, handing a document to the usher who walks it to Rosenberg in the witness box. Rosenberg glances at it briefly and looks up.

'Yes. It was on my stall when I went to set up one day last June.'

'Did you see how it got there?'

'No, but Baz was the only person around. It was early. We used to set up and then go for breakfast together, before the punters arrived. And he was looking at me.'

'Looking at you?'

'Yeah. In a funny way. Staring. Like he was waiting to see how I'd react.'

'When you found the letter on your stall, what did you do?'

'I opened it and read it. I was shocked. Disgusted. I never knew he was one of them, you know … a poof.'

'Did you recognise his writing?'

'No. He'd signed it "Baz" but I'd never seen him write nothing longer'n a price ticket before.'

'What did you do then?'

'I didn't know what to do. I never said nothing. Just took it home that night and showed me mum.'

Charles turns to see Mrs Rosenberg's eyes flick from her son in the witness box to the boy in the dock and then back again. Rosenberg continues to speak.

'She was shocked too. She said I had to take it to the police.'

'Did you ever speak to the accused about it?' asks Adams.

'No. Mum said to keep clear of him from then on, so I did.'

'Yes,' says the barrister, leafing briefly through his papers. 'Yes, thank you. Please remain there.'

Adams sits.

Charles stands and allows the court to fall completely silent before he speaks. The jury members lean forward slightly in anticipation of his first question. It takes everyone by surprise.

'Do you usually do what your mum says?'

'What do you mean?' asks Rosenberg.

'It's a simple question, Mr Rosenberg. Do you usually do what your mum says?'

Rosenberg shrugs, a gentle smile on his lips. The expression makes him look even younger than his years.

'S'pose so,' he says.

'Does she ever work on the stall?'

'We all do. It's a family business.'

'But not that morning?'

'No.'

'So it was definitely you who found the letter?'

'Yes.'

Charles points to the card bearing the oath on the usher's desk, and addresses the usher. 'Please can you hand that card back to the witness?'

The usher looks to the judge for confirmation, and he nods.

'That's the one from which Mr Rosenberg read the oath, yes?' asks Charles.

'It is, your Honour,' replies the usher to the judge.

She walks back across the well of the court and hands the card back to the witness.

'Can you read the words again from the card?' asks Charles.

'Sure. I swear by Almighty God that the evidence I shall give shall be the truth, the whole truth, and nothing but the truth.' Rosenberg's voice is bored.

'Thank you. Now please return the card to the usher. Usher, would *you* please read aloud the words on the card that Mr Rosenberg has just handed you.'

The judge again nods permission to the usher.

'"I" — then there's a blank for the name — "do solemnly, sincerely and truly declare and affirm…"'. She falters, her voice grinding to a halt. She turns to the judge. 'I'm really sorry, your Honour, I must have given him the wrong card. There was a disturbance at the back of the court and I must have been distracted.'

'Your point, Mr Holborne?' challenges the judge. 'I shall ask the witness to read the oath again, this time from the correct card.'

'I'm afraid your Honour misses the point. Mr Rosenberg was given the affirmation card but what he "read" was the oath. Entirely different words.' Charles turns again to the usher. 'Usher, please hand Mr Rosenberg the New Testament. It's there, on your desk.' The usher complies. 'Now, Mr Rosenberg,' continues Charles, 'please open the Bible. I'd like you to turn to the first page, that's the first page with writing all down it in two columns.'

'Yes.'

'Now I'd like you to read to us the first few lines.'

There is a pause before Rosenberg answers. He looks up, first at the judge and then at the back row of the public galley. His face is suddenly pale.

'I can't see what this has got to do with anything,' he says, flustered.

'Just read it for us, please, Mr Rosenberg.'

Rosenberg looks down again at the book in his hand. His eyebrows contract into a frown and his face screws up in concentration. Head bowed, his forefinger traces each word at a snail's pace.

'In … the … the … be … begin … beginning … God…'

His face flushes a deep red. His voice falters and stops. He looks up.

'You can't read, can you Mr Rosenberg?' The young man does not answer. 'You weren't reading the oath off the card at all. You memorised it.'

Rosenberg's head remains bowed. 'I have trouble with me letters,' he eventually says quietly.

'When you told us you read the letter you found on your market stall that morning, you were lying, weren't you?' Rosenberg stares down at the witness box railing. 'You didn't read that letter, did you?' persists Charles. 'You couldn't have.'

Still the witness does not answer.

'Shall I ask the usher to give you the letter, Mr Rosenberg, so you can read it to us?'

Rosenberg finally shakes his head.

Tears form in his eyes, one dropping like a small diamond onto a hand as it rests on the edge of the witness box. He hurriedly wipes the hand on his trouser leg.

'And someone taught you the oath, didn't they?' continues Charles. 'So it would look like you were reading it.'

Charles swivels swiftly towards the back of the court and fixes a stare on Mrs Rosenberg. Everyone's eyes in the court follow Charles's. The woman juts her chin defiantly at him.

Still staring at Mrs Rosenberg, Charles continues: 'Did you really find that letter on your market stall that morning, Mr Rosenberg?'

He turns back to face the witness. The young man's face is wet with tears and he looks up to lock apologetic eyes with his friend in the dock. He shakes his head.

'And we know you couldn't have written it, don't we?' There is a long pause. 'Do you know who did?' asks Charles.

There is no answer.

'You mother didn't like you being friends with Mr Gandapur, did she?'

Again Rosenberg offers no answer, but he shakes his head.

Charles turns again to stare at Mrs Rosenberg who is now looking down into her lap.

'I have no further questions for this witness, thank you, your Honour,' concludes Charles, sitting. He looks across at the jury and notes with satisfaction that all of them are staring hard at Rosenberg's mother.

Half an hour later Charles is again standing on the busy steps leading into the court building, lighting a cigarette. His brief is neatly re-tied in its pink ribbon and is clamped under an arm. His red bag with his court robes rests by his feet. He can just see Gandapur and his mother, at the far end of the street, turning the corner towards the station.

A sweaty bearded man in his forties, arms laden with bundles of court documents, runs out of the court and down the steps towards Charles.

'Holborne? Charles Holborne?'

Charles turns. 'Yes?'

'Bill Dewar. I've been looking for you everywhere. Where's the client?'

'Gone,' says Charles, simply.

'Gone? Done a runner?'

'No,' explains Charles. 'He's on his way home.'

'Were we adjourned?' asks the solicitor, puzzled.

'No,' repeats Charles. 'The trial's finished.'

'What, already?' It takes Dewar a moment to understand what Charles is telling him. 'He was acquitted?'

'He was, and no thanks to you. No witness statements from his family, no handwriting expert, no pre-trial con. And you couldn't even be bothered to turn up. You're a fucking disgrace.'

The force of Charles's attack takes Dewar completely by surprise. Counsel are not supposed to speak to their solicitor clients like this. His face flushes and his eyes open wide.

'You can't talk to me like that,' he manages.

'I just did.'

'I'll report you to your head of chambers,' blusters Dewar.

'Be my guest. Let's see what the Law Society has to say about *your* performance, shall we? But for an enormous slice of luck, your negligence would have got that young man wrongly convicted.'

Charles grinds out his cigarette on the step, picks up his court robes and walks off, leaving the astonished Dewar to gape after him.

CHAPTER TWO

Charles thunders up the Dickensian oak staircase in the Temple, the professional home to most of England's barristers. As always, he takes the stairs two at a time, leaving little puffs of wood dust in his wake. He opens the door to the clerks' room to find it unusually peaceful.

'Where is everyone?' he asks of Barbara McIntyre, Chambers' senior clerk, as he strides to the pigeonholes. 'Another fire alarm?'

Barbara, deep in consideration of some documents on her desk, takes a moment to reply.

'Jeremy's bringing Mr Appleby's papers back from the Royal Court of Justice, Clive is at lunch and pretty much everyone else is in court. You're not usually here at this time of day, sir,' she says as she totals a column of figures.

Satisfied with her calculation, she lifts her head to regard the clock on the wall and focus on Charles properly.

'In fact, why *are* you here? Weren't you listed for two days?'

By way of answer Charles throws his brief onto her desk. Barbara cranes her neck to look at Charles's endorsement on the front.

'Acquitted,' she reads.

'With Defence costs.'

'Well done, sir. Mr Dewar must be pleased.'

'Mr Dewar is a joke, and should be struck off,' replies Charles, still angry.

Barbara's face falls. 'Oh, sir, what happened? More importantly, what did you *say*?'

Barbara likes Charles Holborne, which is something she cannot say of many of her guvnors. He's a team player — this case was a last-minute return which two other barristers refused — and he's a rainmaker. He's also very good with the pupils and junior members of Chambers. But, as he will cheerfully admit, he was behind the door when diplomacy skills were handed out. Despite the sophisticated accent and mannerisms, polished first in the RAF and then as a scholarship boy at Cambridge, the much more rough and ready Cockney underneath still has a tendency to break surface. She and the other clerks have had to smooth things over with solicitor clients more than once, and Holborne has a way of getting under the skin of some of the more senior, more traditional members of Chambers. Although, where Barbara would say "traditional", Charles would say arrogant, snobbish, anti-Semitic and class prejudiced. Given a drink or two, he'd add several earthier epithets too.

'He hung that boy out to dry.'

'He's not a man to upset, sir. He sends all his work to us, and he's always very busy.'

'Too busy to put forward a defence, it would seem. Anyway,' says Charles as he turns from the pigeonholes, skimming his post, 'I'd rather not work for him again.'

'Will you get the chance?' asks Barbara dryly.

'Probably not. What's this?'

Charles holds up a slip of paper.

'Ah, that. Well, an … interesting man called for you. He announced himself as "Duke." Not "Mr Duke" or "Duke" anything. Just "Duke." Although he pronounces it "Jook" and, if I'm any judge, he wasnae a member of the aristocracy.'

Charles laughs. 'What did he want?'

'I'm afraid I couldn't tell you. Perhaps it was some sort of Cockney code. The only thing I *did* gather was urgency. I do wish you'd remember Chambers' policy on private telephone calls, sir,' she says pointedly, her voice clipped.

Charles admires Barbara's ability to make her displeasure known merely by adjusting her Edinburgh accent. She's an expert at managing a diverse group of competing, privileged and entitled members of the Bar, all of whom consider her their intellectual and social inferior.

'He may be a little rough and ready,' says Charles with a twinkle, 'but you'd warm to Duke if you met him.'

'Hmm,' she replies doubtfully, bending her head to her task again.

'He's a hero — parachuted into the Caen Canal in the D-Day landings, in the first wave. He got a DCM for conspicuous bravery under fire, despite having broken both legs on landing.' Barbara looks up as Charles continues. 'He does a lot of charity work for disadvantaged kids. And he loves his mum.'

Barbara laughs, softening. 'Well, like I said, it's apparently urgent.'

'Okay, thanks.'

Charles runs up to the second floor corridor. He pushes open the door of his room with his foot and looks across at Peter Bateman's desk. Peter, formerly Charles's pupil at Chancery Court, is now Charles's closest friend at the Bar. They continue to share a room, but Bateman's still in court, the seat behind his desk almost completely obscured by the wall of documents on his desk awaiting his attention.

Charles drops his papers onto the frayed leather inlay of his desk and picks up the telephone. Once provided with an outside line, he dials the familiar number. The receiver at the other end is picked up almost immediately.

'Kennington Institute,' comes a gravelly Cockney voice.

'Duke, it's Charlie,' says Charles. 'What's up?'

'Thanks for gettin' back to me. I wouldn't usually ring you at work, but I need a favour.'

'What's that?' asks Charles, absently opening some new instructions on a murder brief.

'Trev was s'posed to be taking the Under Tens, but he can't make it.'

'Drunk again?'

'Yup. 'E was nicked after some fracas in the boozer. An' 'e can't get bail 'til 'e's sober.'

'Sorry, Duke, but I can't this evening. I'm flat out here, and I've got to leave early.'

'It ain't evening, it's this afternoon at four, an' it's only an hour. And you know 'ow much the lads like you. A couple have arrived already. Go on, Charlie, help me out, will you?'

When Charles retired from competitive boxing just before his fortieth birthday he toyed with the idea of giving up the sport altogether. He'd been a member of the boxing club since a boy and many of his friends were involved in the sport. On the other hand Sally was tired of him coming home with split eyebrows and bloody noses — in other words, looking as he does right now — and he had to admit that the injuries only served to perpetuate the gossip in the Temple that he was a thug. Perhaps, he thought, it was time to find an alternative method of keeping fit.

Then he was asked to take a group of youngsters and teach them some basics. Rather to his surprise, he discovered he was a good teacher. His classes became very popular; whenever Charles's name appeared on the schedules pinned to the grubby noticeboard, they filled up in hours. Despite his expensive suits and West End lifestyle, Charles remains an East

Ender at heart. He's a Mile End boy, born and bred. He lived rough on the streets during the Blitz, worked as a lighterman on the Thames, and still counts some of the more dubious denizens of the area as his friends. Despite having gotten posh, he is still "one of them" and, particularly within the boxing fraternity, Charles Holborne, born Charlie Horowitz, is something of a celebrity. To the youngsters, he is a hero.

'One hour, you say?' says Charles, checking his watch.

'On me life.'

Charles considers. 'All right. On my way.'

Charles walks up and down the line of youngsters practising their shuffles backwards and forwards and to left and right. To guide them in their foot movement he has drawn a large chalk cross on the floor in front of each of them. He pauses beside one sparrow-chested seven-year-old wearing his older brother's vest.

'Stop a second, Billy. Are you orthodox or south paw?' The child stops moving and frowns. 'Right-handed or left-handed?' clarifies Charles.

'I write wiv me right, but I bat wiv me left,' explains the boy.

'Okay, but which one do you punch with?'

'This one,' says Billy, holding up a fist.

'Okay then,' says Charles bending down to reposition the boy's feet. 'Remember the rhythm I gave you? One-two … one-two… So start with this foot —' he drags the boy's front foot forward — 'and follow immediately with that one. Good, that's it. Keep it going. One-two … one-two … one-two … now reverse it … Yes! Well done. You've got it.'

Charles continues down the line, correcting and encouraging as he goes.

'Bend your knees, Stewart … better. You trying to do the splits, Barney? Keep your feet the same width as your shoulders!'

The door opens and Duke's flattened nose and cauliflower ears appear. He signals to Charles by tapping his wrist. Charles waves in acknowledgement.

'Okay gentlemen, that'll be enough for this afternoon,' says Charles to the class. 'Off you go and get changed. Remember, you can practice this at home. Try it to music if it helps. It's important to get the rhythm. But don't go drawing crosses on your mum's lino without permission.'

The class breaks up. Charles can see through the doors that one or two parents are already waiting in the corridor. Two boys come up to Charles with extracts cut from newspapers showing Charles's photograph, seeking his autograph. He's tried telling them he's not famous, but they're not having it. "Mr H" is in the papers, defending murderers; *of course* he's famous. So Charles scribbles something with the proffered pens and the boys scamper off happily.

Charles looks up as two men enter the room. His heart rate instantly accelerates. He knows both of them. The larger, a six foot Glaswegian oval of fat and aggression, is named "Big Pat" Connolly. Charles has particular history with Connolly. The other is "Scotch Jack" Dixon, smaller, neater, and if anything more dangerous. While Connolly relies on his size for the purposes of intimidation, Dixon is reputed to carry a gun at all times. Both are employed by Ronnie and Reggie Kray, London's celebrity gangsters, and are trusted members of their "Firm". One of the Kray twins' tactics is to move their muscle around from city to city so that whenever the police arrive, like Macavity, they were never there. Charles expects that, by way of exchange, a couple of Cockney heavies are now adjusting to a sojourn in Glasgow.

The men approach without speaking, their shoes squeaking softly. Charles tries to judge their demeanour. Both appear relaxed but little weight can be placed on that. He knows Dixon only by sight, but Connolly on the other hand can slip into violence for no other reason than someone blinks at him aggressively. If it comes to a fight, Charles hasn't a chance. He's taken off his jacket and tie but otherwise is still dressed for court, and his leather-soled shoes have little grip on the polished floor.

The door opens again behind them and Duke appears. The old trainer's fighting days are well behind him but Charles is relieved at least to have a witness in the room. Charles doesn't know if it's the noise of the door but the two gangsters come to a halt a couple of yards from him.

'All okay, Charlie?' calls Duke from behind the men.

'I don't know yet.' He addresses Connolly. 'Are we all right, Pat?'

'That's up to you. You need to come with us.'

'Why do I need to do that?'

'Ronnie and Reggie want a word.'

Charles looks at the clock above the men's heads. 'I can't,' he says simply.

'No such thing as "can't",' says Dixon softly, smiling dangerously.

'No, boys, I'm serious. I've got to be somewhere else and I should've left already. It's important. Tell them I'm happy to talk to them, but not tonight.'

'We were told to bring you.'

'I'm sure you were. But tell Ronnie and Reggie that I'll pop by the Regal tomorrow — or any other time they like — but I really can't do it tonight.'

'Look, Horowitz,' starts Connolly menacingly, taking another step towards Charles, 'you're a big bloke, but there's two of us. Don't make this difficult.'

'I'm not trying to make anything difficult. I've genuinely got an important appointment that I can't change. I'm not refusing, I'm just saying, not right now. I'm not in the Firm and I don't keep my diary free on the off-chance that Ronnie Kray wants tea with me. Okay?'

'We can make you,' says Dixon.

'Maybe. But I'm not going to cooperate, so we'll all end up bloody and bruised, your lovely suits'll be ruined, and I'll miss my appointment. And in addition to Duke there, there's at least half a dozen other boxers in the changing rooms. On the other hand, as I've said, I'll come willingly tomorrow.'

While Connolly and Dixon regard one another for a moment Charles hooks off his shoes and socks and steps back into his fighting stance.

'So, what's it to be?' he asks.

Connolly pulls an undecided face and Dixon shrugs.

'Tomorrow, you say?' asks Dixon.

'Any time.'

Dixon makes an executive decision. 'Come at ten.'

'Morning or night?'

'Ten pm.'

'I'll be there.'

Getting across London from Kennington to Gower Street during rush-hour is a nightmare, and Charles soon realises that he is going to be late, which means he's going to be in trouble.

He runs through the doors of University College Hospital, strides to the reception counter and almost shouts for directions to the Antenatal Clinic.

Before the nurse can answer, he hears his name called.

'Charlie. Forget it.'

He turns towards the voice. Sally is sitting on a bench a few feet away. Charles walks swiftly over and sits next to her.

'I'm so, so sorry!' he says earnestly.

'Forget it,' she repeats. 'You wouldn't have been allowed in anyway.'

'No?'

'A couple of other husbands came for their first appointments and were sent packing.'

She sounds miserable and angry, and Charles bends to look at her lovely face. Her eyes are filling with tears. For the last couple of months her emotions have been all over the place.

Sally Fisher, Charles's live-in girlfriend, is pretty, petite and an East Ender like him (good things), non-Jewish (bad — indeed, unforgiveable — in the eyes of Charles's parents), and pregnant (jury still out).

Charles reaches into his pocket, finds a clean handkerchief and offers it to Sally, who blows her nose noisily.

'You can't imagine how demeaning it was, Charlie. I'm glad you *weren't* there.'

'Why? What happened?'

'We were all lined up outside this, well, it looked like a caravan, in a yard at the back of the hospital. All sitting on long wooden benches clutching our bottles of urine. The nurse came in and barked at us to take off our underwear beneath the waist. So we all had to remove our knickers and tights. The poor girl in front of me was wearing trousers, so she had to strip off in front of all of us and put her trousers back on again. When she went in we could hear the doctor shouting at her for wasting his valuable time while she took them off again.'

'It sounds awful.'

'I won't even go into the examination. I'm telling you, Charlie, no one's going to be touching me down there for some time.'

Charles takes her hand tenderly. 'I think we should complain,' he says.

'No,' she replies, shaking her head firmly. 'They'll just mark my card as a troublemaker. I've got to come back.'

'But it oughtn't be like that. It's 1968, for Christ's sake.'

'It felt like 1868. They even showed us the instruments of torture.'

'What? Why?'

'So we all understood that everyone gets an episiotomy, whether they need it or not.'

'Jesus! When do you have to come back?'

'Next month. Only once, thank God, for a class. C'mon,' she says, standing. 'I need a drink.'

'There's a pub on the corner of Euston Road,' says Charles, taking her hand again and leading the way.

'Why were you late anyway?' asks Sally.

'I got held up,' he evades, and Sally, still replaying the humiliation of the last hour, doesn't think to cross-examine further.

CHAPTER THREE

Charles listens intently up the stairs. It's all quiet from the bedroom and he assumes that Sally is asleep. Maria, their jazz pianist lodger, is away on tour and they have the house to themselves.

They decided to grab a quick meal at a local restaurant rather than cook when they got home and, by the time they returned to Wren Street, it was almost nine o'clock. Sally was exhausted and went straight to bed, distractedly kissing the top of Charles's curly head as he settled to a couple of hours' work in his study.

Sally is ten weeks pregnant, tearful, exhausted and frequently nauseous, although the symptom that bothers her most is the constant metallic taste in her mouth, which puts her off cooking and eating. They have delayed telling their families; it's only a few months since she suffered two miscarriages in quick succession.

Charles pads downstairs to the garden room, part-kitchen and part-living room. He leaves the lights off, and picks up the telephone receiver. Even if awake, Sally is unlikely to hear him from the top floor.

He dials the number of West End Central Police Station, a number he knows by heart. While waiting for the line to connect, he stares out of the glass ceiling of the kitchen extension at the night sky. There is less light pollution in this part of the city, where a greater proportion of the buildings are still warehouses rather than shops, and the black sky above him is studded with stars.

The line is picked up at the police station.

'Is DS Sloane on duty?' he asks the station officer.

'I think so, sir. Who's calling?'

'Charles Holborne of counsel.'

'And the nature of your enquiry?'

'It's DS Sloane's enquiry, actually.'

'Just a moment, sir,' says the station officer, and there are several clicks on the line.

After a few moments the call is put through and Charles is greeted by Sloane's soft Irish accent.

'Charles,' he says. 'Are you well?'

'Hi Sean. I'm fine, thank you. And you?'

'Grand.'

'Still loving the job?'

'Very happy.'

Charles has known Sloane for several years. When still a green detective constable in the Buckinghamshire Constabulary, Sloane was part of the team investigating the murder of Charles's late wife, Henrietta. He was the only member of the team to keep an open mind and not leap to the conclusion that Charles was the killer, despite apparently damning evidence. They solved that case together, both suffering gunshot wounds in the process. It cemented a firm friendship.

'So, Charles, what can I do for you? Or is this a social call?'

'Not social, I'm afraid, though it would be nice if the four of us could get together soon.'

'What then?'

'I haven't worried Sally about it, but I had a visit today from two members of the Firm requesting forcefully that I make myself available for an interview with Ronnie and Reggie Kray.'

He hears Sloane sighing at the other end. 'They won't leave you alone, will they?'

'No. But I wondered if you had any idea what might have prompted this invitation.'

'Me?'

'Aren't you still part of Nipper Read's task force?' asks Charles.

Detective Superintendent Read had been tasked, secretly, by Assistant Commissioner Peter Brodie, to build a team to gather evidence sufficient to put the Krays away. Read only accepted the job on condition that he would be based outside Scotland Yard, which leaked like a sieve. He also demanded the right to choose his own team, men he could trust not to sell information to the Krays or the newspapers. Brodie agreed. Read was given space in Tintagel House, on the Albert Embankment, the far side of the Thames from Scotland Yard. He was also given a cover story; his team were supposedly conducting a high-level disciplinary enquiry into a major corruption allegation.

It was all to no avail. The truth leaked out, as it always did, and now Read and the Krays are playing a dangerous game of chess. As Read quietly approaches peripheral and ex-members of the Firm to enquire if they will give evidence against their former bosses in return for protection and immunity, the Krays are several steps ahead of him, threatening and bribing people into silence, putting them out of Read's reach.

'Now, you know I can't give you any information on that score,' says Sloane. 'Please don't put me in a difficult position.'

'I don't want operational details. But is something happening?'

'I can't tell you.'

'All I need to know is whether someone's been poking the hornet's nest.'

'I can't discuss it,' insists Sloane. 'All I can do is repeat what was released to the newspapers already. The Murder Squad detail board in Scotland Yard shows the boss's name against the enquiry into a murder in Ireland.'

'A new cover story?'

'Not as far as I know. Hear about the woman found on Dublin beach?'

'I read about it.'

'So it's a genuine case, and I can only assume that the boss's attention is elsewhere at present.'

'Okay, fair enough. Thank you.'

'No worries. How's your darling girl?' asks Sloane.

'Got a minor health issue at the minute, but she's fine,' says Charles.

'Have you proposed yet?'

Charles laughs. 'No, but we've an understanding.'

'An understanding, is it? Don't wait too long, Charles, or someone else'll snap her up. She's a keeper, that one.'

'Of course she is, but … it's not straightforward.'

'You think I don't know that? But if I can face down my Catholic mam, you can face down your Jewish one.'

Sloane, from staunchly Catholic farming stock, has recently announced his engagement to Dr Irenna Alexandrova, a prominent Jewish political refugee from South Africa's apartheid regime. He seems to have got away with it.

'Have you met my mother?' jokes Charles. 'She's Joe Stalin to your mother's Eleanor Roosevelt,' but there is someone else's voice in the background and Charles realises that Sloane is no longer listening.

'Sorry, mate, I have to go,' says the detective sergeant brusquely, and the line is broken.

Charles hangs up, disappointed. He had hoped that Sloane could explain the Krays' sudden interest in him. The Irishman was seconded to Detective Superintendent Read's team in 1966. At that time Read, known to everyone inside and outside the force as "Nipper" due to his diminutive size, was tasked with cleaning up the West End of London in advance of the World Cup Final. However, Sloane's incorruptibility and his personal loyalty to Read resulted in him being kept on for Read's next job: gathering intelligence and evidence aimed at taking down the Kray twins. After years of criminality, including several murders where it seemed that everyone in London except the juries trying their cases knew the Krays were responsible, there was, at last, the political will to end their reign of terror.

The authorities' inability to secure convictions, despite several attempts, had a simple explanation: the East End was terrified of the Krays. It had become commonplace for members of their own Firm to be stabbed, slashed or shot for actual or suspected "grassing", and members of the public, unlucky witnesses to the Krays' criminality, had been known to disappear. As a result, ever since the Cedra Court debacle, the Met had simply turned a blind eye to the Krays' activities. Too many careers had been dashed on those rocks; it was easier to focus on other crimes and less prominent criminals. Now, at last, Nipper Read and his team had accepted the challenge, and Charles needs them to succeed.

He looks at his watch. It's approaching ten. He considers for a moment and leaves his desk.

Ten minutes later Charles slips silently out of the house, jogs to Gray's Inn Road, and hails a taxi.

'Kentucky Club, please,' he says as he climbs in.

'Right you are, chum,' says the cabbie.

The taxi rattles through the deserted streets of Charles's past: Blooms kosher restaurant at Aldgate East, where his parents used to take him and David for long Sunday lunches; his old primary school, where he and David were regularly bullied, chased and robbed for the offence of being part of the wrong gang, namely, Jewish; British Street, the site of his childhood home before Hitler flattened it during the Blitz; lastly, Goldie's *spieler*, the illegal gambling den where, aged seven, he was sent regularly to fetch his great-uncles from wasting their spare time and cash on poker, pontoon and Jewish Faro.

By the time Charles left Cambridge University — by then the son-in-law of a speechlessly appalled viscount — and was called to the Bar by the Honourable Society of the Middle Temple, he fully expected these dingy streets to be consigned to an exotic past; the subject of racy anecdotes at dinner parties.

The years since have demonstrated otherwise. For reasons which long eluded him, he is forever being dragged back here. For a while he blamed his defence practice; too many of the people he used to call friends had become his criminal clients. He continues to blame Ronnie and Reggie Kray, those childhood acquaintances who have shadowed him for most of his adult life and who now hold powerful leverage over him. For the most part, he now thinks it is simpler than that; the East End of London is in his DNA. Fundamentally, for all his cut-glass English accent; his qualifications; his cultured interests in fine art and jazz; and his aristocratic Establishment friends, it is these streets, on which he grew up, which represent "home"; where, counter-intuitively, he feels safest.

The cab pulls up outside the Kentucky Club on Mile End Road. Charles gets out and digs into his pocket for the fare.

''Ere,' says the cabbie, 'ain't you Harry Horowitz's boy?'

Charles looks at the man's face for the first time. He frowns. 'You know my dad?'

'Course I do, son. It's Morris, his old partner!'

Charles leans forward, and does indeed recognise the old man. 'Good heavens! Uncle Morry,' he exclaims. 'What're you doing in a cab?'

Morris Freeman was Harry Horowitz's partner in the early days of his furrier's business, back in the 1920s. Charles thought he and his wife had emigrated years ago.

'I did the Knowledge,' says the old man, 'when I came back after Dot died.'

'Auntie Dot died? I'm so sorry to hear it.'

'Yeah, well, what can you do? Cancer. Anyway, both Susan and Andy had moved back, and I missed me grandkids so I thought, "Fuck it", 'n' sailed back too. Chingford, actually. I just do the odd night shift to add to me pension. Your parents all right, Charlie? Still with us?'

'So-so. Dad had a stroke a year or so back and Mum's memory's not what it was, but they're both still here. I'll tell them I saw you.'

'Do that.'

Charles hands over a pound note and waves away the change.

'Tell your dad he can contact me through the old *shul*, yeah?' says Morry.

Charles hesitates, but decides not to mention that his parents have both been in residential care for a year. 'Will do.'

'Hey, Charlie,' calls the cabbie as Charles makes to cross the pavement. 'Want me to wait? It can get a bit tasty up there.' He nods towards the lit windows on the first floor from which music and chatter can be heard.

'I know. That's why I'm here. No, you get off, Morry. But thanks.'

'Righto. Stay lucky, Charlie.'

Charles waves in reply, pushes open the pavement door and climbs the steps to the club. There is only one bouncer at the head of the stairs, a musclebound young man whom Charles does not recognise.

'Ronnie and Reggie want a word with me,' he says.

'They ain't here.'

'Right. Mind if I have a quick drink before I go?'

By way of answer the man stands aside and pulls back the heavy velvet curtain, allowing Charles to enter.

The Kentucky Club replaced the Krays' former drinking establishment, the Double "R", a few years earlier, and because it was largely Reggie's venture (Ronnie was in prison at the time) it is slightly more upmarket in that although the club remains a magnet for local lowlife, Reggie requires them to wear suits. The attendance of women is also encouraged, and the club offers occasional live music. Celebrities from the worlds of TV and sport like to boast of drinking here as they rub shoulders with the men of violence.

Charles stands on the threshold and scans the room. Two of the small round tables are occupied by people he recognises. He buys a drink and saunters over to the one furthest from the door. Two men are deep in conversation, their heads close to one another. Charles stands at a respectful distance until he is noticed. The men look up at him simultaneously.

'As I live and breathe, Charlie Horowitz,' says one, a tall man with a long head that is entirely bald. Even his fair eyebrows and lashes are so insubstantial as to be almost invisible. Joey the Nut.

'Hello, Nut. How's tricks?'

'Not bad, considering. What brings you back to the manor?'

'Just passing through.'

'Yeah? Well, wanna join us? You've got the look of a man with somefink to say.'

'I will, if I may.'

Charles draws up a chair from an adjoining table and joins the two men.

'This is Milky,' says Joey, introducing the man sitting opposite him, a little man with darting eyes and thin lips which seem to be twitching or speaking soundlessly.

'Milky,' says Charles, offering his hand. The twitching man knocks back the last of his drink and scurries off, straight through the velvet curtain and out of the bar. 'Something I said?' laughs Charles.

'Nah. 'E's a bit funny in the head. Useful bloke, though. So, Charlie, what's up?'

Charles looks around the bar. 'I was looking to catch Ron or Reg. Have you seen them?' he asks innocently.

Joey shakes his head. 'I ain't seen them all night. In fact, not for a bit.'

'It's odd, isn't it?'

'Wassat?'

'There's no one here from the Firm at all. I don't even recognise the bouncer. Have the boys taken everyone on a seaside outing or something?'

'No idea, mate. Got to go,' and before Charles can say another word he too has scurried off, leaving most of his drink intact.

Charles turns around and looks at the other table where he recognised an occupant, but the barmaid is clearing empty glasses and wiping the table down. He stands, knocks back the last of his scotch, and heads for the door.

He looks at his watch. They'll be calling last orders soon, but he probably has time to get to one or two other boozers before closing time.

He heads west, but with no greater success. Even at *The Grave Maurice* in Whitechapel Road there's been no sign of the Krays or any members of the Firm for several days. This is particularly odd as, although the Krays don't own the pub, it's Ronnie's favourite and he holds court there several times a week. This time Charles asked the cabbie to wait, and within five minutes he's on his way back to Wren Street having wasted his evening, deep in thought.

If Nipper Read had his soldiers lined up and had swooped on the gang, Charles is certain he'd have heard about it. It follows, therefore, that the absence of the Krays from their usual haunts is because they are up to something.

But what?

CHAPTER FOUR

E. Pellicci's establishment at 322 Bethnal Green Road (its menu of simple fried food makes it more a "caff" than a café) is an East End institution. Still graced by genuine Art Deco interior and wood-panelled walls, it has been in the Pellicci family since 1900. The "E" was Elide Pellicci who, having given birth to seven children in the flat above, took over the day-to-day running of the business when her husband, Priamo, died in 1931. Its present owner, Nevio, second youngest of the seven, is now in charge.

It is very early on a Thursday morning, and Pellicci's is deserted except for the two identical men in almost identical suits who sit drinking tea at a corner table. The staff keep well out of the way when not actually serving the men.

Nevio exits the kitchen with two plates piled high with chips, eggs, bacon, sausages and beans, and places them in front of his only clients.

'Thanks, Nev,' says Reggie Kray, slipping out of his jacket and hanging it on the back of his chair.

'Anything else I can get you, gents?' Nevio asks, turning first to Reggie and then to Ronnie. 'Sauce, mustard?'

'Nah, but keep the tea coming,' says Ronnie, also hanging up his jacket and tucking his tie into his shirt.

'Of course. *Buon appetito.*'

The use of Italian is a harmless affectation; although the older generations of the family still speak Italian upstairs, Nevio Pellicci is as Cockney through and through as the Kray twins. The gangsters have been coming here for meals, especially breakfast, since the late 1940s.

The Krays give themselves over to the serious business of eating. Both are tired, having had little sleep in the last few weeks and none the night before. A belly full of cholesterol and carbohydrate is just what the doctor ordered to perk them up.

Ten minutes later, Ronnie wipes the plate down with his buttered bread, mopping up the last of the tomato sauce and egg yolk, and pushes the plate away, satisfied. 'Right, now,' he says, lighting a cigarette immediately. 'Who's left?'

'There's six, but top of the list are Ronnie Hart and Horowitz,' replies Reggie, still finishing his food.

'And Leslie Payne,' adds Ronnie.

Reggie sighs and shakes his head. 'We've been through this, and I wish you'd listen to me for once. Leave Payne be. He'll never talk.'

Ronnie turns away, ignoring his brother. 'Still nothing from Hart?' he asks, after a pause.

Reggie shakes his head, chews and swallows. 'I ain't worried yet. 'E's still moving from place to place.'

'Wales?'

'That's what I heard, but I don't think so. He's got various people giving out duff stories to keep Old Bill off his tail. Got anything out of Tintagel House?'

Ronnie takes a drag of his cigarette and shakes his head. 'Not a squeak. It's tighter 'n' a drum over there.'

'How much have we offered so far?'

'A monkey.'

'Up it to a grand, yeah?'

'I was thinking more.'

Reggie considers the suggestion, his fork poised in mid-air between plate and mouth. 'Offer too much and it'll attract time-wasters. How about another monkey, but depending on results?' he suggests.

'Fair enough.'

Ronnie calls to the back of the caff. 'Another cuppa over here, Nev!' he shouts. He turns back to his twin. 'What about Horowitz?'

'Let's see if he shows up tonight.'

'He's got a fucking liberty,' says Ronnie. 'Who the fuck does 'e think 'e is, tellin' us to wait? Arrogant arsehole!'

'I agree, and I've taken steps.' Reggie sees Ronnie checking his watch. 'You in a hurry or something?'

'No. I told McVitie to meet us.'

'Why?'

'Cos I'm gonna give him Payne to sort out,' he says belligerently.

'Don't, Ron. Honest, it's a mistake.'

'Yeah, you've already said, and I disagree. You know what? You've lost your fuckin' nerve!' he hisses. 'Like always, when it comes to the dirty work, you ain't got the balls.'

'It ain't that, an' you know it, it's —'

Ronnie nods towards the door. ''Ere he is.'

The door of the caff opens and a man puts his head in. He scans the room quickly to make sure there are no other customers, and enters. 'All right Ronnie? Reggie?' he says cheerfully.

He approaches the table. He's a shortish good-looking man in his early thirties wearing a jacket and a trilby hat set at a jaunty angle. He has deep rings under bloodshot eyes.

'Jack,' says Ronnie in greeting. 'Take a seat.' He turns to the counter. 'And another cuppa, Nev,' he calls.

The newcomer hangs up his jacket, leaves his hat on and pulls up a third seat. Reggie Kray examines his face, eyes narrowed. 'How're you feeling?'

'I'm fine, thanks.'

'You don't look it. Are you on something?'

'No. I'm clean.'

Reggie looks at his brother, his expression doubtful, but Ronnie ignores him.

For months, Jack "The Hat" McVitie has been consuming an increasing proportion of the Drinamyl — purple hearts — he is supposedly distributing for the twins. It amounts to skimming their profits and the twins have rowed over it. Initially Ron wanted to teach McVitie a lesson but keep him on the books, while Reg was inclined to excuse the rather pathetic addict with the sick baby daughter. But then McVitie started supplementing the purple hearts with the enormous pep pills he called "Black Bombers" and the combination rendered him useless most of the time. Now the twins' positions are reversed: Reggie thinks he's a liability, and Ronnie is suddenly unconcerned, even wanting to give him a big job. Reggie can't understand his brother, and it infuriates him.

Ronnie fixes his eyes on McVitie, pointedly ignoring Reggie. 'We've a job for you,' he says. 'It's your last chance, so don't fuck it up.'

'What job?'

Ronnie leans forward and drops his voice. 'Tidyin' up a loose end.'

'The man with the briefcase?'

Ronnie's eyes narrow. 'What makes you say that?' he asks, immediately suspicious.

'It's obvious, innit? You've been saying for ages you don't trust 'im no more,' says McVitie, leaning back in his chair.

'Now Nipper's looking for 'im, or if he ain't, he soon will be once people start talking. So you need to get to 'im first.'

'Will you listen to me for a sec —' starts Reggie, about to resume the argument, but he's cut short by his brother.

'No!' says Ronnie, jabbing his forefinger across the table. 'Enough! It's decided.'

Reggie glares at his twin for a second but says nothing. He shoves back from the table and stands. 'I can't be dealing with this,' he mutters, his face contorted with emotion.

'Where you off to?' demands Ronnie.

'Goin' to see Frances,' replies Reggie, grabbing his jacket and walking to the door. 'I get more sense outta her!' he throws back over his shoulder.

The door of the caff opens and closes and Reggie strides off up the pavement. Ronnie and McVitie watch him disappear.

'Frances?' asks McVitie after a moment.

'He's had roses planted on her grave. Goes every day to talk to 'er.' He shakes his head. 'And I'm the one who's off his rocker,' he mutters. He turns back to McVitie. 'Never mind 'im. I want you to see Payne.'

'And offer money?'

'No. It's been tried,' replies Ronnie. ''E don't need it — fingers in all sorts of pies, bearer bonds, securities, even a couple of private banks. We can't trust him to keep *shtum* so we need a permanent solution. You know where he lives?'

McVitie shakes his head.

'Here,' says Ronnie, sliding a slip of paper across the table. 'Take someone with you. Maybe Billy.'

'Exley? He's got a dicky heart. You sure he's the right man for this?'

'He can still drive, can't he?'

McVitie shrugs. 'I guess so.'

46

'Good. Still got that shooter?' asks Ronnie.

'Yep.'

'That's sorted then.'

'Well, almost. How much?' asks McVitie.

'A ton now, and a monkey after it's done.'

'Six hundred? Come off it, Ron, that ain't enough and you know it. Well under market value, 'specially for a big contract like this.'

'Six hundred, and that's it,' says Ronnie firmly. 'You're on probation. If Reg had his way, you'd already be out. But do this one right, and there'll be more.'

McVitie considers and eventually nods. 'When?'

'This week, if possible,' answers Ronnie. 'In any case, as soon as.' He reaches into his jacket pocket and takes out a thick envelope. He slides it sideways across the table and McVitie pockets it.

McVitie raises his hand to beckon Nevio over. The owner of the caff is lurking in the doorway to the kitchen, expecting an order.

'What you doing?' demands Ronnie.

McVitie looks puzzled. 'Nothing. Just gonna order some breakfast, that's all.'

'No, you ain't,' replies Ronnie firmly. 'You're too busy.'

McVitie considers Ronnie in surprise. It takes him a moment to realise that his boss isn't joking. 'Suit yourself,' he says, rising, and collecting his jacket. He pauses. 'Not even a bacon sarny to go?'

'Fuck off, Jack,' says Ronnie, dismissing him.

Sally Fisher closes her front door behind her and tries to slow her rapid breathing and heart rate.

It has just gone five o'clock. Since she started working in the Temple as a teenager, she has never been home this early. It goes against the grain. As senior clerk it is her responsibility to make sure every barrister has his papers for the next day's trial, that fees have been agreed and, if possible, that fee notes for that day's work have gone out in the post. She is invariably the last to leave the clerks' room, the one to lock up.

Not this evening.

Sally is exhausted, and still liable to throw up. Something she smelled around lunchtime — one of the barristers' lunches? — turned her stomach and sent her scurrying to the toilet, where she spent most of the afternoon. Once started, she couldn't seem to stop. She managed to get to the chemist on Fleet Street for something to settle her and eventually returned to her desk, pale and sweating, but she couldn't concentrate and gave up a couple of hours later, leaving everything to the juniors.

However, that isn't responsible for her present distress.

Sally is frightened.

She drops her bags just inside the front door, slips off her shoes and runs up the three flights of stairs to the top of the house. From the bedroom window she looks down onto the street.

He's still there.

Sally first saw him as she left for work. She departed that morning before Charles, hoping to get a head start on the day, and noticed a tall man with fair hair and a cigarette hanging from his lips on the corner of Wren Street and Gray's Inn Road. He wore a distinctive trench coat with its belt tied rather than fastened, and he looked directly at her as she walked towards him to catch the southbound bus. Indeed he almost seemed to smile as she passed him, and for a moment she wondered if he was a resident of Wren Street and she'd failed to recognise one of her neighbours. But he didn't look like a member of any of the families to whom she and Charles had started nodding when passing on the street, and he was too well-dressed to be one of the squatters or druggies in the derelict properties still awaiting gentrification.

Sally thought nothing more of him as she turned the corner and walked to the bus stop. However, as she descended with other passengers from the bus at Aldwych, she saw him jumping off the landing board behind her. He followed her all the way to the Temple, but even that seemed no more than coincidence.

Her suspicions were first raised when she saw him for the third time, that afternoon, when she ran out to the chemist. She looked for him specifically when she gave up trying to work and left the Temple at four thirty and, yes, there he was again, on the corner of Fetter Lane.

Now he has followed her all the way home and is still there, on the opposite side of Wren Street, lurking behind an old van. In fact, now she thinks about it, he has not been "lurking" at all. It's as if he's deliberately allowing himself to be seen. No one could be that careless, surely?

She looks at the bedroom clock. Charles won't be home for a couple of hours. She returns to the front door and double-locks it. Then she checks all the windows at the front and back of the house. The garden doors from the kitchen would be easy to break open, but the garden itself is surrounded by other properties and Sally imagines it would be quite difficult to gain access to it.

She tries to remember whether Charles is in court in London that day, but cannot recall what he said. He did tell her as they were preparing to leave that morning, but she was in such a hurry and her head was so full of all the things she needed to get done that day, she wasn't paying proper attention. She tries his chambers just in case, but he's not been seen since lunchtime and no one knows where he is.

She is so concerned that she returns to the top floor and opens the wardrobe. She takes out Charles's baseball bat. Charles and some American friends used to play in Regent's Park on Sunday mornings and, by way of souvenir, one of them gave him a genuine Chicago Cubs Little League bat when he returned to Illinois.

She catches sight of herself in the mirror as she walks from the bedroom, bat in hand: barely five foot with an oval, pale face framed by a dark Mary Quant bob. Hardly very frightening, especially to a well-built man a foot taller than her. Feeling foolish, she returns the bat to the wardrobe.

She considers telephoning the police, but decides against it. They wouldn't do anything; the man has committed no offence. What if he does, after all, live on or near Wren Street and happens to work somewhere near Fleet Street?

She descends to the kitchen and starts preparing the evening meal. Something simple, with no onion, garlic or strong spices. Every now and then she goes to the front window and looks up to the pavement. She can still see the man's feet and shoes on the far side of the road.

When there is a noise at the door she almost jumps out of her skin. Still holding a knife with which she had been slicing carrots, she runs up to the ground floor and peers out into the corridor. Charles's familiar shape can be seen through the stained glass of the front door. He rings the doorbell and Sally remembers that she double-locked the door and left the keys in it. She opens up for him.

'Hello,' he says, puzzled. 'Why's it locked?'

Sally pushes past him and looks outside to the far pavement. Both the van and the man have gone. She looks up and down the road: deserted. She closes the door and locks it again. 'Come downstairs and I'll explain.'

Charles follows her down. As Sally resumes the meal preparation she tells Charles what has happened.

'Okay,' he says, 'describe him again for me, would you?'

Sally looks up, wooden spoon in hand, and concentrates hard. 'Very tall, probably a little taller than you, slimmer than you, blonde hair cut very short — almost a crewcut — early thirties I'd say, thin lips. He was wearing what looked like an American trench coat, you know, the sort you see in 1940s gangster films. And loud shoes,' she adds.

'Loud?'

'Not in style. Very clip-cloppy. I could hear them behind me.'

Charles drops into a kitchen chair and thinks, chewing his lip.

'Well?' asks Sally.

Charles hesitates. 'I didn't want you to worry about this — it may be nothing — but you might as well know now. Two of the Krays' thugs turned up at the gym yesterday and demanded that I go with them. Ronnie and Reggie want to see me. I refused, but promised to pop into the billiard hall tonight.'

'See you? What about?'

'I don't know. Maybe they're looking for a brief. Nipper Read's breathing down their necks.'

'Then they'd instruct Sampsons as normal and meet you in Chambers for a conference. What's the point of sending heavies to collect you?'

'They've had their little beauty parades of barristers in the past. Maybe this is another.'

'And you think the man in a raincoat was also sent by them? Why?'

'It's exactly the sort of thing they do. They remind you they can get at you whenever they want.'

'So the man following me was threatening you?'

'I have no idea. I'm just speculating.'

She frowns, thinks for a moment and then shakes her head. 'I don't buy it. They've no reason to frighten me if all they want to do is persuade you to act for them. You've represented them before, haven't you?'

'Sort of.'

'And you didn't need to be threatened.'

'Not exactly. I wasn't keen, as you know.'

'But you did it because the Cab Rank Principle required you to, as it does now. So it's something else. But what?'

Charles shrugs. He can't tell her — not because he doesn't know, but because he hasn't the courage.

Although their affair has been continuing for years, Charles and Sally only started living together at Wren Street the previous Christmas, after an earlier and failed attempt at making a life together. An attempt that was ruined by Charles's heavy drinking, his late-night working, his failure to give sufficient time or energy to their relationship and, eventually, his fling with an actress which ended, literally, in murder.

As far as Sally was concerned the relationship had been over.

It took months for Charles to persuade her to give him one last chance; he loved her, he said but, then, she'd never doubted that. The question for her was, could he commit to her, to *any* relationship, when he trusted no woman and found intimacy so difficult? Yes, he said. He could change; he *would* change.

It seemed he had. He reduced his whisky intake, stopped working until midnight or later in Chambers; cut out most of his solo pursuits and became part of a couple. As the months passed, Charles watched Sally's love for him being rekindled and, probably for the first time, he fell truly and completely in love with her. He grew increasingly certain that he wanted to spend the rest of his life like this, with her.

He *had* changed.

When Sally fell unexpectedly pregnant she couldn't tell him at first. She was terrified he'd say he — their relationship — wasn't ready. But he surprised her again by being delighted, and his unexpected joy only made Sally love him more. Sixteen years his junior, she looks up to him, admires and respects him. She wants him to be the father of her children. Everything is going well. They are happy.

How then can he now admit to her that he is not the man he purports to be? Charles Holborne, perennial defender of the underdog; the only barrister in his chambers regularly to take pro bono work; the barrister who's fought corruption all his professional life — how can he confess that he's not, after all, a *mensche*, the "righteous man" as his Old Testament father would have put it?

Charles hasn't been able to tell Sally that the Krays have evidence on him which would end his career and send him to prison; that their continuing silence puts him in their debt. He can't tell her that the debt is about to be called in.

There have been opportunities. As their relationship deepened, as Charles began at last to let Sally into his interior life, moments arose when he came close to confiding in her. But the opportunities came and went, and the longer he delayed the more impossible it became.

'So,' repeats Sally, 'what do they want?'

Charles shrugs again. 'No idea. But we'll know by tonight.'

CHAPTER FIVE

The Regal Billiard Hall, Eric Street, just off Mile End Road and in the centre of the Krays' manor, is the twins' spiritual home. They have had interests in numerous other pubs and clubs since the 1950s including, for a period, Esmeralda's Barn, a sophisticated drinking and gambling establishment in the West End where they entertained politicians, celebrities and members of the aristocracy — and fleeced them mercilessly.

The Regal, however, is where the boys can be themselves. A genuine billiard hall with fourteen tables, a long bar and lockers where business partners can hide weapons, stolen goods and other criminal paraphernalia, it is here they relax and entertain their closest associates. In years gone by, before Ronnie's mental illness gripped him by the throat, he was the acknowledged ringmaster of the circus, pulling all sorts of hilarious stunts for the entertainment of members of the Firm. Years after the event, regulars still speak of the time he brought a donkey into the billiard hall, complete with straw boater, and claimed he was teaching it to speak.

The Regal is also the place where members of the Firm deliver the takings of the "Milk Run", the weekly collection of protection payments from bars, restaurants and *spielers* across London. It is where some of Ronnie's most outlandish schemes have been hatched, and from where he used to launch his "little wars" on rival gangs, before there were no more rival gangs to fight. And it is where no policeman ever enters, except to sell information or collect a bribe.

It is a couple of minutes before ten o'clock, and Charles stands on the corner of Eric Street and Mile End Road, preparing himself for the interview. There are two bouncers on the door. He knows one of them, "Chunky" Morgan, a thug with a lifelong loyalty to the twins and a good-natured way of dispensing violence on their orders. He doesn't recognise the other. As Charles hesitates, Chunky sees him and raises his arm in greeting. Charles sets off towards the door, fixing a smile to his face.

'Been expecting you, Charlie,' calls Chunky as Charles approaches.

'Yeah?' Charles comes to a halt in front of the big man.

'People taking bets on whether you'd show or not. I said you would.'

'Taking bets? I can't imagine why,' says Charles, frowning.

'Cos it's dangerous to give Ronnie the brush-off,' says the other man, a lanky youngster with a mouthful of blackened teeth. '"*I'll fit you in tomorrow, if my diary permits,*"' he quotes, in a cartoon imitation of a posh voice.

'Is that what they're saying?'

Chunky nods. 'You ain't 'alf a chancer, Charlie,' he says good-naturedly, shaking his head sadly.

It begins to dawn on Charles how tricky this interview might be.

'You got balls,' says the youngster, 'I'll give you that. Whether you'll still have 'em when you come out's another matter.'

'Is that how it is?' asks Charles. 'Best face the music then, boys. Can I go in?'

The two men part and Charles enters.

The cigarette smoke inside the billiard hall is so thick that for a moment Charles halts on the threshold to get his bearings. The billiard tables are all occupied, the bar is lined with drinkers, some sitting on stools and some standing to be served, and there's a lot of noise. Charles squints through the smoke, looking for either of the twins. One of the barmen looks up, notices Charles hesitating at the entrance, and beckons him over.

'Mr Holborne?'

Charles leans on the bar to hear more clearly over the noise. 'Yes. I've an appointment to see Mr Kray.'

The barman points to the far end of the room. 'Over there. By the doors. Show him, will you, Dennis?'

Another man serving behind the bar dries his hands on a cloth and slips out to lead Charles. Charles follows, weaving his way through the crowd. He recognises several of the men drinking and playing billiards. Indeed, a couple are not only old acquaintances but old clients; Charles recognises one as someone he defended recently. He notes that although the noise levels do not diminish, most eyes follow him as he progresses to the dim recesses of the hall.

Charles's guide comes to a halt at a small circular table in the corner of the room.

'Mr Holborne to see you, Reggie,' he says, and he leaves Charles standing by the table and exits the room through double doors.

Reggie Kray looks up. 'Hello, Charlie,' he says. 'Nice of you to pop in.'

He speaks softly and Charles has to bend to hear him.

'Evening, Reg,' he replies, raising his voice slightly. 'Sorry I couldn't come when Pat asked. My Sally had a hospital appointment.'

'You still with Robeson's girl, then?'

'You know I am. You had her followed all day.'

'Did I?'

'You did. Thank you, by the way. I might've forgotten our appointment otherwise,' says Charles equably.

'You should've come when told. Disrespectful.'

Reggie Kray wears an expensive Italian suit in dark blue, but his silk tie is loosened, he has a newspaper on his lap, and a bottle of whisky and an empty glass sit on the table before him. Superficially he seems relaxed, but the smile playing around his lips doesn't reach his eyes. The last time Charles was in the Regal, after a remarkable court success of which the Krays were the beneficiaries, he'd been offered a drink. Not this time.

'Be reasonable, Reg. You dropped everything when your Frances was poorly. There's no disrespect involved. I just had to be somewhere else. But I'm here now.'

'Yeah.' Reggie stands. 'Come with me.'

'Can I get a drink first?'

'When we're finished.'

Reggie turns his back and goes through the same double doors as Dennis did a few moments before. Charles takes a deep breath, and follows.

He finds himself in a corridor with doors opening off to both sides, one marked as a toilet. The corridor smells of stale beer and urine. A pile of barrels and a loaded sack barrow narrow the space further. Ahead of him Reggie Kray's back is disappearing through an outside door into what looks like an open yard.

One of the doors opens and a young man emerges from the urinal. He nods to Charles and squeezes past him, heading back to the billiard hall. As Charles takes the last couple of steps towards the outside door his arms are grabbed from behind and he is shoved hard. He is propelled out of the doors into the yard and something flies towards his face. He has no time to duck or evade, merely to close his eyes.

He is struck partly on his cheek and partly on his nose and his eyes water immediately. The hold on him from behind loosens but he has insufficient time to react before another blow lands on his abdomen. His knees sag and a third blow, the most powerful yet, thunders into his face, catching him full on the mouth. He feels the shock travelling from his teeth all the way to the back of his head, rattling his eyes.

Charles drops, his knees striking cold cobbles. He curls up to protect himself from further anticipated blows. None come.

'That'll do,' says someone.

Charles takes a few moments to collect himself. His mouth is full of blood and one of his bottom incisors feels loose. He spits blood onto the cobbles and looks up.

Ronnie and Reggie Kray stand in front of him. Ronnie also has his jacket off and his sleeves rolled up. He is examining his fist.

'Fucking cut myself on his teeth,' he complains.

'You aimed too high,' says Reggie. 'He was already dropping.'

Of the twins, Reggie was always the more technical boxer, remembers Charles. Ronnie was the slugger, wild and careless.

'Right,' says Reggie, taking charge, 'get him cleaned up and bring 'im back to the bar when you're done,' he orders someone.

A fourth man hands Ronnie his jacket and the twins return inside. Charles is hauled to his feet, pushed inside after them and guided into the toilet.

One man stands guard over him while Charles splashes his face with cold water and examines it in the mirror. There is a raised and tender bruise on his cheekbone. Testing his nose produces pain but no movement, which is something. His bottom lip is split and blood dribbles down his chin. The tooth is painful and moves at pressure from his tongue, but he has suffered that sort of injury in the ring and knows that, with luck, it should re-bed itself.

He rinses out his mouth a couple of times and dries his face. He straightens his tie, brushes down his trousers and finally folds a paper towel into a pad, and applies it to his lip.

'Ready?' asks the guard.

Charles nods, and is escorted back down the corridor and into the billiard hall.

The Kray twins are now seated at the table and a third chair has been added for Charles. In front of it is a glass with an inch of amber liquid. Ronnie points to the chair and the drink, an instruction to Charles to sit down. Charles complies. He reaches for the glass and takes an exploratory sip — Scotch and water, exactly as he likes it — tipping his head back in an attempt to have the spirit miss the mouth injuries. He winces.

'Now,' says Reggie. 'We need a word about Nipper Read.'

'You know what 'es up to, doncha?' says Ronnie. It's a statement, not a question.

Charles shakes his head. 'Not really,' he mumbles, but the damaged lip and the bloodied paper towel make his words indecipherable.

'Wassat?' demands Ronnie. 'Can't understand yer.'

'Well, whose fault's that?' says Charles, lowering the pad. Blood drips onto the table.

'Consider yourself lucky, Charlie,' says Reggie. 'If you was anyone else, you wouldn't be talkin' at all.'

'Been pushing your luck for years, Horowitz,' says Ronnie angrily. 'I've told you this before. Don't think we ain't got limits. Now: Read.'

Charles takes another sip. 'What of him?'

'You really don't know what's going on?' demands Ronnie, disbelieving.

Charles answers carefully. 'I know as much as everyone, and probably less than you. He's got a team at Tintagel House, and he's talking to people. But no one admits speaking to him, and no one knows what he's investigating. I hear long firm frauds.'

The twins look at one another.

'Yeah, we hear that too, but we don't believe it,' says Reggie. 'He's speaking to people who weren't involved in 'em.'

'I also heard the Dublin beach murder,' adds Charles.

The twins look at one another again. That scrap is news to them.

'From who?'

'A copper mate in the team. He wouldn't lie to me.'

'Interestin',' says Ronnie thoughtfully. 'So, we're on the back burner, you think?'

Charles shakes his head. 'No, I don't. Read may be in Ireland, but the rest of the team aren't.'

Reggie nods in agreement. There is a pause, and Charles senses the atmosphere changing. When Reggie speaks again, the suspicion has left his tone. 'Fair enough. We've a job for you.'

'What sort of job?'

'Don't worry, it's your day job. You're gonna represent Ronnie Hart.'

Charles knows who Hart is but has never met him. East End lore has it that Hart presented himself on the Krays' doorstep at Vallance Road a couple of years earlier and announced that he was their cousin. He'd just been released from prison, he said, and wanted to join the gang and learn how to become a "proper criminal". The brothers were sceptical at first but Hart's story checked out. Since then he has gradually wormed his way into the twins' trust and has become an integral member of the gang.

'Represent him. For what?'

'Never you worry about that,' replies Ronnie. 'You'll be told when we see exactly what the charges are.'

'What does Hart think about this?'

'He'll do as he's told. Like you. We don't want to hear about clashes in your court diary, holidays booked or nothing like that. The brief comes, you take it.'

Charles looks from one twin to the other. 'So you've given me a hiding just to get me to represent someone, which is my job anyway?'

'No, you wanker!' says Ronnie. 'You got a hiding because you took diabolical liberties.'

'And everyone knew it,' adds Reggie, hitching a thumb in the general direction of everyone else in the club. 'Can't let that go, can we?'

'Right. You'll hear soon as Read makes 'is move,' says Ronnie, standing up and dismissing Charles. 'Sampsons will be in touch.'

Sampsons are known to Charles, indeed to all criminal barristers in London. A small one-man solicitor's firm headed by a quiet, clever, Jewish solicitor named Manny Fryde, it is a favourite among the high-profile criminal gangs in the Metropolis.

Charles also stands and, carefully, finishes his drink. 'What makes you so sure he's going to make a move?' he asks. 'If everyone stays *shtum* I don't see him doing anything.'

'We need to be ready if he does,' says Ronnie, moving off.

Charles looks down on Reggie, who is calmly picking up his newspaper again.

'Where does this leave me, Reg?' asks Charles. 'Do I get that evidence back?'

Reggie smiles. 'We'll see.'

'And you'll leave Sally out of it?'

'You know us better than that.'

'It used to be no women and children.'

'Still is.'

'Then why —'

'To make you realise you needed to show up, that's all. Go on, off you get. We'll be in touch.'

Charles walks back towards the door. Heads turn and follow his progress, many observers smirking and pointing at his battered face. He sees money changing hands.

I hope they got decent odds.

The cooler air on the street is refreshing. He walks to Mile End Road and pauses, looking at his watch. In times gone by he would've walked all the way back to Wren Street, or at least taken the Central line tube from Mile End to Chancery Lane. But Sally will be worried, probably waiting up for him. A line of unoccupied cabs is approaching from the east, their "For Hire" lights illuminated, and he hails the first.

'Wren Street, mate,' he says to the cabbie through the window, and gets in.

Twenty minutes later they pull up outside Charles and Sally's home. The lights are still on in the kitchen.

With a heavy heart Charles opens the front door and descends the stairs.

Sally is waiting at the kitchen table in her dressing gown. She looks up as he enters, takes one look at his face, and shakes her head. 'I knew it,' she says, standing, and going to the sink. 'So, I guess you didn't win the beauty parade.'

'*Au contraire*,' says Charles, attempting a grin. 'You should've seen the others.'

'Sit at the table, and I'll see what I can do.'

Charles takes off his jacket, collects the whisky decanter and glass from the shelf, and sits heavily in a kitchen chair. He notices for the first time that his shirt is stained with blood. Sally brings a packet of frozen peas from the refrigerator's icebox for Charles's cheek, which is now swelling nicely, and a bowl of water to clean up his cut mouth. She stands in front of him, lifts his head to examine the damage and again shakes her head sadly.

'If you're going to pour yourself a drink, do it now, and then stay still,' she instructs.

Charles pours a large shot, takes a sip, and gingerly applies the frozen peas to his face, keeping his head tilted upwards so his mouth is available for Sally's examination. She turns his head from one side to the other, peering at the cut, and gently pulls his lip away from his teeth to look inside his mouth.

'Well,' she concludes, 'your bottom lip's split, but I guess you know that. I think you'll get away without stitches. It's also a very interesting purple colour on the inside.'

'Where it hit my teeth,' mumbles Charles, trying to keep his mouth as still as possible. 'Eating's going to be fun for a few days.'

'You sound like Ray Alan,' she says, referring to the TV ventriloquist, as she sponges the dried blood tenderly off Charles's chin.

'Which makes me Lord Charles.'

'Exactly. You're the dummy. So, this was Ronnie or Reggie?'

'Ronnie, though Reggie pulled the trigger.'

'And now's the time for you to tell me the truth.'

Charles takes a deep breath and nods. 'If I do, Sal, please believe me, I didn't want to keep it from you.'

'But?' she asks, sceptical.

He laughs briefly, embarrassed. 'I was scared.'

'Scared? Of the Krays?'

'No. Well, anyone'd be a fool not to be scared of them, but that's not what I mean.'

'Well then?'

Charles reaches up to take Sally's wrist and still her moving hand. 'Sally Fisher, you are the love of my life. I hope you believe it now, finally. The last few months have been wonderful. I've really believed that this,' he says, indicating the comfortable room, 'and this —' he places a hand on her flat belly with the life growing inside it — 'was the future.'

'So have I,' she replies, now a little nervous.

'I didn't want to say anything that would make you doubt me. I've been on probation, remember?'

She frowns. 'What have you done? You must have done something for those bastards to have this hold over you.'

He nods, breaks eye contact with her and reaches for his drink. 'Remember when I was representing Merlin?' he asks.

'Your cousin, the lighterman? Izzy Conway?'

'Yes. Merlin was his river name. And do you remember that you and I had a bit of a ... bust-up around that time?'

'One of several, as I remember.'

'You came to the flat at Fetter Lane, very late one night, and I wasn't there. You were very upset.'

'I remember.'

'I never told you the whole story. I was on the Thames with an old lighterman mate of mine. I was looking for evidence to attack that corrupt waterguard, Vermeulen.'

'So?'

65

'So, to find it, I did one or two things. Bent some rules.'

'As I recall, the Krays had a contract out on you at that time.'

'They did and, if you remember, Izzy was innocent but he was still going to be hanged. Vermeulen was as bent as a nine-bob note, but I hadn't the evidence. And I found some.'

Sally nods and restarts cleaning up Charles's face.

'Which involved a bit of breaking and entering,' he says.

'To expose a bent waterguard? Doesn't sound that bad to me.'

'Bad enough for an officer of the court. But I was forced to do much worse to get us over the line.'

'What did you do?'

'I used what I found to blackmail him. I got him to change his evidence.'

Sally becomes very still. 'Jesus,' she whispers. 'His evidence on oath? As in, in court?'

'Yes.'

Sally drags a chair out and sits next to Charles. 'Oh, Charlie!' she exclaims softly. 'You'd know better than me but ... well ... that's prison time, isn't it?'

'Yes,' he replies. 'I had no choice. My life was on the line, as was Izzy's. They'd already tried to kill me, remember? The knife attack in the phone box? I almost bled to death.'

'Sure, but that wouldn't save you from going inside, would it? Even if you could prove it.'

'No.'

'And the Krays?'

'They've got all the evidence. Vermeulen gave them everything — or sold it to them, I suppose. It was his parting shot. Including something very damaging in my handwriting.'

'Jesus,' she repeats.

They fall silent.

'And what do they want now?' she asks.

'They want me to represent one of the Firm, their cousin, a guy called Ronnie Hart.'

She looks up at him, not understanding. 'So? That's not so hard, is it?'

Charles shakes his head. 'There's more.'

'What?'

'I don't know yet. But there's definitely more. There always is with them.'

'What're you going to do?'

'I don't know. Nipper Read wants me to give evidence for the Crown. He's been approaching members of the Firm, confidentially, offering immunity if they give evidence against the twins.'

'And he'd do the same for you?'

'He says so. But even if I get immunity from prosecution, I'll be disbarred. It'll be the end of everything. Back to square one, an unemployed East End Jew with a dodgy past and an association with the Krays. What do we do then?' He points to Sally's belly.

He drains the rest of his drink, stands, walks to the refrigerator and puts the frozen peas back in the ice box. He returns to Sally. He is suddenly very tired and wants to crawl into bed. 'Look, Sal, I'm knackered, and I need to lie down. If you want me to go to the spare room, just say.'

Say looks up at him, puzzled. 'What on earth for?'

He shrugs. 'I don't know. Maybe you don't feel the same way about me now. Now you know I'm not the honest man I pretend to be. The incorruptible crusader, swimming alone against the tide of venality,' he says with heavy irony. 'All that bollocks.'

She stands and puts her hand up to stroke his cheek. 'And that's what's been worrying you?'

'Well … yes.'

She smiles tenderly at him. 'You're a fucking idiot, Charlie Horowitz.'

'I want you to be proud of me,' he says simply. 'I didn't want you thinking I was like all the others. Or a hypocrite.'

'I'll never think that. You're the most honourable, decent man I've ever met. I know how much the law means to you. I saw it, don't forget, when you defended Dad. You're still fighting for what's right, when most of the rest are either outright bent or treat it like a game. It's like your skeleton; everything else hangs around that.'

'Yes, but —'

'Charlie, I'm no wide-eyed innocent. With the Krays and their bent coppers, and with innocent people's lives on the line, sometimes you have to fight fire with fire. I know that.'

He smiles. 'Still your hero, then?'

'Always.'

Charles takes her hand from his face and kisses her palm. 'I love you,' he says.

'I love you too. But we need a plan, don't we?'

'Yes,' he replies. 'But not tonight.'

At exactly the same time as Sally leads Charles up to bed, a little over six miles from Wren Street, in a quiet road in south London, two men sit waiting in a car. They are in a suburb named Tulse Hill, a pleasant part of the capital with comfortable middle-class homes on wide, tree-lined streets and well-tended parks. The orderliness of the area, indeed its very *lawfulness*, make Jack McVitie and Billy Exley uncomfortable. This is not their milieu; they feel conspicuously out of place.

The two amateur hitmen sit in Exley's car, parked under a large tree on the opposite side of the road to the quiet house they are observing. They've been waiting there for an hour. The street is deserted, with many of the houses already in darkness, but there remains a light shining from one of the downstairs rooms of this particular house.

'What's Payne look like?' asks Exley, suddenly and belatedly aware that he wouldn't recognise their target even if he did walk past them on his way home.

William Exley is in his forties, about a decade older than the twins and, like so many in their inner circle, an ex-boxer. Even before he took two decades of battering in the ring he was not the sharpest tool in the box. A pleasant-looking man with a square jaw and straight hair swept backwards, he was surprised to be picked for this job. He does, genuinely, have a heart condition and believed it would rule him out of anything more arduous than tending the bars in the twins' drinking establishments; maybe straightforward debt collection where no trouble was anticipated. But he's a good soldier and does whatever the twins order.

'Ain't you met him?' asks McVitie.

'Don't think so.'

'He looks like a toff, tall, blond, like a guardsman. Wears a bow tie.'

They sit in silence for a few more minutes.

Finally: 'Sod this. I'm going over,' announces McVitie.

'Doncha want to wait a bit longer?' asks Exley, looking at his watch. 'It's not that late.'

'No,' replies McVitie. 'He must be home by now.'

McVitie reaches behind his seat and comes up with a large and very heavy revolver.

'Fucking hell, Jack, it's a bleedin' cannon!'

'It'll do the job proper, then. You coming?'

Exley hesitates. 'I'm not supposed to, am I? Ain't I just the getaway driver?'

McVitie shrugs. 'Ronnie didn't specify.'

'Nah, I'll wait in the motor, ready for the off.'

'Fair enough. Won't be long.'

McVitie opens the passenger door, looks both ways up and down the quiet street, and crosses to the opposite pavement. He walks silently up the garden path, the gun at his side, comes to a halt at the front door and straightens his jacket. He settles his trilby at its perfect angle — not in any attempt at disguise but because he likes it, just so — hides his gun arm behind him, and knocks on the door.

There is a noise from inside and he can see through the glass that somebody is approaching. The door opens inwards and a slim middle-aged woman stands before him. She wears curlers and a dressing gown and appears ready for bed.

'Yes?'

'Is Mr Payne at home?'

The woman shakes her head. 'No,' she says guilelessly, 'I'm waiting up for him.'

McVitie pauses for a moment. 'That's all right,' he says.

He turns and retraces his steps down the garden path. The woman regards McVitie's departing back, shrugs with some surprise and closes the front door. McVitie re-crosses the road and slides into the passenger seat of the car.

'Well?' asks Exley.

'He wasn't in. Good job. I'd have blown his fucking head off. Let's go.'

'Ain't we gonna wait?'

70

'No. We'll get him another time. Fancy a quick pint?' McVitie reaches into his pocket and draws out the envelope given to him by Ronnie Kray. 'It's on Ronnie.'

CHAPTER SIX

Toilet smells — principally, but not exclusively, urine — hit Charles as soon as he steps out of the lift. He wrinkles his nose. It's always like this, and Sunshine Court has as good a reputation as any residential care home in North London. Residents who have suffered "accidents" are washed and re-dressed as soon as the event is discovered, and carpets and upholstery are blotted and cleaned. Nonetheless, they have severe physical and mental disabilities and the staffing levels are inadequate; accidents, and smells, are inevitable.

Charles and his brother David searched for months for a Jewish care home where their parents, Millie and Harry Horowitz, would feel comfortable and where they would be served kosher food. It turned out none existed. The brothers had to settle for somewhere in North London where, due to its catchment area, a good number of residents were in fact Jewish, and some attempt was made to cater specifically for their tastes and interests. This one, housed in a crumbling early Victorian building that was once the local workhouse, is the best they could find but, even here, the poor standard of care has shocked the brothers. For that reason, one of the family comes every day. They bring food, cooked either by them or bought from the local delicatessen, and do what they can to keep Millie and Harry cheerful. More than once Charles has found himself assisting his mother to the toilet or shaving his father when the staff were too busy.

Some residents appear to have no family available or willing to support them. A few receive no visitors at all. Charles has noted that these unfortunates receive less diligent care than residents who have family members to witness what goes on. He and David make it their business to be known to all staff members and to be very visible. Charles even knows most of the night staff because Millie dozes throughout the day and is awake most of the night, either refusing to go to bed with the others or, having been settled for the night, getting up and prowling round until falling asleep on one of the couches or, once, in someone else's room.

He looks around for his parents and spots them on the far side of the lounge, sitting in adjoining armchairs in a circle of residents. It is teatime and Harry is slowly lifting a piece of sponge cake towards his mouth. The stroke left him with reduced strength in his right side. Physiotherapy has enabled him to regain some movement, but it is weak and jerky. He is now largely wheelchair-bound. Millie is beside him, asleep, her tea and cake untouched.

Charles skirts the circle, greeting the carers as he passes, and reaches the back of Harry's chair. He leans down and places a kiss on his father's soft cheek.

'You're looking very dapper this afternoon, Dad,' he says, crouching at his father's side.

The staff report that Harry is often difficult to deal with when he wakes, sometimes refusing to be shaved or showered until mid-morning when his mood improves. At first Charles refused to believe it. His father, Harry, was always the mildest of men and when Charles saw him, unshaved, his hair on end and still in food-stained pyjamas, he assumed it was another example of poor care. Then he witnessed it for himself. He arrived early one Saturday to find his father fighting off a carer who was doing her best to get him dressed. Harry saw Charles, stopped fighting and dissolved into tears.

'I'm sorry, son,' he sobbed. 'It's just so frustrating.'

Charles hugged him, but could say nothing. He could imagine how it must feel to wake every morning from blissful oblivion to find oneself disabled anew. He would rage. Harry calmed down and apologised to the carer who, in Charles's opinion, took it very well.

Charles checks that the chair beside Harry is dry before lowering himself onto it. He has been the unintended victim of more than one accident in the past.

Harry's head turns slowly. 'Hello, son,' he says.

'How are you, Pops?' asks Charles.

Harry gives him a thumbs up. 'Can't complain,' he says.

Charles looks across Harry's chest towards his mother. Millie Horowitz, a beautiful woman in her youth, was once vain and fastidious about her appearance. A milliner by training, she made most of her own clothes and was the most stylish dresser of their circle. Until a very few years ago she was still perfectly turned out: a small, slender, upright woman with steel grey hair and steelier blue eyes.

However, today she wears baggy trousers which Charles doesn't recognise and suspects are not her own, and a blouse stained with dribbled food. Her hair has not been styled or coloured in months.

'How's Mum?' Charles asks his father.

Harry turns his head slowly to his right and studies the face of his sleeping wife. He shrugs sadly but nods. He doesn't need to reply. Charles recognises his father's expression. It says, better than words, "*What can you do?*", the Jew's eternal resignation to centuries of injustice.

Perhaps it is the sound of Charles's voice, but at that moment Millie's eyes open.

'So you're here, then?' she says, her voice dripping with sarcasm.

Charles looks at his father enquiringly but Harry avoids his glance. 'Yes, Mum, I'm here. How are you today?'

'How should I be? How would anyone be, here, imprisoned by their own family?'

Charles sighs. So, it's going to one of *those* visits. 'You know very well, Mum, you haven't been imprisoned.'

'I don't know what else you'd call it,' she says bitterly. 'I'm ashamed to call you my son. You think I don't know who's idea this was? David would never have agreed if you'd not bullied him into it. That's my one remaining blessing; at least I have one son who's a *mensch*.'

'We've been through this hundreds of times. You can't look after Dad, even —'

She interrupts him with a wave of her hand. 'And having locked us up, you can't even be bothered to visit,' she spits. 'Your clients get more attention than I do.'

'I was here yesterday, and on Sunday!' Charles protests. 'I come as often as I can!'

Millie snorts dismissively and turns her head away.

This has been the pattern of Charles's relationship with his mother for all his life. He doesn't know what started it but for some reason, and as far back as he can remember, nothing he ever did could please the exacting Millie Horowitz; no matter how much he helped at home as a child; no matter how well he did at school. Even being a twice-decorated wartime Spitfire pilot and then a barrister, the first professional in the family, were insufficient to achieve even a minor thawing of the shard of ice that passed for his mother's heart. Something about Charles and his life choices were a red rag to a bull where Millie was concerned, and she seemed unable to forgive him. Then, when he married out and changed his name to

Holborne, he gave her something she *really* could use to beat him, and beat him she has, ever since.

Her present condition leaves Charles with confusingly mixed emotions. Her Alzheimer's disease means that her short-term memory is appalling, so much so that she was a danger to herself and to her husband. On the other hand, except for some occasional word-finding difficulties, she remains as articulate — and, to Charles, as vitriolic — as ever. To someone speaking to her for the first time, she could appear perfectly normal. Charles is happy that her disease has spared most of her intellect, but she now seems unable, or perhaps unwilling, to see how much effort (not to mention money) Charles devotes to ensuring she and Harry are safe and well looked-after at Sunshine Court.

'Don't let your tea go cold,' he says, pointing and hoping to move the conversation into safer waters. 'There's cake too, in front of you.'

She reaches forward and lifts the cup without further comment.

Charles looks round the circle at the damaged people who now live with his parents. Some, like them, can still feed themselves; others are being assisted.

Notwithstanding Millie's condition, it is in fact Harry's stroke which causes both of Charles's parents to be here. Until that occurred he and a carer who came to the house regularly were able to support Millie. She was no longer safe in the kitchen, but Harry and the carer managed to run the house between them, and in the familiarity of her own home, Millie could function reasonably well. Harry's stroke rendered that arrangement impossible.

The irony is that, although Millie is the one who complains constantly about her new living arrangements, it is Harry who suffers more, and in silence. While Millie sleeps through much of the day, Harry is awake and has little to engage him. He reads the newspaper and still, laboriously, manages the crossword in his spidery handwriting, but for the most part he is bored out of his largely undamaged mind because he refuses to be parted from his wife of half a century. Here he can hold Millie's hand for much of the day; he can raise his left arm to stroke her thinning hair, which he does very frequently; and the face she remembers and loves best will always be at her side. They share a couple's suite so Harry can keep Millie tethered to the here and now for as long as possible. Loyal and constant to the last, Harry Horowitz is still in love with his wife, and it warms the hearts of all who witness it.

Charles chats to Harry about his week. When he mentions Sally, as he does once or twice, his eyes flick warily towards his mother's face, watchful for her next acerbic comment.

When Charles and Sally got together and Charles brought yet another *shiksa* into the Horowitz household, he expected the worst. They all discovered, to their astonishment, that the Horowitzes already knew Sally. Her mother worked for the family business as an outworker before the war and as a small child Sally was a frequent visitor to the factory. That history blunted Millie's antipathy, at least to Sally herself. However what she represents is not something she can ever forgive.

Charles is relieved to see that the mention of Sally's name produces no response on this occasion. Millie's attention appears to be on the television on the far side of the circle of residents. He decides to take the plunge.

'Dad, Mum,' he starts. 'I've something important to tell you.'

He and Sally have discussed for weeks how the news of her pregnancy is to be broken to Charles's parents. If Millie reacts badly — as she did years ago when she cast Charles out of the family for "marrying out" — he wants Sally out of the firing line. He also wants to shield Millie from the consequences of her own venom. He is inured to it; whatever she might say, he remains her son and he will tolerate it, for Harry's sake if nothing else. But he can't expect Sally to be so forgiving. Were she to become the target of his mother's tongue-lashing, lasting damage might be caused within the family.

So Sally and Charles have agreed that if Charles judges the circumstances appropriate, and an opportunity arises, he should deliver the news, even if Sally is not present.

Charles expects to have to repeat himself, but Millie surprises him by turning towards him and giving him her entire attention. Charles waits while Harry turns his head towards him. Both his parents are now waiting for him to speak.

'I've some good news,' he says, forcing his features into a broad smile. 'Sally is pregnant. Three months. We didn't want to tell you until we were sure.' He looks from one of his parents to the other.

Harry's hand moves haltingly down the arm of his armchair and reaches Charles's. He grips it, a lopsided grin emerging on his face. '*Mazeltov*,' he says. As Charles watches, his father's eyes fill with tears and he grips Charles's hand tighter. 'I'm pleased for you, son,' he says slowly, articulating his words with care. 'She's a lovely girl, and she obviously makes you happy.'

'Thanks, Dad.' Charles finds his own eyes stinging too. He turns to his mother. Her face hasn't altered and he isn't sure she heard what he said. He is about to repeat himself when she speaks.

'Well, we've been expecting this, haven't we, Harry?'

'You have?' asks Charles, surprised.

'You've been living with her for long enough. She's a young woman; she'll want children.'

It seems to Charles that she's about to say something further, but she stops speaking abruptly and turns her head to watch the television again.

'So?' he prompts. 'Is that all?'

'What more should there be?' says Millie, still watching the screen. 'If this is what you want, I'm pleased for you. Sally is a very nice girl.'

'Thank you,' says Charles.

'Of course, you understand,' she says, turning back to him, 'I could never love this grandchild the way I do Jonathan.'

'Sorry?'

'I could never feel the same way about him or her as I do Jonathan. Any child of David's, in fact.'

Charles shakes his head in bewilderment. He glances at his father, whose head has dropped to his chest. Harry's good hand covers his forehead and eyes. He doesn't want to hear this. 'Why on earth not?' manages Charles after a pause, hoping this is a moment of confusion.

'Because it won't be Jewish.'

'But … but why should that make any difference? It'll be an innocent baby, your grandson or granddaughter, the same as Jonathan.'

She shakes her head. 'No, it won't. Jonathan is part of us, part of me. Part of our tradition. He'll follow in the footsteps of all the males in this family, footsteps that go back five thousand years. His *bris*, his bar mitzvah and, please God, his marriage under the *chuppah*. Perhaps your child will be perfectly nice, who knows, but, to me, it'll be alien, like a foreigner. So I can't love it in the same way. You're a clever man, Charles; I'm sure you understand.'

Charles stares into his mother's eyes which meet his without a flicker. He sees no confusion and no apology. She means every word. 'Yes,' he says quietly. 'I understand perfectly.'

It is early evening and dusk is settling over the River Thames. Charles walks from Temple underground station along the Embankment, the setting sun at his back. It's only a hundred yards or so to the entrance to the Temple but, if he has time, he likes to cross the road for that short distance to walk next to the river. Despite the traffic noise to his left, he can hear the water sloshing against the Embankment wall only a few feet below him. It's slack tide, the period when the river is at its fullest, before ebbtide. During the Blitz, when life was simpler and he worked the river as a lighterman, he liked to imagine this moment as the Thames taking a deep breath, holding it for a while, and then slowly exhaling, its lungs emptying as the water changes direction and flows back towards the estuary and the English Channel.

He reaches the point where he must now re-cross the traffic and enter the southern entrance to Middle Temple Lane, but he pauses for a moment, his elbows on the wall overlooking the river. The sun has emerged briefly from behind dark clouds and the tips of the waves are now pink-flecked.

I'd really miss this, he thinks sadly.

His mind settles, as it frequently does since Nipper Read and the Krays began their phony war, on Sally's father. He too was drawn into the twins' orbit; he too found himself incarcerated, late in life and for the first time; he too had his reputation and career destroyed. In Robeson's case, it was his own fault. Initially the Firm's legal "fixer", he chose to get his hands dirty and paid the price. But Charles remembers what the wily old solicitor told him in the cells at the Old Bailey: he said he was relieved. He'd been looking for a way out for years and his conviction provided it. When he was finally released from prison, assuming he survived the sentence, he'd be of no further use to the Krays.

Charles still clings to the faint hope that he might avoid that fate altogether. Perhaps, like him, other potential witnesses will remain too frightened to talk. Perhaps Nipper Read will run into the same impenetrable wall of fear and wilful blindness as halted all the earlier investigations. Perhaps.

Another, more realistic, part of him recognises the wishful thinking. Read is not like his predecessors. He is a patient, methodical and skilful tactician. His team is honest and utterly devoted to him. If anyone can bring down the Krays, it is him.

Now, after years of having the sword of Damocles hanging over his neck and months of apparent stalemate between Nipper's team and the Firm, Charles is desperate to have the situation resolved. If he is to go to prison, so be it; bring it on. It might indeed be a relief to focus on his sentence and come out the other side. But before that can happen, Read has to make his arrests and decide who is to face what charges. The Krays will call in Charles's debt. Only then can Charles come up with a strategy. Ever impatient, it is the waiting, with everything outside his control, that makes Charles edgy.

He banishes these thoughts from his mind, turns abruptly, looks both ways and jogs through the traffic to Temple Gardens. He heads up Middle Temple Lane. The gas lamps are being lit by one of the uniformed Temple employees. Charles watches him reach up with his eight-foot pole, deftly flick open the glass door, turn the tap, illuminate the gas jet and close the door again. It's as if the Temple is taking the opportunity to remind him how rich his life is and how much poorer it would become if he did indeed lose his profession and his liberty.

Charles climbs the steps to Middle Temple Hall.

'We're not open tonight, sir,' says the porter.

'I know,' replies Charles. 'It's Moot Night. I'm judging it.'

Moots are simulated court trials, organised by the Inn to educate its students, and tonight is the final of the competition. Usually Moots are limited to legal argument, but Charles persuaded the Inn that a full criminal trial would be a valuable learning exercise, so this one is a mock trial with an accused, prosecution and defence counsel and witnesses. Over several nights some of the best and brightest of this year's student advocates have been staging the trial before a jury of their peers, with Charles sitting as judge. The Moot is expected to end tonight with the final witnesses, speeches and jury deliberations. Thereafter Charles will host a discussion concerning the trial and the learning points the young barristers should take from the exercise. Several Benchers of the Inn have been watching the proceedings to see how the experiment progresses and to "mark" the participants.

'Ah,' says the porter, reaching inside his door for a sheet of paper. 'Mr Holborne?'

'Yes.'

'Thank you, sir,' says the porter, standing aside to let Charles enter.

Charles runs down the stairs to the cloakroom to get robed. He heard a recent suggestion in the Inner Temple tearoom that Moots should cease to be held in full court dress, but Charles disagrees, and has insisted that all the actors here play their parts to the full, including being robed. The more realistic the Inn can make it, the better for the students. Furthermore, there is something about the ancient Tudor hall that demands formal dress.

Wearing wing collar, bands, robes and wig, Charles carries

the case papers back up to the foyer and walks into Hall.

He has been a member of the Inn for eighteen years and he enters Hall several times every week, but the sense of awe and wonder it generates in him is still as powerful as on his very first day. When he was a student, it was this building more than anything else which made up Charles's mind — instantly — that it was the Honourable Society of the Middle Temple to which he would apply, rather than any of the other three Inns of Court.

He looks up at the enormous chandeliers hung beneath the hammer beam roof of the Great Hall; the long trestle tables with lamps at each "set" (groups of four place-settings); the huge portraits of the kings and queens, from Elizabeth I right through to Elizabeth II, each of whom in their era graced the Hall with their patronage and presence; and the wood-panelled walls bearing the heraldic shields of all the famous sons (and now, for the first time, daughters) of the Inn. When proudly showing the Inn to his brother or other visitors, Charles always points out the shield of Sir Walter Raleigh and the "cup board", the slab of oak, now used as a table, that started life as the cabin hatch of Sir Francis Drake's *Golden Hind*.

'No less than the five of the original signatories to the American Declaration of Independence were Middle Templars,' he would say with pride, 'and seven signed the first draft of the United States' Constitution. When you sit at these benches, you may well be sitting in the very place where they ate their dinners.'

Charles's family never understood why the threads of English history appealed so much more to him than did his own rich, five-thousand-year history that stretched back to the days of Moses. Charles has never been able to explain it fully. For him, standing in a synagogue where women are relegated to second-class citizens; reciting prayers in Hebrew and Aramaic, neither of which he understands; praying to an all-powerful God who chooses not to use that power to dispense justice in the world; none of that makes sense to him. It actually creates distance and, if he ever had any spark of faith, the distance became too great for the spark to leap it.

Here, however, he is actually walking in the footsteps of men of history, dining and speaking from the very positions where they dined and spoke. Their likenesses hang on the walls above him; their heraldic shields bear testament to their achievements. In this very room Shakespeare acted in the company of the Chamberlain's Men for the inaugural performance of *Twelfth Night* before Elizabeth I and her court. Every time Charles enters the building, he is surrounded by the ghosts of English history. It's this connection which makes him so proud to be English, despite the fact that so many of his English professional colleagues treated him then, and treat him still, as if he were a dirty foreigner.

The end of the room has been set up as if it were a court, and the students making up the advocates and jury are already assembling. Charles knows most of them by first name. He was only asked by the Inn a year ago to take part in the Moots, and he was initially reluctant. He was too busy to take time away from his desk or court to read the papers or to draft judgments, let alone spend valuable evening hours listening to students' legal arguments, many of which were pedestrian at best, some positively tranquillising.

However, after the first couple he was hooked. Rather like his time spent training the youngsters at the boxing gym, he found that he had a flair for teaching, and working with the pupils was energising. His informal approach and his ability to make them laugh, even when correcting them, won him many fans. When walking through the Temple, he is now often accosted by young barristers whom he encouraged to use his first name, an informality previously unheard of between pupils and senior members of the Bar.

The pupil barristers present their cases. Charles is particularly impressed by the prosecution barrister, a Nigerian student, who is tenacious in her cross-examination of the accused and his witnesses while remaining at all times completely courteous. As Charles always says to his students, "Cross-examination should never be *cross*" and she manages it perfectly. If the young woman intends to practice in England, he reflects, she'll have an uphill battle due to her colour and sex, but not due to lack of ability. She is far more polished and incisive than most students with her experience.

The evidence and speeches complete, Charles gives a very shortened summing up and the "jury" retire to consider their verdict. They take less than ten minutes to convict their fellow student, who throws himself melodramatically to his knees, confesses all and pleads for mercy, to general laughter. Charles sentences him to six months for the offence and a further six for dreadful acting, and the Moot comes to an end.

There is a burst of applause for the actors in Hall. Charles calls the students to order and opens a discussion, allowing the Benchers a time to decide on the participants' marks. Forty minutes later the results are given. To Charles's bewildered outrage, the prosecutor receives no mention at all.

'Twas ever thus, he thinks sadly.

He brings a formal end to the proceedings and the "court" breaks up.

As the excited participants mingle with the Benchers, glasses of sherry in hand, Charles manages to break away from the groups of chattering young barristers. They will all be dining in

Hall but Charles has declined the invitation and decided instead to leave early. Sean Sloane is working a late shift, and has agreed to cross the river for a bite to eat and a catch-up, rather than eat in the canteen.

Charles pops into Chambers to drop off his robes. Once at his desk he decides to call Sloane to say he's on his way.

'I'm so sorry, Charles,' replies the detective sergeant, 'but I can't make it. Something's blown up.'

Charles can hear tension and excitement in his friend's voice.

'Not even for a sandwich?'

'Sorry, mate, not even for that. I don't think I'll be leaving here for the next couple of days.'

'I see. Sounds important.'

'Gotta go. I know this is the second or third time and promise I'll make it up to you. Next time we meet I'll have some interesting news.'

'Righto. Understood. Hope it goes well.'

'Cheers mate.'

Sloane rings off.

At last! thinks Charles. *The game's afoot!*

CHAPTER SEVEN

'Look at this,' says Charles, spinning the newspaper round on the kitchen table, and stabbing at a headline on the front page with his cereal spoon. He strides to the radio on the sideboard and reduces the volume of Jack de Manio who, rather than reporting on the serious news, is in the middle of a "Today" interview with a man who claims to eat light bulbs.

'"KRAYS HELD IN DAWN RAID",' reads Sally from the *Daily Mirror*. '"Twin brothers Ronald and Reginald Kray, well-known in London sporting and club circles, were among twenty men detained by Scotland Yard detectives yesterday. One hundred detectives and twenty policemen took part in a series of raids — one of the biggest and most secret operations in the Yard's history. The first call by the police was on the 34-year-old Kray twins and their brother Charles, 41, at dawn."' She looks up at Charles. 'Is this Percy's story?' she asks.

Percy Farrow is Charles's gargantuan gourmand friend, a former police officer and now the best-informed crime reporter in London.

'Doesn't look like it. See there, the byline? But I'm going to give him a call.'

He dials Farrow's number at the old *Sunday Pictorial* building. The receiver is picked up instantly.

'Farrow,' announces the voice at the other end.

'Good morning, Percy,' says Charles.

'Charles. I expected you to call. I guess you've read the early edition,' replies Farrow.

'I have. Is there anything you can tell me, more than is in the paper?'

'Maybe, but not by telephone.'

'Why not?'

'Just trust me, all right? Can you make lunch?'

'Not one of your "proper" lunches, no,' laughs Charles. 'I haven't time right now for a four-hour gourmet experience, nor the inevitable hangover! But if you'll accept my company for a single course and maybe a glass of wine, yes, I'd be delighted, thank you.'

'That's very disappointing, Charles. You know I don't like eating alone. But I'll forgive you on this occasion. There's a new chef at the Wig and Pen Club, and I've been meaning to give him a try. Noon, for a preprandial glass of something?'

'I'll do my best. I may be a few minutes late.'

'Very well. I'll see you later.'

The Wig and Pen Club, known by the Royal Mail as 229–230 The Strand, is said to have been built on Roman ruins in 1624. The original building still stands today, a leaning five-storey Tudor survivor sandwiched between taller twentieth-century offices. It was originally constructed for the gatekeeper (and sometime illicit exacter of taxes) of Temple Bar, the gate into the City of London from the fields and villages to the west that eventually became the City of Westminster. Forty years after its construction, it survived the Great Fire of London, the only building in The Strand to do so.

In a square mile that is home to dozens of historic inns and taverns, the Wig and Pen Club may justifiably claim to be the most celebrated. For over four hundred years it has been the watering hole of some of England's most famous and infamous journalists, lawyers and parliamentarians. Oliver Cromwell is reputed still to haunt the building.

Charles stands outside on the busy pavement, looking up at the overhanging first floor. He has drunk (and been drunk) at the Club on several occasions and even dined there once or twice, but it's not his sort of place. It is the very essence of the "Establishment"; the sort of club where decisions of international import are taken, like White's in St James's, although the latter is a relative newcomer, having been established as recently as 1693.

Taking a deep breath, Charles enters the dark interior and gives his name. He is directed to the basement restaurant where Percy Farrow awaits him at a corner table for two. Farrow half-rises to shake Charles by the hand.

Every time Charles meets his friend, he worries anew about his health. The journalist is extraordinarily fat, with numerous chins squeezed inside a stiff wing collar, Saveloy sausages for fingers and an increasingly ruddy complexion. He wears, as always, a three-piece suit, the waistcoat of which — the circumference of a large barrel — is fastened by buttons that strain their threads and threaten to fly off at the slightest provocation. Farrow lives in a flat in Wembley with his spinster sister, who does not include cooking among her many accomplishments, and accordingly is usually the guest of one chef or another most evenings of the week. It shows.

Charles takes his seat.

'I hope you don't mind, Charles, but knowing the kitchen and the fact that you'll run off after thirty minutes, I ordered for you. Calvados Guinea Fowl, together with a lovely Saint-Nicolas-de-Bourgueil. I hope that meets with your approval?'

'I'm sure it'll be fine. How are you, Percy?'

'I'm very well indeed,' says the journalist, pouring wine into Charles's glass for him.

Charles leans forward. 'What can you tell me?' he asks.

'Oh, Charles, I know it bores you, but at least pretend some interest in the social niceties! It's always business with you.'

'Sorry, Percy, you're absolutely right. But I've got skin in this game, remember?'

Farrow sighs and shakes his head. Refusing to be hurried, he savours the final mouthful of his hors d'oeuvre, lays his fork down deliberately, reaches for his glass and takes a sip of wine, rolling it around in his mouth before swallowing. He dabs his lips fastidiously with his linen napkin and, finally, sits back. 'Very well. There will probably be a half dozen trials, three of murder.'

'Three? I guessed Frank Marshall and George Cornell, but who's the third? By the way, this —' Charles lifts his glass — 'is rather nice.'

'Jack "The Hat".'

'McVitie? He's not dead is he?'

'Apparently. No body yet, but strong evidence.'

'But he was an integral part of the Firm.'

'He was. But he took money from Ronnie to kill Leslie Payne, and notwithstanding the fact that he didn't complete the job, went and spent it. That's what Ronnie calls a "*something, something, something liberty*".'

He leaves Charles to fill in the expletives for himself. Despite having spent his entire adult life in the two most foul-mouthed professions, the Metropolitan Police and Fleet Street journalism, Farrow is the son and nephew of churchmen and will not tolerate profanity. 'In fact, it's the one likely to prove the Krays' downfall,' he adds.

'Why is that?'

Farrow leans forward and lowers his voice. The restaurant is in any event so busy Charles doubts that anyone at an adjoining table would be able to overhear, but Farrow is obviously nervous. 'This is what I couldn't tell you from the news desk. Charles, this is absolutely and completely confidential, understand?'

'Of course.'

'No, not "of course". I need your word as a gentleman that you will not tell *anyone* what I'm about to say.'

'You have it. Not even Sally.'

Farrow stares at Charles, evaluating him. 'Very well. Bear in mind, only a couple of Nipper Read's team know this. If it got out, the source of the leak would certainly be traced back. He'd lose his job and it could undermine the entire prosecution. All right?'

'If it's so confidential, why are you telling me?' asks Charles.

'My dear fellow, I'm telling you because, as you so crudely put it, you have skin in the game. I'm telling you because … it's possible you've been named.'

Charles's heart leaps. 'Named? By whom? In what context?'

'What do you know about Leslie Payne?'

Charles shakes his head impatiently. 'Not much, and no detail. They call him "The Man with the Briefcase".'

'They do — except Mr Ronald, who apparently refers to him as "Brains".' Farrow grins. 'That psychopath watches too many cartoons, I suspect.'

'I know Payne used to run the Krays' business empire. They say he pretty much created it for them.'

'Correct. It appears that Ronald took out a contract on Payne, a contract which McVitie didn't complete. He was certain Payne would talk to Read, and wanted to make sure he didn't. Ironically, it was the bungled assassination attempt which finally persuaded Payne he had no choice. Nipper met him several times before then and got nowhere. But after McVitie turned up on Mrs Payne's doorstep, Nipper confirmed that Mr Payne was on Ronald's "List". Payne realised he'd had a lucky escape, and changed his mind. I doubt he'd have talked otherwise. And for the last three weeks, nine to five, he has been sitting with Read and one of his sergeants in the library of a police section house in Marylebone, giving a statement.'

'Are you sure? How do you know?'

'Charles,' chides Farrow, sounding hurt. 'I'm an investigative journalist, remember? Like you, I have my sources. And I'm absolutely certain of this. Mr Payne's statement is 146 pages long, and tells everything. It's a blueprint of how the Firm has operated, all its contacts, all its criminal enterprises; everyone who has ever had any dealings with the Krays.'

'Will Payne give evidence?' asks Charles.

Farrow shrugs his enormous shoulders. 'Who knows? But right now it doesn't matter. Nipper's had all his suspicions confirmed. All the little threads of evidence he's been gathering for months have been tied up nicely. He now knows exactly who did what to whom, when and where. He knows where to apply pressure. He's so confident, he's been able to arrest almost everyone in one fell swoop.'

'And you think my name's somewhere in that statement?'

Farrow leans back in his chair and raises his eyebrows. 'You tell me.'

Charles also sits back to reflect. At the same time their meals arrive. The two men start eating in silence.

Although Charles knows who Payne is and his role in the Firm, he has never actually met him. He runs through in his mind all the occasions in the past few years he has had dealings with the Krays. More often than not he was acting in self-defence — either of himself or of someone else — and the Krays' aggression towards him gave them no leverage. That was not the case with regard to Merlin's trial and death, but

Payne wasn't involved in that in any way. But could he have known about it?

Then there was an incident in a recent trial when the twins tried to bribe a juror. It backfired, and Charles was instrumental in helping prevent a wrongful verdict. He certainly crossed the line then but, again, nothing to do with Payne. Would the Krays have mentioned it to him?

Charles has consumed his guinea fowl, untasted, by the time he has considered all the possibilities. Farrow, still savouring the meal, is not half-way through his plate.

'Well?' asks Farrow.

'Yes, it was lovely, thank you,' replies Charles distractedly.

'No. I mean, are you likely to be named?'

'Oh. I don't know. It's unlikely, but not impossible.'

'What are you going to do?'

'I don't know. I have no control over events. It'll depend on Nipper Read on one side and the Krays on the other.'

'Oh dear. You really are between Scylla and Charybdis, aren't you, old chap?'

'Yes,' replies Charles heavily. 'But I'm very grateful to you.'

CHAPTER EIGHT

Charles does not have to wait for long. His journalist friend might incline to Greek myth but Charles is more comfortable with the American "between a rock and a hard place". It is the hard place of the Krays and not the rock of Nipper Read that makes the first move. Forty-eight hours after his luncheon with the journalist, Charles arrives in Chambers to be grabbed by Barbara before he can even say "Good morning."

'Follow me, sir, if you will,' she says, striding towards him as he stands on the threshold of the clerks' room. She brushes past him and leads the way into the conference room. Charles follows.

Barbara opens the door for him, slides the "Conference in Progress" plaque across the door, and shuts it firmly. 'This arrived this morning,' she says.

She hands him what looks like a single sheet of paper with a bow of pink ribbon around its waist. Charles pulls the bow and unrolls the sheet. It is headed "*Brief to Counsel*" but it looks like no Brief Charles has ever seen before.

Briefs to counsel are usually several inches — sometimes several boxes — thick. The Instructions act as an index, listing the enclosures such as depositions, records of interview and copy charge sheets; they identify the proposed client and the charges faced; they explain what the solicitors require of counsel, such as an advice on evidence or attendance at a certain court.

Instead of all that useful information, this piece of paper simply says: *Conference. Brixton Prison, 11:30 today.*

Charles turns the sheet over in his hands. 'I don't understand,' he says, looking up at Barbara. 'Who's the client? What are the charges?'

'Apparently that will all become clear when you arrive,' she says angrily.

'It's a joke, surely?'

'No. That … *document* —' she cannot even bring herself to describe it as a "Brief" — 'came from Sampson and Co., and when I rang to protest they told me it was intended to be your Instructions, but they would give no further information. You are to meet Mr Ralph Haeems at the prison. He will explain.'

'Not Manny Fryde? Has he retired then?'

'No, but he's taking a back seat from now on.'

'So, we're to assume this is the Krays' case,' says Charles, heavily.

'That's my guess. I've assumed you'll go and I've put the conference in your diary. However, I would like you to make it absolutely clear to Mr Haeems that these chambers do not do business in this manner. I don't care what special arrangements he may have with his favoured chambers or what they might put up with, but this is a professional, long-established set, we are due some respect, and we will not be treated as Sampson and Co.'s back office.'

'I understand,' says Charles, but Barbara has not finished.

'How on earth can I do my job if I don't know the name of the case, where it's to be heard, how long the trial will last? How do I check availability? How do I check the lists? I've dealt with Mr Fryde before and he's always seemed very experienced and efficient. I can't believe he would allow Instructions to go out like this. I can only assume that this is his clerk, Mr Haeems.'

95

'I don't know about that, but I will make sure your views are communicated.'

'Thank you, sir. Please do.'

With which, she opens the door and storms back to the clerks' room, still fuming.

HM Prison Brixton always reminds Charles of a run-down council estate: a complex of buildings in yellowish London brick, lining narrow streets that house poverty, social dysfunction and lawlessness. Indeed, in that the prison lacks the burnt-out cars, the stained mattresses abandoned on the pavement and the graffiti so ubiquitous in some urban developments, it is rather *more* wholesome.

Charles walks down the access road and presents himself at the small side door for legal visits. His name is taken and he is allowed through the first series of locked gates to be searched.

He is an old hand at this. He has learned that, if possible, it's best not to bring bags or briefcases; he removes his jacket before being asked and lifts the collar so it can be searched for razorblades; he opens his two packets of cigarettes — part of his standard visiting paraphernalia, even for non-smoking clients who need prison currency — so they may be examined for drugs; he empties his pockets into the stainless steel dish before being frisked. Had he been provided with more than a single sheet of paper for his Instructions, he would have fanned the documents out on the desk to demonstrate that no hole had been cut into them, no receptacle for contraband.

Within ten minutes of arriving, a further barred door is being opened to him and he is shown into the conference suite. A man sitting with his back to the door stands to greet him. 'Mr Holborne?' he says.

'I'm Charles Holborne. Mr Haeems?'

'Yes. Pleased to meet you. Take a seat.'

Charles does so, examining the other man. He knows that Fryde's managing clerk was born into a Jewish family in India, but Haeems's skin colouring is lighter than Charles expected, more North African, Egyptian maybe, than Indian. Furthermore he is much younger than Charles supposed, probably not yet thirty. He is smartly dressed, with large framed spectacles and wavy hair brushed back from a slightly doughy face which Charles suspects will eventually tend to fat.

You must be something special, thinks Charles, *if you're being given conduct of such high-profile cases.*

'I must apologise for the way in which you were instructed, Mr Holborne,' starts Haeems. 'Everything has moved at great speed since last Thursday. I assure you that this is not the normal way in which I proceed. However, Sampsons have been instructed to represent most of the dozen accused, and my lay clients have provided me with a list of barristers they would like to consider, but precisely which barrister for which client has yet to be decided. To make matters more difficult still, the police have distributed my clients all around the country.'

'Presumably so they can't speak to one another.'

'That's what I suppose.'

'Are you able to tell me what charges the police have preferred so far?'

'Various defendants have been charged with conspiracy to murder and harbouring an escaped prisoner. What I have started calling the "second tier" defendants are charged with being accessories both before and after the fact of murders. These are the ones I expect Superintendent Read is hoping to turn. There are then third tier defendants facing less serious charges.'

'Does the first group include the Krays?' asks Charles, taking out his blue counsel's notebook and starting to make notes. 'Are they charged with murder or conspiracy?'

'Not yet.'

'Am I even here to see the Krays?'

'Yes, you are, but whether it's one or both I don't even know myself. I have two other clients to see as well, so I'm afraid I shall be shuttling backwards and forwards between here and another conference room. I hope that won't cause you any professional difficulties.'

Under normal circumstances it is not appropriate for a barrister to discuss the case with his client unless there is a solicitor or his representative present. However, on the basis that Charles is not yet instructed to act on behalf of the Kray twins — or, indeed, anyone in particular — he consoles himself with the thought that he is, probably, just about, within his professional rules. Haeems's delicacy makes him smile; the absence of a witness to this conversation is laughably insignificant compared to what the Krays are about to demand of him.

'Unless and until I am actually instructed for a specific client, I don't think there's any difficulty,' he says smoothly.

There is a noise outside and Ronnie Kray appears. As a prisoner on remand he is still able to wear his own clothes, but Charles is surprised to see that he is not in his trademark Italian suit and silk tie. He wears comfortable slacks, an open necked shirt and a woollen jumper. He looks as if he's about to play a round of golf. A prison officer escorts him into the room and leaves, closing the door behind him.

Ronnie takes a seat without making eye contact with Charles.

'Would you mind if I had a private chat with Mr Holborne, Mr Haeems?' Ronnie asks the solicitor's clerk respectfully. 'Just social matters, you understand.'

Haeems shares a glance with Charles. 'No, be my guest. One of my other clients is waiting for me with counsel, two doors down. I'll start there. Is that all right, Mr Holborne?'

Charles nods without replying, and Haeems departs. Ronnie Kray waits for his footsteps to recede.

'Right,' says Ronnie, coming straight to business, 'you're gonna be counsel for Ronnie Hart for the murder of McVitie.'

Charles makes a note. 'So Jack McVitie is dead, then?'

'So they say. Although, as you'd put it, that's hearsay, cos I got no direct knowledge, have I?'

Ronnie looks into Charles's eyes, challenging him. He is smiling, a mocking expression on his face, and Charles knows without a flicker of doubt that Ronnie killed his former employee or, if he didn't actually administer the *coup de grâce*, he ordered it.

'I see. Has Hart been charged yet?'

'Nah. Nipper missed him.'

'What? You mean he's not in custody?'

'Not yet.'

'Then how do you know he's going to be charged with murder?'

'Cos 'e's going to put 'is hands up to the actual stabbing. All right?'

So, McVitie was stabbed. I wonder what they did with the body?

'He's agreed to that, has he?'

'He will.'

Charles puts his pen down and examines the man sitting opposite him. Since his mental illness began some years back, Ronnie Kray has suffered periodic fluctuations in his contact with reality. During those spells he alternates between paranoia, when he sees assassination plots all round him, and drug-induced somnolence, when his eyes droop, his voice is slurred and he's a zombie. Right now he looks tired, but his eyes are bright, wide-open and intelligent.

Nonetheless, Charles remains sceptical. He picks his next words carefully. 'You've thought this through, have you, Ronnie? It's all very well having a plan, and maybe Hart's even agreed to it, but promises are cheap, especially if he's still at large. He'd say anything to keep you off his back, wouldn't he? That's a very long way from standing in the dock and actually pleading guilty. The prospect of a life sentence ... well, people get cold feet.'

'Yeah, we know that. Don't you worry. He'll plead, and if he wavers, you're gonna persuade him.'

'No amount of persuasion can make a man volunteer for a life sentence. Especially if he's got a shout at being acquitted,' points out Charles.

'It won't come to that. But if it does, you'll make him see sense.'

'Make him?'

'You heard me.'

'But —'

'If you ain't up for it, I'll find someone who is. And those documents you want so bad will be on Mr Read's desk. No skin off my nose. In fact, I'd almost prefer it, having you in the dock next to me, you arrogant little fuck. Time you was taken down a few pegs.'

Charles believes him. He studies the gangster whom he has known since boyhood. Kray is relaxed, smiling, relishing Charles's anguish.

He really doesn't care. Part of him would indeed get more pleasure in bringing me down than in helping himself.

Charles has learned over the years that Ronnie Kray has a genius for intuiting others' vulnerabilities. He is a sociopath, devoid of all conscience or sense of remorse, and a sadist; a man who derives his greatest pleasure when manipulating others to betray their fundamental selves.

Look what he did to the Reverend Stanley Sharpe, Charles reminds himself.

Only a year or so ago Ronnie went out of his way to have a man of God falsely convicted of murder. It wasn't the life sentence that got his juices going; it was having Sharpe condemned publicly as a hypocrite.

The gangster stands. 'Don't let me keep you, Mr Holborne,' he says with snide formality. 'Would you mind knocking on the other door and telling Mr Haeems I'm ready for 'im?'

Charles waits at the bus stop on Jebb Avenue for the 159 bus to Victoria. Once there he can take the tube to Temple. He could get back to Chambers much more quickly by taxi but he needs time to think, and he can do that better as part of an anonymous mass of human movement where everyone is going about the business of their daily lives.

How can anyone force a man to take a murder conviction "for the team"?

More importantly, thinks Charles, how could *he* force Hart to do it, when it runs against everything he's ever stood for?

But perhaps Hart is actually guilty?

That thought is consoling, but only for a moment. Even were Hart to confess to the murder, how could Charles believe it, knowing the pressure the Krays will have exerted over him and his family? Charles will never learn the truth, whatever Hart says.

The conversation with Ronnie Kray has at least settled one thing in Charles's mind: he knows he won't help the gangster escape justice yet again, not this time. Nor will he help convict an innocent man.

Charles has witnessed injustice and abuse of power throughout his life. The businesses of innocent, law-abiding Jewish shopkeepers, wantonly destroyed by Oswald Mosley's black-shirted thugs; grandmothers — not his, but *somebody's* grandmother — beaten up and put in hospital on the streets of the East End; Hitler's bombers flattening his community during the Blitz; innocent men framed and sent to prison by corrupt police officers; the same police officers lining their pockets with money from the very men they were supposed to apprehend; and politicians abusing their positions, and in some cases children, because there was no one to call them to account. Finally, and more recently, the injustice and prejudice displayed by his "honourable" and "learned" friends to Jews, people of colour, women — in fact anyone not in their illustrious club.

He has seen it and hated it all his life, and it developed in him a visceral determination to do his part in redressing the balance.

Charles devoted his life to the Law because, every now and then, it is capable of correcting the imbalance between the powerful and the powerless; to rein in the mighty and bring them to account. He knows the system is flawed, sometimes systemically and sometimes by the very forces bent on defeating it, but Charles still believes in it. Legal aid, perhaps the greatest democratising force ever invented by Parliament, permits the weakest, most invisible members of society to hold the most exalted to account on equal terms. It doesn't always work, but it's all there is.

Without the rule of law, everything collapses.

The bus arrives and Charles gets on with a group of cheerful West Indian women who look askance at his white skin and formal clothing, but who say nothing to him. Charles takes a seat on the empty upper deck. His thoughts return to Ronnie Hart, the twins' younger cousin.

Perhaps Nipper won't find him.

Charles considers and rejects the idea immediately. Ronnie Hart can't evade Nipper Read indefinitely. In any case, it doesn't matter; the twins would surely find someone else to take the fall for them, and Charles would be back where he started, merely with a different client. The task set him by the twins is to facilitate their coercion of some poor minion, *any* poor minion, to take the rap for McVitie's murder.

The problem is, I'm working blind. All the other players know more than I do; I'm just reacting.

That thought is more helpful. He needs to get some control over events, get into the game. He wonders again what Payne's statement might say about him, considers asking Sloane directly, and again rejects that idea. Sloane is a man of principle. He has shown complete loyalty to Read and he loves his job. It's taken him years, but he's finally found his tribe within the Met, and he's thriving. He would never put that at risk, despite his friendship with Charles. In any case, Charles couldn't ask it of him.

What then?

Charles's thoughts drift off and before he has reached any useful conclusions, he has arrived at Victoria.

He runs down into the underground and fights his way onto an eastbound District line train. Fifteen minutes later he is entering Chambers. He thinks he might risk Barbara's ire and bypass the clerks' room for once, but as his foot is about to land on the staircase leading up to the next floor the door opens and Jeremy sticks his head out.

'I thought it was you, sir. A DS Sloane has been trying to get you all morning. He's called four times. Please can you call him urgently?'

Now what?

'Sure,' says Charles with a heavy sigh. 'Can you get him for me? I'll be at my desk in thirty seconds.'

'Yes, sir,' replies the junior clerk. 'Right away.'

By the time Charles reaches his desk the phone is already ringing. He picks up the receiver.

'Detective Sergeant Sloane for you, sir,' says Jeremy.

The line clicks and Charles hears Sloane's voice.

'My boss needs to see you. It's urgent,' he says without preamble.

'Sure. I'm not in court on Friday so —'

'No, Charles. He wants to see you today, this afternoon if possible.'

Charles feels his stomach clenching. 'Sorry, but I can't. I've been out all morning —'

'Seeing the Krays. Yes, we know. Have you been instructed?'

Charles answers hesitantly. 'That's ... not decided yet.'

'Then you need to see us.'

'I need some time, Sean.'

'No, you don't, you need to come and speak to my boss. Don't let this opportunity go, Charles, because it may not come again.'

Charles draws a deep breath. 'Fine,' he says reluctantly. 'Where and when? Not at the *Prospect*.'

'No, we weren't thinking anywhere public. Know *The Black Friar* in Queen Victoria Street?'

'I think so.'

'There's a side entrance just under the bridge which bypasses the bar and goes straight to the upper floors. At the top of the steps on the second floor there's an old private function room. Four o'clock?'

'Okay.'

'Good. See you later.'

Charles hangs up.

So, he's being followed by the police. Or perhaps someone at HM Prison Brixton is reporting to Tintagel House, which is marginally more likely. It then occurs to Charles that the Krays probably have someone watching him as well. In fact, it wouldn't surprise him in the slightest if it were the same person. It's happened before, a nark reporting alternately to each side and doubling his money.

I need to start being much more careful.

Charles heads out to Mick's, the legendary greasy spoon on Fleet Street. It's not in his nature to be miserable for long, especially with a stomach full of artery-busting fried food. As he enters the steamy door he is hit full in the face by a tide of bacon fat, cigarette smoke and laughter.

Charles loves everything about the famous grubby café, from its all-day gargantuan breakfast for one and six, to its greasy Formica counters, cast off newspapers and legal and journalistic banter. He orders his standby cure-all, a comforting bacon and fried egg sandwich with brown sauce, washed down by two mugs of strong tea.

As he is finishing his second mug, he looks around at the other diners. The room is alive with talk and laughter — often shared between tables — and Charles realises that this place is the poor relation of the Wig and Pen Club. It too is a meeting place between lawyers and hacks, but it is as unpretentious as the Wig and Pen is grandiose. Here too one can meet movers and shakers, happy hacks and Bailey briefs, but instead of whispered state secrets, the diners here share scurrilous news desk stories and hilarious courtroom gossip.

Cheered, Charles returns to Chambers in a better state of mind and manages to do a little work before his time to meet Sloane.

At quarter to four he slips down to the ground floor. Making sure no one sees him as he passes the clerks' room, instead of heading down the main stone staircase he turns towards the back of the building and descends to the basement. Pushing carefully past stacks of unused chairs, an old noticeboard on wheels and boxes of antique law books mouldering in piles of their own dust, he finds the door to the basement corridor which runs underneath the pavement. This passageway is unknown to most people, even Temple tenants and residents. Charles's only risk here is of bumping into junior clerks having a crafty cigarette in a dark corner, or engaged in sweatier, more intimate, recreation.

He walks to the far corner of the courtyard before venturing up to ground level. Before stepping out he looks up to the pavement to scan his surroundings. There is a lot of purposeful pedestrian movement; no one is lurking suspiciously. Satisfied that the entrance to Chambers is not being watched or, if it is, his escape thus far has not been noticed, Charles emerges onto the pavement and swiftly exits the Temple via Tudor Street. From there he strides down to the Embankment and five minutes later he is crossing the road at the traffic lights opposite Blackfriars tube station.

The back door to *The Black Friar* is where Sloane said it would be. Charles hesitates. The last time he met Sloane's boss, Detective Superintendent Read, it was not a happy event and it damaged his friendship with Sloane. This time he is better prepared. He knows, or can guess, why Read wants to meet him. More importantly, Charles might be able to learn something of use; in particular, whether he is named in Leslie Payne's long statement. He pushes open the door to find a narrow staircase facing him. He climbs the steps to the second floor.

His approaching footsteps are heard. As he arrives on the second floor landing a door at the end of the corridor opens and Sean Sloane puts his head out.

'Charles,' says Sloane by way of greeting.

Sloane briefly and intensely locks eyes with Charles as he approaches, trying to convey something. A warning to be careful, wonders Charles? Or merely emphasis that Charles needs to be open to anything Read might offer? Sloane steps back, allowing Charles to enter.

The plot on which *The Black Friar* stands is triangular, shaped like a slice of cake, and the room which Charles enters is at the fat end with windows over two aspects, to the right looking across New Bridge Street and to the left onto the railway line spanning Queen Victoria Street. It is furnished with two desks, one wall of filing cabinets and another completely covered in pin boards. A man unknown to Charles is hurriedly pulling sheets over the boards to hide what is displayed, but Charles catches sight of portrait photographs with lines of tape joining them and cards full of handwriting under each. He has insufficient time to see if his photograph features in the rogues gallery.

Superintendent Leonard Read stands from behind the larger of the two desks. 'Mr Holborne,' he says, extending a hand. 'Thank you for coming. Sergeant Sloane you already know, and that —' he points at the third man — 'is Sergeant Hemingway. Take a seat.'

He indicates a seat in front of his desk and Charles sits, conscious that the two sergeants are behind him, flanking him one to each side.

This is the first time Charles has seen Nipper Read for some months. He is again struck by the fact that Read looks so different to the common perception of a police officer, particularly one employed in the Met. He is short, probably no more than five foot six inches, and he has a benign square face with light brown hair brushed from a neat parting. The little man looks tired, and his face is pale, almost as if he himself had been in prison for some months. *I suppose in one sense,* thinks Charles, *he has.*

'I heard about Tintagel House,' says Charles, 'but I didn't know you'd taken over London's landmark pubs as well,' he says, looking around at the room.

'It's a very complex investigation, as I'm sure you can understand. Lots of balls to keep in the air at the same time,' says Read with a wave of his hand. 'It actually helps to keep certain parts of it separate. Do you know why I've asked you to meet me?'

'I assumed it was for the same reasons as you spoke to me a few months ago. You want me to give evidence against the Krays.'

'That's a slight over-simplification. But we are interviewing a lot of people,' replies Read opaquely.

'I'm sure you are. But I'll bet you're not interviewing John Platts-Mills, Ivan Lawrence or any of the other defence barristers, are you?'

'They don't have the same history with the twins as you. As a matter of interest, have you been instructed to represent anyone in the Firm?'

'I don't have to answer that, Mr Read. Both the fact and content of any instruction I might have are protected by legal professional privilege.'

Read shrugs lightly, and smiles. 'It's not really of much interest to me,' he says. 'Although were you eventually to give evidence against the Krays or any of the other defendants on the indictment, that might be a little embarrassing to you, professionally speaking, wouldn't it? I don't see how you could continue to represent one of the defendants if you were giving evidence.'

'Not in the same trial, no,' confirms Charles.

'Anyway, more importantly, I want to repeat the offer I made to you a few months ago when we first met. It's the same offer as I am making to other potential witnesses. I am authorised to consider offers up to and including complete immunity from prosecution for accomplices of the Krays who give evidence against them.'

'I have never been the Krays' accomplice. I've told you this before. I have more often been their victim.' Charles speaks confidently, but is aware that his heart rate has accelerated. This is Read's opportunity to reveal that he now knows more about Charles's law-breaking than when they spoke the previous year. However, instead of challenging Charles, he continues speaking and his manner of delivery suggests that this is a stock speech, made many times before.

'For anyone who chooses not to assist the Crown, but against whom evidence of wrongdoing is found, I intend to prosecute them to the fullest extent of the law.'

Charles doesn't answer immediately. He waits, letting Read's words fade away, giving space for the policeman to continue. If he has evidence against Charles, this would be the time to mention it. Traffic noises and the toot of a train horn can be heard faintly through the windows. The silence in the room lengthens further.

Maybe he doesn't know.

Charles teaches pupil barristers that it's dangerous to ask a question to which you don't already know the answer. Nonetheless, Read's silence and Charles's gut instinct tempt him to take a chance.

He plays his card. 'But you haven't found any evidence of wrongdoing against me, have you?' he asks, 'or you'd be using it now to twist my arm to help you.'

'Our investigations are still not complete,' replies Read guardedly. 'But your name has come up, more than once.'

Charles's confidence heightens a notch. 'Gossip, but no evidence, right?'

'I'm not in a position to reveal —'

Charles interrupts. 'You see, Mr Read, the one thing I know about you, is you're straight. Unlike most of your brethren in the Met, you don't bend the rules. Which means if you had anything, even for reasonable suspicion, I'd have been cautioned by now.'

Pause.

'Well? Are you going to caution me?'

Read doesn't reply.

'What's more,' continues Charles, now increasingly sure and prepared to take an even greater risk, 'you won't find any evidence. As I have repeatedly told you, the rumours of my involvement with the Firm are false.'

'Why would anyone spread false rumours that you were a member of the Firm?' asks Read testily. 'What've they to gain?'

'Oh, come on! Are you really so ... lacking in imagination? I'm an East End boy who was a tearaway in his youth, a bit too ready to use his fists, who speaks with a Cockney accent. I grew up with a bunch of kids on the streets during the Blitz, many of whom now make their living as criminals. On top of that, I'm a Jew. Worst of all, I knew the Krays as a youth, boxed with them at the same club, even shared the same trainer for a while. Now, put that kid in the RAF, give him a scholarship to Cambridge and teach him to speak properly. Have him qualify as a barrister and instal him in chambers with a bunch of privileged, entitled, anti-Semitic, class-conscious toffs. Finally, watch him compete on equal terms *and* take their work from them. What do *you* suppose is going to happen?'

The length and energy of this speech surprises even Charles. Every word of it is true and is meant, vehemently, but he can't remember ever putting it all into one package. It comes out with more emotion and more violence than he intended, and it leaves the room silent for a long time.

Charles looks briefly over his left shoulder and sees that even Sloane, his friend of several years, is surprised.

Well, it may have revealed more of me than I wanted, but perhaps it'll convince them.

When Nipper Read replies, he does so softly, as if he were sad. 'You never struck me as a coward, Mr Holborne. I'm surprised.'

Charles is so astonished that for a moment he can't formulate a reply. 'What?' he manages eventually. 'Did you hear a word of what I said?'

'I heard.'

'Then how do you conclude I'm a coward?'

'I conclude that you could help us if you wanted, but you're too frightened. I've got statements from barmaids, minor criminals and members of the public, all coerced by the twins into assisting them. All brave enough to step up. You know the law and you can handle yourself, but *you're* too scared.'

'Anyone who isn't scared of the Krays doesn't know what they dealing with,' says Charles bitterly, thinking of his dead cousin and the knife attack he, Charles, suffered.

Read presses on. 'In some respects you're closer to the Krays than any of the others. Your evidence could make all the difference.'

Charles leans forward. 'I am not a member of the Firm and I never have been,' he hisses. 'I know nothing of what they get up to. And you know how they test you, before they allow you in? They give you something dangerous and dishonest to do — intimidating a witness, bribing one of your lot, being an accessory after a crime — to create leverage right from the start. From that moment you can never go to the police, and you get drawn in deeper and deeper, whether you want to or not. Even if I agreed to help you, it's too late! They'll never let me in now. I can't prove myself because you've arrested everyone.'

'That's not the only way —'

'I'm coming to that,' interrupts Charles. 'What you really want is for me to be instructed by one of them.'

'I've not asked you to do that.'

'No, not expressly, but I ask myself, what's your motive for continuing to pressurise me, and that's the only conclusion I can reach. My particular … my *unique* use to you, would be to feed you information once instructed by the Krays or one of

112

their lieutenants. In other words, break all my professional principles. Ironically, it's exactly what Ronnie Kray wants me to do!'

Read's face hardens. 'That is not what I'm asking! I wish to make that absolutely clear. That would be completely improper. It might even undermine the entire case we're building.'

'Then we have nothing further to say to one another. I have no evidence I can give you.'

'Explain to me how the Krays were involved in nobbling the jury when you acted for Dr Alexandrova.'

'I can't.'

'Explain to me the circumstances which led to your cousin's death on the river two years ago while you were in company with Ronald Kray and Patrick Connolly.'

'I can't.'

Read sits back in his chair and looks from one of his sergeants to the other. 'Very well,' he concludes. 'You know where to find us if you change your mind. But I warn you: this is a time-limited offer. Eventually indictments will be drawn, and if you haven't jumped by then you may find yourself standing in the dock next to your childhood friends. Do you understand me?'

Charles stands and, without another word, descends the stairs to the street.

CHAPTER NINE

Charles walks back to the Temple, lost in thought. Whatever Payne's statement contains, he thinks, it can't name him. Or, if it does, it's not enough to give Read sufficient leverage. That's the good news. On the other hand, Charles is no further forward, still stuck in the middle; undecided.

In his pigeonhole is a note asking him to call Sally at Chancery Court. He heads upstairs. Peter Bateman is in, his trial having finished. It's a Friday afternoon and he has his feet up on his desk as he leafs through a newspaper.

'Busy?' teases Charles as he enters.

'Run off my feet,' says Bateman, turning a page resting on his long legs, 'as you can see. Fancy popping into *The Clachan* for a glass of something?' he suggests. 'You look as if you could use it.'

Charles looks at his watch. 'A bit early, don't you think?'

'Yes, but I'm feeling very Fridayish, the weather's lovely and they've put some tables outside in Hare Place. Come on, I'll treat you to a glass of bubbly.'

'Tempting. But I'm supposed to call Sally,' says Charles, brandishing the scrap of paper. 'Let me do that first.'

Charles asks for an outside line and dials the familiar number of his former chambers. A young man picks up the phone, a voice unknown to Charles. He asks to speak to Sally, is required to identify himself, and is eventually put through.

'Who was that?'

'That's our new junior clerk, Simon. He's Stanley's nephew.' Stanley was Charles's senior clerk for years, but has now retired. 'You haven't forgotten tonight, have you?'

'Tonight?'

'I knew it! Your head's been all over the place the last few days. Friday night supper at Sunshine Court? Remember?'

For an additional payment, the home offers its clients the use of its guest dining rooms and kitchen staff. It enables families to be entertained on birthdays and anniversaries or, as in this case, Friday nights, and it helps in the illusion that the residents still have the same facilities for entertaining that they enjoyed in their own homes.

'Shit! I'd completely forgotten.'

'We have to go, Charles.'

'Do we? It's not the same as being invited to their actual home…' he evades.

'Yes, it is,' insists Sally. 'We'll have all the candles and wine stuff, right? The blessings? And your mum's the hostess?'

'Nominally, I suppose. The home actually arranges everything, but, yes.'

'Then there's no difference at all. You know exactly what she'll say if we *don't* go.'

Charles sighs heavily. Sally's right.

'And,' persists Sally, 'David and Sonia want to celebrate our pregnancy. Whatever your mum might think, they *are* genuinely happy for us. So we have to go.'

'Yes, of course. You're right,' he says. 'Sorry. I'll pick you up at home. Six o'clock?'

'Good boy. See you later.'

He hangs up and turns to Bateman. 'Sorry, mate, that glass of bubbly will have to wait,' he says.

'So I gather. Not to worry, another time.'

Charles checks his watch again and stands. 'I'd better get going. That flower shop on High Holborn's still there, isn't it?'

'Tut tut, Charles. If you'd been doing your duty by Sally, you'd know the answer to that.'

'Well?'

'It was there this morning.'

'Thanks. Have a good weekend,' replies Charles, hurrying from the room.

He puts his head into the clerks' room to announce his departure.

'Oh, sir!' calls Jennie as he's about to leave.

Jennie is Jeremy's counterpart. Known throughout the Temple compendiously as "JJ", they are the two junior clerks in Chambers.

'Yes?'

'This arrived earlier,' she says, brandishing a new set of Instructions. 'I've just booked it in. I thought you'd like to see it before you go.'

'Who's it from?' he asks, about to say it can be left in his pigeonhole for Monday.

'Sampsons.'

Jennie watches Charles's face turn suddenly pale. He enters the room fully and goes to her desk. He picks up the pink-ribboned brief and reads: "*Brief to Counsel — The Queen v Ronald Hart*".

It's only six hours since Charles saw Kray at the prison. So, Ronnie knew the brief was on its way. Charles was banking on having time, a few days, maybe even weeks before Hart was arrested, to come up with a strategy.

The decision he now makes is not the result of a careful evaluation of his position as between the threats posed by the Krays and by Superintendent Read. He makes it out of anger and a stubborn refusal to be coerced.

'Is Barbara in?' he asks.

'Yes,' replies the Scotswoman, entering behind him, her arms full of files. 'Oh, you've seen it. Congratulations.'

'Congratulations?'

'Half the Bar is angling for instructions in those trials. Hart's one of the big names in the Firm, isn't he?'

The tall clerk weaves her way to her desk and deposits the files on it.

Charles sees the court diary on Barbara's desk and spins it around so he can read it.

'Sir! You know we don't like members of Chambers going through the diary,' she protests.

'I know, I know, just give me a moment,' he says, distractedly. 'I promise I'm not looking at anyone else's entries.' He flicks ahead several pages. 'There,' he says, pointing to an entry. 'I can't take it. I've got something right in the middle of the trial period.'

Barbara takes the huge diary and forcibly turns it around again to read what Charles is indicating. 'That's nothing, a simple false accounting case. Anyone could do that. Don't worry about that, sir, I'll speak to the solicitors and move it elsewhere.'

'No, I'm not happy to do that. Who are the solicitors? Yes,' he says reading upside down, 'Allen and Overy. I've not worked for them before, and I'd like to. I don't want to let them down on my first outing.'

Barbara studies the entry and then looks up at Charles. Her expression is one of total bewilderment. 'But Allen and Overy didn't ask for you specifically; I just allocated it to you because you were free. I don't even think they know your name's against it yet. They might even ask for one of their regulars. Honestly, sir, don't worry about that case.'

She picks up an eraser, clears the case name from Charles's line in the diary and replaces it against another set of initials. 'There you are. You're free.'

Charles shakes his head. 'No, Barbara, if you don't mind, I'm not happy with that. Give the Sampsons brief to someone else.'

The noise levels in the normally hectic room drop. Charles is aware of at least two other barristers behind him, one who was talking to a secretary and another standing by the pigeonholes, both now listening intently.

Charles's ears are burning and he feels clammy.

'Are you saying you don't want to accept Sampsons instruction?' asks Barbara very distinctly so there can be no suggestion of misunderstanding.

'Yes. That's what I'm saying. I'm sticking with the Allen and Overy brief. As I'm obliged to do under the Cab Rank Principle. It came in first.'

Barbara shrugs and shakes her head. 'Everyone else in Chambers would bite Ralph Haeems's hand off for that case, but if you're sure…'

'I am, thank you. Well, I'll be off,' he says cheerily, ignoring the tense atmosphere. 'Have a good weekend, everyone.'

Charles heads for the door, aware that his progress is being followed by several sets of eyes.

Charles and Sally sit in Charles's newish Rover outside Sunshine Court just off the North Circular. Every now and then Jewish families pass the car on foot, knock on doors, are greeted warmly and disappear inside. Sabbath will start at dusk and, for Orthodox Jews, the embargo against work includes the operation of a car. No one living or visiting here drives on a Friday night.

Except Charles.

In the years since the war, East End Jewry has moved en masse to the suburbs. Hendon, Golders Green, Hampstead, Chingford and Ilford all have their own local synagogues, kosher restaurants, delicatessens, bakeries and double-parked Volvos on Sunday mornings.

They have been sitting in the car for twenty minutes. Sally has seen Charles's parents on a couple of occasions since he announced the pregnancy and both were polite, Harry even affectionate. Nonetheless Millie remains unpredictable. Sally is anxious to go in; she'll feel better once she's gauged the unpredictable mood of her future possible mother-in-law. Charles, on the other hand, wants first to bring Sally up to date on the events of the day.

'So, in short, you've said no to both sides, Nipper Read and the Krays?' she says, after hearing Charles's account.

'Exactly.'

'But it's the Krays who pose the most immediate danger, isn't it? If Ronnie carries out his threat, you could be arrested tomorrow.'

'Unlikely. I've no idea where the documents are, but they sure as hell aren't in his prison cell. So I probably have a few days at least. Plus, I don't think Reggie will let him do it yet.'

'Why?'

'Reggie's a tactician. If they think I can still be manipulated, they'll keep the threat hanging over me. The minute they hand me to Read, I'm no further use to them.'

Sally shakes her head. 'But you always say that when Ronnie loses his rag, Reggie can't control him. What if Ronnie's so furious with you refusing to play ball, he just orders one of his boys to deliver the papers to Read? In a fit of anger.'

'Then I'm screwed. But I can't do it, Sal. That's about the only thing I'm sure of. If it comes to a choice between sending an innocent man to prison for life, or putting my hands up to what I've done, then...' He shrugs and leaves the sentence unfinished. 'But I think it'll be okay.'

She snorts. 'How can you say that?'

''Cos I'll think of something. Come on,' he says, 'let's get this over with at least.'

Sally takes two deep, calming breaths, and then nods. 'Yup.' She still doesn't move. She looks across at Charles, her face contorted. 'I don't know who I'm more terrified of, the Kray twins or your mother.'

'No contest: my mother, every time. Ready?' he asks, his hand on the door handle.

Sally takes another deep breath and nods.

They get out of the car and walk up the path between neatly-tended flowerbeds. The smell of the Sabbath greets them as the door opens to admit them: chicken soup and *Challah* bread.

They travel up to the second floor. The dining area is being cleared following the residents' meal, and some are already being taken to their rooms for the night. Charles leads Sally towards the private dining room and opens the door.

David and Sonia are playing with their son, Jonathan, on a small couch. Harry is in his wheelchair at the table, wearing a suit and tie and his yarmulke. Millie, standing by the table, is fussing with the candles in their tall silver candlesticks. She looks elegant in a blue jacket and skirt that Charles remembers. She is even wearing her pearls, which someone must have remembered to bring from David and Sonia's home where all her valuables are now kept.

'The last to arrive, as always,' she says, not making eye contact with Charles. 'Anyone'd think you didn't want to be here, Charles. Hello, Sally,' she says, with noticeably greater warmth.

The next few minutes are taken up with kisses, hugs and solicitous enquiries. Charles listens intently for any acidic comment from Millie about the pregnancy, but he hears nothing untoward.

Is she dissembling, or has she forgotten?

The staff have made a real effort, and the room looks lovely. There are vases of flowers on the table and sideboard and the oval table has been prepared for a Sabbath meal. Judith, the duty team leader, hovers in the corner. She *is* Jewish, and her contribution is obvious. The table is laden with the foods of Charles's childhood, and a bottle of *Kiddush* wine and six goblets stand on a silver platter in the centre of the table awaiting the blessings. After everyone settles, David hands round glasses of champagne to toast Sally and the bump. Judith leaves to alert chef and the kitchen staff, and Sonia gently and discreetly guides Millie through the prayers over wine and bread. Then she too slips out to assist with bringing in the food.

Charles finds himself sitting beside his father.

'Everything all right, son?' asks Harry in his slow drawl. Charles has to listen carefully and watch his father's face to understand him clearly. 'You look as if you've the weight of the world on your shoulders.'

'I'm fine, thanks, Dad. It's just been a busy week.'

Harry regards his older son gravely. Harry Horowitz was a successful businessman. A furrier by training, he built a business, first as a manufacturer of fur goods, then as a retailer. The walls of his shop were covered in signed photographs of the rich and famous, including film stars, who were his former patrons. He retired early, leaving the everyday running of the

121

business in the hands of two competent managers, employees for thirty years or more, and when the fur trade began to decline he took the decision to sell the business as a going concern. Despite the stroke, mentally Harry remains sharp. He says little, and misses nothing. 'You know, Charles,' he says, articulating his words even more carefully, 'I read an interesting article in the paper this week.'

'Oh, yes?' says Charles, unsuspecting.

'Yes. That Superintendent Read fellow. He's arrested the Kray boys and the whole of their gang.'

'Yes? Come to think of it, I read something about that too.'

Harry smiles. 'That must be quite a weight off your mind.'

Charles tries to fix a smile to his face but finds it turning sour. He takes a deep breath, preparing to launch into platitudinous reassurance, but finds he hasn't the energy for it. 'Not really,' he manages.

He gives his father and brother a brief, and edited, summary of his difficulties. The family is well aware of Charles's connection with the Krays, because in fact the relationship began in the generation above. Harry used to take Charles and David to the boxing gym in Kennington when they were very small, and not only did he meet the twins and their older brother, Charlie Kray, but he knew their father from before the war. So Harry and David have no illusions as to how dangerous the Krays can be. But they are unaware that Charles has done some ill-advised things which have left him in their power.

He would rather die than tell them.

'So the Krays want you to represent one of the gang, and Read wants you to give evidence against them,' summarises David.

'Yes,' confirms Charles, 'that's it, in a nutshell.'

'And you've turned them both down.'

'Yes. But the twins won't let it rest. They don't take kindly to "No."'

'Is there anything we could do to help?' asks Harry. 'I might be able to have a word with Vi.'

'When was the last time you spoke to Violet Kray?' asks Charles.

'Shortly after the war, I expect.'

'There you are. Thanks, Dad, but I'm not sure it'd do any good — unless you happen to know how to get hold of Ronnie Hart, who's at liberty somewhere, and doing a better job than me at avoiding both sides.'

'If you've turned down the brief for Hart, why do you want to contact him?' asks David.

'I might be able to persuade him to help Read. I need Nipper Read to get his skates on and take the Krays out of circulation.'

'Ronnie Hart, you say?' interjects Harry. 'Any relation to Terry?'

'I've no idea,' answers Charles. 'Why? Who's Terry?'

'I used to know a couple, a nice couple, in Bethnal Green called Thomas and Mary Hart. They had two boys, and I think they were called Ronald and Terence.'

'What makes you think they're the same people?' asks David.

'I don't, but it's a coincidence, the names being the same.'

'How do you know so many people, Dad?' asks David, smiling.

'Don't patronise me, Davie. I may be in this thing —' he slaps the arm of his wheelchair — 'but I've still got most of my marbles.'

'Sorry, Dad,' says David, contrite. 'I didn't mean —'

'The East End's a small community,' interrupts Harry, 'and was even smaller before the war. All the local businessmen knew one another. We were all members of the same livery companies, the same Guilds, the same *shuls*. Everyone in the fur trade and the *schmutter* business used the same suppliers, the same outworkers and so on. And some were councilmen, like me and Thomas Hart. So, Charles, if it *is* the same people, would you like me to put you in touch with Ronnie Hart?'

'Sure, Dad,' replies Charles laughing gently. 'And if you could have a word with the trial judge and the Benchers of my Inn, that would also be very helpful.'

'You can make *geshpet* if you like —' starts Harry, mock-offended.

'No, no, Dad, I'm not making fun of you,' reassures Charles, reaching out to pat his father's knee.

'But if you'd like my help —'

'Honest, that'd be fantastic, if you can.'

The two brothers share a glance unnoticed by their father.

'Fine, I'll ask,' says Harry. 'But don't hold your breath, as they say. It's probably just a coincidence.'

CHAPTER TEN

Charles sits in the kitchen at Wren Street and pours himself another cup of coffee. Sally left for the Temple over an hour earlier.

He has a couple of days free of court commitments but Peter Bateman has secured himself a nice juicy instruction to prosecute a million-pound Post Office fraud and needs their room for a day-long conference. So, rather than work in the library, Charles brought a load of work home. He finds that he often accomplishes more in his study than when in Chambers, where he is constantly interrupted by telephone calls from solicitors and questions from junior barristers asking to pick his brain. So he will work here until late afternoon and then walk in, taking whatever he's completed to the typists. He is due in the Temple in any case at six o'clock for a Chambers meeting.

Music comes from the transistor radio in the background. At this moment Joe Cocker is explaining that he gets by with a little help from his friends. His hit was at number one but, despite slipping down the charts, is still receiving a lot of airtime on Radio Caroline.

Charles takes his coffee, reaches for his cigarettes and, in deference to Sally's wishes, opens the French windows and steps into the garden.

What was an area of broken fencing and rampant weeds when he moved in has been transformed over the last two years by Sally into a beautiful, restful space full of colour. He is about to lower himself onto the teak bench acquired earlier that year, when he hears the telephone ring. He leaves his cigarette burning on the arm of the bench and returns to the kitchen.

'Terminus 1525,' he says on picking up the receiver.

'Is that Mr Holborne?'

'Yes. Who's speaking?'

'My name's Terence Hart. I think our fathers know one another? Anyway, I got a message to call you, about my brother, Ronnie.'

Charles is so astonished that for a moment he can't reply. He hadn't believed for one minute that his father could conjure up a contact with Ronnie Hart.

'Are you there?' asks Hart.

'Yes! Mr Hart! Thank you for calling. It's a bit of a long story but, in short, your brother's in a bit of bother.'

'You don't say.'

'I don't know if you were told, but I'm a barrister, and I received some rather odd instructions to represent Ronnie. But I don't think he's been arrested or charged with anything yet.'

'No, he ain't.'

'Well, Sampson and Co. want me to represent him, but I can't do anything till he surrenders or is caught and faces charges. Are you in contact with him?'

Hart doesn't answer for a moment. 'I know how to get hold of him,' he says cautiously.

'Well, I think it'd be in his interests to speak to me. He can't run forever, and Superintendent Read is offering deals.'

'Deals?'

'Yes. He's completely focused on potting the Krays for murder. George Cornell and Jack McVitie certainly. He's saying that anyone who can put murder weapons in the Krays' hands and turns Queen's Evidence will be given immunity. Would your brother fall into that category?'

126

'I couldn't tell you.'

'Do you think you could arrange for me to meet him?' asks Charles.

'I don't know,' replies Hart. 'I've been telling 'im to hand himself in, but he's scared.'

'Look,' says Charles, 'he can meet me anytime, anywhere. Nothing he says to me will go any further, but I really think he should listen to what I've got to say, especially if he was on the fringes of one of those murders. Read has spoken to me, and he's definitely offering deals.'

There is silence at the other end of the line as Hart considers this. 'Complete immunity?' he asks finally.

'For the right evidence, yes. But it does depend on what Ronnie can say. That's why I need to see him. Completely off the record, wherever he likes. But as soon as possible.'

'I'll see what I can do,' says Hart, and the connection is broken.

Charles hangs up, lost in thought, and lights another cigarette, having forgotten the one burning away outside in the garden.

At half past five Charles packs up his papers, leaves a note to Sally telling her she should eat supper without him, and departs.

It is a beautiful summer's afternoon and he enjoys the walk south down Gray's Inn Road and Chancery Lane. He enters the Temple via the Mitre Court Gate which, unusually, has a Temple official managing those entering and departing.

'Afternoon Jimmy,' says Charles to the official as he comes to the front of the short queue of people waiting to enter. 'I didn't know it was that day, again. Aren't you a bit grand for this job now?'

The young man looks at Charles and his face breaks into a smile. 'Hello Mr H,' he says. 'We all do an hour or two, but it's such a lovely afternoon, I ain't complaining.'

Once a year the Temple enforces its legal rights by reminding its users that they enter the enclave only by permission, by closing the gates and re-opening them for each and every person coming through. It creates queues on both sides of the gate.

Charles has known Jimmy since he was a teenage junior employee and has watched him progress through the uniformed ranks of the Inn. The two men recognise something in each other. Both had troubled starts to their lives — in Jimmy's case a spell in Borstal for burglaries — but both have worked hard to pull themselves up by their bootstraps.

'Have a nice evening, sir.'

'And you,' replies Charles as he passes through the gates.

Charles reaches the clerks' room in Chambers before the typists leave and drops in their wire basket the papers now needing to be typed. In his pigeonhole he finds the agenda for that evening's meeting. There is only one item, the proposal that Chambers opens an annex on the south coast.

The vast majority of barristers practising in England work from one of the four Inns of Court in London. There are small chambers in other major cities but the London sets treat them as if they were slow-witted country cousins; the assumption is that any barrister who can't build a practice in London must be a duffer. The same arrogant condescension applies to annexes. Despite the fact that a provincial annex is clerked by the same staff and serviced by the same barristers as those based in London, they are still somehow not the "real thing". How can a few rooms above a bank overlooking the sea possibly be taken as seriously as a thriving set of barristers in the heart of the Metropolis?

As is often the case, Charles's attitude is different. If provincial towns are good enough for the solicitors who send all their work into London, why not offer a better service than the competition and actually work out of the same town? He does quite a lot of work in Lewes Assizes, and for long trials can think of nothing more pleasant than to use an annex in one of the nearby seaside towns, rather than commuting every day; get to know his instructing solicitors properly; build relationships. Nonetheless, as always within Chambers, the older and more traditional members resist change of any description, and Charles finds himself leading the youngsters in advocating a tentative entry to the twentieth century.

'I need a word with you, please, Charles,' says a voice behind him.

Charles turns. The speaker is Adrian Yelland QC. The tubby little man is the new deputy head of Chambers, but he has at least four toadies on the management committee who follow his lead in all things, so he effectively runs the set.

'Afternoon, Adrian,' says Charles.

'My room?' says Yelland, and he heads without further word to the first floor corridor. Charles follows.

Yelland's room is as large as Charles's but he doesn't share it with another barrister. It is clear that he has spent a considerable amount of his own money on it. The freshly-polished floorboards are covered in the centre by a thick Persian rug and Yelland's desk, placed at an angle in the opposite corner so that anyone entering the room will come face-to-face with its occupant, is huge, dominating the space. The walls are covered with oil paintings which, to Charles's untutored eye, appear to be originals.

Yelland closes the door behind Charles and waddles swiftly to his desk, where he sits. Charles is left stranded in the middle of the room and is not invited to pull up a chair. He has the sudden impression that he is about to be told off like a disobedient schoolboy.

'Now look here, Charles,' starts the other man, 'I've just had a very difficult conversation with Jeremy Stevenson QC at the Bar Council.'

'Yes?'

'Yes. Apparently a complaint has been made about you. You're going to be reported for breaching the Cab Rank Principle.'

'What?' exclaims Charles angrily. 'I have never broken the Cab Rank Principle in my entire career! If a brief comes in with my name on it, in my field of work, I take it. Who made the report?'

'Well, now, that really doesn't matter, does it?' replies Yelland, rather evasively.

'Of course it does. It's got to be either a Chambers client or one of the other barristers here, hasn't it?'

Yelland finds something to fiddle with on his desk. He looks distinctly uncomfortable.

'Was it a member of Chambers?' demands Charles.

'Frankly, it doesn't matter even if it was. The fact is you are accused of refusing a properly marked criminal brief.'

'Oh, I see,' says Charles as the tumblers fall into place. 'This is to do with that Sampsons brief, isn't it?'

'Yes, it is,' says Yelland after a pause.

'Which means it was someone in Chambers who overheard my conversation with Barbara. Have you spoken to her about it?'

'Not yet, no. I thought I should give you the courtesy of a heads-up first.'

'Well, thank you for that, but if you speak to Barbara you'll discover there was another case in my diary right smack in the middle of the trial period and I insisted that it should *not* be moved. It was because I was bound by the Cab Rank Principle that I *couldn't* accept the Sampsons brief. Somebody in Chambers is stirring up trouble. And not for the first time!'

Yelland's face assumes a strange expression which at first Charles cannot decipher. It takes a moment to realise that Yelland is relieved.

That's let him off the hook. He won't have to go into bat for a troublesome member of Chambers and risk upsetting the worthies at the Bar Council.

The little man has always struck Charles as a coward; for a barrister, whose every working day involves conflict, he has a steadfast aversion to battle.

'And Barbara will confirm that?' he asks.

'She will. There were several other witnesses present too.'

'Well, that's perfectly all right then,' says Yelland, standing. 'Probably just a misunderstanding. No doubt you'll receive the standard letter, but if you reply telling them what you've told me, all should be well. Good.'

He stands and starts ushering Charles out of his room.

'Never a good idea to upset the Bar Council, is it?' he says. 'That sort of mud can stick. Oh, look at the time! They'll be starting in a moment. Are you coming to the meeting?'

Charles is still so angry that he is about to refuse and head for a stiffener at the nearest pub. The prospect of looking around the table and wondering which of his learned friends is trying to have him censured or, worse, suspended from the Bar, makes him feel sick.

Fuck them!

'Wouldn't miss it for the world,' he says defiantly.

Charles and Sally are eating a hurried breakfast together the following morning. Charles is reading passages from the newspaper, quoting from the report of Enoch Powell MP's speech given that spring. It is still news.

'"The River Tiber foaming with blood"?' Sally repeats.

'*Much* blood,' corrects Charles.

'So he reckons West Indian immigration's going to cause civil war, then?'

'Seems so,' replies Charles, folding the paper. 'What an appalling man. We're supposed to send them all back, after we encouraged them to come and help rebuild the economy.'

Sally starts clearing the cereal bowls from the table.

'Trouble is, he's so articulate, he almost makes it sound reasonable,' says Charles.

'No. The trouble is, a lot of people agree with him.'

'Right-wing racists.'

'Not just them. People like your mother.' She sees Charles's shocked expression, but she presses on. 'I know she'd never say it out loud but for the dementia, but isn't that what she really thinks?'

'No!' insists Charles, finding himself in the novel position of defending his mother. 'It's not because of the colour of their skin. It's the pace of change. She grew up in an exclusively Jewish environment. Everything's changing too fast for her, and she's frightened.'

Sally locks eyes with Charles for a moment, shrugs and walks to the sink. 'Whatever you say.'

Charles falls silent.

In the East End it was common to hear members of his parents' generation use a pejorative Yiddish term to refer to West Indians. Charles never understood it. Hadn't the Jews suffered exactly the same sort of discrimination? And weren't the West Indians "strangers in a strange land", as the Jews had always been, doing their best to work hard and build lives? If Jews couldn't feel kinship with immigrants, who could?

His parents, always polite and respectful, never used the expression, certainly not in his presence. But then, during an episode of confusion when Millie wandered off and tried to board the Tube in her nightclothes, she threw it at the West Indian ticket collector who barred her way.

It rendered Charles intensely uncomfortable. As much as he tried to excuse the outburst as a manifestation of Millie's deepening dementia, he had since found himself privately asking the question now posed openly by Sally. For a while he managed to reassure himself, not least by recalling the charm and kindness demonstrated by his parents to Maria. Charles's mixed-race ex-pupil, now a permanent resident with him and Sally at Wren Street, is an integral part of their household. She had even been invited to the Horowitzes although, now Charles thinks about it, he can't remember an occasion when she actually accepted. Perhaps he's been missing something, he muses; something that Maria can detect, an attitude perhaps, which he cannot. He resolves to speak to her about it.

'I forgot to ask,' says Sally brightly from the sink, her tone indicating a sharp change of subject, 'how was the meeting last night?'

Her words shake Charles out of his reverie.

'Long and difficult,' he says heavily.

'And?'

'Well, the good news is we voted to open an annex somewhere on the south coast. Probably Hastings, as it's central to the firms who send most of the East Sussex work.'

'And the bad news?'

'The vote was very close, and it's conditional upon my agreeing to go.'

'You? Why?'

'I kind of walked into a trap,' replies Charles, pouring the dregs of the coffee into his cup. 'If it's to be successful, Chambers has to be taken seriously, so they want senior members available down there. As I was the strongest advocate in favour, the juniors looked at me to take the lead.'

'Not unreasonable.'

'I agree. And of course the others, the starched shirts, would be delighted to see the back of me.'

'What did you say?'

He shrugs. 'What could I say? I said I couldn't go, not right now. I didn't say you were pregnant. I just said "for personal reasons".'

'Could you commute?' suggests Sally.

'What, stay on the south coast during the week and come back at weekends? Hardly ideal. What if something happens? No. I want to be part of this, and not just at weekends.'

'So, how was it left?'

'Unless I agree to go, I think the project's dead in the water.'

Charles stands, collects the remaining crockery from the table and takes it to the sink. 'I'm pretty much ready to go,' he says. 'I'll do these while you pack your bag.'

'Okay.'

Sally runs upstairs.

Fifteen minutes later they are walking together down Gray's Inn Road towards the Temple.

Sally reverts to one of her favourites topics, her list of possible names for their forthcoming child. Charles listens with only half his attention. He hasn't told her of the professional complaint to be brought against him. He knows he could do so — she was completely supportive when he informed her of the Krays' blackmail — but he can't bear to add anything further to her existing burden of anxiety. The late miscarriage she suffered only a few months ago still weighs heavily with him. He had no choice but to explain why the Krays gave him a beating, but this he can manage himself.

They part, kissing briefly, on Fleet Street and enter the Temple by different gates.

Charles is the first to arrive that morning. He unlocks the huge studded oak door and steps on something white. He bends to pick it up. On the mat behind the letterbox is an envelope with his name on the front and the typed words "Private and Confidential". It bears the insignia of the General Counsel of the Bar. Charles tears open the envelope.

Inside he finds the letter which Adrian Yelland QC warned him was on its way. It informs Charles that a complaint of serious professional misconduct has been made against him, namely a breach of the Cab Rank Principle. As particulars, it is said that Charles Holborne Esq., without reasonable justification, refused to take a properly marked brief in the field in which he purports to practice, namely a criminal matter entitled The Queen versus Ronald Hart.

The letter continues to give procedural details of the disciplinary hearing before the Bar Council, the submission of evidence and so on.

Still holding the letter, Charles goes over to Barbara's desk, sits in her seat and opens the diary. He looks for the Allen and Overy case which will let him off the hook.

He can't find it. His feels his heartbeat speed up. He flicks diary pages backwards and forwards with increasing urgency, but is finally forced to the obvious conclusion: it's no longer there. He suddenly feels clammy. Then he looks more closely at each entry against his name for the whole of the next quarter. He finds the page. The pencil entry is still faintly visible, but it has been rubbed out.

He goes back to the beginning of the quarter and checks carefully the name of every barrister in Chambers. It's not there either; it hasn't been transferred to a colleague. The case has simply disappeared and, with it, Charles's defence against the Bar Council charge.

His choice is now simple: he either admits the charge, and is censured or even suspended, or he does Ronnie Kray's bidding and accepts the instruction in Hart's case.

How on earth did Kray manage this?

No.

He reassesses. The Krays have no concept of the professional niceties of the Cab Rank Principle. This is too subtle, too clever by half. The only people familiar with the arcane rule, designed to ensure that barristers cannot pick and choose only winning cases or likeable clients, are barristers. And, of course — and here Charles's heart sinks — solicitors.

Sampsons? Could they have pulled Allen and Overy's strings, persuaded them to remove the brief from Chambers? Even that seems pretty unlikely.

The other possibility and, it seems to Charles, the most likely, is that someone in Chambers is simply trying to cause him trouble. Plenty of Charles's colleagues can't stand him and, as Charles said to Yelland, it would hardly be the first time.

So, on balance of probabilities, a coincidental confluence of malice.

Charles ponders for a few minutes more but eventually realises that it's pointless. He slams shut the diary. It doesn't matter who is responsible. He has to make a choice. It's that simple.

He takes the letter upstairs to his corridor, unlocks the outer door and goes to his desk. From the drawer he takes a sheet of paper and he begins to write a reply to the Bar Council. It is a short letter.

Dear Sirs.

I refer to your letter of 3rd relating to an alleged breach of the Cab Rank Principle. You assert that I have refused an instruction for the Defence in the case of The Queen versus Hart. I don't know the source of this information, but it is false. I am instructed in the Hart case and I have accepted the instruction. I invite you to contact my clerks who will corroborate the foregoing. Please confirm by return that no disciplinary proceedings will follow.

Ten minutes later he hears the junior clerks chatting as they enter Chambers and he descends to the clerks' room, completed letter in hand.

'Good morning, you two.'

'Good morning, sir,' Jennie and Jeremy say in unison.

'Do you happen to know what happened to the Allen and Overy trial that was in my diary?'

'Yes, sir,' replies Jennie. 'They phoned yesterday and moved it out of Chambers.'

'Do you know why?'

Jennie shakes her head. 'Sorry.'

'Okay. What happened to the Sampsons brief? You know, the Krays' trial. Have you allocated it elsewhere yet?'

'No, sir,' replies Jeremy. 'Barbara told us not to. She hoped you'd change your mind.'

Charles sighs and smiles grimly. 'I've changed my mind.'

'Very good, sir. Do you want me to put it back in your diary?' asks Jennie.

'Yes, please. Oh, and can you post this letter to the Bar Council? Their letter to me is there too. I suppose we should keep copies. By the way: did you happen to notice which members of Chambers were in the room when Barbara and I were discussing the Hart case?'

Jennie and Jeremy look at each other.

'Was one of them Mr Knight?' asks Jennie.

'No,' replies Jeremy, 'he was still on holiday.'

Jennie shrugs. 'In that case, sir, sorry, but I don't remember.'

Charles sighs. 'All right, thank you.' He hands the letters to Jeremy. 'Not a word of this to be discussed outside this room, got it?'

Both youngsters nod. They might be young, but they both understand the implications.

'I'm going to put the kettle on,' says Charles. 'Could one of you locate the papers and bring them up now? I'll start on them right away.'

Charles heads back to his floor.

Round two to Ronnie.

It's early in the bout, but Charles is losing on points.

CHAPTER ELEVEN

Charles opens the Brief and starts to read.

THE QUEEN
- and -
RONALD HART
BRIEF TO COUNSEL

Enclosures:

1. *Deposition of Oswald Tennyson*
2. *Deposition of Carol Skinner*
3. *Statement of Colin Tyldesley, Scenes of Crime Officer*
4. *Statement of DS Frank Cater*

Counsel is instructed on behalf of Ronald Hart. At the time of drafting these Instructions Mr Hart's whereabouts are unknown. However it has been indicated via intermediaries that he is shortly to surrender to custody at which time he will be charged with the murder of Jack Dennis McVitie on or about 28 October 1967. Our present instructions, to be confirmed by our client in due course, are that he will enter a guilty plea to the charge.

In order to assist in Counsel's preparation of the case, Instructing Solicitors include herewith the statements served by the Crown in respect of the prosecutions of two other defendants, namely Mr Anthony Barry and Mr Christopher Lambrianou. Counsel will be able to gather from the enclosures the evidence likely to be led by the Crown against our client. Counsel will be kept up-to-date with developments in respect of any further evidence served that relates specifically to Hart. Once our client is in custody Counsel will be invited to meet him in conference with a view to

advising on evidence, mitigation and likely sentence.
Sampson & Co.

Charles pauses in his reading. 'These are, without doubt, the oddest Instructions I've ever received,' he says out loud.

Peter Bateman, who has just arrived for the day, looks up from his desk. 'How so?'

'Have you ever been instructed for a client yet to be caught, yet to be charged and yet to instruct solicitors? And for murder? But the sols say that, despite not having met their client, he's going to plead guilty!'

'This is Sampsons, right?' asks Bateman.

'Yes, but not Manny Fryde. I don't know anything about this guy —' Charles leafs to the signature at the end of the Instructions to remind himself of the name — 'Ralph Haeems, the managing clerk. Ever heard of him?'

'I heard he's taking over more of Manny's cases,' replies Bateman. 'That's all.'

'Any suggestion he's dishonest, or in the Krays' pocket?'

'No, nothing like that. But I suppose they could be pulling the strings.'

Charles considers that possibility for a moment. 'But Fryde has the reputation of being a straight arrow, and I can't imagine he'd allow it,' he concludes.

He turns to the statements.

Deposition of Oswald Tennyson
Occupation: *Barman*
Address: *c/o The Regency Club, 240A Amhurst Road, Stoke Newington, London N16*

Magistrates Court Rules 1952: *This deposition of Oswald Percival Tennyson, Barman, is sworn before me, Kenneth Barraclough, Justice of the Peace, on 18 July 1968, in the presence of the accused, Christopher Lambrianou, at Bow Street Magistrates' Court.*

Signed: *Kenneth Barraclough*

Signature of deponent: *O. P. Tennyson*

Oswald Tennyson WILL SAY AS FOLLOWS:

I am a barman employed by the Barry brothers, John and Anthony, who own the Regency Club and Restaurant at the above address. I have been employed at the club as a barman and occasional doorman since it opened in 1960. Everyone knows me as "Ozzy".

On the evening of 27 October 1967 I was working at the nightclub on the door. At around 9 o'clock a group of men arrived. I recognised several of them, including two of the Lambrianou brothers and Ronnie Hart, a cousin of the Kray twins. There are five Lambrianou brothers and I don't know them all by name but one of them was definitely Christopher, known by everyone as "Chrissie". At the time when this group arrived, Mr Anthony Barry was just inside the door at reception. It was clear to me that the group had been drinking. They smelt of alcohol and they were speaking loudly and aggressively.

One of them asked Mr Barry if Jack McVitie was in the club. Mr Barry said that he was inside. One of the others, I think it was Ronnie Hart, said that they intended to kill him. I couldn't believe he just said it out loud, in front of Mr Barry and me, and at first I thought he must be joking, but they all looked serious. Mr Barry asked if they meant to kill McVitie in the club, to which the answer was "yes". Mr Barry was outraged. I could tell he was frightened of the men but he insisted that they couldn't kill anyone in his club. He said the Regency would be shut down and he would be ruined, and there were dozens of witnesses. The men wouldn't listen at first but Mr Barry continued to insist that he wouldn't allow them in to commit a murder.

Eventually they seemed to agree. One of them, I can't remember which, put a gun on the reception desk and told Mr Barry to look after it.

The two Lambrianou brothers went into the club to keep an eye on Mr McVitie and make sure he didn't leave. The others left.

About an hour or so later Ronnie Hart returned. Mr Barry and I had remained on the door to make sure there was no trouble. Hart told Mr Barry to bring the gun to the basement flat at 97 Evering Road, which is a short walk from the club. Mr Barry asked why Hart couldn't take it himself as he was going back there in any case, but Hart insisted that it had to be Mr Barry who carried it. Mr Barry said he couldn't leave his club while it was still open, and Hart should take the gun, but Hart was adamant and threatening. I could see that Mr Barry was very frightened. He picked up the gun and left the club with Hart. He returned twenty minutes or so later. I asked him what had happened and he told me it was best if I didn't know.

The two Lambrianou brothers were still in the club, drinking with McVitie. McVitie had been drinking all evening and was quite jolly. At about 1:30 am a man came in and whispered in Chrissie Lambrianou's ear. The two Lambrianou brothers then spoke to McVitie. I didn't hear all that was said, but I did hear something about a party at "Blonde Carol's flat". The three men then left the club together. It did not look to me as if McVitie was forced to leave. He still seemed happy and was laughing and joking with the Lambrianous.

I have been asked if either of the Kray twins was present during the course of these events. The Krays are regular visitors to the club and I know what they look like. I did not see them at any time.

I am prepared to give evidence in court about what I saw that evening.

Signed: *Oswald Percival Tennyson*

Deposition of Carol Skinner

Occupation: *Housewife*

Address: *97 Evering Road, Stoke Newington, London N16*

Magistrates Court Rules 1952: *This deposition of Carol Skinner, housewife, is sworn before me, Kenneth Barraclough, Justice of the Peace, on 22 July 1968 in the presence of the accused, Christopher Lambrianou, at Bow Street Magistrates' Court.*

Signed: *Kenneth Barraclough*

Signature of deponent: *C. Skinner*

Carol Skinner WILL SAY AS FOLLOWS:

I am a housewife and the mother of two children living in the basement flat at 97 Evering Road, Stoke Newington. On the evening of 27 October, 1967 I was at home. I had a few friends around. It wasn't a party as such, just an impromptu gathering. We were playing records on the record player, but not very loud because my two children were in bed asleep. There was a knock on the door and I opened it to find three men on my doorstep. I knew two of them as "Ronnie", Ronnie Hart and Ronnie Bender. I knew these two men from having met them in local pubs and at a couple of parties. They had always been friendly towards me, and they had been to my flat before. I did not recognise the third man.

The men told me to go out for a while as they needed the flat for a party. At first I refused. I told them that it was late and the children were asleep, but they were very insistent. They seemed to be in a hurry and I was virtually ordered out of the house. They told me to go across to a friend's house.

I have met the Kray twins at several clubs and pubs in the area, and I knew Ronnie Hart and Ronnie Bender were members of their gang. Ronnie Hart is the Krays' cousin. I knew that the men who arrived at my door that night were all very dangerous. I was frightened and I didn't feel I could refuse. My friends were all leaving and I felt vulnerable, so I got the children out of bed, put them in their dressing gowns and took them over the road to a neighbour's house.

I didn't know what time I could return but I thought they would have finished with the flat by the early hours of the morning. At about 2 am I left the children in bed at my neighbour's and went back to my flat. Ronnie Bender came up the steps and wouldn't allow me to go in. He said "There's been a bit of a bother". He was wearing a pair of my son's socks over his hands, and I could see they were bloodstained. You can see into the bathroom window from the pavement if the window is wide open. I saw another man, also a member of the Krays' gang called Chrissie Lambrianou, pouring a bowl of dark liquid down the toilet. I insisted on being allowed into my flat, and eventually they let me go down. The carpet in my front living room had been taken up and the underlay was covered in dark stains which I believed to be blood. A man unknown to me was cutting it up and taking it out the back where there was a fire in the garden. He was putting sections of the underlay on the fire. When I went into my bedroom I saw that my candlewick bedspread had gone as well.

I knew that something terrible must have happened in the flat but I was too frightened to say anything to the police. Everyone knows that if you inform against the Krays you can be hurt or even killed and I had the children to think about.

A few days after these events a man called Albert Donoghue arrived in the flat and redecorated it completely, including hanging new wallpaper.

I was given no money either to let the men use my flat or to remain silent. Only after the Krays and their gang were arrested did I feel it safe to tell the police what actually occurred.

Signed: *C. Skinner*

Charles pauses in his reading to make some notes in his blue counsel's notebook. He then sits back to consider the evidence he has read.

'Well?' asks Bateman.

Charles sighs. 'It's obvious that both witnesses know the twins, and the people they do name are Firm members. But the barman specifically says the twins weren't involved and "Blonde Carol" implies the same.'

'So the Krays are off the hook?'

Charles shakes his head. 'It inconceivable that so many of their lieutenants would be involved in a murder of one of their own without their directing it.'

'It's happened before though, hasn't it?'

'Not really. Members of the Firm have killed for their own unrelated business interests, once or twice to settle a score. And there have been a couple of drunken fights which left bodies. But there are no fewer than five named Firm members involved here, either in the run-up or the aftermath of the killing. Five! Two Lambrianou brothers, Ronnie Hart, Ronnie Bender, and Albert Donoghue, the decorator. Five of them acting together without the Krays' approval? Never. And the way in which McVitie died? It's got Ronnie's fingerprints all over it. No, either the Krays ordered it or, more likely, were directly involved. These witnesses have been paid, or more probably frightened, into leaving them out of their statements.'

Charles flicks through the remaining two statements. The first is from a Scenes of Crime Officer who was involved in stripping back the wallpaper of Blonde Carol's flat and who found widespread bloodstains. The second is from another police officer who interviewed Chris Lambrianou, who answered every question put to him with "No comment".

'Is there enough to convict Hart?' asks Bateman.

Charles sits back and considers the question. 'Neither witness puts him actually in the flat at the time of the murder, and the barman only *thinks* that it was Hart who said they were at the Club to kill McVitie. And, as we know, *thinks* is not the same as sure beyond reasonable doubt. But this is definitely enough for conspiracy, maybe even murder as part of a joint enterprise. As for an accessory before or after the fact — he wouldn't have a hope.'

'Maybe Hart actually did it,' says Bateman, expressing Charles's deepest hope. 'That's why he's pleading.' He studies Charles's frowning face. 'But you don't think it's that simple?'

'It's never simple with the Krays.'

'You'd know more about that than me.'

Charles look up sharply at his friend. 'What's that supposed to mean?'

Bateman looks flustered. 'I didn't mean that the way it came out. Sorry.'

Charles gives his former pupil a hard stare. 'Of all the barristers in the Temple, I wouldn't have expected that from you,' he says.

'Sorry,' repeats Bateman. 'What I was trying to say is ... well, watch out. You're playing with fire with those two. I wonder if your first instinct — to decline the instructions — wasn't the right one.'

'I tried that. Someone in Chambers reported me to the Bar Council. And the Allen and Overy case has mysteriously disappeared and, with it, my defence. So I've no choice.'

CHAPTER TWELVE

Dawn has retreated. The cloud cover is so low that it seems to be getting darker rather than lighter and rain hammers down with such force that it bounces back off the pavements to ankle height, soaking the turn-ups of Charles's trousers.

Charles reaches the end of Wren Street and looks up and down Gray's Inn Road. No welcoming yellow "For Hire" signs. Several taxis sweep past him, sending sprays of water to knee height, all occupied. He grips the handle of his umbrella more firmly and angles it to face the wind, realising that his suit will be drenched by the time he reaches the Temple. He turns around. It's only a mile or so, but he'll collect the car and drive in.

But for that decision he wouldn't have spotted the man loitering outside his house. As Charles runs back towards his steps, he sees, on the other side of the road, a short man wearing a raincoat and hat. The man seems to be undecided. He stands on the kerb, right opposite Charles and Sally's front door, gazing up at the lit bedroom window. He seems to be about to step onto the road, to walk towards the front door, when he hears the sound of Charles's running feet. He freezes. At the same moment, Charles's front door opens and Maria steps out. The man's gaze fastens on the young woman and there is something about his posture which suggests surprise. It seems that the combination of Charles's approach and the sight of Maria leaving the property breaks his resolve. He spins on the spot and sprints away from Charles towards the far end of the road, his feet splashing through puddles.

Charles slows to a halt at his front steps just as Maria reaches the pavement.

'What was all that about?' she asks.

Charles squints through the rain to the far end of the street. The man has disappeared round the corner. 'Haven't a clue,' he says, frowning. He turns to Maria. 'Decided to take the car. Can I give you a lift?'

'If you don't mind going the wrong way,' shouts the young pianist over the noise of the downpour. 'I've a train to catch from King's Cross.'

'Let me get the keys. Want to come back in for a second?'

'Sure.'

They both re-enter the house. Maria stands on the hall mat to avoid dripping on the tiles while Charles runs upstairs.

Sally is dressed but still drying her hair from the shower. 'What did you forget?' she asks.

'Nothing. The weather's too bad to walk in. But there was someone loitering outside the house.' Charles explains quickly what he saw.

'Who do you think it was?' she asks.

'No idea. Someone from the Firm? One of Read's men? But I had the impression that he was coming to the door. He wasn't hiding. I just scared him off.'

'I can't afford to wait to find out,' says Sally. 'I'll come with you, if you give me thirty seconds.'

They drop Maria off at the station. Then, instead of heading south directly towards the Temple, he and Sally circle back to check the house. There are a couple of pedestrians scurrying through the rain on their way to work, but no sign of the man. Charles turns the car south on Gray's Inn Road towards the Temple.

Charles works steadily on papers throughout the day. Rather than popping into Hall for lunch as they usually do, he and Bateman, who is also under pressure of work, eat sandwiches at their desks. Charles works later than usual, knowing that Sally has a doctor's appointment.

At half past seven that evening he finally switches off his desk lamp. 'I've had enough,' he says. 'Quick glass at the *Witness Box*?' he suggests to the barrister working opposite.

'Can't,' says Bateman, stretching. 'Still loads more to do. Nice offer though.'

'Okay. I'll be off, then.'

Charles packs up and leaves Chambers.

The narrow cobbled lanes and courtyards of the Temple are largely deserted. The sounds of twentieth-century traffic can be heard faintly from Fleet Street to the north but otherwise the Temple has sunk back into eighteenth-century twilit torpidity.

The weather has improved steadily all day and for the first time there are patches of sky visible between the heavy clouds, but it is dusk, the time of day when shadows seem to gather between the ancient buildings and the gas lamps produce soft balls of yellow light — pretty, but offering little illumination.

As Charles walks through the arch into Essex Court towards his car he is aware of movement out of the corner of his eye, a stirring of the shadows. He maintains his pace and heads towards the cars parked in the centre of the rectangle of tall buildings, now certain that he is being followed. In the reflection offered by the windows of a Bentley parked at an angle to his right he sees, twenty yards or so behind him, a shortish man in a dark raincoat.

That's the chap from this morning.

On impulse Charles walks straight past his Rover and out of the far side of Essex Court. Increasing his pace, he strides into the passage leading to Outer Temple and thence the Strand. It is a narrow alley, a gap between tall Dickensian buildings little wider than a man's shoulders. It is also completely unlit, with a dogleg half way along its length. As soon as he passes the dogleg, Charles stops and leans flat against the wall, holding his breath in the darkness. He listens intently.

Yes!

Footsteps echo in the narrow space, but they are slowing. Whoever is following is apprehensive, afraid of the dark and of what might lurk in it around the corner.

Charles waits. The footfalls slow further and then stop. The man is only a couple of yards from Charles, waiting, stationary, just before the turn in the alley. Charles imagines his indecision; to continue into the dark or retrace his steps, giving up? Five seconds becomes ten, and ten, fifteen. Charles hears a high-pitched squeak as the man spins, grinding grit against cobble as he turns to go. Charles leans out and looks back towards Essex Court. Charles can see the man clearly, silhouetted against the evening light as he walks away.

Charles takes two running steps and launches himself into a rugby-tackle. It is well-judged. Charles's right shoulder hits the back of his pursuer's thighs as he simultaneously wraps his arms around the man's waist. The man hits the ground with Charles's fifteen stones on top of him and Charles hears the breath *Oomph!* from his lungs. His hat goes flying and rolls out towards the end of the alley, but he is agile and fast. With barely a pause he wriggles and kicks, one heel striking Charles's head, and within a second he has squirmed free. He rolls onto his back and half-sits.

'You can't see it, but I gotta gun pointed straight at your chest!' he gasps.

Charles is on his knees, feeling the water from the day's rain soaking into his trousers. He can't see any gun and for a split-second is about to ignore the bluff. Then he hears the double-click of a revolver hammer being cocked.

'Okay. Fair enough. Who are you? And why're you following me?'

The man with the gun stands slowly. Charles remains on his knees, intensely conscious that he's already in the conventional position for an execution.

Is this it?

'I was told you wanted to see me.'

Relief washes through Charles like a warm wave. 'Hart? Ronnie Hart?'

'Yeah.'

'Why the fuck didn't you just speak to me, like a normal person?' demands Charles angrily, but not yet daring to stand up.

'Thought it was a trap. You're the Krays' bent brief, right?'

'No. I'm definitely not the Krays' bent brief!' insists Charles vehemently. 'Look, can I stand up? I'm not armed.'

Hart hesitates.

'I just want to talk,' says Charles. 'I'm up against them just like you. Please?'

Charles leads the way into the basement bar of the *Witness Box,* Hart right behind him. He has guided Charles to the pub, his hand not moving from the revolver now hidden in his pocket. The *Witness Box* is one of the Temple's favourite watering holes, but by late evening most of the regular clientele have drifted off towards their homes, and the gloomy basement bar is always less busy than the saloon upstairs. A good choice for this meeting, thinks Charles.

'Over there,' says Hart from behind Charles. 'In the corner. That's me brother.'

Charles sees another man sitting at a table. He half-stands as Charles and Hart approach. Charles stops at the table.

'For fuck's sake, Ronnie,' he says, gesturing towards Hart's pocket, 'I told you that weren't necessary.'

'It was. Bloke fucking attacked me!'

'That's not exactly what happened,' says Charles patiently. 'So, you're Terence?' he asks, holding out his hand. 'Terence Hart?'

'Terry. Brother to the idiot behind you,' he replies, shaking Charles's hand readily enough. 'You're Charles Holborne.'

'Yes. You know my dad, then?'

'Not really. But he 'n' our old man go way back. Take a seat. Drink?'

'Wouldn't mind. Scotch, straight up.'

Terry moves towards the bar. Charles and Ronnie Hart sit down facing each other.

Now Charles sees Ronnie in decent light, he is surprised at his youth. Probably in his mid-twenties, he's as handsome as a pop star, with an oval face, dark bushy eyebrows, a strong chin and brown hair cut in a mop-headed style. He could easily pass for one of the Tremeloes or Gerry's Pacemakers. For all his good looks, he has a haunted look around his eyes and his cheeks are pale.

The two men sit in silence until Terry brings back some drinks.

'You're a brief, yeah?' says Ronnie Hart. 'A proper brief?'

'Yes.'

'All right. Terry says I gotta listen to you. I'm here. So, talk.'

Despite the fact that there is no one in the bar except the barmaid, and she's some distance away, Charles drops his voice to little more than a whisper. 'The Krays say you're going to cop a plea for killing Jack the Hat. Is that true?'

'What's it to you?'

'They want me to represent you, and they say you're going to plead. Are you?'

The young man's eyes flash momentarily with anger. 'That's what they want.'

'But what do *you* want?'

'Are you fucking kidding me? I never touched 'im!'

'I've seen some of the prosecution statements. They've got witnesses placing you at the Regency Club and Blonde Carol's flat,' points out Charles.

'Yeah, that's as may be. But I weren't involved in killing the bloke.'

'The point is, Mr Hart, I've been talking to Superintendent Read who's leading the investigation. He's speaking to everyone in the Firm, now and in the past, and he's offering deals.'

'To grass.'

'To turn Queen's Evidence, yes. And to walk.'

'Nipper's never going to let me walk. Not once I tell 'im the whole story.'

'I think you're wrong. He wants the twins. There are no witnesses except members of the Firm. He said if they want convictions, they've got to go down into the sewers to get them.'

Ronnie Hart grins mirthlessly. 'Fucking charming.'

Charles shrugs. 'He's not wrong, is he? From the witness statements I've read, someone *butchered* McVitie in that flat. You may not have held the knife, but in any other circumstances you'd probably be facing conspiracy to murder. You might still.'

'Ron,' says his brother, 'if you're being offered an "out" for turning QE, you'd be a bloody fool not to take it.'

Ronnie Hart turns on his brother. 'Once I admit anything, I've no way back!' he hisses angrily. 'What if Read don't keep his side of the bargain? I'm in for murder. What if I give evidence but they don't get their conviction? The Firm's back in business and I'm a dead man!'

'It's a gamble, I know that,' replies Charles. 'But look at your choices. You can't stay on the run for ever. Nipper's got pretty much everyone else, and now they're looking for you. Top of their list. Got a false passport? Money stashed abroad? Anywhere to go?'

Ronnie Hart scowls and shakes his head.

'I didn't think so,' continues Charles. 'Sooner or later, they'll nick you. Once you're on remand the twins'll force you to take McVitie's murder. You know the sort of pressure they can exert, and not just on you. You've a wife, right? And there's Terry, and your parents. The boys won't hesitate. You know that better than anyone.'

Charles stares hard at the frightened young man. Ronnie Hart drops his head. Charles can hear his laboured breathing from across the table.

'So, you'll end up pleading guilty; you won't have a choice. Gonna be happy with life inside — for something *they* did — while they walk free? Personally, I couldn't stomach it. Okay; that's one option. Now let's look at your other choice, Nipper Read.'

The other man doesn't seem to be paying attention. Terry reaches forward and places a calming hand on his forearm. Ronnie snatches it away angrily, but he does look up at Charles.

'Second option: you tell Read everything, give evidence along with everyone else, and make sure the evidence sticks. The Krays go down for life, probably a minimum of twenty or thirty, and you're free. Start again. It is a risk, I agree. But your chances are much better with Read.'

'How can I trust 'im? Or you, for that matter. I don't know you from Adam! Why's Ronnie Kray so keen for me to use you? There's loads of briefs.'

Charles sits back. He expected this. Ronnie Hart *doesn't* know him from Adam, and the Krays' insistence that Charles must be the barrister to represent him must look deeply suspicious.

No wonder he came tooled up. He probably thought he'd been set up.

Charles takes the only tack he can. He tells the truth. 'You can trust me, Mr Hart, because I'm in exactly the same position as you. Read is trying to force *me* to give evidence for the Crown.'

'You? I don't understand. You've got evidence against the twins?'

'I've got something, less than Read believes, but something. But I'm less frightened of him than I am of the twins. They *do* have something on me, and they're using it to twist my arm to represent you.'

'Why?' demands Ronnie.

Charles answers instantly. 'To make sure you're convicted.'

The brothers stare at Charles.

'Get me *convicted*?' exclaims Ronnie. 'That settles it. Why the fuck would I instruct you if you're gonna shaft me?'

'Why are you telling us this?' asks Terry more calmly.

'I can decide whether to talk to Read,' insists Ronnie, turning to his brother. 'I don't need a bent brief for that!'

155

'I'm not bent, but no, you don't need me for that. But I do urge you to talk to Read, and instruct me to defend you,' says Charles.

'Mr Holborne, why are you telling us this?' insists Terry, sensing more.

Charles speaks without taking his eyes off the young man in front of him. 'Because your brother needs a brief. And it should be me.'

'But you just said —' starts Ronnie.

'I know. The Krays want me to make sure you go down for the murder. But the reason you can trust me is … I think I've a way out. For both of us.' Charles's words hang in the air. 'I've not worked it out completely, but give me five more minutes of your time, and I'll tell you what I have in mind.'

It's later that evening and Charles and Sally have finished eating. They sit at the kitchen table at Wren Street in silence. Charles has Sally's small white hand in both of his paws. He has just finished telling her of his meeting with the Hart brothers and his next move.

'So that's it,' he says, watching her face, waiting. 'What do you think?'

'Honestly? I think you're mad. It'll never work. There's too much that could go wrong.'

'It's risky, yes.'

'Risky? It's completely bonkers!' she protests.

'Maybe. But can you see any other solution?'

'No, but that's no reason —'

He releases Sally's hand and reaches behind him, pulling the telephone down onto the table.

'You're doing it?'

Charles starts dialling. Sally pushes back from the table and starts pacing round the room agitatedly.

'No, please, Charles —'

Charles puts his finger to his lips.

'West End Central Police Station,' answers the station officer.

'DS Sloane, please,' says Charles.

'Who may I say is speaking?'

'Charles Holborne.'

'And what does it concern?'

'The whereabouts of a certain man you're seeking. Mr Ronald Hart.'

'Please hold the line, sir.'

There is silence for a while, followed by a number of clicks and different ring tones. Charles imagines the call being put through first to the Murder Squad and from there to Tintagel House. If there is any way of contacting Nipper Read's team directly, he is not aware of it. Although the whole of the Met and the London criminal fraternity now know of Read's squad and its purpose, it is still, officially, a secret.

After another few moments Sloane's gentle brogue comes on the line.

'I don't know how many times I have to tell you, Charles. I can't give you any information about our enquiries.'

'I don't want you to. This time the boot's on the other foot. I've some information for you.'

There is a pause at the other end of the line. 'Well?'

'I suggest you and Superintendent Read are at Tintagel House by five a.m. tomorrow morning.'

'Why is that?'

157

'I think I've persuaded Ronnie Hart to surrender to custody. And if he does, make sure your boss remembers who did him the favour.'

Charles hangs up. He looks up at Sally at the other end of the kitchen table.

'Well?' she asks.

'That was the easy part. Now for Mr Haeems.'

Charles reaches for a set of papers already opened on the table, and selects one before dialling again. 'This is Charles Holborne for Mr Ralph Haeems,' he says when the phone is picked up at the other end.

Someone evidently goes to find the managing clerk.

'Mr Haeems? I'm sorry to trouble you at home but you gave me your number for this sort of eventuality. Could you arrange a prison visit for me to meet Ronnie Kray as soon as possible? Yes, I have news … I've seen him. He says he's going to hand himself in at Tintagel House tomorrow morning, between five and six a.m.… Yes, he's going to ask for you. Yes … I expect you'll be called before they start the interview … Okay, thank you. No, if you're already at Tintagel House by then, by all means send someone else. Thank you. Yes, it is good news. Again, I'm sorry to have disturbed your evening.'

Charles hangs up again. 'All set,' he says.

CHAPTER THIRTEEN

Charles is once again at HM Prison Brixton sitting across the desk from Ronnie Kray. With them sits a young boy, no more than sixteen or seventeen years of age, one of Ralph Haeems's outdoor clerks. He gabbled excitedly and without stop while he and Charles queued to be allowed in and then while they were being searched. It's the first time he has ever been inside a prison and, what's more, he's meeting the notorious gangster, Mr Ronald Kray. He could barely contain his excitement, and informed Charles, at least twice, that he couldn't wait to tell his mum. He even wondered if Mr Kray would give him his autograph. Now actually in Kray's presence however, he seems to have been terrified into silence. He refuses to look at either man, and sits with a pad open on his knee and a pencil gripped so tightly in his hand Charles expects it to snap.

'And he'll definitely plead to McVitie?' Ronnie Kray is saying.

'That's what he says. You'll find out soon enough; Haeems is sitting in on the interviews as we speak.'

'What about Reg and me?'

'What about you? You weren't there, were you? You had nothing to do with it, right?'

Ronnie looks at Charles through narrowed eyes for a long moment. 'Yeah, exactly. We knew nothing about it. Private beef between the others.'

'So, I've managed to persuade him to hand himself in, he's putting his hands up to the murder, I've agreed to take the case and I'll do his plea in mitigation, for what that's worth. So, are we square?'

Ronnie sits back in his chair expansively, takes a deep drag on his cigarette and nods slowly. 'If you've pulled this off, Horowitz, you've done a good thing.'

'Yes, but are we square? What about the documents? The evidence.'

'You'll get it back soon as he pleads.'

'No.' Charles casts a sideways look at the boy. 'I'll need them sooner than that. I've done everything I was told to do.'

'Well, we've been thinking about that, me and Reg. As you pointed out, there's a long way between Hart giving a statement to Read and actually pleading when the indictment's put to him. He could bottle it, go for trial. So you'll be our eyes and ears. Plan B. Then you'll be in place to defend him at any trial.'

Charles turns to the boy, still laboriously trying to record the conversation. 'You don't need to record this.'

'Yeah?' says the lad hopefully, flexing his wrist which is evidently aching from all the note-taking.

Charles examines the notebook. The smudged pencil record is well behind the conversation and pretty much incomprehensible. Had Charles not actually been party to it, he doubts even he'd be able to make sense of the scrawl.

'Yes. Take a breather.' Charles returns his attention to Ronnie Kray. 'I want those documents back, now.'

Ronnie smiles. 'No. You can manage without them for a while longer. It's important evidence. We can't have it falling into the wrong 'ands, can we?'

Charles examines Ronnie's smirking face, and realisation dawns.

I'm never going to get those papers back, whatever I do for him. He'll keep asking, and I'll keep giving in. He's enjoying this too much.

'No, I'm sorry, Ronnie, but that doesn't work for me. Once Hart's made a full confession, you're safe. Haeems will report back, maybe even by the end of today. I want the evidence then.'

The smile fades from Ronnie's face. 'Are you saying you won't cooperate?'

'I'm saying I already have, and you've got what you want. Now it's your turn.'

Ronnie shakes his head. 'Once he pleads. Or, if he changes his mind, once the jury convicts. Not before then.'

'What do you mean, exactly, "*once the jury convicts*"? No one can guarantee that! Counsel have no control over the evidence or the witnesses. And you know for yourself that juries are unpredictable things … even when you pay them.'

Charles points directly at Ronnie, eyebrows raised. 'Remember?'

Ronnie waves away Charles's objection. 'We've seen you working. You'll have plenty of opportunities to fuck up any nonsense defence Hart runs,' he says, full of assurance.

'Sabotage my own client's defence, in open court? I'd never get away with it.'

'Nah, you're clever enough. Just don't ask some important questions. Ask a couple of daft ones.'

'It won't work, and even if it did my career would be over.'

Ronnie shrugs. 'I don't see why. Everyone has an off day. And your mind's elsewhere, ain't it?'

'What do you mean?'

'Your dad? Had an 'eart attack, I hear. People make mistakes when they're under pressure, right? No one'll notice a thing. Anyway, you say he'll plead, so you ain't got no worries.'

Charles want to punch the smug, grinning, gangster in the face. He wants to beat him to a pulp. In fact he wants to kill

161

him. He even thinks he might be able to do it before the screws come running to pull him off. Instead he closes his notebook and stands.

He turns to the boy. 'Come on. We're done here.'

The Krays' next move arrives in Chambers three days later in the form of Additional Instructions to Counsel from Sampson and Co.

THE QUEEN

- and -

RONALD HART

ADDITIONAL INSTRUCTIONS TO COUNSEL

Enclosures:

5. Note of Interview

Instructing Solicitors apologise to Counsel, who they know has been making attempts to contact Mr Haeems of this office. Mr Haeems has been very busy dealing with a number of the accused men charged in relation to the activities of "the Firm".

However, as hoped, Mr Hart surrendered himself to custody last week. Those instructing thank counsel for his efforts in persuading Mr Hart to turn himself in. In fact Mr Hart changed his mind several times, and it was only at 4:45 am that his brother telephoned to say that Hart was actually on his way to Tintagel House.

Mr Hart has been charged with the murder of Jack McVitie. He was interviewed under caution by Chief Inspector Moody and Sergeant Frank Cater. Mr Hart has yet to be brought before a court for committal proceedings, and so we are unfortunately still unable to tell Counsel what evidence will be led against our client. Furthermore, no statements from Superintendent Read or Sergeant Cater have yet been served. However Mr

Haeems of this office attended to represent Mr Hart and was able to take reasonably comprehensive notes. The enclosure herewith is a transcript thereof. It is entirely self-explanatory, and no attempt is made to repeat its contents here.

Instructing Solicitors will contact counsel's clerks as events unfold.

Sampson & Co.

Charles turns to the only enclosure within the pink ribbon. It consists of a manuscript transcript of two interviews with Ronnie Hart, with a short gap in time between the two. He reads the interviews twice, the first time quickly, feeling their flow, the back and forth of question-and-answer, question-and-answer, and the second time slowly, marking certain passages with his pencil.

Then he sits back in his chair and stares out of the window at the River Thames, gathering his thoughts.

His first response is one of pity. Jack McVitie wasn't just murdered in that grim basement flat; he was hacked to pieces, unmanned, crying and pleading for his life. Charles has seen statements and interviews regarding all sorts of crimes, including murder. He has seen photographs of bodies, both whole and partial, and of terrible wounds inflicted on them. Nonetheless, something about the description of this murder seems more shocking than any of them. McVitie simply couldn't understand what was happening to him. People he considered to be friends and colleagues got him drunk, took him to a party, turned on him and butchered him.

His second response is an even firmer conviction that the two actual killers were Ronnie and Reggie Kray. That Ronnie would have taken part in such a brutal killing is no surprise. He has always been capable of extreme and illogical violence when his blood was up. Charles is no psychiatrist, but he has seen

163

enough over the years to know that Ronnie Kray only feels truly alive when swept away in the throes of uncontrolled violence.

It is Reginald Kray's part in it that initially surprises Charles. Reggie has demonstrated repeatedly that he has no compunction using violence when there are sound business reasons, but it doesn't excite him the way it does Ronnie. Charles has heard him say, more than once, "*Where's the profit in it?*" and that simple question has often been enough to dampen Ronnie's rashness. Indeed Charles suspects that, had Ronnie remained safely locked up in mental institutions after his initial diagnosis, Reggie would eventually have gone straight. He'd have moved gradually into clean businesses or, at least, businesses no more dirty than any of the others in the City of London.

Yet Charles can think of no sensible business reason for this murder. True, McVitie failed to honour his contract to kill Leslie Payne, and then spent his advance payment — something Ronnie would have called a "diabolical liberty" — without completing the job. But grounds for murdering a trusted long-term lieutenant before so many witnesses? No.

Charles can only assume that Reggie must have been goaded into taking part by his twin. Charles saw it while growing up. Reggie could never bear to think he was in any way "less than" Ronnie. He had an irrational terror of losing face in his brother's eyes and that, from time to time, allowed him to be led into insane, illogical missteps. Murdering Jack "The Hat" McVitie would appear to be the most recent, and most egregious, example. Charles wonders if it will prove the brothers' undoing.

Charles puts aside consideration of the psychodynamics of the Kray twins' relationship to focus on their cousin, and his putative client, Ronnie Hart. The transcript makes it clear that, when finally faced with the opportunity of implicating the twins in return for immunity, Hart lost his nerve. As a result, his interview constitutes the worst of all possible outcomes for him: he admits being an accessory both before and after the fact; he admits actually being in the flat at the time of the murder and witnessing it; but he fails to name either of the Krays as the men who gave the orders or did the deed.

'Done up like a kipper,' says Charles out loud, shaking his head. 'And you've done it to yourself.'

On the other hand, he thinks, perhaps Hart has done *him* a favour. This evidence is now more than ample to have him convicted.

Maybe he'll even plead?

Which, of course, would let Charles off the hook.

The phone on his desk rings.

'Sir,' says Jeremy's voice, 'I've got Ralph Haeems on the line for you. He's in a call box.'

'About fucking time! Okay, thank you, please put him through.'

'Mr Holborne?' comes Haeems's soft voice.

'Yes, Mr Haeems. I'm just reading the Notice of Additional Evidence you sent me.'

'You might as well stop. Did the office call?'

'No. Why?'

'Then you won't have heard. We've been sacked. Mr Hart says he's instructing other solicitors and has demanded his file back.'

'Jesus. Did he give a reason?'

'No reason at all. That's why I'm calling you.'

'We've had no further contact with him in Chambers. I've been waiting for you to send me the committal papers. But as far as I know we've not been told to return the brief anywhere. Looks as if I'm still instructed.'

'Well, that's something, I suppose. Of course his new solicitors may want to use their preferred counsel. Would you be kind enough to let me know what happens if you have contact from them? As a matter of courtesy?'

Courtesy, huh?

'Of course. *If* I hear anything. More often than not we're just asked to return the papers and that's the end of it.'

'Yes, I understand. Thank you. I expect Mr Kray will want to speak —' but the pips go, cutting Haeems off in mid-sentence.

Charles lowers the receiver slowly and permits himself a small smile. Hart may have lost his nerve, but the plan could still work. In fact, maybe this is even better.

CHAPTER FOURTEEN

Sally arrives home at just before eight. She warned Charles that she had to work late, so he took the opportunity to meet some football friends for a drink. She encouraged him to go. He needed a few hours away from everything, and even an evening spent discussing West Ham's useless defence over a few pints would give him a much-needed break.

She kicks off her shoes, throws her bags onto the kitchen table and goes directly to the fridge. She missed lunch, and she is famished.

She opens the door to find a covered bowl of salad. She takes it out, frowns, and only then sees Charles's note for her, on the counter under a washed-out mustard jar. She smiles, a surge of love for him filling her.

Cooking is not Charles's strong suit. He managed adequately when he lived alone, but he readily admits that the quality of his diet improved considerably once the two of them began living together. Nonetheless the salad includes fresh leaf, tomatoes, chopped peppers, boiled eggs and what looks like poached chicken. He obviously found the two chicken breasts in the fridge which needed cooking. He's even made fresh croutons. Then she looks more carefully at the mustard jar and realises that it contains half an inch of oil and vinegar dressing.

'Oh, you sweetie!' she whispers to herself.

Throwing her jacket over a nearby chair, she takes a fork from the kitchen drawer, carries her dinner to the table, and starts eating directly from the salad bowl.

She is halfway through her meal when the doorbell sounds. She puts the fork down, wipes her mouth and climbs the stairs to the hall. She opens the door.

An elderly man stands before her. He's in his late sixties with salt and pepper hair and grey sideburns. He wears an expensive suit but it hangs off him, and his shirt collar, although buttoned up, gapes, revealing a stringy neck.

He smiles.

Sally's hand goes to her mouth in shock and her eyes open wide. 'Dad?' she gasps.

'Hello, Sally. You're a sight for sore eyes.'

'But … what are you doing here? You're not due out yet.'

'Weekend licence.'

Sally stands on the threshold, her hand still on the doorknob, staring at her father. The former solicitor has lost a great deal of weight since he was imprisoned. Before his trial he was fit and bronzed, a successful man who looked younger than his years, the very picture of vitality and prosperity. Now Harry Robeson looks old, tired and defeated.

Sally saw him a couple of times during his incarceration but she found it so upsetting when she had to leave at the end of the visits that, eventually, he told her to stop coming. Full of guilt, she followed his advice, but she continued writing to him for a while. Receiving no replies, even that contact gradually stopped.

'Well, are you going to invite me in?' he asks.

Sally is startled back to her manners. 'Of course! Please!'

She stands back to allow her father into the hall, closes the door, and leads him down into the kitchen.

'This is lovely,' he comments as he follows. 'Have you been here long?'

'A couple of years,' replies Sally over her shoulder. 'How did you find me?'

'I asked your mother. I assume that's okay?'

'Yes, of course. I didn't know you were still in touch with her.'

'A little. I wrote to her once or twice from prison.'

They arrive in the kitchen.

'Oh, I've interrupted your meal,' he says.

'Don't worry about it.'

'Still eating out of the bowl?' he says with a smile, pointing at the table.

'I was five, Dad. I'm on my own, and I missed lunch. Can I get you anything?'

'I'll have a drink, maybe, when you're finished.' He looks around. 'Charles not here?'

'No.'

Sally picks up the salad bowl and her fork and clears them from the table. 'I'll put the kettle on. Would you like a hot drink? Or maybe something stronger?'

'Tea would be lovely.'

She watches him pull out a chair at the table and sit. He moves slowly, as if all his joints were stiff. Sally realises that she has not kissed or hugged him, and neither has he approached her. 'Where are you staying?' she asks.

'I managed to hang on to a couple of the rental properties. One of them is quite a nice little flat in Mayfair. That's where I'll go when I get my eventual release.'

'That's good.'

'How's Charles?'

'He's very well, thank you,' replies Sally, brightly. She knows instinctively not to mention Charles's current difficulties.

'And you two are happy?'

This she can answer with a full heart. 'Very. More than I thought possible. I don't mean specifically with Charles; I mean with anyone.'

'That's good. I'm very happy for you, darling. He's a good man.'

Sally doesn't answer. There is too much in her father's response that makes her bridle. The word "darling" — never before used by him — rings a completely false note, and the reference to Charles is especially sour coming from a man who, for years, was the Krays' consigliere. Charles was manipulated by them into breaking the law and his professional rules, and now his liberty is threatened. What might Robeson have done to protect Charles had he wanted to?

Suddenly angry, she turns from the kettle to face Robeson. 'What are you doing here, Dad?'

'I'm seeing my daughter for the first time in years.'

'Yeah, but why now? You're only out for a weekend. You got friends, other family, two other daughters and a bunch of grandchildren. Have you seen them?'

'No, but I will.'

'And this has nothing to do with the arrest of your former bosses?'

Robeson is suddenly still. The noise of the kettle coming to a boil fills the room. He takes a deep breath. 'I wanted so much to see you again. I'm so proud of you, of what you've achieved.' He waves his hand around, apparently indicating the beautifully restored Georgian house. 'But I'll be honest with you, Sally, I have been asked to help out, too.'

'So you're still working for them?' she says angrily. 'Ain't you learned, you old fool? You kept on saying, the only upside of doing a stretch was you'd no longer be useful to them. "Off the hook", you said! And here you are, first weekend release, and still running their errands! You're a fucking idiot!'

'Just hear me out —'

'No! I ain't letting you involve Charlie. Or me!'

'Now, now, Sal, let me explain. I can help him.'

'Yeah?' she retorts angrily. 'In your whole life, you've never helped anyone unless it helped you first!'

She sees that the last remark really stings Robeson. He stands and takes a couple of steps towards her, but she backs away from him as if he were armed.

'No!'

'Sally, Sally! Please! I've got one thing to say, just hear me out, and then I'll go.'

'We ain't interested!'

'Think, girl! Charles would say to listen. Well, wouldn't he? He'd want as much information as possible before making a decision. No one ever gained anything by sticking their head in the sand.'

Sally does think. 'Okay, then. What've you got to say?'

He pauses, collecting his thoughts.

'Spit it out and leave,' she insists impatiently.

'Right. How much has he told you about Ronnie Hart?'

'Everything.'

'So you know that Hart has sacked Sampsons.'

'Yes.'

'Charles needs to hang onto the brief. He needs to find out who Hart is now instructing, and schmooze them. Make sure he's retained as counsel.'

'Why would he do that? If the brief's gone elsewhere, he's off the hook.'

'Don't be so naïve! What lets him off the hook is dealing with the Hart case and getting that incriminating evidence

171

back. If it's not this time, it'll be something else. The twins will still have him by the throat. This is his chance! Hart's been charged with murdering McVitie, and he's all but admitted it. Conspiracy's a stone-cold certainty. All Charles needs to do is see it through to the end.'

'So you've seen the evidence have you?'

'I'm a solicitor. Of course I have.'

'You ain't a solicitor anymore. You're just the Krays' gofer. And what you mean by "*see it through to the end*" is make sure Hart is convicted.'

'It won't come to that. He's admitted it in interview and he hasn't named the Krays.'

'What if he backs out? What if his new solicitors come up with something?'

'Well, then...' Robeson raises his eyebrows to her, leaving the sentence unfinished.

'There's the problem, Dad. You of all people ought to know. Charles hasn't got it in him deliberately to screw up his own client's defence. He couldn't do it.'

'Even if his life depended on it?' He drops his voice to little more than a whisper. 'Or yours?'

That's a question to which even Sally has no answer.

'You know what the twins are capable of,' continues Robeson.

'But that's only half the problem! We don't trust them to hand over the documents. Or they'll keep copies. They'll never hold up their end of the deal.'

'You don't need to trust them,' says Robeson, his voice soft, his hands spread wide as if demonstrating his good intent. 'You just need to trust me.'

'You?'

'I can get the documents, hold them as stakeholder, someone trusted by both sides. And I can assure you, with absolute certainty, there are no copies.'

Sally finds herself suddenly unsure. The old man before her stirs her pity, and he is still her father. He seems sincere and she wants to trust him. He'd never lie to her face, promise to help, only to betray her and Charles so shamelessly. Would he?

Robeson takes another step towards her, his hands outstretched before him, as if begging for alms. 'Let me do this for you. Let me make amends. I know I let you down, Charles too. I'm trying to make it good. With the evidence back, the twins'll have no hold over him. It won't matter whether they're convicted or not — though, believe me, they *will* be convicted. They're looking at life even without McVitie's murder. Either way, you and Charles are free of them.'

'Why should we trust you? You lied to both of us.'

His head drops and he addresses the floor quietly. 'I've had a lot of time to think. I love you, and Charles is a good man. I hurt you both, I know that. I want to make amends. And the Krays have played directly into my hands, presented me with this opportunity.'

There is a catch in his voice. Sally has never heard her father like this. He was always so strong, so self-assured. There was no situation, no people, he couldn't manage. The man before her is pathetic, vulnerable, and he's begging for a last chance.

'I promised myself I would never trust you again,' she says, but she feels herself wavering. 'If we do as you suggest … honestly, Dad, if you let us down again —'

'That won't happen.'

'If you let us down again…' she frowns, pauses for a moment and then forges on, '…you'll never see your grandchild. I'll make sure of it. Never.'

Her hand goes, almost unconsciously, to her belly. He follows her gesture with his eyes and a smile slowly illuminates his face. 'You're pregnant?'

She nods.

'Does he know?'

'Of course he knows.'

'And he's on board? I mean … well … are you sure?'

'Yes, of course I am,' she says, irritated afresh. 'I love him, and I'm absolutely sure he loves me.'

'But is he in for the long haul? Are you getting married?'

'For God's sake, this is the sixties! We don't have to be married to be committed to one other!'

'Maybe, but … now, please don't take this wrong, but … he does have a pretty chequered history with women, doesn't he?'

This last comment astonishes and infuriates Sally, and once again she is unable to control her anger. 'And you don't?' she shouts. 'Who the hell are you to talk? He's never dumped me like you did! You walked out and left us for that bloody woman, without a word. I didn't hear from you for thirteen years! How dare you!'

Robeson raises his hands in submission and tries to shush her. 'Yes, yes, yes, I'm sorry! I'm sorry. I shouldn't have said that. I'm just worried for you. You're my little girl, and I don't want you to end up with someone…'

'Someone like you?' she snarls.

'Yes, okay, someone like me. There're a lot of similarities between Charles and me. Have you never noticed?'

'He's not like you in one important respect. He's honest. And as for … the rest … he's changed. I see him every day and I see how hard he tries to be the best person he can be. I haven't doubted him once in the last two years. Anyway, you and I are not discussing my relationship with Charles. Out of bounds, Dad! You've said your piece. Now get out.'

'But —'

'Go!'

There is silence for a moment as father and daughter stare at one another. Sally's eyes blaze with hostility and pain; Robeson's are soft with fear and anxiety.

'Okay,' he says, turning towards the kitchen door. 'Please talk to him. Tell him what I said.'

'Get out, Dad.'

Charles arrives home at 10:30 pm. He finds Sally in bed, reading. Her face is pink and her hair still damp from the shower.

'Hello,' he says, entering the bedroom.

'Hi. Have a good time?'

'Yes. It was good to see Roger and the others, forget about … everything.' He leans over the bed and kisses her softly. 'You smell nice. How was your day?'

Sally puts down her book. 'Dad turned up,' she says simply.

'At Chambers?'

'No, here. He's on weekend licence.'

Charles turns from taking off his clothes to look at her. 'What did he want?'

'You were right. The Krays have upped their offer.'

'How so?'

'He says he has the documents, or will have, and he'll hold them as honest broker.'

'"Honest broker"!' scoffs Charles.

Sally doesn't answer for a moment. She fiddles with the book on her lap. 'Please, Charles.'

Charles starts to speak, but stops himself. He takes a deep breath. 'Yes, I'm sorry. He's still your father, and of course you love him. But I can't forget what he did to me.'

Charles has been dreading Harry Robeson's release from prison. How could he ever treat the disgraced solicitor, the man who betrayed him, as his "father-in-law"? It might have been possible if Robeson were, finally, out of the game, off the Krays' hook; a retired solicitor, living quietly, enjoying his grandchildren. Maybe then. But now he pops up unexpectedly, while on weekend release, and is still running the Krays' errands?

No. Robeson might get round Sally, but Charles will never trust the ex-solicitor.

'He *is* still my father,' says Sally softly. 'And, for what it's worth, he seemed sincere. I think he does want to help us.'

'Yes. But at what cost? What if Hart pleads not guilty? You know what they want of me then.'

'Yes.'

Charles sits on the bed next to Sally. He can feel the heat of her body through her thin nightie. 'Did he say anything about copies?'

'He says there aren't any.'

'How would he know that?'

Sally shakes her head. 'I didn't ask him. Sorry.'

She is silent for a moment. Then Charles realises that her shoulders are heaving. He lifts her chin up to find that she's crying.

'Oh, sweetheart!' he says softly.

'You should've seen him, Charles,' she sniffs. 'I didn't recognise him at first. He was just some scrawny old bloke. He's aged twenty years! It was such a shock.'

'I'm sure. Prison's a tough place, especially for a soft middle-aged businessman who's never been there before.' Charles slides down the bed until he is lying next to Sally. He puts his arms round her. 'It's going to be all right,' he says into her ear.

'How can you say that? You don't know. There's so much could go wrong.'

'Yes, but as the man who fell off the Empire State Building said as he passed the thirty-second floor … "*So far so good.*".'

Sally snuffles a half-laugh into his chest. 'The old ones are the best,' she says.

Her breathing gradually calms as Charles strokes her hair and places little kisses on her cheek.

'Are you tired?' he whispers.

'Yes.' She reaches behind her, flicks off the light and turns back to him. She insinuates her leg between his. 'But not that tired,' she says, huskily.

CHAPTER FIFTEEN

The Krays' committal proceedings start in May. The purpose of committals, like the grand jury system in America, is to ensure the prosecution has credible evidence to lay before a jury. Many go through "on the nod", the Defence keeping its powder dry until the actual trial. However, in this case, the fact that Nipper Read has done exactly as he threatened by "going down into the sewers" to find his witnesses, presents the Defence teams with a rare opportunity. They hope to do such damage to the motley selection of co-conspirators, gangsters and prostitutes on whose evidence the Crown must rely, that the cases are thrown out early. All have instructed counsel to attend Bow Street Magistrates' Court, and all are up for the fight.

It is a combustible, heady mixture of violence and sex, and the newspapers can't get enough of it. With over a dozen accused men, scores of charges including three murders, and many of the biggest beasts of the Bar instructed, every day brings new titillating headlines. Some of the allegations printed are indeed extraordinary, including evidence of multiple assassination plots involving crossbows, trick briefcases and lethal injections. The Krays, looking like businessmen in their smart suits, are relishing the publicity. Ronnie gets the biggest laugh and the best headline when, the court having heard evidence of the mechanism in the briefcase designed to deliver a fatal injection to a victim's legs, he scoffs loudly from the dock and asks if James Bond will be giving evidence in the case.

Charles, not instructed for any of these defendants and thus not involved at this stage, is feeling left out and twitchy. The case is speeding past him and all he can do is watch it flash by.

One sunny Monday morning, having finished an inconsequential trial the previous week, he decides to walk from the Temple to Covent Garden and gauge the atmosphere in court for himself. It might also give him an opportunity to play his next card in this increasingly high-stakes poker game.

He walks down Fleet Street to the Aldwych, skipping out of the way of the liveried bellhops at the Waldorf Hotel as they hustle across the pavement the two dozen items of luggage and instrument cases of some departing rock stars. He vaguely recognises a couple of them as he hurries past. Charles is a jazz fan, not as up to date with rock and pop as Sally who is sixteen years his junior, but as he turns the corner into Drury Lane he realises that two of the men he saw climbing into the limousine were David Gilmour and Roger Waters. Charles has just pushed through the entourage of The Pink Floyd who, on Saturday, played the free concert in Hyde Park.

Charles walks up Drury Lane and cuts through to Bow Street. As he passes a telephone box on the corner of Drury Lane and Broad Court a young woman steps out and almost collides with him. Both halt and apologise. Then Charles notes that she is wearing a see-through top with no bra, a miniskirt and knee-length boots. In her hands she has a roll of Sellotape and sheaf of printed cards offering various thinly-disguised sexual services.

'Marketing day?' he asks, smiling, and pointing to one of the cards which has just been taped above the telephone.

'It's a game I play with Westminster Council,' she replies with a grin and a surprisingly cultured accent. 'They keep taking them down and I keep putting them back up again. But it does get expensive.'

Charles laughs. 'I've never considered you girls' printing and stationery costs. I hope your accountant sets them off against takings. It's a deductible business expense, you know,' advises Charles.

'If I ever pay tax, I'll bear it in mind.'

Charles makes to move on but she puts a gentle hand on his forearm. Charles looks down. Her fingers are long and white, her nails painted purple.

'I don't suppose you're looking for business, are you?' she says, looking Charles up and down. 'I could do with some time off my feet. These boots are killing me.'

Charles smiles. 'No, sorry. I'm working too.'

'Pity,' she says, her eyes twinkling. 'You'd have been no chore.'

'Neither would you,' replies Charles. 'See you,' he says as he moves off.

'No need to flirt with me, soldier,' she calls after him. 'I'm what they call a dead cert!'

Charles raises his hand and waves without looking back.

The Bow Street magistrates work in a beautiful Greco-Roman building almost directly opposite the Royal Opera House, which marks the threshold of Covent Garden. The court, in existence since 1740, is one of the most famous in English history. It was the birthplace of Britain's first police force, the Bow Street Runners, created by Sir Henry Fielding and, over two centuries, has seen dozens of famous prosecutions, from Dr Crippen to Oscar Wilde. For a beautiful building of such historical and legal importance, Charles is always shocked and saddened by its decrepitude. The interior, as he steps inside, is ill-lit and grimy, litter gathers in the corners of the entrance and the foyer, and it stinks of sweat, cigarette smoke and stale food.

Today the main hall is eerily quiet. No throngs of barristers, solicitors, police officers and witnesses; no hastily-convened legal conferences on the steps or in corners; no need to raise one's voice above the clamour. For the next several weeks the stipendiary magistrates will be engaged exclusively in the task of deciding which members of the Firm have cases to answer at the Old Bailey, and no other work is being listed. Everyone concerned with the Krays' cases is already packed into the courtroom, not wanting to miss a moment of the drama.

The fact that the antechamber is almost completely deserted intensifies Charles's impression that he's been left out of something important, and he crosses the marble floor impatiently and pushes open the wooden doors to the court. He slips inside and manages to find a space at the end of the reporters' bench close to the door.

John Platts-Mills QC, leading counsel for Ronnie Kray, is in the middle of an interminable, convoluted question regarding the evidence on one of the murder charges. It is clear from the expression of the woman in the witness box that she has lost the thread of the question and has no idea what is being asked.

Charles allows himself to settle into the comfortable rhythm of question and answer. He has not brought his notebook — there's no need for him to record this evidence — which makes for a pleasant change. Unusually, he is able to sit back, relax and spectate.

After a few minutes his eye is caught by someone looking directly at him from the well of the court. Ralph Haeems has twisted round from his position in the solicitors' bench behind counsel and is pointing at Charles with eyes raised. He then indicates the door. Charles nods, points to the court clock and raises a single finger. Haeems understands: they will talk at one o'clock, at the adjournment for lunch.

Charles continues listening to the evidence but, as is often the case even with sensational charges, it soon becomes dull. The court has moved on to deal with some technical evidence involving the timing of two interviews, which is of little interest to anyone except the lawyers and the judge. Matters are not helped by Platts-Mills, whose style is rambling and dry. There is a palpable air of impatience from the barristers queueing behind him, anxious for their chance to get at the witnesses and land some decent punches.

At two minutes before one, Haeems leans sideways to a colleague, gives some whispered instructions, and rises quietly from his place on the bench. He walks up the aisle, looks at Charles pointedly, and indicates with his head that Charles should follow. Haeems is waiting outside for Charles as he leaves the courtroom.

'Mr Holborne,' he says.

'Good afternoon, Mr Haeems,' says Charles, lighting a cigarette. 'You wanted to speak to me?'

'Yes, please. Mr Kray would like a word as well.'

'Which one? Or both?'

'Mr Reginald Kray.'

'Paul Wrightson might have something to say about me talking to his client,' points out Charles.

'We're not asking you to speak to him as his lawyer,' says Haeems enigmatically.

Charles considers, and then shrugs. 'I don't mind having a word. When?'

'How about now? We can go to the cells and you can speak to Mr Kray when court rises. It should only be a minute or two.'

'Okay.'

'Thank you.'

Haeems leads the way across the floor to the door to the cells and rings the bell. It takes some time before they hear anyone's footsteps on the stairs behind the door. Charles realises that most of the custody officers are still in court, standing guard over the numerous defendants. The wicket in the door opens and Haeems leans forward.

'Solicitor and counsel to see Mr Reginald Kray. Is it all right if we come in and wait for him to be brought down?' he asks.

'Court just rose, so they're on their way down now, sir. Yes, in you come.'

The wicket closes, keys jangle in locks, and the door swings open. Charles follows Haeems down the stairs as the gaoler re-locks the outer door.

The smell, as always, is indescribably awful.

'Have they still not sorted out the drainage problems?' says Charles as he descends, trying not to inhale.

'It's the Victorian sewers,' says the gaoler as he descends behind them. 'Apparently it's a big job, and everyone's arguing over who's to pay for it, and whether the court has to be closed while the work's going on.'

'I don't remember it being this bad,' says Charles.

'It's always worse in the summer,' replies the gaoler. 'You get used to it after a few hours. Right, gentlemen, can I take your details, please?'

Haeems and Charles have their names recorded, but otherwise the security is almost non-existent.

'We're very full, as you can imagine, so you'll have to see him in the cell. And he won't be alone, so I'm afraid you won't get any privacy.'

'That's fine,' says Charles.

'I'll see a couple of the others, then,' offers Haeems.

Charles glances at the managing clerk but his face gives nothing away.

'If you wait there, then, sir,' the gaoler says to Haeems, 'I'll be right back. You follow me,' he says to Charles.

Charles is led further into the bowels of the cells. The gaoler opens the wicket in the final cell door, checks who is inside, and unlocks it for Charles.

'Counsel to see you, Mr Kray,' he says.

Charles steps in and the door is locked behind him.

Both Kray twins are sitting on a bench set into the wall in front of Charles. There is a third man whom Charles does not recognise, pacing up and down. The space is foetid, with no window and no ventilation.

Reggie Kray stands. 'All right, Charlie?'

'I'm fine, Reg. What's up?'

'Where the fuck is Hart?' says Ronnie Kray, standing suddenly and crowding Charles back towards the door. His aggression is so surprising that Charles is caught off guard.

'I've no idea,' says Charles. 'I've still got the brief in Chambers but I've heard nothing from the new solicitors yet.'

'He should be here with us,' says Reggie, more calmly than his brother.

'Well, he's confessed, right?' says Charles, 'and he's pleading guilty, so not necessarily.'

'What do you mean, "*not necessarily*"?' demands Ronnie.

The third man, sensing trouble, backs into a neutral corner.

'I mean, the solicitors have probably decided not to contest the committal. What's the point of cross-examining witnesses if he's going to plead? My guess, it'll go through on the papers.'

'Who are the solicitors?' asks Reggie.

Charles takes a deep breath. 'Now, boys, hear me out on this and don't lose your cool. I've been thinking about this and — for good reasons — I'm not going to tell you.'

Ronnie crowds Charles even further, squaring up to him, fists ready. 'You'll do as you're fucking told, Horowitz!' he hisses, keeping his voice down so as not to be heard by the officials outside.

'Not this time. I know what you'll do if I tell you. You'll put them under pressure and risk getting me sacked.' Charles tries to keep his voice level. He lowers it further still. 'How do you think some country bumpkin solicitor's going to react if he's suddenly coerced by the Kray twins? He'll throw the case back and I'll lose the brief. At the moment, he's just delighted to have landed a big case, and with experienced counsel already on the team. It gives me free rein because he'll do whatever I tell him. You need me for the trial, and at the moment I'm still on the inside. Leave well alone.'

'Country bumpkin?' asks Reggie.

'So I'm told,' replies Charles.

'And you're still instructed?'

'Yes,' confirms Charles. 'Still waiting for committal papers.' He pauses to allow the gangsters to weigh his words. 'It's the right call,' he says after a moment's silence. 'Trust me.'

There is a pause as the twins look at one another.

'That's the problem,' says Reggie. 'We don't trust you.'

Charles laughs grimly. 'You don't say? Well, it's mutual. But whether we like it or not, we're in this together now.'

'Where the fuck is Hart?' repeats Ronnie angrily.

Charles raises his hands. 'I've told you. I've no idea. Presumably somewhere in the prison estate, being kept as far from you as possible. Isn't that what Read's done throughout?

185

Moved you all over the country to stop you talking to one another?'

The twins again look at one another. The tension in the tiny cell seems to dissipate slightly, but Ronnie takes another step forward so that he is only inches from Charles. He raises a warning finger and wags it. 'Be real careful, Horowitz,' he threatens quietly. 'We know where your brother and that little baby of his lives. And your parents. You double-cross us, whatever happens to them is on you.'

Charles raises his hand slowly, closes it around Ronnie's forefinger and moves it away from his face as if turning back the hand of a clock. 'I understand that. I have always understood that.'

Charles gets home first that evening, changes out of his suit and tunic shirt, and heads for the kitchen. He browses through the refrigerator, trying to remember what Sally told him was there for their evening meal. He finds a beef casserole cooked over the weekend and remembers that he is supposed to prepare some vegetables, so he gets on with that.

By seven o'clock Sally hasn't arrived. He is not yet worried — she sometimes doesn't get in until almost seven thirty — but she usually telephones to warn him. They have fallen into the practice of calling each other's chambers if they are likely to be home after seven. By five to eight Charles has tried ringing Sally's desk, but without answer. He goes up to the bedroom to see if there are any clues there. On one occasion, earlier that year, she was invited to play tennis with a girlfriend in Highgate and had rushed out of the house so quickly she forgot to leave Charles a note.

He learns nothing. All her clothes are hung neatly, her sports bag is on the floor of the wardrobe and everything looks exactly as it was when he left for the Temple that morning.

Telling himself that she's probably gone for a drink with one of her clerk colleagues, Charles manages to reassure himself for a while that he's worrying over nothing.

By half past nine, he is becoming seriously concerned. Even if Sally had gone out with colleagues, she would certainly have telephoned by now, knowing that they had agreed to eat together that evening. Wondering if something might have happened to Nell Fisher, Sally's disabled mother, he rings the number in Romford. There is no answer. That too is odd, because Nell very rarely goes out in the evenings. Her ability to leave the house at this time of day is governed by the availability of carers prepared to work overtime. Charles starts ringing round their friends.

No one has heard from her, and all agree to call Wren Street if they do.

Finally, at quarter past ten, he starts thinking about calling the police. He paces up and down the kitchen, allowing a further ten minutes, then fifteen, to elapse. He doesn't know what to do. His first instinct is to call Sean Sloane, but the Irish copper is almost certain to ask if Sally's disappearance might have something to do with the Krays, and Charles cannot answer that either honestly or helpfully. In the end he decides to call the local police station. The station officer doesn't exactly fob him off, but he says it's far too early to complete a missing person's report and, in any case, he couldn't do that over the telephone. Charles would need to come into the station. The sergeant recommends leaving it until the morning. If Sally is still unaccounted for by then, Charles should come in.

He replaces the receiver with impatience and frustration. He tries Nell Fisher again, but still receives no answer. The tension of pacing around the empty house, waiting for Sally to turn up, is getting to him. He needs to take action. He thinks about driving to Romford — surely Nell can't remain out all night? — but at the same time he is reluctant to leave the telephone in case Sally calls.

Then he thinks of the hospitals. Perhaps she's had a fall? Maybe she's been involved in an accident and is unable to give her details. Charles grabs the telephone directory and compiles a list of all the hospitals in central London and their telephone numbers. He starts calling those most likely to have picked somebody up on the route between the Temple and King's Cross. Half an hour later he has called six Accident and Emergency Departments, some of them miles away and highly unlikely to have been involved. None has a record of a patient being brought in who matches Sally's description.

Finally, at eleven fifteen he calls David.

'Hello, David?' he says as the phone is picked up.

'No, it's Sonia. Is everything all right Charles? It's very late.'

'I'm really sorry to trouble you —'

'We're in bed.'

'Sally's not there by any chance, is she?'

'Sally? No. Why would she be here?'

'I don't know. I've run out of ideas. She didn't come home this evening, and I don't know where she is.'

Charles hears bedclothes rustling and the receiver being handed to someone else. His brother's voice comes on the line.

'It's me,' says David. 'I heard that. Sally's missing?'

'I don't know. Probably not, but I don't know where she is and she hasn't been in contact. She should've been home five hours ago. I've tried everywhere, hospitals, all our friends, her chambers.'

'The police?'

'Yes. She's an adult, and they won't categorise her as missing until tomorrow at the earliest.'

'Would you like me to come over?' asks David.

'Thanks, but I can't see any point. The thing is…'

'What?'

'Well, remember what I told you about the Krays?'

'You think it might be them?'

'Possibly. I saw the twins today at the magistrates' court. They were pretty pissed off with me, and Ronnie did make a sort of veiled threat against the family.'

'Why were they angry?'

'Does it matter? We disagreed over tactics.'

'Did you tell the police that?'

'No. Look, David, thanks, but I'm going to go to Romford. I can't raise her mother either and I'm wondering if the two things might be connected.'

'Charles, what can we do to help?'

'Nothing. Thank you. It's fine. I'm going now.'

'Okay. Please call us when you've some news. It doesn't matter how late, okay?'

'Okay.'

Charles hangs up and runs upstairs. He pulls on some slacks and a shirt, races back down, collects his car keys, and leaves the house. It feels better to be doing something.

The road eastwards to Nell Fisher's house in Romford takes Charles through the city of London and the East End. As he is passing Blooms on Aldgate it occurs to him that before going to Romford he should look in the Temple. He has a vision of Sally lying at the foot of the stone steps to the basement of

Chancery Court, calling in vain for help. He executes a U-turn and speeds back down Lower Thames Street. The river to his left is unusually still, a pane of glistening darkness. Charles loves the Thames and feels completely at home on it — it was his friend even when he was working through air raids as a lighterman during the Blitz — but for the first time he can remember, it looks sinister and dangerous.

I wax desperate with imagination.

At the entrance to Middle Temple Lane he ignores the "No Right Turn" sign and turns into the Temple. He pulls up in Essex Court and runs to Chancery Court.

The building is deserted. No light shines from any of the barristers' windows. He climbs the steps and pushes open the street door. He tries each floor in turn but the main door to every corridor is locked. He leaves the building and descends the stone staircase to the basement area, where he pictured Sally's fall. It too is deserted. Not much relieved, he turns and retraces his steps to ground level.

The Rover races eastwards through empty wet streets. Charles ignores speed limits and drives as quickly as the traffic conditions allow. He usually enjoys travelling this route, through the streets of his childhood and young adulthood. Now they too seem alien. The black yawning windows of the closed shops, the litter everywhere and the bins on the pavement awaiting collection are indifferent to him, hostile. The world couldn't care less that Sally, wonderful, kind, sexy … *pregnant* Sally is missing, maybe injured … maybe …

Nightmare scenarios force their way into his head. Sally, stabbed and bleeding out from some random mugger's knife attack; Sally, mangled under the wheels of a lorry; Sally, pale, still and growing cold under a sheeted hospital gurney. Finally, and somehow more frightening than the other terrifying possibilities, Sally, gagged and tied somewhere, a member of the Firm regarding her with cold fish eyes, speculating about removing her clothes.

And the baby! *The baby*!

Charles fights the incipient panic, forcing himself to breathe slowly and to ease off the accelerator.

The journey to Romford takes forty minutes. He enters the quiet residential street.

There is nowhere to park. Both sides of the pavement are lined with vehicles. It takes him ten minutes to find a space in an adjoining street, and he is in a state of high anxiety by the time he locks the car and runs back to Nell Fisher's tidy little home.

He is surprised but relieved to see lights shining from both downstairs and upstairs windows. He walks swiftly down the garden path to the front door and rings the bell. The door opens almost immediately.

'Charles?' says a young woman.

'Hi Tracey,' he says.

Sally's younger sister, an elongated Sally, almost as pretty but taller and thinner.

'What're you doing here? Is Sally all right?'

'She's not here, then?'

'No,' she replies, puzzled.

'Then I don't know where she is. I don't know what's happened to her.'

Tracey opens the door wider. 'Mum!' she calls behind her. She addresses Charles. 'You'd better come in.'

Charles steps into the narrow hallway. At the far end, just outside the kitchen door, is Nell. She leans on two elbow crutches while her other daughter, Michelle, helps her out of her coat. The three women appear recently to have returned from an outing.

'Charles?' says Nell, seeing him for the first time. 'What's going on?'

'Sally's missing,' explains Tracey.

The movement ahead of Charles in the hallway stops.

'Missing?' says Nell.

Charles's relationship with Sally's mother has never been easy. His age, his notoriety, his historical connections with the Krays — all make him, in her eyes, an unsuitable partner for her middle daughter.

'What have you done now?' she challenges.

'Nothing,' says Charles, colouring.

'I don't believe you. Aren't you involved in the Kray trial?'

'Not directly.'

'*Not directly*? So you are, then. What have you done?'

Charles can't answer.

'I knew something like this would happen,' she says, pointing an accusing finger at him. 'Sooner or later.'

'I'll call you as soon as I've news,' says Charles, turning to leave.

'Shall we call the police?' asks Michelle.

'I already did,' replies Charles, backing away down the path.

'If anything's happened to her, it's on you!' shouts Nell after him in an uncanny echo of Ronnie Kray's threat of a few hours earlier.

Charles heads back to his car, opens the door, and collapses into the comfortable leather seat, sweating.

Nell's right: this is my fault. It's got to be the Krays. It's got to be.

The more he thinks about it the more sure he is. If Sally had been injured in some attack or accident either he or Nell would have heard by now. The fact that she's not been in touch means that she's being held somewhere, *prevented* from being in touch.

So much for Reggie's assurances concerning women and children.

But then, Reggie's assurances don't always cut much ice with Ronnie.

Charles has known the Krays since the three of them were schoolboy boxers at the Kennington Institute. He has never trusted Ronnie. He was a sociopath then and he's a sociopath now. He has always treated people as objects, objects to get what he wants or objects in the way of what he wants.

However, to a limited extent Charles *had* trusted Reggie. Over the years there had been several examples of an unspoken understanding between them, a grudging mutual respect, despite the fact that they ended up on opposite sides of the law. Charles believed that, by his own lights, Reggie Kray did operate according to a sort of moral code. Kidnapping Sally to ensure Charles's obedience was crossing a line, a line Charles didn't think would be crossed.

The fact that Reggie must have let his twin do it shows how rattled the Krays are. Nipper Read has managed something no one has ever done before: he has turned enough members of the Firm to arrest the whole gang at the same time.

Charles turns the ignition and sets off towards Wapping and the River Thames. He drives through dark deserted streets.

He knows what he must do.

The timing's all gone to hell, but we're still on track. Just about.

As always, now he is acting, following a plan, he is calm, clear-headed. He's about to make himself even more unpopular than he is in Romford, but he has no choice.

He stops briefly at the first phone box he finds and, leaving the engine idling, tries his own number at Wren Street. He is disappointed, but unsurprised, when the phone rings out.

CHAPTER SIXTEEN

At just after three a.m. Charles steps into a dark alley alongside a four-storey end of terrace house in Wapping. He is so close to the river here that he can smell the water; when the wind changes direction he can even hear it lapping against the quayside. A sudden longing grips him, but he repels it; this is no time for nostalgia. He has used up too much time and goodwill to locate this address. Even now he is not sure he's at the right place.

The depths of the alley are lost in complete darkness and Charles pauses, uncertain. Then, as if on cue, the clouds clear for a moment and Charles sees, right at the far end, the outline of a staircase, its wet treads picked out in faint moonlight. Charles flicks alight his cigarette lighter, steps carefully around the bins which narrow the entrance of the alley, and heads towards the staircase.

Constructed in rough timber, the stairs zigzag their way to the top floor of the house where they terminate in a small landing. Charles starts climbing. He arrives on the landing to find a door set in the gable end of the property. The door has a window in it, but it's covered by a curtain on the inside. The room beyond is in darkness. He leans forward, his ear against the cold glass. Silence, but he can detect the faint odour of bacon. He grips the door handle. It turns, but the door is locked and doesn't budge.

Charles straightens up and raps gently but firmly on the glass. Still silence.

Charles knocks again, with slightly more force.

The night is so still he can't believe that anyone inside wouldn't have heard him, but there is again no response. He raises his hand to knock for a third time, worried now that he'll disturb neighbours, when he detects something behind the curtain, not a movement exactly, more a change in the quality of the darkness.

'Johnny, I know you're in there,' says Charles urgently.

Nothing.

'It's Charles Holborne,' he says. 'Charlie Horowitz.'

Still no response, and no change in the darkness beyond.

Did I imagine it?

Deciding to make one last attempt before abandoning his mission, Charles knocks for a third time, this time loudly. He hears immediate movement, footsteps, a shoot-bolt being retracted, and the door opens a couple of inches. Charles steps forward again.

'What the fuck are you playing at, at this time of night?' comes a voice in reply. 'You'll wake the landlord!'

Charles is confused. Johnny the Jar is known throughout the criminal fraternity as the doppelgänger of the TV and film actor, Terry-Thomas. He looks like Terry-Thomas, sounds like Terry-Thomas and cultivates the same aristocratic cad persona, even down to the pencil moustache, the 1930s slang and the affected cigarette holder. Yet the voice hissing from the darkness is pure Plaistow.

'Jar? Is that you?' asks Charles urgently.

'Yes, and you woke me up!'

'I'm really sorry, Johnny, but I need your help.'

'Then come back in the morning, old chap,' says the voice, a trace of the familiar accent returning.

'That'll be too late. I know it's out of the blue, but I have two hundred reasons in my pocket why you should hear me out.'

The door remains motionless for a moment longer before opening further.

'Mind the cats,' says the occupant as he stands back to let Charles enter.

Charles steps into a darkened room. The smell of stale cooking is stronger here but is overpowered by the odour of well-used cat litter.

Charles squints as a lamp is illuminated. As his eyes adjust he sees that he's in a kitchen. Every surface is covered with dirty crockery and saucepans. There are three cat baskets under the Formica-topped table in the centre of the room but only one is occupied. The other feline inhabitants of the premises — and there can be no fewer than six — lie on the kitchen counter, on a bookcase used to store dried goods and on the table itself.

Charles turns his attention to his host. Tall, thin, with a yellow pallor to his face, Johnny the Jar has seen better times. His hair is greasy and he hasn't shaved for some days. Bony ankles protrude from the bottom of frayed striped pyjamas.

'There are matches on the side,' says Johnny, pointing. 'Get the kettle on, there's a good fellow, and I'll make myself presentable.'

An hour later the door closes again. Charles steps back out onto the staircase and feels his way to the ground floor. He retraces his steps to the Rover, his footsteps echoing from the opposite side of the empty street. Dark windows look down at him.

As he turns the corner he shivers, and something makes him turn. He looks back at the flat he has just left to see the Jar's silhouette moving swiftly away from the curtain at a front window. Charles is suddenly assailed by doubts.

Is this a mistake? Is he up to it? And, more importantly, can I trust him?

Charles has known Johnny the Jar most of his life. The two men's paths have crossed many times but they have never been friends. The Jar started life as a teenage pickpocket, and the speed of his hands made him a legend throughout the East End between the wars. It was like observing a skilled stage magician at the top of his game. You watched, and watched, and came away thinking "How did he *do* that?"

For most of his professional life the Jar made a living as a conman. His "bread and butter" con, where he worked alone, involved selling "jars" or "jargoons" — zircons — and passing them off as diamonds, but he gave that up a decade ago when his lightning-quick fingers started losing their dexterity. The Jar told Charles that he was semi-retired, although the state of his accommodation and his obvious ill-health suggested that "on the skids" would be a more accurate description.

Charles remains on the pavement, looking up at the Jar's windows until the lights are extinguished, and only then does he move off again. The truth is, he has no other options, not in the time available. He knew this would be risky.

He returns to the car and allows himself the luxury of closing his eyes for a few moments. It's some years since Charles worked right through the night on a case, but the exhausting workload demanded of popular junior barristers is standing him in good stead. He feels pretty good. The tiredness will hit him later that afternoon.

'Okay,' he says to himself, opening his eyes again. 'Smithfields.'

While the rest of London sleeps, the Smithfield meat market, an 800-year institution, is a hive of bustling activity. From 2 am to 10 am every weekday it supplies every morsel of meat consumed in London and the south-east of England. There, carcasses of pork, mutton and beef are unloaded, barrowed and cut up by big men in white hats and coats, fat-streaked leather aprons and bloody Wellington boots.

Charles finds his way into the market blocked by a tangle of lorries, trolleys and barrows and their arguing drivers. Executing a neat U-turn, he retraces his route down West Smithfield, circles around Rotunda Garden and enters the hospital grounds, parking outside St Bartholomew the Less. He leaves the car and walks back.

As always, the market is a bustling, crowded, stinking mass of men hauling, carrying, sawing, cutting, weighing and shouting over meat. The businesses under the dome are crammed with the jostling representatives of all the major restaurants, hotels and catering institutions of London, laughing, joking and haggling with the vendors. This is not Charles's milieu, but even his mood is lifted by the noise, the excitement and the banter ringing all round him.

Charles is almost run down by a young man speeding down a ramp barely in control of his barrow.

'Mind out the fucking way!' shouts the lad as the wheel bumps over Charles's shoe.

Charles grabs the boy's arm as he goes past. 'Miller and Stone?'

The boy points. 'First right, down the end!' he shouts.

Charles waves his thanks but the boy has already gone.

He follows the directions, pushing his way through the crowds. He finds the wholesale outlet and gets in what he hopes is the queue. Two men behind the counter pack slabs of raw meat into bags. Then Charles spots a little booth to the right where an elderly man is taking money. He moves to a shorter queue in front of the booth. Eventually he reaches the front.

The old man reaches out. 'Ticket?' he demands.

'No, sorry, I'm trying to locate a cutter named Andy Tyson.'

'Dun't work here no more.'

'Since when?'

'Since 'e cut off his hand, for a start.'

'He cut his hand off?'

'He did.'

'Jesus. Do you know where I can find him?'

The old man shrugs, looking over Charles's shoulder to the next customer.

'Look, it's really urgent,' insists Charles.

'I ain't seen him for a coupla days. You could try *The Fox*. Look for a dandy.'

'A dandy?'

'You'll see.'

'Thanks,' says Charles, but the old man is already dealing with his next customer.

Charles pushes his way out of the press into the cold night air and crosses the cobbles. He averts his eyes as he passes the Head Shop (it's too early in the morning for that amount of gore) and reaches *The Fox* on the corner of West Smithfield.

It's 5 am on a damp Wednesday morning, and the pub is as lively as a Christmas eve.

It is illegal to sell intoxicating liquor after 11 pm anywhere in England. There is, however, an exceptional enclave tucked away in Smithfield, known only to a select group of London's night workers. Big men shifting two hundred pound beef quarters over an eight-hour shift require sustenance, and *The Fox* is one of the small handful of hostelries permitted to provide it.

Charles pushes open the door and is hit in the face by the smell of grilled meat. His mouth waters immediately and his stomach rumbles in answer.

It was Charles's pupilmaster, Wally Otkins, who first introduced him to *The Fox*. That was shortly after the war, when everyone in England was still on ration cards and a good steak as rare as a self-confessed Nazi. Having read for libel overnight at one of the Fleet Street newspapers, Wally told Charles to grab his coat and hat and together they walked up Fleet Street, left into Farringdon Street and right into Smithfield. Despite having lived in London all his life, Charles had never been to the market. Wally installed them in a corner table at *The Fox* and bought Charles the largest and rarest steak the young barrister had ever eaten, a slab of meat on a plate with a few burnt onions for decoration.

'These were running around a field yesterday,' said Wally, pointing with his fork as he tucked in.

Charles has been coming ever since.

The pub is, as always, packed full of market workers, cutters, salesmen and tellers. The three bars, one on each floor of the building, are so crowded that the temperature inside is ten degrees warmer than on the street. Everywhere Charles looks, wooden trestle tables are full of men eating, talking loudly and laughing, and bar staff rush back and forth trying to serve those queueing at the bar.

Charles's clothing marks him out as an outsider but no one troubles him. He takes his cutlery from the bar and waits. He wants a space at one of the ground-floor tables where he can watch the doors, so he has to be patient. Eventually a gap opens up and he squeezes himself onto the end of a table.

Smithfield is a closed shop, run by the union, with jobs passing father to son through the generations. As with the lighterage business with which Charles became familiar during the war, it has its own slang and customs. Charles listens with only half his attention to the hubbub surrounding him, understanding little of it. His meal arrives and he starts eating.

The steak is excellent, huge, succulent and perfectly cooked, but he barely notices it. He slows down, to the point where the last few mouthfuls are cold, but after twenty minutes he has finished and has spotted no one who could possibly be described as a "dandy". The downstairs bar is beginning to look less crowded as market workers finish their breaks and return to their stalls. Charles already has his hand in the air to attract the waitress's attention when the door opens again.

In walks a young man in smart clothes, indeed smarter than Charles's own. He wears a light-coloured tailored suit with a claret waistcoat, silver watch chain, and a striped tie over a double-cuffed shirt fastened with cufflinks. A rose, matching the waistcoat, adorns his buttonhole and he wears grey calfskin gloves. Charles's heart lifts briefly, but falls again: this man has both hands.

Wrong dandy?

The newcomer, tall and broad shouldered, circulates round the tables and, notes Charles, seems known to many of the workers from the market. He banters good-naturedly as he passes, slapping one or two on the shoulder, asking after mutual acquaintances. Charles sees that he is leaving flyers or notices on each table as he passes.

Finally the man approaches the table where Charles sits. He is about to say something to one of the men sitting there when he notices Charles studying him.

'What?' he demands.

'Sorry, mate,' apologises Charles, 'I'm looking for someone called Andy Tyson. But I don't think it's you.'

The young man's brow furrows. 'What do you want with Andy?'

Something about the man's expression makes Charles wonder if this is, after all, Tyson. 'A mutual friend thought we might be able to help one another out, that's all,' he replies cautiously.

'Friend?'

'The Jar.'

The newcomer's face relaxes. He steps over the bench and takes a seat at the table, pulling off his gloves. With a shock, Charles sees that the only complete fingers of his right hand are his thumb and index finger. The rest have been amputated at the first knuckle and the vacant fingers of the glove are stuffed with something.

Tyson holds out what remains of his right hand. 'I'm Andy Tyson.'

'Charles Holborne,' says Charles, and after a second's hesitation, he shakes gently. 'I was told you lost that,' he says, nodding at the maimed hand.

'That's the story everyone tells the apprentices, but it weren't that bad.'

'Mind me asking how it happened?'

'Usual malarkey. Coupla lads playing a practical joke. They hid me chainmail gloves and put a smaller pair in their place. Claimed me hands must've swelled up overnight. So, just for once, I worked without 'em and...' He holds up the hand.

'Shit.'

'Yeah. Hurt like fuck. And that was the end of me career as a cutter. Dad was gutted. The stall'd been in the family two hundred years.'

'You look as though you're doing okay though,' says Charles indicating the other's clothes.

'The whistle? It's me new job. Here,' he says, reaching across the table to one of his flyers. He slides it over to Charles.

'*The Cockney Cutter*?' reads Charles. 'You're a barber now?'

'I came back to the market after the accident and tried working as a bummaree, but it weren't the same. I was too slow, and it was too much of a comedown. So I moved into another area, as you might say, which is how I met Johnny. That didn't go so well neither. Got two years in Springfield. But there I discovered I still had some skill with me 'ands.'

'As a prison barber,' says Charles.

'Exactly.'

'And now you're a barber on the outside?'

Tyson indicates the flyer. 'I asked meself: where d'you get eight hundred men every night who never 'ave time to get an hair cut? Answer? Smithfield. They're all asleep during the day, see? So what if I opened up me own barbershop, just round the corner from the market, and did the same hours as them?'

Tyson seems comfortable and chatty — Charles can see how he'd be good at putting clients at ease — but there's a guardedness about his eyes. This is all fluff; he's waiting for Charles's pitch.

'How's it working out?'

Tyson shakes his head. 'Slow. Anyway, enough chat, Mr Henderson. What do you want?'

'It's Holborne, and you can call me Charles. Got time for a steak while we talk?' Charles doesn't wait for an answer, but interrupts the waitress as she passes with a stack of used plates. 'Same again here,' he says, pointing at Tyson, 'and two pints of mild. Okay with you?' he asks Tyson.

Tyson shrugs. 'Rare,' he says to the waitress, 'and make mine a mug of tea.'

Charles waits for the waitress to move off before leaning forward. 'Johnny says you might be able to help me out. I've a proposition for you.'

It is seven a.m. by the time Charles coasts to a halt outside his own home. A familiar car is parked directly outside his front door.

'Oh, David!' he mutters.

Charles locks his car door and walks the few feet down the pavement to his brother's Volvo. He peers inside the windows. The vehicle is empty. Frowning, Charles climbs the steps to his front door and opens it.

As he passes, Charles looks inside the open door to the darkened lounge.

'Charlie?' comes a sleepy voice.

'David. What are you doing here?'

The coffee table lamp illuminates and David sits up from where he had been lying on the couch under his overcoat. 'Any word on Sally?' he asks.

Charles shakes his head wearily. 'No. Why are you here?'

David yawns. 'I want to help. What time is it?'

'About seven.'

'Are you going to bed?'

'Nope. Too late for that. I need coffee now. Did Maria let you in?'

David unwinds his long legs and stands. 'I was waiting outside and she saw the car.'

'Go up to the spare room and get another couple of hours,' suggests Charles.

'No. I'm awake now.'

'But —' Charles starts to protest.

'No, Charles. I want to know what's going on. There must be something I can do to help.'

Charles looks at his brother, his earnest, religious and completely moral brother. They are so different, in looks, attitudes and values. But Charles has always known that, if push came to shove, there is nothing he wouldn't do for David, and vice versa.

He smiles. 'I've been thinking about this. In fact, there is. But you won't want to do it.'

'Try me.'

Charles shrugs. 'Come down to the kitchen. I'll fill you in on what's happened so far.'

CHAPTER SEVENTEEN

Charles is bellowing. 'If you don't let me see Mr Haeems this minute, I'll be back with the police!'

The receptionist at Sampson & Co. colours but doesn't back down. 'As I've already explained to you, sir, Mr Haeems is seeing a client, and as soon as he's finished he's leaving for court. He's involved in a very important case at the moment, and he's extremely busy. But if you leave your name and telephone number I'll make sure he rings you as soon as he —'

'No! I need to see him right now!'

The door opens behind the receptionist and a tall balding man in a three-piece suit puts his head out. 'What's all the commotion, Karen?'

The receptionist jumps up. 'I'm so sorry Mr Fryde! This man insists on seeing Mr Haeems. I've explained the situation but he won't listen.'

Fryde looks at Charles.

'Mr Fryde? Emmanuel Fryde?' asks Charles.

The man, who Charles notes distractedly looks a little like one of his uncles, narrows his eyes.

'I know you, don't I?' says Fryde.

'We have met actually, but a long time ago, while I was in pupillage. Look, Mr Fryde, I need to speak to Mr Haeems. It really is a matter of life and death.'

Fryde opens the door to his office wide. 'You'd better come in,' he says.

Charles hesitates. He has no idea who is pulling the strings at Sampson & Co. For that matter, he doesn't know which of the Kray twins, or indeed other member of the Firm, might be pulling *the lawyers'* strings. But he finds it hard to believe that this respectable solicitor approaching retirement could know anything about the Krays' threats or Sally's disappearance.

'Come on,' encourages Fryde, his eyebrows raised.

Charles precedes the man into his office and the door is closed behind him. The solicitor returns to his desk where he was evidently working before the disturbance.

'Take a seat,' he says, indicating one in front of the desk and screwing the top back on his fountain pen.

'No … thank you.'

'Tell me what this is about, Mr …'

'Charles Holborne, of counsel. Your Mr Haeems instructed me to represent Ronnie Hart in the murder trials.'

Fryde nods. 'Yes, I think I know about that. But Hart sacked us, didn't he?'

'Yes. But I'm still instructed by another firm.'

'It's probably not appropriate for you to talk about Mr Hart's case then, is it?' says Fryde.

His lips barely open when he speaks. As if he's so parsimonious that every word has to be weighed before he will consider expending it. Dashiell Hammett's expression, "a close-mouthed man", pops into Charles's head.

'I don't propose to talk about Mr Hart's case,' replies Charles, 'except that I'm being put under pressure by your firm's clients to persist with it.'

'Under pressure?'

'Yes. Ronnie Kray made some threats a few days ago. And now my girlfriend's disappeared.'

Fryde continues to evaluate him without expression. 'I see,' he says finally. 'And are you suggesting that either I or Mr Haeems are aware of these alleged threats? That we might have had anything to do with this … disappearance? That would be a very grave assertion.'

'No.'

'Neither I nor my clerk are parties to any alleged criminal actions of our clients. But, if you think someone has committed an offence, you must go to the police.'

Fryde stands. Charles remains where he is, hesitant.

'Have you reported your girlfriend as missing?'

Charles does not reply.

'It's time for you to leave, Mr Holborne. I understand you're upset, but I can't have you causing a disturbance in my offices. Seems to me you should be in a police station, not harassing my receptionist.'

Charles's shoulders slump. He turns towards the door. 'Please would you give Mr Haeems a message to pass on to Mr Kray?' he says.

'What is that?'

'Merely that Hart's trial is to start tomorrow at Thameside Assizes, and I will be representing him. The Krays need do nothing … rash.'

Frye doesn't answer, but instead opens the door for Charles and waits patiently for him to go through it.

Charles shakes his head, but he leaves.

Back on the pavement, he stands motionless, undecided. It should have been obvious to him: he can't rely on Fryde, or Haeems for that matter, to get the information to the twins. Maybe not at all, and certainly not in time. So, who else is there? There must be peripheral members of the Firm still at large who could carry his message, but who? And how to contact them?

Who do I know who is guaranteed still to be in touch with them? And who will deliver a message immediately? Who?

He takes several deep calming breaths. With an effort of will, he lets go of his anger and anxiety. He has to think coolly.

He starts to pace up and down the pavement in front of the solicitors' office. This is how he thinks best. Most of his best speeches and most devastating cross-examinations have been developed while walking or pacing up and down his room in Chambers.

Then he smacks his forehead in exasperation.

Of course!

Braithwaite House, Bunhill Row, is a new nineteen-storey tower block in Shoreditch, situated a few hundred yards north of London Wall, the site of the original Roman fortification around London. It is common knowledge in the East End that Violet Kray moved out of the terraced family home in Vallance Road when Ronnie and Reggie presented her with the keys to a brand new flat on the ninth floor of the block.

Charles takes a deep breath and presses the intercom button. A woman's voice answers.

'Yes?'

'Is that Mrs Violet Kray?' he asks.

'Who's asking?'

'I'm an associate of Ronnie and Reggie's. A lawyer. I need to get a very important message to them urgently, about their trial. They're expecting to hear from me.'

There is a long silence from the intercom. Finally: 'If you're their lawyer, you don't need me to —'

'No! I didn't say I was *their* lawyer, but I am involved with their case. I promise you, Mrs Kray, they'll want to hear this. Is there any way you can get a message to them?'

Another long silence, then, 'What's the message?'

'Please tell them that Hart's trial starts tomorrow at the Bailey overflow court.'

'Overflow court?'

'Yes. Thameside Assizes.'

'Is that all?'

'Yes. Thank you.'

'What's your name?'

'Charlie Horowitz.'

PART TWO

CHAPTER EIGHTEEN

IN HER MAJESTY'S ASSIZES AT THAMESIDE
Case No: T6760062
Date of hearing: 25.11.68
Start time: 10:30 *am*
Finish time: 1:05 *pm*
Before: THE HONOURABLE MR JUSTICE KINDER

R E G I N A
-v-
RONALD JOSEPH HART

Mr Desmond Cullinane QC appeared on behalf of the prosecution
Mr Charles Holborne appeared on behalf of the accused

CLERK: *Are you Ronald Joseph Hart of 38 Bacon Street, Bethnal Green, E2?*
ACCUSED: *Yes.*
JUDGE: *Just a minute. Mr Holborne what's happened to your client?*
HOLBORNE: *He was attacked while on remand by other prisoners.*
JUDGE: *Is he fit to proceed?*
HOLBORNE: *He has nasty cuts to his face, hence the bandages, but he has been stitched and given painkillers. He tells me he is well enough to proceed. His speech is slightly impaired, but not enough to make him incomprehensible. I've had no difficulty taking instructions.*
JUDGE: *Very well.*
CLERK: *Ronald Joseph Hart, you are charged that on or about 28*

October 1967, at Stoke Newington, London, you did murder one Jack Dennis McVitie. How do you plead? [Pause] Did you hear me, Mr Hart? Shall I put the charge again, my Lord?

JUDGE: Mr Holborne, your client appears either not to understand the charge or to be wilfully silent.

HOLBORNE: Please may I take further instructions?

JUDGE: Yes, but be quick about it. We were informed that this case was effective.

[Short adjournment]

JUDGE: Now, Mr Holborne, are we ready to proceed?

HOLBORNE: Thank you for allowing me that time. I believe we are ready, my Lord.

JUDGE: Very well. Stand up again, Hart.

CLERK: Ronald Joseph Hart, you are charged that on or about 28 October 1967, at Stoke Newington, London, you did murder one Jack Dennis McVitie. How do you plead?

ACCUSED: Not guilty.

JUDGE: (to Clerk) Have we a jury in waiting?

CLERK: Yes, my Lord.

JUDGE: Mr Cullinane, Mr Holborne, I'm told we have a jury in waiting. Are the parties ready to proceed on the basis of a trial?

CULLINANE: The Crown is ready, my Lord. My learned friend was good enough to alert me, informally, that despite earlier indications to the contrary, his client might plead not guilty when arraigned, and we took the precaution of lining up sufficient of our witnesses to proceed today if necessary.

JUDGE: Excellent. What is your position Mr Holborne?

HOLBORNE: We're also ready.

JUDGE: Then let's get on with it. Bring in the jury in waiting.

[Jury sworn in]

JUDGE: *Thank you. Members of the jury, before we start this case, I wish to thank you for your patience. I know that the court facilities are a little … basic … at the moment due to the building contractors. You will notice that there is no work going on at present and so the Lord Chancellor in his infinite wisdom ordered that Court 1 here be reopened to assist with the lists at the Old Bailey, which means we have no choice but to work in these very unsatisfactory conditions. The canteen remains closed, so we shall be bringing in sandwich lunches for you, and the jury bailiff will give you forms to fill in for that purpose. It is very important that you take care when using the building and respect the signs that direct you away from the scaffolding and machinery. The jury bailiffs are here to assist you, and will ensure you remain in the accessible areas. This case is listed for two to three days, and I am informed by counsel we shall be finished in that time, so we'll soon have you back in the Bailey for the rest of your jury service. Mr Cullinane?*

CULLINANE: *Thank you, my Lord. Members of the jury, I appear on behalf of the Crown in this case and my learned friend Mr Holborne, who sits nearest to you on the bench, represents the accused. This is a notorious case. No one in Britain can be unaware of the arrest of the Kray twins and their associates and the serious charges they face. It's been all over the newspapers and TV. You might even have read about this particular charge of murder.*

But it is absolutely essential that you put everything you may have read or heard out of your minds completely. You have to focus exclusively on the evidence you hear in this court. As I'm sure you know, newspapers frequently make mistakes, indeed the more cynical of us might say they even make things up from time to time, and they never, ever, have the full story. So please ignore anything you may have heard or read, from whatever source. No one is interested in what they think; the world is waiting to hear what you think. You have a great responsibility, members of the jury, because you are in the fortunate, or perhaps unfortunate, position of being the only people in the world who are actually going to hear the evidence relating to Mr McVitie's death and what the Crown say was the accused's part in it. You are the sole arbiters of the facts in this case, not the press, not me, not Mr Holborne, and not even his Lordship. And it is you who will decide this case, on the evidence you hear from the witness box or, in certain limited cases, what is read to you as agreed evidence.

Now, on that subject, my purpose in addressing you now is not to give you evidence. What I say is not evidence. My purpose is simply to give you a framework so that when the evidence is called you will understand how it all fits in. If I say something that doesn't fit with the evidence, you ignore me. Follow the evidence!

This accused is charged with murder. Both he and the victim, Mr Jack McVitie, were members of the Krays' gang, "the Firm", as they liked to call themselves. That is until Mr McVitie fell out with the Kray twins. The Crown has no intention of proving what caused that internal strife within the Firm. That is irrelevant. It is the upshot of that strife which concerns us, and it was this: Mr McVitie was stabbed to death in a flat in Stoke Newington in the early hours of 28 October last year.

As you will hear, it was a horrible and gruesome attack, and you are going to have to steel yourselves to listen to some of the evidence. Mr McVitie's body has never been found, but the Crown is absolutely confident that when you have heard the evidence you will be satisfied so that you are sure that McVitie was indeed murdered at that place and at that time by, amongst others, this accused. Do not concern yourselves with the others who were involved. There are other trials to take place. You are concerned only with this man, Ronald Hart.

You will hear that the basement flat at which the murder occurred, 97 Evering Road, Stoke Newington, belongs to a woman called Carol Skinner. A plan was hatched to lure McVitie to her flat by pretending there was a party to which he was invited. Carol Skinner, who was in fact *holding a gathering of her own friends that evening, was forced by the people who hatched the plan to leave her own flat, taking her guests and children with her, thereby leaving the premises available for the crime to take place.*

You will hear from a Mr Tennyson, a barman at the Regency Club where Mr McVitie was drinking that evening. He will tell you that a group of men including this accused came to the reception and demanded to know if Mr McVitie was inside. This accused then said that they had arrived to kill Mr McVitie and he actually revealed the gun to be used. The owner of the club refused to allow the men to enter. Hart left the gun there, presumably for safekeeping, and departed. Two other members of the group, brothers named Lambrianou, went inside to buy drinks for McVitie and ensure he didn't leave.

You will hear from Mrs Skinner who says that the accused was one of three men who arrived at her flat unexpectedly and demanded that she take her guests and her children and leave. She will tell you that she knew the accused and the two men with him from previous meetings, so there can be no doubt about her identification.

Mr Tennyson will tell you that some time later, this accused returned to the Regency Club and insisted that the owner of the club, a Mr Barry, bring the gun to Mrs Skinner's flat.

So, the scene was set. Another member of the Firm was sent back to the club to tell the Lambrianou brothers that all was ready, whereupon they invited McVitie to the party at 97 Evering Road. He readily accepted, being somewhat the worse for drink by then, and went, in all innocence, to the basement flat. There, shortly after he arrived, a gun was put to his head and the trigger pulled. It failed to go off. McVitie tried to get away through the window. Then the accused, Mr Ronald Hart, grabbed him, pulled him back into the flat and stabbed him repeatedly —

HOLBORNE: *My Lord, my learned friend is opening facts not reflected anywhere in the prosecution papers! There is no evidence at all of Mr Hart stabbing anyone!*

CULLINANE: *I'm sorry to correct Mr Holborne, but that's wrong. I am referring to the Notice of Additional Evidence served on 19 October—*

HOLBORNE: *What Notice of Additional Evidence? We've received nothing.*

CULLINANE: *The evidence of Geraldine Burns, my Lord. She was at the party.*

HOLBORNE: *I repeat, my Lord, the Defence has never seen any such evidence. [Pause] No. My Instructing Solicitor confirms that nothing has been served on us.*

JUDGE: *Well, Mr Cullinane, do you have a spare copy for Mr Holborne?*

CULLINANE: *Yes.*

JUDGE: *You've got it now.*

HOLBORNE: *My Lord, this is trial by ambush! This is critical evidence and the Defence was entitled to see it before the middle of the Crown's opening!*

JUDGE: *I'll give you time to take instructions.*

HOLBORNE: *Thank you, my Lord, but that's not the point. We have no opportunity to make further investigations. What if we could prove that this witness was elsewhere at the time? Or that she's been pressurised to give this evidence? Such investigations are now precluded.*

JUDGE: *I think you're jumping ahead of yourself, Mr Holborne. Take instructions from your client and we'll see where we go from there.*

[Counsel takes instructions]

JUDGE: *Well, Mr Holborne?*

HOLBORNE: *I am forced to seek an adjournment, I'm afraid.*

JUDGE: *No, I don't think so. You'll have plenty of time to take further instructions before this evidence is reached.*

HOLBORNE: *But this is outrageous! This man is on trial for murder, and the crucial witness in the Crown's case, the very witness who claims to have seen the murder weapon in my client's hand, is served on us in the middle of the trial? How on earth can that be fair?*

JUDGE: *Moderate your tone, Mr Holborne! I have said I will give you further time if needed during the course of the trial, but I am not adjourning it altogether. It's unfortunate, but this sort of thing happens every now and then. You're an experienced advocate and you should be able to deal with it. Now sit down and let Mr Cullinane get on with his opening.*

HOLBORNE: *I must object, my Lord —*

JUDGE: *Sit down, Mr Holborne! I have made my ruling. If you don't like it you can take it up with the Court of Criminal Appeal in due course. But we are going to get on with this case.*

HOLBORNE: *But —*

JUDGE: *One more word, Mr Holborne, and I will hold you in contempt. Now sit down. Yes, Mr Cullinane.*

CULLINANE: *As I was explaining, you will hear from Mrs Geraldine Burns, a lady who was invited to the party by members of the Firm, no doubt to make it look more realistic, that Hart stabbed McVitie until he was dead. After McVitie was dead, members of the Firm went into action to hide all traces of it. For his part, Hart was involved in carrying away men with blood on their hands and clothes in order to get them cleaned up. You will hear that there was a great deal of blood, so much indeed that the flat had to be redecorated.*

As you would expect, the accused, Mr Hart, was interviewed after he was arrested. You will hear from the officer who recorded that interview. In it, the accused admitted going with others to the Regency Club, he admitted it was possible that he had a gun with him, and that he thought he left it at the club when he left. He admits going to Carol Skinner's flat. He admits also that he returned to the club, and accepts that it is possible that he went back to get the gun. Most importantly of all, he admits being in the flat when one of his associates tried to shoot McVitie, and then McVitie was stabbed to death.

It is here, say the Crown, that Hart's account given to the police departs from the truth. Although he describes the knife and where it struck Mr McVitie in great detail, he claims somebody else wielded it. We say, of course, that that is a lie, an ineffective attempt to distance Mr Hart from what he did. He then returns to the truth by saying that he was asked to take men who had blood on them to other premises where they could wash up.

The Crown say that the evidence will be more than sufficient to prove to you, beyond reasonable doubt, that he is guilty of McVitie's murder.

I should remind you that the burden of proving the accused's guilt lies at all times on the Crown, and Mr Hart has to prove nothing. Furthermore if, having heard all the evidence and listened carefully to his Lordship's summing up and directions on the law, you are anything other than satisfied so that you are sure of Hart's guilt, it is your duty to acquit him.

And with your Lordship's leave, I shall call the first witness.

JUDGE: Yes, please.

[Witness called and oath administered]

CULLINANE: Please give your name and address to the court.

SKINNER: My name is Carol Skinner, and I live at 97 Evering Road, Stoke Newington, London N16.

CULLINANE: Mrs Skinner please could you keep your voice up and if you could turn slightly to your left so you're facing between the judge and the members of the jury, I think we shall all be able to hear you better. What is your occupation?

SKINNER: I work as a barmaid when I can, but mostly I'm a full-time mother.

CULLINANE: Please tell us what you were doing on the evening of 27 October 1967.

SKINNER: I was at home with my children. They were in bed and I had invited a few friends round.

CULLINANE: Did anyone arrive at your flat who had not been invited?

SKINNER: Yes. Three men.

CULLINANE: Did you know the men?

SKINNER: I knew two of them, both called Ronnie. Ronnie Hart and Ronnie Bender. I didn't know the third man.

CULLINANE: How did you know them?

SKINNER: Well, they were sort of friends of my husband, but I got to know them better after my husband went ... away.

CULLINANE: Did you know them well?

SKINNER: Quite well. I used to meet them in the local pubs and parties every now and then, and we would chat. Sometimes they'd buy me a drink.

CULLINANE: Had they ever been to your flat before?

SKINNER: A couple of times.

CULLINANE: But you hadn't invited them to your flat that evening?

SKINNER: No.

CULLINANE: What did they want?

SKINNER: They wanted to use my flat for the evening, and told me to take everybody out.

CULLINANE: Did they say what they wanted to use the flat for?

SKINNER: They said they needed it for a party.

CULLINANE: What was your response to that?

SKINNER: I didn't want to leave. My friends and I were having a drink and listening to music, and the children were asleep in bed.

CULLINANE: Did you comply with their request?

SKINNER: It wasn't a request.

CULLINANE: Please explain.

SKINNER: *They were very insistent. They were in a hurry, and there was no time to discuss it or argue. They were very serious. More a demand than a request.*

CULLINANE: *How did you feel about their demand?*

SKINNER: *They weren't trying to frighten me, not exactly, but I knew I couldn't refuse. I knew who they worked for and the sort of work they did.*

CULLINANE: *And who did they work for?*

HOLBORNE: *I object to that question, my Lord. It is highly unlikely that Mrs Skinner has direct knowledge of who those men worked for, only hearsay, and it is in any case irrelevant to what she may or may not have done. Her evidence is relevant only as to what was said or done, on that night, by Mr Hart.*

CULLINANE: *The reason why this evidence is relevant, my Lord, is that it explains why Mrs Skinner was prepared to take her guests and her children out in the middle of the night. I am not suggesting she is right or wrong about who employed these three men, or what they were employed to do. I am leading the evidence to explain her state of mind only.*

JUDGE: *I agree. It goes only to this witness's state of mind, not to the truth or falsity of her belief. You may answer, Mrs Skinner.*

SKINNER: *I knew they were members of the Krays' gang. I knew they were very dangerous men, even though they were friends of my husband and had been pleasant to me in social situations. So I was worried about what might happen to me or the children if I refused.*

CULLINANE: *So, Mrs Skinner, did you take everyone out of the flat?*

SKINNER: *Well, my guests had all gone anyway by then. But I took the children out.*

CULLINANE: *And where did you go?*

SKINNER: *To a friend who lives close by.*

CULLINANE: *Did you go back to your flat that evening?*

SKINNER: Not that evening. At about two o'clock the next morning.

CULLINANE: Did you go alone or with the children?

SKINNER: I went on my own at first, to see if they were finished.

CULLINANE: What did you find?

SKINNER: I arrived at the top of the steps, it's a basement flat, and Ronnie Bender intercepted me. He said I couldn't go back in yet.

CULLINANE: Did he say why?

SKINNER: Not exactly. He said "There's been a bit of a bother."

CULLINANE: Did you notice anything about him that was odd?

SKINNER: Yes. He had a pair of my son's socks, one on each hand, as if they were gloves. I recognised them immediately.

CULLINANE: Did you notice anything in particular about the socks?

SKINNER: They were covered in blood.

HOLBORNE: My Lord, this witness cannot possibly say what stains may or may not have been on her son's socks. There is no suggestion she examined them, let alone had them examined in a laboratory. The proper extent of her evidence can only be that she saw stains on the socks.

JUDGE: If you're going to jump up and down every couple of minutes with these objections, Mr Holborne, this trial is going to take forever. I can recognise blood when I see it, as I expect can the members of the jury. You may carry on Mr Cullinane. Mrs Skinner?

SKINNER: [Distressed]

JUDGE: Usher, get the witness some water. Mrs Skinner, would you like a short break? We all understand how difficult it must be to recall such horrific events.

SKINNER: No, I'm okay. Thanks.

CULLINANE: What happened then, Mrs Skinner?

SKINNER: Well, from the pavement you can see the bathroom window, and it was open. And I saw another man who I knew to be a member of the Krays' gang, pouring a bowl of dark liquid down the toilet.

CULLINANE: What happened then?

SKINNER: *I was angry, and worried about what they'd done to my home. I argued with Ronnie Bender and said I was going down, and eventually I sort of pushed past him, and he didn't stop me.*

CULLINANE: *What did you see when you got downstairs?*

SKINNER: *It was horrible, really horrible. My lounge carpet had been removed, and the underlay was covered in dark stains. [Witness distressed]. Some man … I'd never met him before … he was busy cutting it up and taking it out in sections. To the back garden.*

CULLINANE: *Did you see what was happening to it in the garden?*

SKINNER: *They were burning it. There was a bonfire, in the middle of the night.*

CULLINANE: *Did you form any conclusion as to what the stains were?*

HOLBORNE: *I object to this question too, my Lord. All this witness can say is that she saw stains on the underlay. Unless she examined the stains and had tests carried out she cannot possibly say —*

JUDGE: *I have already made my ruling on this point, Mr Holborne. Please sit down.*

CULLINANE: *Mrs Skinner?*

SKINNER: *They looked like blood to me.*

CULLINANE: *Thank you. Was there anything else amiss in your flat?*

SKINNER: *Amiss?*

CULLINANE: *Anything else wrong?*

SKINNER: *My bedspread had gone. It was on my bed when I left, but it'd been taken off. I never saw it again.*

CULLINANE: *What happened then?*

SKINNER: *Around four in the morning they left, and I went to get my kids. But there were stains all over the living room walls.*

CULLINANE: *What happened about the stains?*

SKINNER: *A few days later another member of the Firm, a chap* called Albert Donoghue, came to the flat and redecorated it.

CULLINANE: *Did you ask him to do that?*

SKINNER: *No. He just turned up with paint pots, ladders and brushes and said he was there to do it. So I let him get on with it.*

CULLINANE: *One last question, please, Mrs Skinner. Did you tell the police about these events?*

SKINNER: *Not at the time, no. It was obvious that something terrible had happened there, but I knew I couldn't say anything about it. More than my life was worth.*

CULLINANE: *But you did eventually give a statement to the police though, didn't you?*

SKINNER: *Yes. Months later, after the gang was arrested. I was approached by the police.*

CULLINANE: *So you felt safer then?*

HOLBORNE: *That's a leading question, my Lord. By the way he phrases the question, my learned friend suggests the answer.*

JUDGE: *Would you like to rephrase the question, Mr Cullinane?*

CULLINANE: *Why did you decide to give your statement to the police later?*

SKINNER: *I did feel a bit safer, yes, but still ... lots of my friends and family told me not to give evidence in case ... you know ... in case he gets off, or maybe the others get off. Then I'd be in real trouble.*

CULLINANE: *Thank you, Mrs Skinner. Please wait there. There may be further questions for you.*

JUDGE: *Mr Holborne?*

HOLBORNE: *Thank you, my Lord. Mrs Skinner, one of the very first answers you gave to my learned friend was that "They wanted to use my flat for the evening, and told me to take everybody out."*

SKINNER: *Yes?*

HOLBORNE: *I'd like you to tell us exactly how the conversation went, the exact words spoken by each of the three men on your doorstep* and by you.

SKINNER: *[Pause] I can't, not the exact words.*

HOLBORNE: *I noted that on several occasions you said "they" said this or "they" said that. Not once did you say that specific words were spoken by a specific man.*

SKINNER: *No, perhaps not, but they all wanted the same thing. They wanted me to go.*

HOLBORNE: *Can you remember any words actually spoken by Ronald Hart?*

SKINNER: *No, not exactly.*

HOLBORNE: *So it's possible, isn't it, that Ronald Bender took the initiative in the conversation and that Ronald Hart didn't actually say anything?*

SKINNER: *I suppose so. But they were all standing there together, at my door.*

HOLBORNE: *That's as maybe. I'm asking about what Ronald Hart actually said, and you can't remember if he said anything. Now, you mention that they were all standing there at your door. Your front door is down some steps from the pavement, isn't it? It's a basement flat.*

SKINNER: *That's right.*

HOLBORNE: *How far away is the closest streetlight to your front door?*

SKINNER: *I don't know. Maybe fifty yards?*

HOLBORNE: *And there is no light above the basement front door, is there?*

SKINNER: *No.*

HOLBORNE: *And no other light in the basement yard where you keep your bins?*

SKINNER: *No.*

HOLBORNE: *I suggest to you that it's very dark at night in that area, the little courtyard onto which your front door opens, isn't it?*

SKINNER: *It's not very well lit, no.*

HOLBORNE: *It's quite difficult to see people's expressions, isn't it? People outside the door on the steps.*

SKINNER: *Not really. The hall light was on so when I opened the door it would have thrown light on the men.*

HOLBORNE: *It was Ronald Bender who was at the front of the group, the one actually standing there when you opened the door, was it not?*

SKINNER: *I don't really remember. I remember seeing Ronnie Bender first.*

HOLBORNE: *Thank you. The third man was behind him and Mr Hart was further away still, standing on the higher steps leading up to the pavement, was he not?*

SKINNER: *Possibly, I don't remember.*

HOLBORNE: *Do you remember looking at Mr Hart's face?*

SKINNER: *Not really.*

HOLBORNE: *It's my instructions that Mr Hart was extremely drunk. He had been drinking since early that afternoon. It is further my instructions that he was half-way up the steps and took no part in the actual conversation. Do you dispute either of those things?*

SKINNER: *He could have been behind Bender, I don't remember. As to whether he was drunk or not I couldn't tell you.*

HOLBORNE: *Because it was impossible to tell in the poor light conditions what his facial expression or his demeanour were like.*

SKINNER: *I suppose so. I didn't really notice.*

HOLBORNE: *Thank you. I only have one further thing to ask you, Mrs Skinner, and it's to do with your belated decision to give evidence. You have a motive, don't you, to make sure that Mr Hart is convicted?*

SKINNER: *I don't know what you mean. I'm telling the truth.*

HOLBORNE: *You told my learned friend a moment ago that your friends and family have warned you against giving evidence in case Mr*

Hart or other members of the Firm are acquitted. Because then you'd be in danger.

SKINNER: *If you lived in the East End you'd understand. Everyone knows you don't cross the Krays.*

HOLBORNE: *Precisely. So, the only way to make sure you and your children remain safe, is to make sure Mr Hart and the Krays are convicted. As I suggested, that's a motive to get a conviction. It taints your evidence.*

SKINNER: *I'm telling the truth! I've told you exactly what happened!*

HOLBORNE: *But you fear that your life might be on the line, is that what you're saying?*

SKINNER: *I don't know whether they'd … I don't know what they'd do! But I know they'd take revenge.*

HOLBORNE: *Exactly. Having been persuaded to give evidence against Mr Hart, you now have a powerful incentive to exaggerate or say he was involved where he was not, to make sure that it doesn't come back to bite you.*

JUDGE: *That's a matter for your speech to the jury, Mr Holborne, not for this witness. You may ask her if she's exaggerating or making any of it up, but that's as far as you can take it. Mrs Skinner: are you exaggerating any of this evidence or making any of it up because you are frightened?*

SKINNER: *No, your honour. I am frightened, but I've told the truth.*

JUDGE: *Anything further, Mr Holborne?*

HOLBORNE: *No, thank you, my Lord.*

JUDGE: *Any re-examination, Mr Cullinane?*

CULLINANE: *No, thank you, my Lord. I next call Oswald Tennyson.*

[Witness called and oath administered]

CULLINANE: *Please give your name, address and occupation to the court.*

TENNYSON: *I'm Ozzy Tennyson ... actually it's "Oswald" but I never use it ... and I'm a barman at The Regency Club, 240A Amhurst Road, Stoke Newington.*

CULLINANE: *Were you at work at the club during the evening of 27 October 1967?*

TENNYSON: *Yeah, I was. Partly on the bar and partly on reception.*

CULLINANE: *Do you remember a group of men arriving at around 9 pm?*

TENNYSON: *Yeah.*

CULLINANE: *And who were they?*

TENNYSON: *I think there were four or five men. Two of them were Lambrianou brothers. There's loads of Lambrianou brothers, but only two I know. One of them is known as "Chrissie".*

CULLINANE: *And the other members of the group?*

TENNYSON: *The only other man I knew by name was Ronnie Hart.*

CULLINANE: *Did you know these men before they arrived?*

TENNYSON: *Yes. They all work for the Krays. Ronnie Hart's the twins' cousin, or something. I know he's supposed to be related to them.*

CULLINANE: *And how did you know these men?*

TENNYSON: *I had served them at the club on lots of occasions. The Regency was a favourite place of the Krays, and they'd often come in with their... associates.*

CULLINANE: *Do you have any doubt in your own mind that the men who arrived were two of the Lambrianou brothers and Mr Hart?*

TENNYSON: *No. I'm certain it was them.*

CULLINANE: *Thank you. Now, where were you when you first saw these men?*

TENNYSON: *On reception with one of the two owners, Mr Barry.*

CULLINANE: *Did you hear what was said?*

TENNYSON: *One of them asked Mr Barry if Jack McVitie was in the club. Mr Barry said he was. Then one of the others, Ronnie Hart, said, straight out, that they intended to kill him.*

CULLINANE: *Mr Hart said in front of you and Mr Barry that they intended to kill Mr McVitie?*

TENNYSON: *I couldn't believe it either.*

CULLINANE: *Did Mr Barry say anything?*

TENNYSON: *He asked if they meant to kill McVitie in the club, and they said yes.*

CULLINANE: *What was Mr Barry's response?*

TENNYSON: *He put his foot down. He refused to let them in. He said they couldn't kill anyone in his club in front of a load of witnesses. Someone was bound to talk. And the club would be closed down. He kept saying to think about it and what was bound to follow.*

CULLINANE: *Did he seem frightened by them?*

TENNYSON: *Christ, yes! Mr Barry's a decent bloke, a businessman. He's not a gangster. They come into the club, the Krays and their gang, quite a lot, and they're always polite and pay their bills. Everyone knows who they are and what they do, but they're just having a drink. So we're told to be polite to them and not make any trouble. But you could see he was frightened. But he stood his ground, kept saying he couldn't let them in if they were going to commit a murder. In the end he persuaded them not to do it.*

CULLINANE: *What happened then?*

TENNYSON: *Well, they had a little chat between them, and one of them got out a gun. I thought for a second it was all going to kick off — I actually ducked — but he put it on the reception desk and told Mr Barry to look after it. Mr Barry didn't want to, but Mr Hart and the others all left, leaving the two Lambrianou brothers at the club. They went into the bar. Mr Barry had no choice. He hid the gun under the reception desk.*

CULLINANE: *What happened then?*

TENNYSON: *The brothers went into the bar and sat next to Mr McVitie. They bought him a drink, well, actually, lots of drinks.*

CULLINANE: *And then?*

TENNYSON: *After about an hour or so Ronnie Hart returned. I was still on the door because Mr Barry wanted to make sure there was no trouble.*

CULLINANE: *What happened?*

TENNYSON: *Mr Hart went up to Mr Barry on reception and told him to bring the gun to the basement flat of 97 Evering Road. It's just around the corner from the Regency. Mr Barry said he couldn't leave the club and if Mr Hart was going to the flat, why couldn't he take the gun with him? But this time he couldn't persuade Hart. Hart was insistent that Barry had to carry the gun.*

CULLINANE: *What did Mr Barry do?*

TENNYSON: *He got the gun out from under the reception desk, put it in his coat pocket, and left with Mr Hart.*

CULLINANE: *Was that the end of the matter?*

TENNYSON: *No. The Lambrianou brothers stayed in the club drinking with Mr McVitie until quite late.*

CULLINANE: *What was Mr McVitie's state by then?*

TENNYSON: *Oh, he was drunk. Not falling down drunk, but very happy, laughing a lot, loud, a bit unsteady on his feet.*

CULLINANE: *What happened then?*

TENNYSON: *A man came into the club and spoke to the Lambrianou brothers. I was working on the bar by then.*

CULLINANE: *Did you hear what was said?*

TENNYSON: *He said there was a party at Blonde Carol's flat and that they were all invited. The Lambrianous told McVitie, said they were going, and invited him to go with them. He seemed happy to go. So they all left.*

CULLINANE: With McVitie?

TENNYSON: Yes.

CULLINANE: Thank you, Mr Tennyson. Please stay there.

JUDGE: Any questions, Mr Holborne?

HOLBORNE: If it please your Lordship. Mr Tennyson, please describe the demeanour of the men when you first saw them.

TENNYSON: I thought they'd been drinking. They smelt of alcohol and they were loud and aggressive.

HOLBORNE: So you wouldn't dispute it if I suggested to you that Mr Hart was very drunk?

TENNYSON: It depends what you mean by "very drunk". I thought they'd all been drinking, and perhaps quite a bit, but he didn't seem "very drunk". He was able to speak coherently.

HOLBORNE: You said "one of them" got out a gun. You don't remember which one of the men it was who had the gun, do you? Or else you would have said so in your statement.

TENNYSON: No, I didn't see who had it. I saw a hand place the gun on the reception but I couldn't tell you whose hand.

HOLBORNE: So it could have been one of the others?

TENNYSON: Yes.

HOLBORNE: You gave evidence that it was Mr Hart who said they were going to kill Mr McVitie.

TENNYSON: Yes.

HOLBORNE: I want to make it clear to you that Mr Hart disputes that completely. I suggest that he didn't actually speak at all on that occasion.

TENNYSON: I think it was Mr Hart.

HOLBORNE: But you're not sure?

TENNYSON: Pretty sure.

HOLBORNE: But it's possible it was one of the others?

TENNYSON: I suppose. But I think it was Hart what said it.

231

HOLBORNE: *Thank you. You weren't a member of this gang, were you?*

TENNYSON: *Of course not.*

HOLBORNE: *And neither was Mr Barry, was he?*

TENNYSON: *No, though he was forced to carry a gun, and now look, he's on a murder charge with all the others.*

HOLBORNE: *Yet someone in this group of men simply volunteered, in public, that they were there to commit murder, just like that?*

TENNYSON: *Yes. Like I said, I couldn't believe it. I thought, at first, maybe they were joking.*

HOLBORNE: *If you weren't a member of the gang, how did they know that you wouldn't simply call the police? [Pause] Sorry, Mr Tennyson, but a shrug isn't recorded on the transcript. I need you to answer.*

TENNYSON: *Dunno.*

HOLBORNE: *Can I suggest two possible reasons? The first is that you were part of the conspiracy, so they knew you wouldn't report it.*

TENNYSON: *No, that's not true. I've never been —*

HOLBORNE: *And the second is that they relied on the fact that you'd be too frightened to do anything.*

TENNYSON: *Yeah, exactly.*

HOLBORNE: *You're saying they took advantage of the fact that you would be too frightened to report it?*

TENNYSON: *Yeah.*

HOLBORNE: *Do you know of anyone else who is frightened into silence by the Krays?*

TENNYSON: *Pretty much everyone in the East End.*

HOLBORNE: *Even members of their own Firm?*

TENNYSON: *Of course. I don't know if they're true, but everyone's heard stories about them stabbing or shooting people. Even their mates. You don't cross them.*

HOLBORNE: *Now I want you to think about the next question very carefully please Mr Tennyson. You've already agreed with me that Mr Hart had been drinking and may have been drunk. You've already agreed with me that you can't say if it was Mr Hart who produced the gun. And you've already agreed with me that it is possible that he didn't speak on that occasion. Now, here's the question: If I suggest to you that Mr Hart, like you, was in fear during that first transaction; that he was being forced to go along with it for fear of his life; did you see or hear anything which makes that suggestion wrong?*

TENNYSON: *I don't get you.*

JUDGE: *No, Mr Holborne, I don't understand the question either.*

HOLBORNE: *I am putting to this witness that he did not see or hear anything from Mr Hart which would contradict my assertion that Hart too was being forced to take part in this event. Because he too was terrified of the Krays.*

TENNYSON: *I understand. No, I suppose not.*

HOLBORNE: *Thank you. Now, you say that later in the evening Mr Hart returned and demanded that the gun be brought to the party by Mr Barry. Mr Barry is not a member of the Krays' Firm, is he?*

TENNYSON: *No, definitely not.*

HOLBORNE: *But he was coerced into carrying the gun to Evering Road?*

TENNYSON: *Yeah.*

HOLBORNE: *Because he was terrified of the Krays as well?*

JUDGE: *Don't answer that. Mr Holborne, this witness cannot say what may or may not have motivated Mr Barry.*

HOLBORNE: *Very well. Mr Tennyson did you see Mr Barry when this request was being made of him?*

TENNYSON: *Yes.*

HOLBORNE: *Did you see his expression?*

TENNYSON: *Uh-huh.*

HOLBORNE: *Describe it for us.*

TENNYSON: *He was sweating and he looked absolutely terrified. You could tell he didn't want to do it.*

HOLBORNE: *My Lord, I would be grateful if Mr Cullinane would confirm that as a result of his involvement in carrying the gun, Mr Barry has been charged with murder along with other members of the Krays' gang.*

CULLINANE: *That is right, my Lord.*

HOLBORNE: *So, Mr Tennyson, it is your evidence that Mr Barry was so terrified of what might happen if he refused the request, that he took the gun to the party, and as a result has found himself charged with murder.*

TENNYSON: *That's right.*

HOLBORNE: *Thank you, Mr Tennyson, for your honest evidence.*

JUDGE: *Mr Cullinane? Any re-examination?*

CULLINANE: *Yes, my Lord. Mr Tennyson, it's been suggested to you that Hart was in fear of the Kray twins. When you saw Mr Hart in the Regency Club before this event, was he in company with other members of the Krays' gang?*

TENNYSON: *Usually.*

CULLINANE: *Did that include the Kray twins, Ronald and Reginald, themselves?*

TENNYSON: *Sometimes.*

CULLINANE: *And did you have the opportunity to observe Mr Hart on those occasions?*

TENNYSON: *What do you mean?*

CULLINANE: *Well, did he look relaxed in their company?*

TENNYSON: *Sort of, I suppose. He'd be drinking with them, laughing and joking, like the others.*

CULLINANE: *On those other occasions, did it look to you as if he was being forced into their company?*

TENNYSON: No.

CULLINANE: And now, on this occasion, the night that he and the Lambrianou brothers arrived to kill Mr McVitie, was his demeanour any different from the previous occasions you saw him in the club?

TENNYSON: Not really. I didn't see anything different.

CULLINANE: Thank you, Mr Tennyson. Does your lordship have any questions of this witness?

JUDGE: No, thank you. Is that a convenient time for us to break, Mr Cullinane?

CULLINANE: Sorry, my Lord, I didn't notice the time. Yes, that would be convenient.

JUDGE: Members of the jury, we shall break there for lunch. I'm going to give you a warning now which will apply to every break we have between now and the end of the case, when you are asked to go out to consider your verdict. As Mr Cullinane has told you, it is very important that the decisions you reach in this case are yours alone. For that reason I must instruct you not to discuss this case with anyone outside your number until the case is finished. I'm sure that your friends and family will be curious to know what you have heard today, but you must resist any temptation to discuss the case at all. The trouble is that once you start talking about it, they are bound to say something, to offer their opinions, and as soon as they do so there is a risk that something they say will affect your mind. As soon as that happens, the decision will no longer be that of you and you alone. So it's better to say nothing at all, do you understand? In fact I recommend that you avoid even discussing the case amongst the twelve of you at this stage, because you have heard very little of the evidence. It's best to leave discussions until the end when you have the whole picture, together with my directions on the law. Now, please go with the jury bailiff and she will take you to where you are to have your lunch. Five past two, please, gentlemen. Take the accused down.

USHER: All rise!

CHAPTER NINETEEN

IN HER MAJESTY'S ASSIZES AT THAMESIDE
Case No: T6760062
Date of hearing: 25.11.68
Start time: 2:05 pm
Finish time: 4:10 pm
Before: THE HONOURABLE MR JUSTICE KINDER

REGINA

-v-

RONALD JOSEPH HART

Mr Desmond Cullinane QC appeared on behalf of the prosecution
Mr Charles Holborne appeared on behalf of the accused

JUDGE: *Your next witness, Mr Cullinane?*

CULLINANE: *My Lord, Mr Holborne has informed me that he does not dispute the contents of the depositions of the next two witnesses. They are Mr Colin Tyldesley, the Scenes of Crime Officer responsible for the forensic examination of the basement flat at 97 Evering Road, and Dr Williamson, the forensic scientist who examined the stains in the floorboards and elsewhere and determined they were human blood. Due to the absence of any body it has not been possible to attempt a comparison between that blood and that of Mr McVitie. Your lordship will find the statements starting on page 17 of the bundle.*

JUDGE: *Mr Holborne, is that correct? Do you dispute any of this evidence?*

HOLBORNE: *No, my Lord. The fact of the murder of Mr McVitie* *at the time and place alleged by the Crown is not disputed. Only Mr Hart's part in it.*

JUDGE: Very well. Members of the jury, my clerk will now read the two statements to you. Counsel have agreed that the evidence in those statements is not disputed and therefore you do not need to hear from the witnesses themselves. However, the evidence read to you has every bit as much force as if you had heard it from the lips of the witnesses, do you understand?

[Witness statements read]

CULLINANE: My next witness is Sergeant Frank Cater, my Lord. Page 23.

JUDGE: Thank you.

[Witness sworn]

CATER: My Lord, my name is Detective Sergeant Frank Cater, based at West End Central Police Station, although currently seconded to Detective Superintendent Leonard Read's Team at Tintagel House.

CULLINANE: Thank you, Sergeant. I shall be asking you about an interview you and Chief Inspector Moody conducted with Mr Ronald Hart on 6 November 1968. Will you need to refresh your memory?

CATER: My Lord, I recorded the questions and answers in my pocketbook as the interview progressed. It was therefore made contemporaneously with the events. I would indeed like to refer to that document to refresh my memory.

JUDGE: Yes, you may refer to your pocketbook.

CULLINANE: Thank you, my Lord. Sergeant Cater, where and when was the interview conducted?

CATER: In an interview room at Tintagel House early in the morning of 6 November 1968.

CULLINANE: *And who asked the questions?*

CATER: *My boss, Chief Inspector Moody.*

CULLINANE: *As it's a long interview, my Lord, may I suggest that I ask the questions, taking the part of Mr Moody, and Sergeant Cater takes the part of the accused?*

JUDGE: *Any objection to that course, Mr Holborne? It does make it a lot more comprehensible to the jury.*

HOLBORNE: *No objections.*

CULLINANE: *Members of the jury, Sergeant Cater and I will read the interview as it occurred. I shall ask the questions as they were asked and Sergeant Cater will read the answers as they were given by the accused, Hart. In due course you will be given a copy of the transcript to read for yourselves.*

[Transcript of police interview read as follows.]

Moody: *Just to remind you, Mr Hart, you are under caution, which means you're not obliged to say anything unless you wish to do so, but anything you say will be taken down and may be used in evidence against you. Do you understand that?*

Hart: *Yeah.*

Moody: *Please confirm for the record your full name and address.*

Hart: *Ronald Joseph Hart. As for me address … well … I suppose no fixed abode. At the moment, like.*

Moody: *Please also confirm that in the room with us is Sergeant Cater, who is noting this interview.*

Hart: *Yeah, that's right.*

Moody: *And also Mr Ralph Haeems from the firm Sampson and Co., who is representing your interests.*

Hart: *Yeah.*

Moody: *Thank you. Now I want to ask you about the events of 27*

October and 28 October last year. Do you remember where you were on the evening of 27 October?

Hart: *Yes. I went with some other men to the Regency Club in Stoke Newington.*

Moody: *Who else was with you?*

Hart: *The Lambrianou brothers, Chris and his kid brother Tony, they were there.*

Moody: *Anyone else? [Pause] Ronnie, did you hear my question? Was anyone else there?*

Hart: *I can't remember.*

Moody: *Are you sure? Try to recall.*

Hart: *I can't remember anyone else. We'd all had a lot to drink.*

Moody: *Were Ronald and Reginald Kray with you?*

Hart: *I don't think so. I don't remember them being there. But, like I said, we'd had a lot to drink. My memory of the evening is a bit fuzzy.*

Moody: *Okay. Maybe we'll come back to that. What were you doing at the Regency Club?*

Hart: *We went to get Jack the Hat.*

Moody: *That's Jack McVitie?*

Hart: *Yes.*

Moody: *What were you going to get him for?*

Hart: *I don't know.*

Moody: *Well, who asked you to go and get him?*

Hart: *I don't know. When I met up with the other men, I was told that's what we were doing, and I went along.*

Moody: *What happened when you arrived at the club?*

Hart: *Anthony Barry, he's one of the two owners, wouldn't let us in.*

Moody: *Why?*

Hart: *I can't remember now. Maybe because we had had too much to drink?*

Moody: *Or because he saw that you had a gun.*

Hart: I don't remember having a gun.

Moody: But you do carry a gun, sometimes don't you?

Hart: Sometimes.

Moody: So it's possible you had one on that evening?

Hart: It's possible. I can't think why I'd have one though. We weren't working.

Moody: Mr Barry has given a statement under caution saying that you had a gun and that you were trying to get into the club so you could kill Jack McVitie. His evidence is supported by another independent witness as well.

Hart: I don't think that could be right. I mean, if I had a gun, I can't see Barry preventing me from going in. I mean, he's not that kind of bloke, you know? He ain't tough and he don't use guns.

Moody: But you think it's possible that you did have a gun which Mr Barry saw?

Hart: Yeah, it's possible.

Moody: Okay. What happened then?

Hart: We left.

Moody: What happened to the gun?

Hart: I don't remember.

Moody: Well, if you took it, and showed it to Mr Barry, and he wouldn't let you use it, did you take it away with you again?

Hart: No. I don't think I left with it.

Moody: So you would have left it at the club?

Hart: Possibly.

Moody: I suggest to you that you did leave it at the club. Several witnesses say they saw you leave it there.

Hart: I must have, then.

Moody: Why would you have left it at the club?

Hart: I don't know. I can't remember very clearly. Like I said...

Moody: You were drunk, yes. Did you all leave?

Hart: *No. The Lambrianou brothers stayed.*

Moody: *Why?*

Hart: *I dunno. Maybe they wanted a drink.*

Moody: *Did you see Mr McVitie?*

Hart: *At the club? No. We never got inside.*

Moody: *Very well. Where did you go when you left the club?*

Hart: *We went to a party at Blonde Carol's flat.*

Moody: *That's Carol Skinner, yes?*

Hart: *Yes, that's right.*

Moody: *Do you remember the address?*

Hart: *It's a basement flat at Evering Road. I couldn't tell you the number.*

Moody: *And who left the club with you to go to the party?*

Hart*: I don't remember. I could've been on my own.*

Moody: *But you said "we" went to a party. So you must have been with someone else. If you left the Lambrianou brothers at the Regency Club, who was with you?*

Hart: *Umm…*

Moody: *Mr Hart?*

Hart: *I'm trying to think. I can't remember. Sorry.*

Moody: *Did you stay at the party after that?*

Hart: *I can't recall.*

Moody: *We have witnesses who say you returned to the Regency. Are you saying you didn't go back there?*

Hart: *No, I'm saying I can't remember. Because —*

Moody: *You had a lot to drink, yeah, you already said. Why would you go back?*

Hart: *I can't tell you. I've no recollection after I was at the club early on. Maybe to get the gun? If I forgot it, maybe I went back for it.*

Moody: *I suggest that you went back to tell Mr Barry to bring the gun* to the party. That's what happened, isn't it?

Hart: *I don't think so, no.*

Moody: *I have two independent witnesses who say that's exactly what you did.*

Hart: *Who are they?*

Moody: *I'm not prepared to tell you that, at this time. Are you saying they are lying?*

Hart: *Maybe they just got it wrong.*

Moody: *Come on now, Ronnie. It's not the sort of thing people "get wrong", is it? I mean, how often is a club proprietor, with no criminal history, ordered to bring a loaded gun to a party for a murder to take place? For someone who's never handled a gun before, it would be terrifying, something they'd definitely remember, wouldn't they?*

Hart: *[No answer]*

Moody: *You were sent back to the Regency Club to instruct Mr Barry to take the gun to the party, to incriminate him in what was going to follow. So he couldn't report it without getting himself into trouble.*

Hart: *I don't know.*

Moody: *Tell us what you remember next.*

Hart: *I was at the party, and Jack McVitie arrived with the Lambrianou brothers. That's when it all kicked off.*

Moody: *What kicked off?*

Hart: *Someone tried to shoot McVitie, but the gun jammed.*

Moody: *Who tried to shoot McVitie?*

Hart: *I didn't see. The room was very crowded and there was lots of movement. Everyone was trying to get out the way.*

Moody: *What happened to McVitie?*

Hart: *At first he thought it was a joke and was trying to laugh his way out of it, but then whoever had the gun put it to his head and pulled the trigger again, and Jack realised it was serious, because he started to struggle.*

242

Moody: *What happened then?*

Hart: *He tried to get out through the front window, and it got broken.*

Moody: *And then?*

Hart: *Someone said something like "Come on Jack, stand up and take it like a man."*

Moody: *Who said that?*

Hart: *I don't know, whoever had the gun.*

Moody: *Come on, Ronnie, you were all at a party together in a living room. You must have seen who did it?*

Hart: *No. I didn't know everyone who was there.*

Moody: *All right, we'll come back to that. What happened then?*

Hart: *Jack said, "But I don't want to die like a man."*

Moody: *And after that?*

Hart: *[Sobbing]*

Moody: *What happened after that?*

Hart: *[Sobbing?]*

Moody: *Do you want to stop for a while?*

Hart: *N … no. Just give me a moment.*

Moody: *Feeling better?*

Hart: *Yes, thanks. Sorry about that.*

Moody: *No need to apologise. It must have been very shocking.*

Hart: *Yeah. I've never seen anything like that before. I never wanna see it again, neither.*

Moody: *It's all very well being a gangster, isn't it Ronnie, until something like that happens? Then you realise how brutal it can be. Makes it very real.*

Hart: *Yeah.*

Moody: *If you're ready to go on …*

Hart: *I'm fine.*

Moody: *What happened then?*

Hart: *Someone else grabbed McVitie from behind and then the man who had the gun stuck a knife into him.*

Moody: *Can you describe the knife?*

Hart: *It was really big. Like a kitchen knife.*

Moody: *Do you know where the knife came from?*

Hart: No.

Moody: *Did you see where the knife landed?*

Hart: *In his face at first, and then in his stomach. McVitie was screaming and pleading for his life.*

Moody: *What happened then?*

Hart: *He fell to the floor, and the man who had been holding his arms … took the knife and…*

Moody: *And?*

Hart: *[No reply. Distressed]*

Moody: *What did the man do with the knife?*

Hart: *He shoved it really hard into McVitie's neck, twisting it at the same time. I'll never forget the noise it made. It must have hit bone as well, because there was a terrible grating noise, and then all the blood, and air whistling, and gurgling. I'll never forget that, Mr Moody, never in me whole life. I still dream about it.*

Moody: *What happened then?*

Hart: *Well, McVitie was dead, and there was blood everywhere, on peoples' clothes, all over the carpet, on the window. It even splashed on the far wall.*

Moody: *What happened then?*

Hart: *I was pretty sober by then, so a couple of men asked me to give them a lift.*

Moody: *"A couple of men"? Who?*

Hart: *I can't tell you that, Mr Moody. I don't know them.*

Moody: *Where did you take them?*

Hart: *To a flat they directed me to. They had blood on them and wanted* *to wash up.*

Moody: *So it was the two men who killed McVitie?*

Hart: *Could be.*

Moody: *What happened when you got to the flat?*

Hart: *They washed their jewellery and coins, and burned their paper money.*

Moody: *There must have been a lot of blood, then?*

Hart: *I never knew a man could have that much blood in him.*

Moody: *Then what?*

Hart: *They washed the gun and the knife, and someone else arrived with fresh clothing and took away the men's clothes.*

Moody: *Right, now, Ronnie, I'm going to bring this interview to an end for the moment, so we can all have a bit of a break and you can have breakfast. You'll be returned to your cell for the moment.*

Hart: *Okay.*

[Continuation of police interview]

Read: *Before we start, I have to remind you that you are under caution, that you don't need to say anything unless you wish to do so but if you do say anything it will be taken down and may be used in evidence against you. Do you understand?*

Hart: *Yes.*

Read: *My name is Superintendent Read and I am in charge of this investigation. Please confirm that the only other person in the room with us now is Chief Inspector Moody, who conducted your earlier interview?*

Hart: *Yeah.*

Read: *Good. Were you given some breakfast?*

Hart: *Yes.*

Read: *Good. Now, please stand up.*

Hart: *Why?*

Read: *Because we have decided to charge you at this stage. Ronald Joseph Hart, you are charged with the murder of Jack Dennis McVitie on or about 28 October 1967. You are not obliged to say anything, but anything you do say will be taken down and may be used in evidence against you. Do you wish to say anything?*

Hart: *I thought it might be conspiracy, not actual murder.*

[End of transcript of police interview]

CULLINANE: *Thank you, Sergeant.*

JUDGE: *Mr Holborne?*

HOLBORNE: *Thank you, my Lord. Now, Sergeant Cater, please tell the jury where Mr McVitie's body is.*

CATER: *I'm afraid, my Lord, his body has never been found.*

HOLBORNE: *Have you or any members of your team interviewed members of his family?*

CATER: *His family? No.*

HOLBORNE: *To the best of your knowledge has he been reported missing by his family?*

CATER: *Not to the best of my knowledge.*

HOLBORNE: *Mr Ronald Kray and Mr Reginald Kray are very well known to the police, aren't they?*

CATER: *Yes.*

HOLBORNE: *They have faced trial on many occasions, for offences up to and including murder, haven't they?*

CATER: *They have.*

HOLBORNE: *And over the last several years, each time they have faced trial they have been acquitted.*

CATER: *I believe that to be the case, yes, my Lord.*

HOLBORNE: *They escaped conviction because witnesses were too frightened to testify against them, isn't that right?*

CATER: I wasn't involved in those cases, so I couldn't say.

HOLBORNE: Surely you're not telling us, Sergeant Cater, that you're unaware of the fact that the Kray twins are feared throughout the East End? It's common knowledge, isn't it? I mean, look at the jury, Sergeant. Even they know of the Kray twins' reputation.

CATER: I expect so.

JUDGE: That's quite improper, Mr Holborne!

HOLBORNE: I was just inviting the Sergeant to look at the jury members. He can see their expressions as well as the rest of us.

JUDGE: You cannot ask a witness what is "common knowledge" nor invite him to speculate on what jury members might know of other people's reputations. Members of the jury, you are directed to ignore that question and the Sergeant's answer. Mr Holborne, I know of your reputation and I warn you that I will not have this court turned into a circus. One more stunt like that and I will have you committed for contempt.

HOLBORNE: My reputation? [Pause] My Lord, there is a matter of law which I wish to raise in the absence of the jury.

JUDGE: A matter of law, you say?

HOLBORNE: Yes.

JUDGE: I can't see what matter of law arises out of that, Mr Holborne, but very well. Members of the jury, this occurs in all cases whenever there are issues of law, which are for me alone to decide. If you follow the jury bailiff you should have time for a cup of tea and a cigarette if you like. Thank you.

[Jury retires]

JUDGE: Now, Mr Holborne?

HOLBORNE: I have a difficult application to make, my Lord, and I hope you will believe me when I say that I have never in all my years of practice made such an application before. I make it in full knowledge of its seriousness and after proper consideration.

JUDGE: *Well?*

HOLBORNE: *I regret that I am forced to apply that your Lordship recuses himself from this case on the grounds of bias against me. Your unceremonious dismissal of my submissions, particularly regarding the Defence's lack of opportunity to investigate what will be the central evidence in the case, was inexplicable to me until your Lordship's most recent comment concerning my supposed "reputation". It is my respectful submission that your Lordship, perhaps even unconsciously, has failed to give adequate weight to defence applications because he proceeds from an assumption that I am prone, in your words, to "stunts". Your approach is accordingly coloured from the outset; your starting position is that any application I make is likely to be unmeritorious. Incidentally, the suggestion that I am prone to "stunts" is entirely false, as your Lordship would discover were he to consult any other barrister or judge on this circuit. Nonetheless, the result is that my client is not receiving a fair trial.*

JUDGE: *That is an outrageous proposition! You will withdraw it immediately or you will find yourself in serious hot water with your Inn and with the Bar Council.*

HOLBORNE: *I cannot withdraw it. It is my honestly-held opinion that your Lordship's bias against me personally is depriving my client of a fair trial. It is my duty to call it as I see it.*

JUDGE: *I'm giving you one last chance, Mr Holborne. If you do not withdraw those comments, not only will I report you to your Inn and the Bar Counsel, but I will commit you for contempt of court. For that is what you have demonstrated, sir, a complete contempt for this court. Well, sir, do you withdraw your application?*

HOLBORNE: *I cannot.*

JUDGE: *Sergeant at Arms? Where is the Sergeant at Arms?*

[Delay while Sergeant at Arms summoned]

JUDGE: *Sergeant at Arms, you will take Mr Holborne down to the cells immediately. Mr Holborne, I shall not make any decision as to committal until you have had some time to cool off and reflect on the course you are forcing on me. But be warned: the decision you are about to take will have ramifications for the rest of your career. I shall rise for an hour.*

[Court resumes]

JUDGE: *Well, Mr Holborne? I hope you've used the last hour to good effect. Withdraw the accusation of bias against me, and we shall proceed with this trial. If you persist in it, I will commit you for contempt for a period of fourteen days or until such earlier time as you apply to purge your contempt, the trial will be aborted, and we will proceed afresh with different counsel. What is your decision?*

HOLBORNE: *I apologise to your Lordship. I withdraw the application. I reserve my position for the Court of Criminal Appeal.*

JUDGE: *Which, of course, is your right. That is the proper way to proceed. Very well. Mr Cullinane, Mr Holborne, it is now 3:45, and in view of this afternoon's events I propose to retire early rather than bring the jury in for what will only be fifteen or twenty minutes of further evidence. To make up time we will start tomorrow at 10 o'clock.*

USHER: *All rise!*

CHAPTER TWENTY

IN HER MAJESTY'S ASSIZES AT THAMESIDE
Case No: T6760062
Date of hearing: 26.11.68
Start time: 10:00 am
Finish time: 1:03 pm
Before: THE HONOURABLE MR JUSTICE KINDER

R E G I N A

-*v*-

RONALD JOSEPH HART

Mr Desmond Cullinane QC appeared on behalf of the prosecution
Mr Charles Holborne appeared on behalf of the accused

JUDGE: *Good morning members of the jury. I'm sorry you were unable to return to court yesterday afternoon but the question of law raised has now been resolved. Sergeant Cater, you are still on oath. Do you have any questions for this witness, Mr Holborne?*

HOLBORNE: *I do, my Lord. Sergeant Cater, have you or any members of your team spoken to members of the accused's family since he was arrested?*

CATER: *I don't believe so, no.*

HOLBORNE: *So if, for example, they were being threatened by members of the Firm to secure Mr Hart's cooperation, you would be unaware of it?*

CATER: *I am not aware of any suggestion that Mr Hart's family are being threatened.*

HOLBORNE: *I'm making the suggestion, now. I suggest that Mr Hart was put under pressure by the other members of the Firm to take part in this entire enterprise. He felt his life and that of his family were in danger. Indeed he was put under pressure actually to admit the murder, but he resisted that pressure during his interview.*

CATER: *First I've heard of it, my Lord.*

HOLBORNE: *But it wouldn't be the first time the Krays and their gang have threatened people, put them under pressure, would it? For example, for years no witnesses would come forward to the murder of George Cornell, which occurred in broad daylight in a busy pub. Only since the gang has been arrested have witnesses felt safe to give evidence to the police.*

CATER: *Yes, my Lord, that's true.*

HOLBORNE: *Nor would it be the first time the Krays have put people under pressure actually to commit crimes to secure their silence, would it?*

CATER: *I can't answer that, my Lord. I don't have sufficient knowledge of other cases against them.*

HOLBORNE: *Did you take the statement of Mr Tennyson, the barman at the Regency Club?*

CATER: *I did, my Lord.*

HOLBORNE: *And the Crown put Mr Tennyson forward as a witness of truth, yes?*

CATER: *Yes.*

HOLBORNE: *Someone on whom this jury can safely rely to convict Mr Hart, right?*

CATER: *Yes.*

HOLBORNE: *Mr Tennyson gave evidence that one of the owners of the Regency Club, a man of good character, a man who is certainly not a gangster, was so frightened of the Kray twins that he was forced to take the gun from his club and deliver it to the place where the murder was to occur.*

251

As a result of which he now faces a charge of murder. Is it the Crown's case that Mr Tennyson was lying about that or is he a witness of truth?

JUDGE: *I won't permit that question, Mr Holborne. It's not for this witness to say whether Mr Tennyson is a witness of truth or not. That is for the jury.*

HOLBORNE: *I wasn't suggesting that this witness should determine if Mr Tennyson was telling the truth or not. That is indeed a matter for the jury. I was asking a different question, namely whether the Crown believe that Mr Tennyson was truthful about the pressure put on Mr Barry.*

JUDGE: *What do you say about this, Mr Cullinane?*

CULLINANE: *It will be for a jury in another case to decide if Mr Barry acted under duress or was a willing participant, but not in this trial.*

HOLBORNE: *With all due respect to my learned friend, that is a non-answer. The Crown must surely be saying that Tennyson is telling the truth, or else they wouldn't be calling him in this trial. I heard nothing in my learned friend's opening suggesting that Tennyson's evidence was partly true and partly false. Accordingly, they accept his evidence. And if they accept his evidence that Barry was put under pressure, that is clearly relevant to my client's defence that he was put under pressure as well.*

JUDGE: *Be careful, Mr Holborne. That is a matter for your speech, not to be ventilated before the jury during cross-examination. But I will allow you to rephrase.*

HOLBORNE: *Thank you, my Lord. Sergeant Cater: have you seen any evidence to suggest that Mr Tennyson is lying when he says he saw Mr Barry being put under pressure to take the gun to the party?*

CATER: *If Mr Tennyson gives that evidence in Mr Barry's trial, it will be for the jury to decide what motivated Mr Barry and for the learned judge to give a direction as to the law. That's all I can say.*

HOLBORNE: *I'm not asking you about Mr Barry's trial! I'm asking you about this one! Mr Tennyson told us that Mr Barry was forced to take the gun to the party. Counsel for the Crown has confirmed that, as a result, Mr Barry is now facing a charge of murder, despite the fact that he* says he was forced. I say Mr Tennyson was telling the truth. Does the Crown now say those are lies?

CATER: *It's not for me to agree or disagree. It's for the jury.*

JUDGE: *That's as far as I will allow you to take this Mr Holborne. As I say, you may address the jury on the subject in due course. Move on.*

HOLBORNE: *But —*

JUDGE: *That's enough. I have made my ruling.*

HOLBORNE: *I'll move to a different subject. Sergeant Cater, what is the Crown's case as to motive? Do you have any evidence of any motive why Mr Hart would want to kill Mr McVitie? Any feud between them, of which you're aware? Any argument over the proceeds of crime, perhaps?*

CATER: *No, we don't, my Lord. But they're all criminals, and they frequently fall out amongst themselves. It could be almost anything. In my experience, there is no honour amongst thieves, not these ones, anyway.*

HOLBORNE: *Do you agree with me that the Krays, and indeed other members of the Firm, all have a motive for making sure Mr Hart is convicted of the crime, in place of themselves?*

CATER: *What motive would that be, sir?*

HOLBORNE: *Well, you said it yourself, Sergeant. There is no honour amongst thieves. And if Mr Hart is convicted in place of the real murderer or murderers, it would let them off the hook, wouldn't it?*

CATER: *If Mr Hart was wrongly convicted, yes, of course, that would mean the actual killers escape justice. But if the jury convict Mr Hart, I don't believe they'd be making a mistake. So it would not be a wrongful conviction.*

HOLBORNE: *Thank you, Mr Cater.*

JUDGE: *Any re-examination, Mr Cullinane?*

CULLINANE: *No, thank you, my Lord. Does your Lordship have any questions of this witness?*

JUDGE: *No. Thank you.*

CULLINANE: *My next witness is Chief Inspector Moody, who also* deals with the interview, but as my learned friend asked no questions regarding that, it may be that he is no longer needed. Unless Mr Holborne has other issues in cross-examination?

JUDGE: Mr Holborne?

HOLBORNE: I have no questions of Chief Inspector Moody.

JUDGE: No questions?

HOLBORNE: No, thank you.

JUDGE: Are you quite sure, Mr Holborne?

HOLBORNE: Yes.

JUDGE: Well, you know your case, I suppose. That leaves you free, Mr Cullinane, to comment to the jury should you wish. In that case, who's next?

CULLINANE: Mrs Geraldine Burns, my Lord. The Notice of Additional Evidence is in the bundle at page 26.

JUDGE: Thank you. Can you tell me why this lady was called out of order?

CULLINANE: The Crown hoped to call her yesterday before the police evidence, but she has responsibility for a sick mother and couldn't find anyone to care for her yesterday.

[Witness sworn]

HOLBORNE: [inaudible]

JUDGE: What was that Mr Holborne? I didn't hear you, and I don't think the shorthand writer did either.

HOLBORNE: Sorry, my Lord. I repeated the words, "sick mother". For the purposes of my note, you understand.

CULLINANE: Mrs Burns, please give your full name and address to the court.

BURNS: Geraldine Margaret Burns, 3 Cedra Court, Cazenove Road, Clapton.

CULLINANE: *And your occupation?*

BURNS: *Actress.*

CULLINANE: *Mrs Burns, I'm going to ask you about an event that occurred on 27 October 1967. Do you remember where you were that evening?*

BURNS: *That's the night of the party, right?*

CULLINANE: *Yes.*

BURNS: *Yes, I remember it. I'll never forget it. Awful it was. That man's a monster!*

HOLBORNE: *I object, my Lord. Dock identifications are discouraged as dangerous. The Queen versus Flower. My learned friend is well aware of the law.*

CULLINANE: *I didn't elicit that comment, my Lord—*

HOLBORNE: *Then my learned friend should control his witness!*

JUDGE: *Mr Holborne! You're doing your client no favours by these outbursts. It is not for you to tell the court when a witness should or should not be controlled. Last time I looked, I was the judge here!*

HOLBORNE: *I apologise, my Lord. But on top of the fact that the Defence have had no advance notice of this crucial witness, for her suddenly to volunteer a dock identification like that ... well, my Lord can see the prejudice.*

JUDGE: *Mr Cullinane, my understanding of the authorities is that dock identifications are not actually prohibited, although care should be exercised. Is that right?*

CULLINANE: *That is my understanding as well.*

JUDGE: *Mr Holborne, do you disagree?*

HOLBORNE: *I don't. But the amount of care has to be considered in the context of the rest of the evidence. Where there is only one identification witness, it's obviously crucial. The risk is obvious: she sees a man in the dock and immediately assumes he is the perpetrator, whatever her actual view was, in this case across a busy, crowded room, in poor lighting.*

JUDGE: *Very well. The jury has heard the evidence, and I'm not going to direct them to ignore it. I shall deal with the caution they should apply in my summing up. Would you like to proceed, Mr Cullinane?*

CULLINANE: *Mrs Burns, do you remember what you did that evening?*

BURNS: *I was asked if I wanted to go to a party.*

CULLINANE: *By whom?*

BURNS: *By a man I know, Phil.*

CULLINANE: *Phil what?*

JUDGE: *Madam, a shrug can't be recorded on the transcript. Please answer.*

BURNS: *I don't know his surname. I was at the theatre bar and he bought me a drink.*

CULLINANE: *Do you remember the address of the party?*

BURNS: *A basement flat in Stoke Newington. I don't know the address.*

CULLINANE: *What time did you arrive?*

BURNS: *At half past midnight.*

CULLINANE: *So that would be the early hours of the morning of 28 October.*

BURNS: *Yes.*

CULLINANE: *You seem very sure about the time.*

BURNS: *I am, because I looked at the clock as I went in. It's in the hallway and you have to walk right past it.*

CULLINANE: *How many people were there?*

BURNS: *About twenty or so, I'd say. Maybe a few more.*

CULLINANE: *Tell us what happened.*

BURNS: *We were in the lounge, drinking and dancing and that, when some blokes arrived.*

CULLINANE: *How many blokes?*

BURNS: *I didn't see them coming down the steps but I saw new faces coming into the lounge. I noticed because one of them was wearing a hat. He was the only bloke there in a hat.*

CULLINANE: *What happened then?*

BURNS: *It was all so fast. One minute they were coming in and suddenly the man in the hat was, like, surrounded by other men.*

CULLINANE: *What were the other men doing?*

BURNS: *I thought at first they were, you know, pleased to see him? Like they were clapping him on the back, wishing him happy birthday or something like that.*

CULLINANE: *And then?*

BURNS: *He cried out something.*

CULLINANE: *In words?*

BURNS: *Yeah, but it was too noisy to hear what. The music was on, and it had got much louder.*

CULLINANE: *Louder?*

BURNS: *I didn't clock it then, but afterwards I realised the music had got suddenly louder just as the men came in. As if it had been turned up.*

CULLINANE: *What happened then?*

BURNS: *I saw that man —*

HOLBORNE: *My Lord, I must protest!*

JUDGE: *Mr Holborne she has already identified your client as the man responsible. I can't see what further harm can be done. Go on, Mrs Burns.*

BURNS: *I saw that man bring his arm up, above his head it was, and I saw a knife in it.*

CULLINANE: *What sort of knife?*

BURNS: *Like a large kitchen knife, with a long blade. At least a foot long.*

CULLINANE: *You saw it clearly?*

BURNS: *Oh yes. It glinted in the light.*

CULLINANE: *What happened then?*

BURNS: *He brought it down in an arc and it went into the man's* *shoulder. Then he pulled it out and stabbed him again, somewhere lower on his body.*

CULLINANE: *Where did it land?*

BURNS: *I didn't see exactly. In the chest I think, but there were people in the way.*

CULLINANE: *Were there any other blows with the knife?*

BURNS: *Yes. I saw his arm going up and down two or three times. Blood was spraying everywhere. I got some on me hair, and I was on the far side of the room. It was … it was …*

JUDGE: *Usher, please give the witness some water. Would you like to stop for a moment, Mrs Burns?*

BURNS: *Yes, please.*

[Court resumes]

JUDGE: *Do you feel well enough to continue?*

BURNS: *Yes, thank you.*

CULLINANE: *What happened then?*

BURNS: *It was all over in a few seconds. The man was on the floor, and there was blood everywhere. It all went quiet.*

CULLINANE: *Quiet?*

BURNS: *Yes. Someone turned off the music. And then we were all ushered out. I had to make a fuss to even get my coat back before I was being hurried up the steps.*

CULLINANE: *Thank you, Mrs Burns. Please remain there.*

JUDGE: *Mr Holborne?*

HOLBORNE: *Thank you, my Lord. You're an actress, Mrs Burns?*

BURNS: *That's right.*

HOLBORNE: *On TV? Films?*

BURNS: *Stage, mainly. Though I have done film work.*

HOLBORNE: *And I think you said you were in the theatre bar when* *you were invited to this party?*

BURNS: *Yes, that's right.*

HOLBORNE: *What theatre was that?*

BURNS: *It's a little theatre in the West End. I doubt you'll have heard of it.*

HOLBORNE: *Try me.*

BURNS: *The Carnival.*

HOLBORNE: *Off Frith Street?*

BURNS: *You know it?*

HOLBORNE: *You call it a theatre, but I think the proper term is "strip joint".*

BURNS: *No, it says "Carnival Theatre" outside, in lights.*

HOLBORNE: *I'm sure it does, but calling a chicken an eagle doesn't make it one.*

BURNS: *No, it's a proper theatre, with a stage and lights and proper plays.*

HOLBORNE: *I see. And were you in a play at the time of this party?*

BURNS: *I certainly was. I had the lead role.*

HOLBORNE: *So you were on stage that evening, you met "Phil" in the bar afterwards, and he invited you to a party.*

BURNS: *Exactly.*

HOLBORNE: *And what was the title of this theatrical masterpiece?*

BURNS: *What?*

HOLBORNE: *What was it called? Your play?*

BURNS: *I forget now … let me see … yes! "Dennis Among the Virgins".*

HOLBORNE: *Oh, by Mr Shakespeare? Or was it Mr Marlowe?*

BURNS: *I don't think so. I think the manager wrote it.*

[Laughter]

BURNS: *Is he allowed to take make fun of me like this?*

JUDGE: *Just answer the questions, Mrs Burns. If counsel asks something improper, I will stop him.*

HOLBORNE: *And the show's run-time?*

BURNS: *What?*

HOLBORNE: *What time did it start, and what time did it finish?*

BURNS: *It's every half hour with a ten minute break between performances. The last show's at midnight. Then it's burlesque 'til three.*

HOLBORNE: *Thank you. So, if your last performance starts at midnight and lasts for half an hour, you couldn't have got to the party by half-past midnight, could you? The show ends at half-past midnight. And then you've got to change out of your costume, take off your stage make-up, get dressed, and get from the West End to Stoke Newington. That's five miles or more. Even at that time of night it would take at least half an hour, wouldn't it?*

BURNS: *We didn't do a last show that night. There was … a bit of trouble … in the audience.*

HOLBORNE: *I see. But, even so, you couldn't have reached Stoke Newington by half-past midnight. If the last show started at half-past eleven and ran until twelve, by the time you got out of your costume —*

BURNS: *That doesn't take long.*

HOLBORNE: *Why? Ah, let me guess: you play one of the virgins.*

[Laughter]

BURNS: *Yeah. So what?*

HOLBORNE: *And by the time the play finishes you're not wearing a costume.*

JUDGE: *Would you mind telling me the relevance of this, Mr Holborne?*

HOLBORNE: *It goes to character and credibility.*

JUDGE: *Is it your case that merely because this lady may be, let us say, an exotic dancer, she is not telling the truth?*

BURNS: *I ain't an exotic dancer! I'm an actress!*

JUDGE: *You will speak when you're spoken to, madam.*

HOLBORNE: *I'm happy to move on, my Lord.*

JUDGE: *Very wise, Mr Holborne.*

HOLBORNE: *May I ask you, Mrs Burns, why you went to this party in the first place?*

BURNS: *Well, why shouldn't I?*

HOLBORNE: *Is it your usual habit to meet men in bars, men to whom you have never spoken before, men whose name, character and background are completely unknown to you, and within a few minutes go off with them to a party at an unknown destination?*

BURNS: *I don't see why I shouldn't.*

HOLBORNE: *And you insist on describing yourself as an actress do you?*

BURNS: *I know what you're saying, and you're all wrong. I'm not … I don't do … what you're suggesting. The party sounded like a laugh, so I thought I'd go. Anyway, it weren't just a few minutes. We had a few drinks first.*

HOLBORNE: *For you to have arrived at Stoke Newington by half-past midnight — as you assure us you did — you must have left the theatre no later than midnight, which is when your last show ended. I'd be surprised if there was time for even a single drink.*

BURNS: *Well, there was. Maybe the woman's wall clock was slow.*

HOLBORNE: *What woman?*

BURNS: *The woman whose flat it was.*

HOLBORNE: *Who said the flat belonged to a woman?*

BURNS: *I … dunno.*

HOLBORNE: *Did Phil tell you that?*

BURNS: *I don't remember. Someone did.*

HOLBORNE: Are you saying you met the woman whose flat it was? Your hostess?

BURNS: I don't know. I don't think so.

HOLBORNE: What makes you think you didn't meet her?

BURNS: I dunno. I s'pose cos there weren't many women there. It was mainly blokes.

HOLBORNE: Odd sort of party, with mainly blokes and only a couple of women?

BURNS: That's your opinion. I think they're the best sort.

[Laughter]

HOLBORNE: Let's turn to this supposed identification. What room was the party held in?

BURNS: The lounge.

HOLBORNE: How big would say that room was?

BURNS: Oh, say from me to the end of your bench.

HOLBORNE: I'd say that was about twelve feet. Does my learned friend agree?

CULLINANE: I think closer to fourteen feet, my Lord.

HOLBORNE: Very well, fourteen feet. And about as wide as it was long, would you say, Mrs Burns?

BURNS: No, a bit less wide, maybe to there [points].

HOLBORNE: Ten feet?

BURNS: Around that.

HOLBORNE: Any furniture in the room?

BURNS: Some chairs, like a couple of armchairs, and a table for some crisps and drinks and so on.

HOLBORNE: And a record player?

BURNS: Yes.

HOLBORNE: And records.

BURNS: Yes.

HOLBORNE: *Were the lights on?*

BURNS: *The main light weren't, but there were lamps on the tables.*

HOLBORNE: *Tables? Plural?*

BURNS: *Yeah, I forgot. There was a little table by each of the armchairs.*

HOLBORNE: *So, low level lighting in two corners?*

BURNS: *Look, I dunno. I didn't pay much attention.*

HOLBORNE: *Well, Mrs Burns, you were there and we weren't. So I'm asking you to give us a picture of the room, all right? Do your best, okay? It was lit for a party, wasn't it? Low level lighting in two of the corners.*

BURNS: *Yeah.*

HOLBORNE: *Thank you. So, in this fourteen by ten foot lounge, there were two armchairs, two occasional tables, another table for the food and record player, and twenty-plus people, dancing.*

BURNS: *Yes.*

HOLBORNE: *So very crowded.*

BURNS: *Quite crowded I suppose. It was a party.*

HOLBORNE: *Now you say you noticed the man in the hat arriving in the room.*

BURNS: *Yes.*

HOLBORNE: *And when he arrived he was surrounded by other men.*

BURNS: *Yes.*

HOLBORNE: *So, in this half-lit room, with everyone dancing and moving around as they do at parties, you see a man wearing a hat enter the room, and he is immediately surrounded by other men.*

BURNS: *Yes, but I could still see everything, especially what your client did.*

HOLBORNE: *But you were on the far side of the room, with up to twenty people between you and the door.*

BURNS: *Who said I was at the far side of the room?*

263

HOLBORNE: You did. You got blood on your hair even though you were at the far side of the room. So if McVitie just gets in the door and is surrounded by other people, who you initially think are saying hello, or congratulating him, and you are on the far side of the room when, seconds later, he is being stabbed. You would have had all the other guests between you and McVitie.

BURNS: I could see perfectly. I saw it all. I'll never forget those moments for the rest of my life.

HOLBORNE: Okay, let's test that. How many men were in the group surrounding Mr McVitie?

BURNS: Three or four.

HOLBORNE: Which? Three or four? [Pause] Well Mrs Burns, which is it? You'll never forget those moments for the rest of your life.

BURNS: Four.

HOLBORNE: What were they wearing?

BURNS: I don't remember.

HOLBORNE: Were they short or tall, thin or fat?

BURNS: I don't know. Average I suppose. Though McVitie was quite small.

HOLBORNE: You don't know, average you suppose. And as for McVitie, have you seen photographs of him in the newspapers or on television?

BURNS: No, I don't think so.

HOLBORNE: You must be the only woman in England who hasn't, then.

JUDGE: Comment, Mr Holborne.

HOLBORNE: Yes, my Lord. Sorry. So, in summary Mrs Burns, you can't describe any one of the other actors in this scene, this scene that you will never, ever, get out of your head, with the odd exception of Mr Hart, who you saw with perfect clarity, from across a busy, darkened room and with twenty moving people between you and him. Is that about it?

BURNS: *I saw him. I saw him! I saw the knife in his hand and I saw it go up and down.*

HOLBORNE: *So you say. I suggest to you, Mrs Burns, that this whole story of being invited to this party with a stranger named "Phil" is a complete lie. I suggest you were paid to give this evidence.*

BURNS: *No, it's true, every word of it. On me life.*

HOLBORNE: *I suggest that if you were at this party at all, you were paid to make up this story to implicate Mr Hart.*

BURNS: *No. It ain't true.*

HOLBORNE: *You live at Cedra Court, Casenove Road.*

BURNS: *Yeah? What of it?*

HOLBORNE: *How long have you lived there?*

BURNS: *Since 1961.*

HOLBORNE: *That's the block where Ronnie and Reggie Kray each have a flat, isn't it?*

BURNS: *Who?*

HOLBORNE: *Who? Are you saying you've never heard of Ronnie and Reggie Kray?*

BURNS: *I … I don't… well, maybe.*

HOLBORNE: *"Maybe"? You're certainly the only woman in England who's never heard of the Kray twins! And yet by some mysterious chance, you actually live in the same block of flats as them.*

JUDGE: *Comment, Mr Holborne. Is there a question in there by any chance?*

HOLBORNE: *I'll rephrase, my Lord. Is it your evidence, Mrs Burns, that for several years you've lived at Cedra Court, the infamous venue of Ronnie Kray's sex parties, which were plastered all over the newspapers and television news only a year or two ago, and you were unaware that the Krays were your neighbours?*

BURNS: *Yes.*

HOLBORNE: *And when the media of the world was camped outside*

Cedra Court, you didn't notice a thing? No photographers, no cameramen, no journalists and so on? None of the police officers in their shiny uniforms getting out of their shiny police cars? Nothing?

BURNS: *Maybe I was out. I work long hours.*

HOLBORNE: *You do understand, don't you Mrs Burns, that Mr Hart was formerly a member of the Krays' criminal gang, known as the Firm?*

BURNS: *I didn't know that. I've just been asked to say what I saw that night.*

HOLBORNE: *Did you also know that other men present at the party were also members of the Firm?*

BURNS: *No.*

HOLBORNE: *It seems to me, Mrs Burns, that you saw and heard nothing except what you were paid to see and hear. I suggest you've been paid by someone to give evidence against Mr Hart.*

BURNS: *No. I'm telling the truth.*

HOLBORNE: *And I'd hazard a guess that the someone was Ronnie or Reggie Kray. Am I right?*

BURNS: *No one's paid me nothing.*

HOLBORNE: *You're a liar, Mrs Burns, prepared to lie for money to send a man away for life. Isn't that right?*

BURNS: *No, it ain't. I'm telling you what I saw.*

HOLBORNE: *Thank you, Mrs Burns, I have no further questions. I hope your mother recovers soon.*

BURNS: *What?*

HOLBORNE: *Your sick mother.*

BURNS: *What you on about? I ain't seen my mother since I was six.*

HOLBORNE: *You surprise me.*

JUDGE: *Mr Cullinane, any re-examination?*

CULLINANE: *Yes, if you please my Lord. Mrs Burns, how close do you think you were to Hart when you saw him raising his arm with the* *knife in it?*

BURNS: *About six feet.*

CULLINANE: *Was there anyone between you and him at that moment?*

BURNS: *There were people milling around, but I could see him clearly. He had his back to me and McVitie — the man in the hat — was sort of facing me.*

CULLINANE: *Did you see the knife strike McVitie.*

BURNS: *Yes.*

CULLINANE: *And was it held by Hart at that instant?*

BURNS: *Yes.*

CULLINANE: *Thank you. Does my Lord have any questions of this witness?*

JUDGE: *No, thank you. You are free to leave, Mrs Burns. Is that your case, then, Mr Cullinane?*

CULLINANE: *Yes, my Lord. That is the case for the Crown.*

JUDGE: *Mr Holborne.*

HOLBORNE: *Thank you. I am not calling evidence on behalf of the Defence, but my client wishes to read a statement from the dock.*

JUDGE: *Stand up, Hart. What do you want to say?*

HART: *You've all heard of Ronnie and Reggie Kray. You know they run the East End, and most of the West End too. They have killed people, or had their men kill people, more times than I can say. But you don't need me to tell you that. Anyone who says they haven't heard of the Kray twins, especially when they live in the same block of flats, is lying to you. I had nothing when I came out of prison, no home, no money and no job. I asked if I could work for the twins, as a driver or a barman, for example. I wanted to get away from crime, and they owned lots of businesses and had lots of straight employees. So I thought it would be okay. But gradually they gave me things to do which I knew were wrong and I decided I had to leave the gang. They made it impossible. There is* *only one way to leave the Firm, and that's if you're dead. I knew they wanted to kill McVitie — don't ask me why, they never tell us what they're thinking — and they sent several of us to the Regency to do it. They said if I didn't go, they'd kill me. They also said that they knew where my brother and his wife and baby girl lived, from which I took it that they would harm them as well. I had to go. I had no choice. I'd been drinking all day to give me courage and by the time we got to the Regency I was right pissed. I can't tell you who said what, or if I even had the gun. When Mr Barry refused to let them in I was relieved. I was really happy that he kept the gun as well. I thought I could go back to the Krays and tell them we couldn't do the hit.*

But when we got to Blonde Carol's they sent me back to the club and told me to tell Mr Barry to bring the gun. That's what they do, see, they frighten innocent people to get them involved, and after that it's too late to back out. Mr Barry is now facing a murder charge too, and he did nothing but what the Krays forced him to do. Anyway, I went back to the club and the two Lambrianou brothers brought McVitie to the flat.

I swear on my mother's life, I did not have a knife and I never used it on McVitie. When I got back to the party I just tried to keep out of the way. I didn't even want to see what was going to happen. It was Reggie Kray who stabbed McVitie to death after Ronnie tried to shoot him and the gun wouldn't go off. That woman, Mrs Burns, is a liar. If I did as the prosecution says I did, why haven't they called all the other people at the party as witnesses? The only one they've got is Mrs Burns and she's a complete liar. She's been paid by the Krays to tell you a totally false story, so they get off.

I promise you, I'm telling the truth.

CHAPTER TWENTY-ONE

IN HER MAJESTY'S ASSIZES AT THAMESIDE
Case No: *T6760062*
Date of hearing: *26.11.68*
Start time: *2:05 pm*
Finish time: *4:20 pm*
Before: *THE HONOURABLE MR JUSTICE KINDER*

R E G I N A
-v-
RONALD JOSEPH HART

Mr Desmond Cullinane QC appeared on behalf of the prosecution
Mr Charles Holborne appeared on behalf of the accused

JUDGE: *Mr Cullinane?*
CULLINANE: *Thank you, my Lord. Well, members of the jury, that is all the evidence you are going to hear. It is now my job to sum up the case from the prosecution's perspective. I can take this very quickly because nothing has changed from when I opened the case yesterday. It doesn't appear that Hart disputes the fact that he was sent to the Regency Club to kill McVitie; he doesn't seriously dispute that he had the gun; he agrees it was left at the club and that he was sent back to tell Mr Barry to bring it to the party; and he agrees he was in the room when McVitie was killed. He admits taking part in all the preparation, and in his interview he admits taking part in all the clean-up. He doesn't dispute that interview. So, he admits every element from start to finish except wielding the knife. As to the suggestion that he acted under duress, his lordship will tell you*

269

this, but it is no defence to murder, even if it were all true — as to which you have no evidence whatsoever. His lordship will direct you as to the weight of an unsworn statement from the dock, a statement not tested by cross-examination. That is not evidence.

So, the only part he denies is the actual killing. As to that, you have the sworn evidence of Mrs Burns. You have nothing to set against that. In those circumstances I invite you to share the view of the police and the Crown, namely, that Hart is guilty of the charge of murder, beyond reasonable doubt, and it is your duty to bring in a verdict of guilty.

JUDGE: *Mr Holborne?*

HOLBORNE: *Yes, my Lord.*

Ladies and gentlemen, very few people realise that it's only in the last seventy years that an accused has even been allowed to walk across the court, climb into that witness box, and give evidence in his own defence. It was not allowed. Blame the Court of Star Chamber. The Star Chamber could force accused people to answer questions. Torture them into speaking. If they refused, held the Chamber in contempt, they would face mutilation, whipping, life imprisonment. Without even a finding of guilt. The Court of Star Chamber, like the Inquisition, imposed appalling penalties upon the innocent and upon the political opponents of the Crown.

And so the law was changed at the end of the last century to prevent such abuses of power. It became the rule that the accused person was barred from the witness box. Only then could juries be sure he hadn't been the victim of torture. And, went the argument, making it impossible for the accused to give evidence meant that the prosecution evidence had to be watertight on the evidence, so strong that nothing the accused might say could make any difference.

Why am I giving you this history lesson? Because it remains the inalienable right of any person in the English courts still to sit back and say to the Crown: "You accuse me; then prove it! I will say nothing to help you." The judge will tell you that this is Mr Hart's legal right. The Crown has to prove this case so you are sure beyond reasonable doubt, and it has to do that from the mouths of its own witnesses. If their evidence fails to reach this high standard, it is your duty to acquit Mr Hart. In acquitting him you are not doing him a favour; you are according him the right of every man, woman or child coming before the English criminal courts. It is something we have given the world, and we should be proud of it.

Mr Cullinane is correct to say that most of the surrounding facts in this case are not disputed. That measure of agreement however can't be used to brush over or camouflage the fact that, when you come down to it, the Crown has to prove beyond reasonable doubt that it was Mr Hart who had the knife in his hand and who used it to kill Mr McVitie. That is the central piece of evidence. Without that, the Crown has nothing. It has involvement in the preparation for the crime and afterwards, and of course the Crown could have charged Mr Hart as an accessory, as a conspirator or as party to a joint enterprise. They have not done so. They chose to put their case fairly and squarely on one central assertion: Mr Hart, they say, actually wielded the knife. It is that, says Mr Cullinane, which makes Hart guilty of murder.

So, we can move all the other evidence to the sidelines, can't we, and examine the evidence of the only witness called by the Crown to prove that central fact.

And, let's face it, she was awful, wasn't she?

But before I consider her evidence I have one thing to say about all the peripheral stuff, what Mr Hart did before and after that central moment on which we must all focus. Sergeant Cater was reluctant to admit it, but Mr Tennyson was telling us the truth. The Crown took his witness statement and chose to call him to prove their case. They put him forward as a witness of truth. If they thought he was lying, they obviously wouldn't have called him, because that would have been totally improper, not to mention potentially catastrophic to their case. So when he tells us that he watched another man, Mr Barry, being threatened and forced to take part in this crime by delivering the gun to the party, we can believe him, can't

271

we? And if Tennyson saw Mr Barry being put under that pressure, doesn't that make it so much more likely that Mr Hart was put under similar pressure to go to the Regency Club before the event, and help people to clean up after it? As I say, the prosecution has to prove its case, every element, beyond reasonable doubt. And surely Mr Tennyson's evidence creates a reasonable doubt as to whether Mr Hart was doing these acts of his own free will or under compulsion. Mr Cullinane is right to say that acting under duress is no defence to murder. But it is a defence to the acts which surround the main event.

Anyway, as I say, Mr Hart is not charged specifically in relation to such matters. He is charged with murder because Mrs Burns says she saw him wielding the knife. So I turn to that.

This was a party, with alcohol, food and dancing, all crammed into a small basement room. We've all been to parties like that, lights down low, lots of noise, laughing and movement. If Mrs Burns was there at all, and I'll come back to that, she would have been looking, in half-light, from the far side of the room with all the party guests between her and the door. She says the moment McVitie arrived he was surrounded by other men. So much so that she thought at first they were patting him on the back or celebrating something. How then can she be sure it was Mr Hart's hand holding the knife? We need to be very careful about this, don't we? Even if she were telling the truth as best she could, and I'm going to suggest to you that she clearly wasn't, if she got that split-second wrong, you'd be convicting the wrong man.

But she wasn't telling the truth, or even trying to do so.

Firstly, let's look at her, Mrs Burns, the "actress". At first I thought it was rather sweet, naïve, that she insisted that she is an actress, despite the fact that it's obvious that she is, in truth, a stripper in a strip club. Nothing wrong with being ambitious or having a rather inflated conception of one's work. That's human nature.

But then as we heard a little more, my view of her changed, and I wonder if yours did too. Let's start with the mysterious "Phil". Well, who is he? More importantly, where is he? He took Mrs Burns to the party, so he would've been the ideal witness to support the Crown's case. We've not heard a word about him or any attempt to find him. Can you be sure he existed at all?

Then there is the fact that Mrs Burns went with him. She meets a man for the first time, and mere minutes later she is accompanying him to a party at a place and with people she doesn't know. A complete stranger.

What should we make of that? I suggest there are two possibilities and they both lead to the same conclusion. The first is that she is a woman who might go off with a strange man for sexual purposes, for money. I make no criticism of her for that. She may have no economic choice but to engage in such work. But if her body is for sale, why not her evidence? The second possibility is that she was simply bought, by the Krays; paid to give this evidence. The mysterious "Phil" never existed, or if he did, he was part of the group planning this murder.

I am going to suggest to you that it is this second scenario that is true. Here are three reasons:

Firstly, we know she can't be telling the truth when she says he bought her drinks beforehand because there was simply no time for that. She couldn't have got to the party at half past midnight, a time about which she is so certain, if having finished her performance at midnight, she then had to get dressed, take off her make-up, have drinks in the bar and then travel the five miles across London streets to the party. You can look at a map if you don't know the distances involved. It would certainly have taken thirty to forty minutes in a cab. Much longer on public transport, especially at that time of night.

The timing just doesn't work, does it?

Secondly, the Kray twins. Can we possibly believe her when Mrs Burns says she was unaware that they lived in the very same block of flats as she? How can we believe her when she says she was unaware of all the press coverage around the time of the sex scandals involving government ministers? She was living at the block at the time. She would have to have *pushed her way through the crowds outside on a daily basis. I'm sure you all remember it, don't you? I see several of you nodding. There can't be an adult in the whole of Britain who didn't see the headlines, the press reports, the newscasts on television. It was the biggest story of the year, wasn't it? Can we possibly believe that Mrs Burns is telling us the truth when she assures us she was completely unaware of it?*

The answer is no. She was lying on that point.

Which leads to my third point: why? Why would she lie about knowing who the most famous gangsters in Britain are? Why would she pretend she didn't know they lived in the same block of flats as her? It's a perfectly reasonable question for us to ask, isn't it?

And the answer, surely, is obvious: she's been put up to giving this evidence by the Krays. Can you think of any other reason why she would want to hide her knowledge of them?

If you think she has indeed been paid to give this evidence so as to let the Krays themselves off the hook, or you think it's even possible, then there is only one conclusion: you can't be sure she's telling us the truth of what she saw.

Once we reach that conclusion, that is the end of the case. You see, the Crown have to satisfy you that Mrs Burns is such a truthful witness that you can unhesitatingly rely on her evidence to say that you are sure, beyond reasonable doubt, that Mr Hart had that knife. You have to have complete and implicit trust in that critical piece of evidence given by Mrs Burns. If you don't have such complete and implicit trust, the only possible verdict, the only permissible verdict in accordance with your oaths, is one of "Not Guilty".

JUDGE: *Now ladies and gentlemen of the jury it is for me to sum up the evidence and to give you some directions as to the law. So far as the evidence itself is concerned you have heard it all over the space of less than two days and I don't intend to remind you of all of it.*

First let us deal with the burden of proof. Mr Holborne emphasised on several occasions that the prosecution must satisfy you beyond reasonable doubt. I direct you to ignore that phraseology. The appropriate way to put it, is that you must be satisfied on the evidence so that you are sure the prosecution has established the guilt of the prisoner. There is no need to over-complicate it in the way Mr Holborne has done. As for his treatise on English legal history, I suggest you ignore that as well.

HOLBORNE: *My Lord, I must object. Counsel is entitled to say exactly what he wants in summing up as long as it is not defamatory, scurrilous or irrelevant. In the words of the authority, R versus Wainwright, "anything that occurs to him as desirable to say on the whole case." You are making an error of law by telling the jury to ignore it.*

JUDGE: *Sit down, Mr Holborne. You have had your say and now I'm having mine.*

HOLBORNE: *Unless I mislead the jury on an issue of law, your Lordship is not permitted to tell the jury to ignore anything I have said on Mr Hart's behalf! Nothing I said was inaccurate. It is correct that until recent years an accused person was not allowed to give evidence on his own behalf. It is also correct that the Criminal Evidence Act 1898 prohibits the prosecution from commenting in any way on an accused's failure to give evidence.*

JUDGE: *Last warning, Mr Holborne. You are senior enough to know that counsel may not interrupt a judge's summing up. If you don't like it and you think I have made a mistake, the Court of Criminal Appeal is available to you.*

HOLBORNE: *But my Lord —*

JUDGE: *I don't know what it is with you people. Your arrogance is sometimes breath-taking.*

HOLBORNE: *"You people"? What do you mean by that? [Pause] Well? Go on, have the balls to say exactly what you mean!*

JUDGE: *What did you say? How dare you address me in that fashion? Apologise immediately, or you'll find yourself down in the cells.*

HOLBORNE: *No. I insist, for the record, that your Lordship answers me! What did you mean by "you people"?*

JUDGE: I will not be dragged into a slanging match with you, sir! I can see that you are not yourself, Mr Holborne, and I am giving you the chance to apologise —

HOLBORNE: From the very start of this case it's been obvious that your Lordship has some animus against me, and now you've made it clear that your attitude is coloured by racial or religious prejudice. I object in the strongest possible terms.

JUDGE: Very well. You've had your warning. You are in contempt of court, sir, and I sentence you to six months in prison. Sergeant at Arms, take Mr Holborne down.

HOLBORNE: You can't do this!

JUDGE: I think you will find that I can. Your career as a barrister, sir, is over as from this moment. And I daresay both the Bar and the Bench will be relieved to be free of your antics from now on.

[Mr Holborne removed from the court]

JUDGE: Ladies and gentlemen, I return to my directions on the law. You will find Mr Hart guilty of murder if you find that he struck McVitie with a knife intending to kill him or do him serious harm. I doubt that issue will detain you long. Mr Hart tells you, both in his interview and in his statement from the dock, that the mission he was given that night was to kill Mr McVitie. With that admission, if he then plunges a knife into McVitie's body it's pretty clear, you may think, that Hart's purpose was murder or serious harm. So that is simple.

It has formed no part of Hart's defence to say that he did use the knife but was acting under duress. He denies using a knife altogether. So, I direct you in law that the issue of duress falls away. It doesn't arise in this case. In any case Mr Cullinane is quite right to say that duress is no defence to a charge of murder, and you will note that Mr Hart is not charged as an accessory in respect of the preparatory acts or those which followed the murder, where that issue might have become relevant.

You have heard the evidence of Mrs Burns. As the judge, I am permitted to comment on the failure of the defendant to give evidence if I think it relevant. Although the ancient right of a prisoner to address the jury from the dock still exists, what the prisoner says is to be given very much less weight than what he might have said, on his oath, and having been tested fully under cross-examination. You are entitled to ask yourself why Hart chose not to go into the witness box. You would be perfectly entitled to conclude that he was frightened of the questions he might be asked. You would be perfectly entitled to ask yourself if he was hiding something. That conclusion would certainly be open to you and, you may think, is the most likely one.

So, the evidence of Mrs Burns is unchallenged by any evidence from the Defence. It stands alone. Clever cross-examination points made by Mr Holborne cannot affect the fact that the only evidence you have heard concerning the knife comes from the woman who says she clearly saw Hart plunge it into the body of McVitie.

Now, you are entitled to ignore any opinion I may give on the factual issues in the case, because you and you alone are the sole arbiters of fact, but you might think that Mr Holborne's attack on that woman, who witnessed such an appalling act of violence, was unfair. Whatever she may do for a living, she is still able to use her eyes and tell us, honestly, what she saw. You may think therefore that whether she's an actress or something else is a matter of complete irrelevance. The question is, simply, did she see what she says she saw?

Mr Holborne tried to spin a web of suspicion and innuendo around this woman, largely on the basis that she supposedly lives in the same block of flats as two notorious criminals. But where is the evidence of this? Where is the evidence that the Kray twins live at Cedra Court? The Defence could have laid this foundation stone very simply — production of the rates records is all it would have taken, for example — but did not do so. There is absolutely no evidence before you that the Kray twins live at Cedra Court or that they've ever met Mrs Burns. What Mr Holborne puts to a witness is no more than a suggestion, and if it is not accepted, it has no further weight. It is not Mr Holborne's questions that matter, but the answers Mrs Burns gave, and she denied knowing anything about the Kray twins. That is the evidence. Without some evidence called by the Defence to suggest something else, the whole fanciful, unsupported, conspiracy theory collapses, you may think.

I recommend you focus on the evidence she gave as to what she could see from her position. You will remember she clearly saw Mr McVitie as he entered, and was able to see that he was immediately surrounded by other men, one of whom was the accused, an accused whose admitted task that evening was to murder McVitie. She says she saw the knife clearly as the accused brought it down. If you accept that evidence, as surely as night follows day, the prisoner is guilty as charged.

Now, I will swear the jury bailiff who will take you to the jury room to consider your verdict. Elect one of your number to act as foreman.

[Jury bailiff sworn and jury taken out. Hearing adjourned at 3:25 pm]

JUDGE: Mr Cullinane, I shall adjourn for the present. I shall call the jury back in at around 4 o'clock to see if there is any news, or if I can give them any assistance.
USHER: All rise!

[Resumed hearing at 4:15 pm]

JUDGE: Mr Cullinane I gather we have a verdict. Let's have the jury in.
CLERK: Stand up, Hart. Mr Foreman, please answer the following question either yes or no. Have you reached a verdict upon which you are all agreed?
FOREMAN: Yes, my Lord.
CLERK: Do you find the accused, Ronald Joseph Hart, guilty or not

guilty of the charge of murder?

FOREMAN: *Guilty.*

JUDGE: *Thank you, members of the jury. Mr Cullinane I propose to proceed immediately to sentencing. The penalty is prescribed by law and there is nothing that replacement counsel on behalf of Hart could say to affect the outcome. Do you agree?*

CULLINANE: *Yes, my Lord, I do.*

JUDGE: *Ronald Joseph Hart, I sentence you to life imprisonment. Take him down. You will have the pleasure of sharing the transport with your former counsel on your way to prison. Mr Cullinane, I'm not aware if any members of the press are present, but I further order that, in light of the risk of prejudice to the administration of justice, there shall be no publication of any report of these proceedings until the conclusion of the rest of the trials to be heard at the Central Criminal Court against the Kray twins or any members of their gang. Any such report will be punished as a contempt of court .*

CULLINANE: *I'm sure that has been understood, my Lord.*

JUDGE: *Members of the jury, if you go with the jury bailiff, you will be told whether you are required tomorrow.*

USHER: *All rise!*

CHAPTER TWENTY-TWO

Reggie Kray is shown into a legal conference room by a prison guard. He wears his own clothes, a pair of grey slacks, a light-coloured check shirt and informal leather shoes. In one hand he has a folded newspaper and in the other a mug of tea. He is well-coifed and close-shaved and the guard can smell his cologne. He looks like a businessman on holiday about to relax with the day's crossword.

'Well?' he asks.

The prison guard scans the corridor behind him and slips into the room, closing the door quietly. He opens two buttons of his tunic uniform and extracts a thin sheaf of papers from underneath.

'Here you go. Hot off the press.' He hands the pages to Reggie. 'Got to be a first, eh?' he says.

'What's that?'

'A shorthand writer doing takeaway deliveries – and to a nick!'

Reggie leafs through them and nods, satisfied, 'Well done, Ned,' he says. 'No trouble?'

The prison officer shakes his head. 'Nah, I think she'd have taken less, to be honest Mr Kray. But she kept banging on about disposing of 'em soon's you've read 'em. For 'er sake and yours.'

'I ain't stupid enough to take 'em back to the cell. You're gonna chuck them soon as Ron and I have spoken. And you think she'll keep *shtum*?'

'Oh, yeah. She knows the score. So, how long do you need?' he asks, indicating the papers and nodding towards the wall clock encased in its protective cage.

Reggie considers. 'Give us an hour, yeah?'

'Righto. I'll put the call through then. Need anything else?'

'Another cuppa in half an hour, perhaps?'

'No problem, Mr Kray.'

The officer opens the door again, checks the corridor once more, and slips outside, closing the door quietly behind him.

Reggie Kray settles himself at the small table. The high barred window above him overlooks the prison yard and he can hear the raised voices and scuffles of a football match in progress below him.

He fans the sheaf of papers on the table before him. Every page is headed *The Queen v Ronald Hart*. He starts to read.

Forty-five minutes later he turns over the last page of the transcript. He stares up at the window above him, and a smile emerges on his face. He starts chuckling. The chuckling grows in volume and soon Reggie Kray is laughing so hard that his eyes are watering and his sides aching.

The telephone beside him rings a few minutes later. He picks up the receiver, still breathless.

'Mr Kray?'

'Yes, Ned.'

'Ready for your call?'

'Yup. Put him through.'

'Okay. It's down as a "legal" so you've got an hour.'

There's a slight pause and a click. 'Ron?' asks Reggie. 'You there?'

'Yeah, it's me.'

'How's it going?'

Reggie waits patiently as his brother takes a deep drag of his cigarette. 'Oh, you know,' says Ronnie eventually, 'shit food, shit screws. But there're two or three mates here, including Tommy C, so not too bad. You?'

''Bout the same. Well, have you read it?'

'Yeah.'

'It couldn't have gone better.'

'Nope. Though I still don't see the point of the transcript. The shorthand writer's an unnecessary loose end. Mum's there. She'll report back.'

'Yeah, the result maybe, but not the detail. This is much better, worth every penny. And that woman, Geraldine Burns, what a star!'

'Yeah,' agrees Ronnie, 'but who is she?'

'No idea. One of the others must have brought her to the party. But, blimey, she really came through.'

'The best bit is Holborne being stitched up like a kipper,' says Ronnie with a chuckle. 'That's the icing on the cake for me. I'd have given anything to see his smug fuckin' face as he was taken down.'

'I s'pose. But now he ain't no use to us.'

'Good riddance.'

'So, I'll tell Robeson to hand over the documents to the girlfriend?' suggests Reggie.

'Nah, keep 'em. I want Holborne sweating, even if he is inside.'

'I think that's a mistake, Ron. Listen to me for once. He's got us the result we wanted, and he's no further use to us. Double-cross 'im now, and we push 'im into Read's arms.'

'I don't care,' replies Ronnie. 'What damage could he do?'

'He could give evidence of that attempted jury nobbling, for one. And he'd come across well, better than their other witnesses.'

'Yeah, but what the fuck? We're facing murders. Who cares about jury nobbling?'

'Then there's his cousin, the lighterman.'

'That were an accident.'

'That ain't the way Horowitz'll tell it. You kidnapped the cousin and he ended up dead. Look, Ron, we got enough on our plate already. Why make it worse? Now Horowitz is disbarred, he's got less to lose. He got us the result, so we hand over the papers and keep him onside.'

The line goes silent as Ronnie considers the position. 'Yeah, alright. I suppose so. Shame, though.'

'Right. I'll get a message to Robeson. Now, about McVitie.'

'Yeah?'

'We want to keep it as close as possible to what Hart has said. So, we went to Blonde Carol's but lay it all on Hart. Some private beef, and it all flared up. We knew nothing about it in advance and didn't do nuffing.'

'I ain't happy to say we was there, Reg. And I don't know yet if I want to give evidence. Need to speak to the brief.'

'I ain't saying we give evidence, decide that nearer the time, but we tell the lawyers we went to the party, all innocent, and suddenly there was a ruckus. Nothing to do with us.'

'Fair enough. Agreed.'

'So read the transcript again, get your story straight, and then get rid of it, right?'

'Right. See you in court, as they say.'

CHAPTER TWENTY-THREE

Charles sits in the cell in the bowels of Thameside Assizes, straining his ears for clues as to what might be occurring above him. He has been here for several hours, but the cell is so dark he can't see his watch and he has lost track of time.

He stands again and recommences pacing. The stench of damp and mould that permeates the decrepit building is all-pervasive. It seems to roll at him in waves, as if the old brick and stone surrounding him were exhaling in his face. The floor and all the surfaces are slick with fine dust, evidence of the abandoned building works. The seat of his striped barrister's trousers, the back of his black jacket and the gown that now lies in a crumpled heap on the wooden bench — all are covered in white patches where he has sat or leaned against another surface.

He looks up at the thick green glass tiles above him. They are so opaque that almost no light permeates them, but every now and then they are darkened further by passing pedestrians. As is often the case, the cell is underneath the pavement, and the muffled laughter of young voices can be heard briefly as they walk above his head. Schoolkids, on their way home from the school bus, he supposes.

He settles back down on the wooden bench only to be startled by the noise of keys against metal. A protesting hinge squeals as a door is opened at the far end of the corridor. Charles leaps to his cell door and presses his face to the wicket. The limited view means he can see only directly across, into the open door of the empty cell opposite him. He hears footsteps of at least two people, followed by further clanking as one metal door, and then another, are shut. Footsteps, this time of one person, recede. A final door opens and closes and then … silence.

'Hart?' whispers Charles hoarsely.

No reply.

Charles can't risk shouting. He is desperate to know what has been happening above him in court, but he doesn't know if Hart is close enough to hear him, or if they might be overheard. He returns to the far side of the cell and lowers himself once more onto the bench.

More time elapses.

The faint light from the pavement lights has faded and it is now impossible to tell the glass bricks from the surrounding stone. The cell, unheated and chilly when Charles entered, is now uncomfortably cold and completely dark.

He stands, wraps his dusty gown around him for another layer of warmth, and resumes pacing the perimeter of the tiny room, rubbing and blowing on his hands.

Charles is startled awake. He can't believe it, but he fell asleep on the cold bench. The sound that disturbed him is the dock officer returning. Charles hears metal against metal, the now-familiar squeak, and a male voice: 'Come on, Hart,' it says. 'Time to face the music.'

Charles stands and goes quickly to the door of his cell. He closes his eyes and, using the sounds, traces in his head the events unfolding further down the cell block … the click and ratchet sound of handcuffs being applied to wrists … a cell door swinging back with a clang against the cell wall as Hart is led out … the metal door at the end of the corridor being re-locked … footsteps up the stone steps … the courtroom door being opened … a sudden swell of muttering and excited speculation ... the *knock-knock-knock* on the panelled door that admits the judge ... faintly, in the distance, the call "All rise!" ... the shuffling of feet ... and the silence that follows.

Seconds tick by into minutes.

Then the door to the courtroom opens again and heavy footsteps descend into the cell area. Only one pair of feet this time.

The doors open in turn and the footsteps approach Charles's position ... closer ... they are coming to take him out of his cell. He steps back into the shadows, far enough for the opening door not to hit him in its arc.

'You're wanted in court, Mr Holborne,' says the dock officer.

Charles nods, his heart racing. He holds out his hands for cuffs to be applied, but the dock officer laughs briefly.

'Very funny,' he says, and he turns and retraces his steps down the short corridor. Charles follows; through two open metal doors, and up the steps.

The light in the courtroom is so bright by comparison to the gloom to which Charles has become accustomed, he has to shade his eyes as he steps into the dock.

The court erupts into spontaneous applause and cheering.

Charles lifts his hand from his face and looks across the well of the court to the judge. The Honourable Mr Justice Kinder has removed his wig and is sitting with his feet up on the bench, a lit cheroot between two of his fingers. From counsel's bench, prosecution counsel is grinning from ear to ear at Charles. The jurors are standing and applauding, as is the accused and the last of the Crown's witnesses, Mrs Burns.

Charles takes a deep bow, and addresses prosecution counsel first. He has to raise his voice over the din. 'Well? Vi?'

Peter Bateman, alias Mr Cullinane, points to the public gallery where Andy Tyson sits, beaming.

Tyson calls down. 'I followed her all the way to the underground, and pretended to make a call from the next telephone. I heard every word. Mrs Kray has reported that Ronnie Hart was convicted of murder. And that you're finished as a barrister!'

'Sure?' asks Charles, barely able to believe it.

'Completely,' replies Tyson, smiling. 'She was totally taken in.'

Charles punches the air in triumph. 'Well, if there's anyone the twins trust, it's their mum. Far better than any of Ronnie's boys, or even a bent copper.'

He looks round, frowning. 'And where's our corrupt shorthand writer?' he asks Bateman.

'On her way back,' replies Bateman over the din. 'But she called to say she handed it over, and has even got two hundred of the Krays' money for her bribe!'

'That was an unexpected bonus,' says Charles. He turns to the judge. 'And you!'

'Me, Mr Holborne?'

'You were completely convincing! How on earth did you do it? There were times I almost forgot you weren't a judge!'

Johnny the Jar's sallow face creases in an enormous smile. 'The lessons of a misspent youth, my dear fellow,' he says modestly. He flicks a sheaf of papers on his desk. 'Though your notes were rather helpful too.'

'And you lot,' says Charles, addressing the jurors. 'Thank you! From the bottom of my heart, thank you!'

The foreman rises, his hand on his head to prevent his yarmulke slipping.

'Happy to help,' says David.

Charles looks down the two smiling ranks of six jurors. Two or three are clearly Jewish men, members of David's synagogue

287

he assumes, although none of them wears a head covering. The rest of the twelve are a mixture of law students, Smithfields workers of dubious integrity and musician friends of Maria's. They look like any genuine jury, representing all ages, colours and sections of society.

The man who played the accused is sitting in the bench reserved for leading counsel, laboriously unwinding the bandage from his head.

'Bloody pleased to get this thing off,' says Terry Hart. 'It ain't half scratchy. Was I okay?'

'You did brilliantly,' says Charles, stepping down into the well of the court and going over to his "client". He enthusiastically shakes him by the hand. 'You sounded just like your brother. And to be honest, you look enough like him that we could probably have got away without the bandages.'

'No. I felt a lot safer in me disguise!'

Charles turns to address everyone in the room. 'Right, we have twenty minutes to make it look like we were never here. Make sure you leave nothing behind for the builders to find. George here —' he turns to indicate the dock officer — 'has a torch and will guide you out via the yard in twos or threes. There are no court staff in the building, so please don't draw attention to yourselves as you leave. Be careful as you go — there's no lighting outside this room and the place is a building site. And remember: at least three people's lives depend on this charade not being discovered at least until the Krays' trial is over. So … not a word to anyone. Not a word! And thank you all again.'

In under twenty minutes, the court looks as it did before: an unoccupied government building, covered in scaffolding and tarpaulins, collapsing slowly as departments squabble over which has responsibility for completing vastly under-budgeted repairs to the court estate.

Charles and Bateman walk silently westwards through the evening streets. This part of the East End was densely populated before the war, but the Blitz levelled it completely and it was never fully rebuilt. The court building, one of the very few structures to survive the bombing, now stands alone, an abandoned galleon in a lagoon of vacant tarmac. Accordingly, there are almost no other pedestrians, although a continuous stream of traffic rumbles past them in both directions, heading towards and away from the city.

For a long time neither man speaks. Now the excitement of the "sting" is dissipating, Charles's thoughts turn again to Sally. He is trying to calculate how long it will take the Krays to release her.

'You okay?' asks Bateman, raising his voice above the traffic noise.

Charles nods. 'Yes. Just worried about Sally. Look, I didn't really thank you before, but I can't tell you how grateful I am, Peter. It was a big ask, and you came through.'

Bateman does not answer at first.

Charles sighs. He is well aware how far he has pushed his friendship with his roommate, and despite the other's reassurances, he remains intensely uncomfortable at having to ask him to play the part of prosecution counsel. He prays he has caused no permanent damage to their relationship. Charles has very few real friends at the Bar; to lose Peter Bateman would make him very sad.

'It's fine,' says the younger man shortly.

'I didn't know who else to ask,' says Charles apologetically.

Bateman sighs in his turn. 'I know. And you know I'd do anything for you, and Sally of course … it's just…'

'Yes. Holding a fake trial is above and beyond. But I keep telling you, we did nothing illegal.'

Bateman barks a short laugh, a sound devoid of mirth. 'It felt *completely* illegal!'

'But you did the research, same as me. We haven't perverted the course of justice. Hart's still Read's witness. We just conned the twins into believing he's already been convicted. And in doing so, saved his life. And Sally's. Possibly mine too. We were *protecting* the course of justice.'

Bateman turns his handsome aristocratic head towards Charles. Even in the poor street illumination Charles can see the incredulous expression. 'And what about trespassing on government property?' he demands.

'Well, yes,' says Charles grudgingly. 'There is that. Not a crime though, is it? Trespass sounds in damages, and we caused no damage.'

'And you imagine the Bar Council will buy that, do you?'

'Peter, we held a moot. A fake trial. That's all. The Inns do it every year.'

'But not with intent to deceive.'

'To deceive gangsters. Gangsters who will otherwise kill Sally, and force Hart into taking a murder rap for them. You know, I'll bet we could even persuade the Bar Council that it was a training exercise for the pupils on the jury.'

Bateman doesn't dignify that contribution with a reply, and they walk on in silence.

'So, your next move?' he asks after a few minutes.

'I'm disappearing tonight,' replies Charles.

'Haven't the twins got contacts throughout the prison estate? Surely they'll suspect something when they can't find you anywhere behind bars.'

'They have contacts, yes, but not everywhere. I've managed to hide people on the inside from them before. And I'd be in some soft open prison, while all their confederates are in Cat A with the other hard men.'

'You're uncommonly confident! Where are you going to go?'

'I thought Hastings.'

'The annex? It's not set up yet.'

'We signed a lease yesterday, or so Barbara tells me. I can start sorting out phones, desks, typewriters and so on. And making contact with the local solicitors.'

Bateman laughs at this, a sardonic guffaw. 'Trust you, Charles, to turn this to your professional advantage.'

'Professional advantage?'

'Yes, getting in on the ground floor with all the local solicitors. By the time the rest of us turn up, you'll have cornered the market.'

'I'm doing this to get Sally released in one piece,' he chides gently.

That brings Bateman up short. 'Yes, of course you are,' he says with genuine remorse. 'Sorry. I was only kidding.'

'Don't worry about it.'

'So, you're going to tell Barbara, then?'

'Yes. Her, and you, and no one else. I've already packed a bag.'

'How will you find out if … *when* they let Sally go?'

'I was rather hoping I could leave a note for her at Wren Street to call you. She'll go there first. Would that be okay?'

'Of course.'

They part at Bow Road underground station. Bateman turns to his former pupilmaster. 'Look … Charles … I'm sorry if I was a bit … you know … I'm just anxious. I've never done anything like this before.'

'I know,' replies Charles. 'Mr Goody Two-Shoes.'

Bateman shrugs, and smiles self-consciously. 'Always have been — though I'm not claiming any moral high ground. In my case it's always been fear of getting caught. But I do understand the stakes. I can't imagine what I'd be going through if anyone I loved was being held hostage by the Krays. So, what I'm trying, very badly, to say is … if you need anything else … really, anything at all … just ask.'

'Thank you.'

'I mean it. And for Christ's sake, Charles, be careful!'

Charles loiters at the far end of Wren Street. He has walked the length of the road twice, passing his front door, collar up and head down. He needs to make sure no one is watching the building. Every now and then he has been forced to duck out of sight when people have approached his position, but all turned out to be neighbours. As far as he can see, there is no one on the short street who doesn't belong there.

After waiting for about half an hour he makes a decision. He strides quickly to the front door, keys in hand. As soon as he is inside he peers out of the lounge windows. The street remains deserted.

He runs upstairs in the dark to the top floor. Open on the bed are his half-packed suitcases. He's going to have to remain out of London for several weeks, perhaps months, and the cases are full of clothing, court robes, briefs on which he can work while away, Archbold (the criminal practitioner's Bible), notebooks, pens and other items of stationery.

He collects his bathroom bag, throws it in, and scans the bedroom.

All done.

He runs to his study, pulls a sheet of paper from his desk drawer, and hesitates. Then he writes: *I'm safe, but have joined the Away Club. My roommate has the grisly details.*

He realises that he is probably being over-cautious — it seems highly unlikely that anyone from the Firm would be searching the house to find the note — but he can't be sure. If read, this would lead a Firm member to believe that he was in prison — their imprisoned associates are called "Aways" — but he hopes it will also lead Sally to contact Bateman, from whom she can learn the truth. Assuming, of course, the twins release her. As to that, Charles has no guarantees, but he can't see why they would harm her, the daughter of one of their closest associates, once she has been used to get what they want.

That, at least, is his calculation.

He seals the note in an envelope and leaves it propped by her bedside light.

There is a noise in the entrance hall.

Charles tiptoes out of the bedroom and down the first flight of stairs. Looking over the banister to the ground floor, he sees the shape of someone by the front door. They have a large item with them — Charles can't identify it in the darkness — and they are making no apparent attempt to be quiet.

Charles flicks on the light switch by his elbow. The hall is flooded with light, prompting a woman's sharp scream.

'Jesus, Charlie! You scared me half to death!' complains Sally, looking up. 'What're you doing lurking in the dark like that!'

Charles immediately extinguishes the light. 'Don't move!' he orders. He runs the rest of the distance to the top of the lower staircase, and thunders down it. He grabs Sally in a bearhug as she is half-way through taking off her coat. 'Thank God!' he sighs fervently into her hair. 'Thank God!'

'What's going on?' she says.

Charles plants kiss after kiss on her hair and her face, almost causing the two of them to fall over Sally's suitcase in his eagerness.

'Charlie?' she giggles. He doesn't stop. 'What's the matter? Charlie!'

Her final exclamation stops him.

'What?'

'What's all this for? I've only been gone a week.'

'Only a week? I've been frantic with worry.'

'Why? You knew where I was.'

'No I didn't!' says Charles, the first suspicion forming that something is not as he believed. 'I knew who had you, but not where you were! I had no idea what they might've done to you. I was envisaging … well, all sorts.' That thought causes him to thrust her away from him, still gripping her by the upper arms. 'They didn't, did they? Are you okay?'

'I'm fine. Who's "they"?' And what are *you* doing here?'

'All right … all right…' he says, taking a deep calming breath. 'Let's back up. Where have you been?' he asks, trying to keep his voice as level as possible.

'At Dad's flat, as agreed.'

'Agreed? Agreed by whom?'

'Agreed by … wait! Are you saying you didn't know?'

'I thought the Krays had you.'

Sally's mouth drops open. She is suddenly completely still, her coat still half-way down her back. 'That fucking bastard!' she whispers. 'That utter fucking bastard!'

'Who?'

She looks up at him, her eyes ablaze. 'My rotten, corrupt, lying father! He told me you and he had come up with a plan to keep me out of the twins' way. You were both worried they'd use me to get at you.'

'That's exactly what they did! When I refused to force Hart to take McVitie's murder, Ronnie Kray threatened the family, even the baby! And your father said I'd agreed to this?' She shrugs helplessly. 'Sal, I thought you were being held somewhere by them, against your will. I had no idea if they'd hurt you or what conditions you were being kept in. Your mother is…'

'Blaming you?'

'I was going to say incandescent actually, but yes, that too.'

She grabs him and holds him tight to her. 'Oh, Charlie, I'm so sorry! I'll put her straight, I promise!'

'Where is he now?' says Charles.

He feels his eyes blurring, but whether in relief at having Sally back in one piece or impotent, visceral fury at the duplicitous Harry Robeson, he couldn't say.

'I don't know,' she says into his chest. 'He said he had things to do. Getting your documents back was one of them.'

'So he's out on licence now?' Charles feels Sally nodding in his embrace. 'Good,' he says. 'Cos I'm going to kill him.'

Sally lets that one go. 'Okay, your turn,' she says looking up at him. 'Dad said you were banged up.'

'No! It was the fake trial, as we discussed.'

'You went ahead with it?' she asks, astounded. 'But how? You told me it'd take weeks to organise.'

'I had no choice. Once I thought the Krays had you.'

'And it worked?'

'Yes! They were all brilliant! Johnny the Jar was amazing, and he found someone, a real actress, to play the witness —'

'I thought the Jar was dead.'

'Not quite. And everyone chipped in, Maria, the Smithfield bloke and my brother with jurors, George Robey — remember him? — got out his old uniform, Hattie Dodds from the Bailey did the clerking, and Peter Bateman prosecuted. They all came good.'

'Wow!' she breathes. 'Shows how much they respect you, Charlie.'

'I don't know about that.'

'And the contempt of court?'

Charles smiles modestly. 'A little refinement that occurred to me on the first day. It was one thing having Hart "convicted" but if I'm to get the documents back, I need the twins to think I can never be of any further use to them.'

'Which they now do.'

'Yes, or, at least, I hope so. But I have to go, Sal! It's not safe here.'

'Can't you stay? Even for tonight. I ain't half missed you.'

He shakes his head, but he smiles. 'I've missed you too, and there's nothing I'd like more than to cuddle up with you, but I can't. I can't be seen, or it'll all have been for nothing. Once the twins hear about it they'll have someone outside, making sure. Reggie is nothing if not thorough.'

'Ain't they all banged up?'

'The main players, yes, but there are always peripherals prepared to do a bit of sneaking for a tenner.'

'Where are you going?'

'Hastings.'

She nods. 'Makes sense.'

'And you've got to carry on as normal. As if I was actually in prison. Got it?'

'Yes.'

'No, listen to me, Sally.' He disengages and lifts her chin so she is looking up into his eyes. 'They'll probably follow you, to make sure it's kosher. Always assume you're being watched. Understand?'

'But how long for?'

'Until the Krays' trial starts.'

'But that's January!' she protests, her hands going to her bump. 'The baby'll be here by then!'

'Not till the end of January, and I should be back by then.'

'Babies come early, Charlie.'

'I know they do. But I'm only a couple of hours away if you go into labour. I'll be there, I promise. After all this, we can't take the risk. For the first time in years, I'm a couple of moves ahead of the twins. You do see that, don't you?'

Sally sighs and nods reluctantly. 'Yes, I do see that. Are you driving? Won't they wonder where your car's gone?'

'I've thought of that too. If anyone asks, last you knew it was in a side street near Thameside Assizes, where I parked it. If it's not there, it's probably been stolen. It wouldn't have lasted more than a few hours in that area anyway, so they'll have no trouble believing that.'

'Can I come down? To Hastings?'

'Not for a bit. Maybe not at all. But once I know where I am I'll get a phone number for you. You can call me from work.'

'All right,' she replies in a small voice. 'I've been so looking forward to seeing you.'

'I know. Blame your father. Kidnapping you forced my hand.'

'It wasn't a kidnap.'

'That's how it looked to me.'

Sally is silent for a long time. 'I'm so sorry, Charlie. He's done it again, hasn't he?'

'Yes. Bottom line, the Krays still own him, and we can't trust him.'

'I realise that now.'

Charles pulls her towards him once again. 'I won't kill him, Sal.'

'Good. Thank you.'

'But he and I are going to have serious words when I next see him.'

CHAPTER TWENTY-FOUR

Charles sits in the high-backed armchair, a mug of coffee warming his hands, and gazes out of his sitting room window over the roofs of Hastings Old Town at the sea. The water today is slate grey, a flat sheet of iron which merges imperceptibly with the grey skies. Despite his time as a lighterman on the Thames, he has never lived in close proximity to the sea before, and he is still fascinated by its sheer size and its protean nature. It is constantly changing in texture, colour and mood. A confirmed city boy, someone so at home in London he feels that, like some Cockney superhero, he derives his strength and speed from its familiar streets, buildings and pavements, his enjoyment of his present surroundings has taken him by surprise.

If everything goes tits up, he thinks, *maybe I'll come and live here.*

There is something about the Old Town that reminds him of the East End. His sharp eyes have spotted some slick dealing in smuggled cigarettes and booze on the corners and in pubs. He has spent several afternoons exploring the area around Rock-a-Nore Road, regarded carefully by fishermen with narrowed eyes. He likes its teetering timber net shops, its dingy seafront taverns and the smell of fish. As in the East End, he has observed that it's the denizens of the Old Town who seem to run the place, not the police, who keep a very low profile. If worst came to worst and he lost everything, he could find a niche here. Once the dust has settled. Only as an afterthought does he wonder how Sally might feel about giving up her career to bring up their baby in a small run-down seaside town on the south coast of England.

Downstairs, on the ground floor, Mrs Finlayson sings along with Mario Lanza as she potters from room to room. She has a collection of Lanza's 78s, which she plays, loudly, from dawn to dusk. The house is full of Lanza's voice, every day of the week except Sundays. On the day of rest Mrs Finlayson goes to church and then takes the short bus trip to St Leonards for lunch with her sister and brother-in-law.

Three weeks after moving into the top floor of 14 High Wickham, Charles is coming to the realisation that his new landlady is a genuine eccentric. She wears a different coloured wig every day and smells strongly of sherry by early afternoon. When walking down to the shops in the Old Town she drags behind her a makeshift wooden cart, the sort of thing cobbled together by kids from an old box and pram wheels, and speaks to almost everyone she meets. She sings, constantly, even when out and about.

Her oddities please Charles, even her singing, which is surprisingly tuneful and pleasant.

She looked askance at Charles when he first arrived on her doorstep. Both his cultivated accent and his clothing suggested that he belonged somewhere else. She looked him up and down, and then behind him to the shiny Rover clicking by the kerbside as its engine cooled. She was suspicious that a man in such an expensive suit and driving such a car would be interested in renting her top floor which, even she admitted, needed a lick of paint. He could obviously have taken a room at the Langham or one of the other nice hotels. And in November? Who comes to a poor, run-down, fishing town, on their own, just before Christmas? There was obviously more to this man than he was telling.

But Mrs Finlayson had been alone in the big house for almost three years, ever since her wastrel of a husband ran off with the last tenant, a pert little teacher from Eastbourne. The husband was no loss, but she didn't like the quiet and she needed the money. She felt safer with someone upstairs, and she preferred it to be a man. In particular she had a weakness for handsome curly-haired men, especially ones as charming as this. He reminded her of Gerry, the youngest of her five brothers, a chancer who was always getting into and out of scrapes. Any remaining hesitation evaporated as soon as Charles placed in her hand a roll of notes, more than enough for a month's rent in advance. She opened the door wide.

Since then, Charles has been taking it easy. The upstairs flat is a bit tatty but it is well-furnished, warm and cosy. The hot water is plentiful and the wide double bed, angled in such a way as to provide sea views on waking, is surprisingly comfortable.

He splits his time between leisurely meals — the seafood in the town's restaurants is, as would be expected in a fishing community, excellent — long walks around Hastings and the surrounding area, and introducing himself and Chambers' new annex to the solicitors in the local towns. He has popped into the offices of most of the firms who already send work to Chambers, and his reception has been enthusiastic. Charles had been right; busy local solicitors would be very keen to avoid travelling on poor roads and unreliable trains to the Temple in London, merely for an hour-long conference with counsel. All were excited at the prospect of having a group of London barristers on hand in the town. Not only would the solicitors save hours of unproductive travelling time every week; they'd also have more chance of corralling their unreliable and reluctant clients and witnesses into local meetings than getting them to commit a day to travelling to see counsel in London.

Charles finishes his coffee, rinses his mug in the tidy little kitchen and prepares to go out. Mrs Finlayson has a payphone in the downstairs hall which Charles is permitted to use, but he prefers not to be overheard. The landlady seems blithely uninterested in his comings and goings — one of those people, thinks Charles, who lives for the most part in their own heads — but he takes no chances. Every morning he walks into town, buys himself a newspaper and whatever supplies he needs that day, and telephones Sally from the box outside the Post Office.

Charles steps out of the house under cover of Mario Lanza and turns right, downhill. At the bend in the road he decides for a change to leave the carriageway and take the steps down into the area of grassland and gorse overlooking the harbour. He follows a trail through the trees, descending almost parallel to the line of the steep funicular railway, meeting no one. The sounds and smells of the Old Town are borne up to him on the wind in sudden gusts. He rejoins the carriageway at Tackleway and spots a telephone box. He checks his trouser pockets and, coming up with two shilling pieces, opens the door. He dials Sally's chambers in London. It is she who answers.

'Chancery Court.'

'Hi, Sal, it's me.'

'Charles. I'm glad you called. You need to speak to your brother as soon as possible.'

'Why? What's happened?'

'It's your mum. He's called three times this morning. I wish you'd give me a way of contacting you. This is exactly the sort of thing I was worried about.'

'I'll call you back as soon as I've spoken to David, okay? Where can I reach him?'

'At Sunshine Court.'

Charles rings off and dials the care home. He gets through immediately, but then has to wait impatiently before someone can be found who knows his parents and is aware of what is going on. Eventually a woman picks up the handset.

'Hello? This is Andrea.'

Charles is relieved. Andrea, one of the team leaders, is Dutch, and she speaks perfect English. An experienced nurse, she is one of the few staff members whom Charles trusts. 'Hi Andrea. It's Charles Holborne … Horowitz. I understand something's up with my mum?'

'Yes, Charles. Your brother is with her and the doctor now. Millie was unusually sleepy this morning and her breathing sounded a bit ragged, so I called the doctor in. He says your mum has aspiration pneumonia. You know? She's been having a little trouble swallowing recently.'

'Is she awake now?' asks Charles urgently.

'Yes, but she's not making much sense. I did wonder if she might have a urinary infection as well, as that can often present this way.'

'Could you get my brother, please?' asks Charles. 'I'd like to talk to him.'

'Sure, I'll fetch him. Hold the line.'

Charles hears the receiver put down and then Andrea's footsteps recede. He waits for several minutes. Eventually footsteps return and the receiver is picked up again.

'Charles?' says David's voice.

'Yes. What's the story?'

'The doctor says she has a chest infection and maybe a urine infection too. Mum's very confused.'

'Is she going to hospital?'

'Not yet. The doctor says she doesn't need to go. He's taken urine for analysis —getting that was an awful battle, I can tell you! — and given Mum antibiotics. He thinks the analysis will be back by tomorrow, and he'll come out again then.'

'Why? Surely hospital's the best place for her.'

'I've tried persuading him. He doesn't seem very interested. He keeps saying she's old and demented, and at the end of her life.'

'She's not yet seventy!'

'I've made that point, repeatedly. But if she doesn't respond to the pills, he will consider intravenous treatment in hospital.'

'Okay. Look … how bad is this, Davie? Should I be coming back to London?'

David hesitates before answering. 'It's quite bad, Charles. She doesn't always recognise me or Dad at the moment, and she's pretty distressed. But Andrea made a good point. She says that moving Mum to hospital would disorientate her. She won't know anyone there and Dad won't be there to encourage her to eat. She says it can lead to a permanent step down in cognitive ability.'

'What did the doctor say to that?'

'Not much. But I trust Andrea. She's been doing this a long time.'

'I agree.'

'So I'd say no, there's no need to hurry back right now, but things can change. I need to be able to get hold of you in an emergency.'

'Of course. I'll give you the address and phone number down here. But, please, be careful with the information. Not to be mentioned to anyone at all. Give me a sec…' Charles reaches into his jacket pocket and pulls out a piece of paper. 'Ready?' he asks.

'Yes.'

Charles gives David Mrs Finlayson's address and the telephone number of the phone in her hall. 'I'll call you at home this evening for an update, okay?' he says.

'Okay. How are things down there?'

'Surprisingly enjoyable, actually.'

'No sign of…'

'No, nothing.'

'Good. Listen, I want to grab the doc before he leaves. Speak later.'

David rings off. Charles checks his change. One sixpenny piece. It might be enough. He dials Chancery Court again.

'Sal?' he says as he gets through.

'Yes.'

Charles tells her briefly the situation with Millie. Then: 'Are you being watched?' he asks.

'Yes. Same chap as before, tall, fair-haired, long trench coat. Not all the time, but every now and then.'

'At home or in the Temple?'

'Both.'

'That decides it then. It's too dangerous for you to come down.'

'But I'm enormous Charles! It can't be long now! And it's Christmas —'

'It's only for a couple more weeks. I'll be back as soon as the twins' trial starts; sooner, if the baby comes early.'

Sally doesn't reply for a moment. When she does, her voice is thick with her disappointment in Charles. 'We were supposed to be doing this together.'

'Doing what?'

'The pregnancy? Our baby?'

'We *are* doing it together, but —'

But the pips start, Charles's money has run out, and he has no more change.

The line is cut and Charles is left with the indifferent dial tone and a feeling that he hasn't recognised for a couple of years: the sense that a gap has opened up between him and Sally.

CHAPTER TWENTY-FIVE

Charles wanders along George Street, very slightly drunk. It is a pleasant evening, with a surprisingly warm breeze blowing off the sea.

The news from London is encouraging. David telephoned the night before to say that Millie, who had after all to be admitted for intravenous antibiotic treatment, was to be discharged from hospital after a stay of ten days. She seemed to have recovered from the infections, although she was weak and very sleepy and would require more support once back in the care home.

Charles has been in the snug bar of Ye Olde Pump House for the last few hours, chatting to a group of Norwegian students. The pub is a mock-Tudor cliché rebuilt from a nineteenth-century boot and shoe shop in the mid-50s. Nonetheless it has a pleasant, relaxed atmosphere and serves good food. It is popular with a certain youngish middle-class clientele and, as Charles discovered, has recently introduced Wednesday "curry nights". Charles was a regular visitor to the curry restaurants of Brick Lane for over a decade, but since leaving his flat in the City he has rarely returned. Indeed, the only Indian restaurant he still patronised at all before leaving London was Veeraswamy's off Regent Street and, even that, infrequently. This is the first time he has encountered a provincial pub offering Indian meals and, while the dishes might be slightly blander than to his taste, he has made Ye Olde Pump House his regular destination on Wednesday evenings.

He starts the steep climb to High Wickham, humming quietly to himself. Never a Mario Lanza fan before he moved into Mrs Finlayson's top floor, he now often finds himself with Lanza's songs in his head. Most of the windows he passes glitter and blink with Christmas decorations and lights.

As Charles enters the faded Georgian terrace he notices a new vehicle parked outside Mrs Finlayson's front door, immediately behind his Rover. He freezes twenty yards short of the steps. The car is, unmistakeably, that of Harry Robeson.

The luxurious Austin Princess was once marketed as "the poor man's Rolls-Royce". Tall and stately, and sporting a great rectangular radiator grille, this Austin Princess was, before his incarceration, Robeson's pride and joy. Charles had more than once heard the disgraced solicitor speak lovingly of its thick carpets, its walnut facia and its quiet, sedate, power. A car fit for ambassadors, if not for princesses, he liked to say. Charles had thought the vehicle was sold when Robeson went to prison, but here it is.

The possibility that it now belongs to someone else, and that its appearance outside Charles's "safe house" is a mere coincidence, doesn't even cross his mind. It's presence, here and now, can mean only one thing: Robeson — and therefore the Krays — have found him.

Charles stands motionless, undecided, on the pavement. There is a noise and he looks sharply to his right across the narrow street, but it's merely the wind whipping up East Cliff from the harbour, bending the trees and bushes.

If Robeson were alone, Charles would welcome a confrontation with the man. Once, in the cells of the Old Bailey, he punched the suave solicitor on the jaw, and derived great satisfaction from the way he collapsed. That's an experience he'd enjoy repeating.

But is Robeson alone? All the major players in the Firm are now in custody, fighting for their lives and their freedom, but Charles has no illusions. The Krays still have contacts throughout the criminal fraternity and money enough to pay for a contract on his life. It wouldn't even be a matter of great import to them. To the Krays, Charles is no more than a loose end, one that could be tied up permanently by a payment of as little as £500. Isn't that the price they put on Leslie Payne's head? And he was far more dangerous to the twins than Charles.

But if that is the purpose of the visit, why is the car — a car so easily recognised — parked openly, right there, outside Charles's door?

And what of Sally? Is she still free? His heart speeds up at the thought that, once again, she is at risk, used as a pawn to manipulate him. He half-turns to run back down to a telephone box when he sees the light emanating from Mrs Finlayson's front room changing in quality. The curtains across the bay window are being closed.

Charles can't remember them being drawn before. The terrace of houses, facing out over East Cliff, is not overlooked, and very few people come up here unless they live in one of these old properties. That's what made High Wickham so perfect for Charles. The occupants of the terrace don't usually have to worry about being observed through their windows.

He tiptoes quickly past the house and its drawn curtains to the end of the row of buildings. His bathroom looks out over a scruffy garden at the rear of the property. He has never used the garden, but he thinks he recalls a gate into it. If there's a gate, there must presumably be a path or track leading to it.

The pavement gives way to a narrow overgrown path curving round the end house in the terrace. It continues along

309

the back of the properties. Charles finds the gate leading into Mrs Finlayson's back garden with ease. He opens it silently and creeps into the garden.

The grass is long, tangled and drenched. Keeping to the shadows, he approaches Mrs Finlayson's kitchen window. The kitchen is brightly illuminated, Mrs Finlayson at the counter, pouring water into a teapot. Next to her is a tray on which there are cups and saucers, a tea-strainer and a painted china pot of sugar cubes. She looks relaxed, at her ease, as if entertaining guests rather than acting under compulsion. As she pours the boiling water, she is saying something over her shoulder. She speaks towards the open kitchen door, but Charles cannot see to whom her words are directed.

Teapot filled, Mrs Finlayson places it on the tray and carries everything out of the kitchen towards the front of the house. Charles waits in the garden, hoping that his landlady might return — for biscuits perhaps? — but he waits in vain.

It occurs to him that his best course is simply to run for it, but his car keys are in his bedroom. He has enough money to get away — to London perhaps? — but there won't be any trains heading away from Hastings until the morning. He won't get far on foot.

He will have to go in.

He casts about the garden for a weapon. Behind him he sees a small wooden shed. The clasp and staple are held closed only by a vertical rusty nail. Charles lifts it out, illuminates his cigarette lighter, and peers inside. The only reasonably heavy portable item he can see is a lump hammer propped on its head in a corner. He reaches down and lifts it, the handle sticky and fluffy with spiderwebs. He hefts it: six or eight pounds, he estimates. Too unwieldy for a decent weapon, but better than nothing. Perhaps.

Instead of circling back to the front door, Charles goes to the kitchen door and tries the handle. The door opens inwards silently. He steps inside the warm kitchen. He can still smell Mrs Finlayson's supper: mushroom soup.

From the door leading to the hallway he can hear voices from the front lounge. He is certain there is more than one person beyond the moulded door but he cannot tell who is talking.

Charles covers the short distance to the lounge door in four quiet strides. Taking a deep breath and raising the hammer in his right hand, he pushes hard at the half-open door and barges in.

The first person he sees is Sally, sitting demurely opposite him on the couch, her hands in her lap. She looks much more pregnant than she did when he last saw her, several weeks earlier. Her face is very pale and she seems to be holding back tears. Next to her, facing Mrs Finlayson, who is occupied pouring tea, is Robeson. Beside him, over the arm of the couch, is his leather driving coat with a woollen lining, rather like the aircrew jacket Charles wore in the RAF. His hat balances on top of it, and he is reaching across Sally, holding her hand fast in his.

Charles has the momentary impression of three pairs of eyes turning towards the noise of his entrance as he drops the hammer on the floorboards with a clatter and leaps at Robeson. He swings his left fist in a thunderous blow at the older man at the same instant as Sally screams.

'No, Charles!'

Charles checks his blow, but it still lands on Robeson's left cheek with enough power to connect hard. Robeson's head snaps to the right as if hinged on his neck. He emits a short grunt and his body suddenly loses all rigidity. He tips sideways, arms loose like a rag doll's, and he comes to rest against the thick cushions, his chin on his chest. His eyes are closed, and he remains still. Charles, still not trusting the ex-solicitor, stands over him, fists raised.

'Stop Charles!' shouts Sally, leaping up. She pushes him out of the way and bends over her prone father. 'Dad! Oh, Dad!' she cries, trying to get his head to stay upright. He remains unconscious.

'I'll get a cold flannel,' says Mrs Finlayson. 'I've also got some smelling salts.'

She calmly replaces the teapot on the occasional table, stands and, flashing a brief smile at Charles, leaves the room. Even in the confusion of the moment, Charles cannot but note, with some amazement, her extraordinarily composed demeanour.

Sally kneels on the floor by her father's legs. 'Why did you do that?' she demands, not looking back at Charles.

'What? You know why!' says Charles, his adrenaline and confusion causing him to shout. 'He's a fucking snake! He had it coming!'

'Yes! But not this time!'

Mrs Finlayson reappears, wet flannel dripping and a small brown bottle clenched in her hand, but Robeson's eyes are already opening.

'Here,' says Sally, holding out her hand for the flannel.

Mrs Finlayson gives it to her and Sally applies it gently to her father's cheek, where a red swelling is already rising. Robeson groans.

'Stay still, Dad,' orders Sally.

'Yes,' affirms Charles loudly. 'I'd stay still if I were you.'

A thought strikes Charles and he lifts Robeson's jacket to check for weapons. The pockets are empty. Only then does

Charles see the brown leather briefcase by Robeson's feet. He kicks it away, out of reach.

'I know how it looks, Charles,' says Robeson, his voice faint.

'How it looks?' spits Charles back. 'How it *looks* is how it *is*! You fucking kidnapped your own daughter to ensure my compliance with your bosses.'

'No, my boy. I wanted her out of harm's way,' he says, sitting up cautiously. 'Could I possibly have that cup of tea now, Mrs Finlayson? I'm suddenly very dry.'

Mrs Finlayson hands Robeson a cup in a saucer and Sally lowers her hand to allow Robeson to take a few shaky sips.

'That's complete crap, and you know it,' replies Charles, looming over Robeson and undecided whether he's going to hit him again. 'If it were true, you could've told us what you were planning! Instead you chose to leave me believing the twins had her!'

Sally stands from her position in front of her father and sits next to him. She reapplies the cold compress. 'Charlie, sit down and listen,' she orders.

Charles looks from his partner to Robeson, and then to Mrs Finlayson.

'Don't worry about her,' says Sally. 'We've been chatting since we arrived.'

'I've got things to attend to anyway —' starts Mrs Finlayson as she stands, but Sally interrupts her.

'No, please stay Mrs Finlayson. You're entitled to an explanation. Charles, I've explained who we are, and why we came down. Just listen to us, please.'

Despite Sally's offer, Mrs Finlayson excuses herself, slips past Charles and leaves the room.

313

Charles stares at Sally for a moment longer before reluctantly backing away and perching on the edge of the seat facing the couch.

'Well?' he demands, staring first at Sally and then at Robeson. 'Why else lead me to believe Sally'd been kidnapped? It could only be to put me under pressure to do the twins' bidding. You *were* still working for the Krays.'

'Yes,' says Robeson, his voice firmer now. 'Or, at least, I had to give that impression. I needed to keep up the pretence until they were permanently behind bars. Just as you did.'

'What do you mean by that? I was never working for them.'

'Your mock trial? What was that if not pretending to do as they ordered? Brilliant, by the way. You had to make the boys believe they had the upper hand over you, and you did it. And got yourself supposedly disbarred in the process. But Charles, surely you know that I'd never allow anything to happen to Sally. My own daughter? Whatever else you think about me, you know me well enough on that score. I love her. And if I hadn't volunteered, they'd have sent someone else. Someone who wouldn't have cared a tuppenny damn if she became collateral damage.'

Charles glares at the older man, but he feels his anger receding.

'I believe him, Charles,' says Sally softly.

'Why? It's all too convenient.'

'Show him, Dad,' she says.

'Hand me my briefcase would you, Charles?' says Robeson, pointing at it.

Charles stands and collects the briefcase from behind the door where it landed. He unclips the leather tongue, opens the soft leather and looks inside. Again, no weapons. He gives it to Robeson.

Robeson reaches in and lifts out a manila envelope. He offers it to Charles. 'There,' he says. 'That should go some way to persuading you.'

Charles looks inside and pulls out half a dozen sheets of paper. He gasps.

After all this time, finally, *finally* he has in his possession the documents that would have destroyed him. The evidence the Krays have been holding over him ever since Merlin's death.

Charles looks up. 'How do I know the Krays don't have copies?'

'No one has copies,' replies Robeson, the colour now returning to his face. 'And the reason I can be sure? Because I've had them since the beginning. The boys asked me to keep them in the office safe.'

'How do you know they didn't open it while you were inside?' asks Charles.

'They had no need to. They wanted them kept as safe as possible. The police would never break into a solicitors' office. And also, I was the only one with the combination.'

'Which you could've given to them.'

'No. I told them it was written down, in code, in an old law notebook and that I didn't know it. To open up the safe would have to wait until I was released.'

'I've only your word on that.'

'Not exactly,' says Sally. 'Tell him, Dad.'

'Tell me what?'

Robeson remains silent, so Sally continues. 'Dad's giving evidence against the Krays at their trial.'

Charles looks from daughter to father and back again, astonished. 'You spoke to Nipper Read?' he asks.

Robeson nods. 'Yes. I gave him a full statement — everything I know — in return for immunity.'

315

'But why?' asks Charles, puzzled. 'You've done your time. You're free of them now. After all those years of loyalty?'

'Because this way I forestall any possibility of other offences coming back to bite me. And I don't think there'll ever be a better chance to break the Krays' power once and for all. And it's the only way I can make sure you and Sally are safe. And…'

'And?' prompts Charles.

Robeson looks up and fixes his glistening eyes on Charles's. 'And it's the only way I can make amends to you, my boy.'

Charles at last looks into Robeson's face. He sees an old man, sallow cheeks, hair thinning. Sally's father has shrunk. The big personality, the confident air and the vitality that characterised the former solicitor have all gone. He used to be larger than life; now he is smaller. Life won.

The expression on Robeson's face is also something Charles has never seen before. His eyes are pleading.

He wants my forgiveness.

Sally takes her father's hand gently in both of hers, and the gesture seems to be the last straw for him. The tears in the old man's eyes spill over and run down his wrinkled cheeks.

She believes him.

Charles takes a long deep breath, exhaling the remnants of his fury.

'Okay,' he says at last, albeit with reservations still. 'I'll buy it.'

He might have said more but Mrs Finlayson enters, clean towels folded over her arm.

'I've made up the bedroom on the middle floor for you, Mr Robeson,' she announces, 'and changed the sheets on your bed, Mr Holborne.'

'You have?' says Charles.

'Well, I assume you're not driving back to London tonight? It's very late, and —' she points at Sally — 'your wife must be very tired.'

Charles looks at Sally, who nods. She does look exhausted.

'Did you bring anything with you, dear?' asks the landlady of Sally.

'Yes, I brought an overnight bag.'

'Well, anything else you need, you let me know. Would you like to follow me?'

CHAPTER TWENTY-SIX

By the time Charles and Sally wake the next morning, Harry Robeson's Austin Princess is no longer parked outside the house. An envelope has been slipped under their apartment door and the note inside informs them that he had to leave for London, but that he would call later that day.

Charles leaves the note on the kitchen table, makes them coffee and takes it back to bed.

They sit, propped by soft pillows, drinking and gazing out to sea.

'I've missed this so much,' says Charles.

'The sea?'

'No. Being in bed with you.'

'Really? I'm surprised. Sleeping with a fidgety beached whale ain't that restful. Or sexy, for that matter.'

'I find you intensely sexy,' corrects Charles softly. 'As I think I proved.'

She smiles and rests a hand on Charles's thigh. 'You did.'

'But it wasn't that either, lovely though it was. No, just waking up with you next to me. That's what I've missed most.'

'Didn't I wake you in the night?' asks Sally.

'Not really. I was aware of you going to the loo once or twice, but I fell asleep straight away.'

'Good. I was worried.' Sally lifts her head to look at the clock on the wall. 'I'd better get moving,' she says, reluctantly. 'I don't suppose you know about trains from here?'

'I've been thinking. Can't the juniors manage without you for a couple of days?'

'It's Christmas,' she replies. 'You know how busy it is.'

'Yes, but I'll bet half your guvnors are already off, and the senior courts close next Tuesday. It's more odds and ends, magistrates' court stuff, now, isn't it? Surely they can cope.'

'Are you suggesting I stop work for Christmas now? I can't possibly! I'm going to be off with the baby soon. I need to get my desk clear. And the new bloke's not half way through his training.'

'I'm not suggesting you stop till the new year. Just today, tomorrow and the weekend. Come on, Sal, let's have a little break, now, while we have the chance. Have our own early Christmas.'

'And go back Sunday?'

'Or Monday. Either way, I'll drive you up.'

'And come back here?'

He shrugs. 'Got to.'

'Can you take me back to Wren Street? You can't, surely?'

Charles considers. 'No. But I could drop you at you father's in Mayfair. He can take you home from there. What could be more natural than spending a weekend with your old dad just out of prison, with you, eight months pregnant and husband banged up over Christmas?'

'Husband? I don't remember any proposal of marriage,' she says pointedly.

'Boyfriend, then,' he says with a grin.

Sally places her coffee cup on the bedside table and reaches for Charles. He follows suit. They slide down into the warm sheets, holding each other, their faces barely apart.

'Not sure about this, though,' says Sally, scratching Charles's growth of beard with her long nails.

'Just temporary,' he assures her.

He brushes her dark hair out of the way and plants gentle kisses on each of her eyes in turn. He is not about to propose

319

— they both know that — but there is something unsaid that they both understand.

Not right now, he thinks. *But soon...*

They make a weekend of it. Mrs Finlayson is kind, considerate and discreet. She manages to find a turkey for them from her local butcher, and Charles produces a Christmas lunch in the little upstairs kitchen without too much going wrong. They visit a couple of pubs in the Old Town, wrap up well for walks by the sea, and spend a lot of time in bed, reading, snoozing and, carefully, making love. They feel like honeymooners.

On Sunday afternoon Charles drives Sally up to London and delivers her into her father's care. He returns, late, to Hastings, to find Mrs Finlayson waiting up for him to make sure all went well. They are now on first-name terms, and Charles knows that he and Sally have made a friend. He is even thinking about renting the flat on a long-term basis for use when he works out of the Chambers annex. Assuming all goes to plan.

CHAPTER TWENTY-SEVEN

Christmas has gone, and 1969 starts with a vengeance. Storms hurl rain and snow at the quiet seaside town, the windswept streets are empty and Charles is confined to his flat. He and Janet Finlayson fall into the routine of sharing a drink after their respective dinners, more often in her front lounge but sometimes in Charles's. Charles learns that she is from a large Catholic family, the eldest of seven siblings. Gerry, like Charles, was a bit of a tearaway, which explains Janet's sangfroid during the short-lived fracas with Robeson.

Then, a few days into January, Charles is called down to the telephone.

'It's your clerk,' says Mrs Finlayson, handing the receiver to Charles.

Now completely in Charles's confidence, she looks at him meaningfully and returns to her kitchen.

'Mr Holborne?'

'Yes, Barbara. Happy New Year.'

'And to you, sir. I'll come straight to it. The Krays' trial started last week. They've finished the evidence in the Cornell shooting and, according to Clive, who's been sitting in whenever he can, the McVitie evidence will start on Monday.'

'Thank you.'

'Are you going to come back?'

'Yes. I'll pack up today.'

There is silence at the other end of the line. Charles knows his senior clerk well enough to realise that she is winding up to say something he won't like. He gives her time.

'Are you sure that's wise, sir?' she says finally. 'I mean, why not wait it out down there? What's the point of coming back now, right at the death, and put yourself at risk?'

'For one thing, I'm bored out of my mind here.'

'I can resolve that for you. Yesterday's post brought three new sets of Instructions for the annex, two of them from Hastings firms. Ever heard of Morgan and Lamplugh?'

'No.'

'They're a well-regarded Hastings outfit doing crime and matrimonial law. I can clerk the cases from here until we employ someone down there, and you can have all three.'

'That is tempting, thank you, but I want to watch the trial, or at least some of it.'

'You want to taunt them,' says Barbara with surprising candour.

'Can you blame me? You don't know the half of it. They killed my cousin, for a start. Almost killed me outside the Bailey — remember that? — and threatened my family. I want the last laugh, and I'll get it when they're put away for good.'

There is a long silence from Barbara's end. Charles can hear typing, one-sided telephone conversations and other noises in the background.

'I had no idea,' she says quietly.

'No, well, you preferred not to know, and I was always careful not to make my position in Chambers even worse. Hopefully, if all goes well, it'll be the end soon. But I want to be there for the *coup de grâce*.'

'Very well, sir. Will you be at Wren Street?'

Charles thinks about that. 'No, perhaps not. I'll find somewhere else.'

Charles has seen many an infamous trial at the Old Bailey, the Central Criminal Court, including high profile murders, armed robberies, rapes and woundings. He has taken part in many such trials himself. However, even he has never seen such a scrum as that which awaits him outside the old court building. The entire thoroughfare is blocked by pushing and shouting members of the public — held back by straining bobbies in uniform — hoping to snatch a glimpse of the twins' arrival. Representatives of the press, radio and television from all corners of the globe jostle each other for pavement space. The queue for the public gallery stretches round the block and all the way to Holborn Viaduct.

Charles takes one look at the crowd and realises he will never get through it. He has planned for this eventuality. He retraces his steps and circles round to the rear entrance. Here too it is packed with people awaiting the arrival of the prison van. Charles bypasses the barred entrance to the yard and walks on a little further, towards a narrow pedestrian gate manned by two court officials.

'Hello, Ritchie,' he says to one of them.

'Blimey, Mr Holborne, sir. I almost didn't recognise you!'

'What, the beard?' asks Charles with a grin. 'Thought I'd see what I looked like without shaving,' he explains.

'And the clothes. You look completely different.'

The official indicates Charles's woollen hat, jeans and what looks like an army surplus greatcoat.

'Come on then, sir. We haven't got long.'

He stands back, lets Charles through the gate, and sets off into the building. Charles is led at confusing speed through a complex of staircases, doors and corridors. They finally emerge into a lobby he recognises. He is now at the head of the queue for the public gallery.

Ritchie speaks to an elderly woman who Charles suspects has been waiting on Old Bailey for several hours for a prime seat. 'This gentleman has a reserved seat, madam,' he says. 'Do you mind if he precedes you?'

The woman looks puzzled but shakes her head.

'Cheers, darling,' says Charles in a heavy Cockney accent, as he takes her place at the front of the queue.

'Top row, furthest from the door,' says Ritchie quietly in Charles's ear. 'There's a "Reserved" notice on the seat.'

'Much obliged to you, Ritchie. Give my love to Emma.'

Ritchie waves and hurries back to his duties.

A minute later, the door to the public gallery is opened and the queue files in.

Ritchie has been as good as his word. Charles's seat is perfect. He can look down and get a bird's-eye view of all the participants, but the curve of the panelled wall will allow him to lean sideways, out of sight of the dock.

Number 1 Court, below him, is filling up. He recognises most of the barristers representing the Crown and the multiple defendants: Kenneth Jones QC, John Leonard and James Crespi for the prosecution; John Platts-Mills and Ivan Lawrence for Ronnie Kray; Paul Wrightson and Monte Sherbourne for Reggie; and Desmond Vowden and Ronald Stewart for the twins' older brother, Charles. Including counsel for other members of the Firm and the hapless owner of the Regency Club, Anthony Barry, Charles counts seventeen or eighteen barristers, resembling, from above, three ranks of black and white penguins.

Every seat in the courtroom is taken. The press table and benches are full to bursting, many of the journalists having to work off their laps. Within seconds the public gallery too is full, and the Sergeant at Arms has to bar the way to scores of disappointed members of the public who, this day at least, will miss the criminal trial of the century. Charles sees, below him in the front row of the gallery, right in the centre, the Krays' mother, Violet.

The judge, the Right Honourable Sir Melford Stevenson, is as favourable a tribunal as Charles could have hoped for. A stern looking but not un-handsome man, he enjoyed a sparkling career at the Bar, including the defence of Ruth Ellis, the last woman ever to be hanged in Britain. Since being appointed to the bench however, he has developed a reputation as an eccentric, blatantly pro-prosecution judge and a savage sentencer.

The jury is led in. They have been sitting for several days, hearing the evidence regarding the shooting of George Cornell by Ronnie Kray at the *Blind Beggar* pub, and already they look like old hands, moving swiftly to their appointed seats on their two benches, clutching their pens and notebooks.

'All rise!'

The judge enters, Bar and Bench exchange low bows, and everyone takes their seats. Finally the clerk calls: 'Put up Ronald Kray, Reginald Kray, Charles Kray, John Barrie, Cornelius Whitehead, Christopher Lambrianou, Anthony Lambrianou, Frederick Foreman, Albert Donoghue and Anthony Barry!'

The door to the cells clangs open, and men start filing into the dock. There are so many of them that the clerk is still calling names by the time the first batch have taken their seats.

The three Kray brothers come up first. They look immaculate in expensive suits, freshly laundered shirts and silk ties. All have had their hair cut.

The twins turn immediately to the public gallery, nod and smile at their mother. They then give a half-bow to the judge and a respectful nod towards counsel.

It's a good performance, and for the first time a flicker of doubt flutters in Charles's chest. These men look less like gangsters than affluent company directors. Will the jury believe the barbarity, the unflinching cruelty, of which they are accused?

The accused men sit. Charles read in the newspapers that earlier in the proceedings Melford Stevenson had ordered the prisoners, at that time numbering eleven, to wear identification numbers around their necks. It was, he said, essential to assist the jury in telling one from the other. Protests by defence counsel failed to change his mind. There remained an impasse until, the following day, Ronnie Kray tore off the number from around his neck and threw it to the floor. The other prisoners followed suit, with the exception of Anthony Barry, whose counsel was astute enough to see how compliance would demonstrate his client's distinction from the others. All but Barry were returned to the cells. Melford Stevenson refused to proceed without the numbers and the prisoners refused to proceed with them.

The prisoners won. After further discussion it was agreed that numbers would be attached to the front of the dock to help with identification, but the men themselves would not be numbered like cattle.

Today, the first witness to be called is Mrs McVitie, the victim's widow. Counsel for the Krays asks if she agrees that her husband was a quarrelsome man. She admits that he had once had a row with Freddie Foreman, one of the men sitting just below Reggie Kray in the dock. Foreman is charged with being an accessory after the fact. The Crown's case against him is that he cleaned up the car that took the blood-spattered partygoers away from Blonde Carol's flat and later disposed of McVitie's body. For a short while Charles wonders if the Krays' case is to be that the murder was committed by Foreman as a result of a private feud but, to his surprise, the suggestion is not pursued further.

Mrs McVitie departs after a relatively short interrogation.

Platts-Mills QC stands. 'The Crown's next witness is Ronald Hart,' he announces.

Charles leans forward in his seat, his eyes boring into the Kray twins.

This is the moment, the reason he's taken the risk of coming. He wants to see their expressions.

The twins both turn to look behind them, at the door leading from the dock down into the cells. Ronald Hart, as a convicted murderer, will be produced from custody in his prison clothes. He will have to walk right past them, close enough to touch; he'll have no choice but to see their expressions; he will know exactly the stakes to himself and his loved ones if he says the wrong thing.

But the door doesn't open. There is no sound of footsteps, of keys or of manacles. Ronnie and Reggie look at one another, and frown.

Instead a door opens at the back of the courtroom.

'Ronald Hart?' shouts an usher. 'Mr Ronald Hart?'

There is a further sound from the back of the court and footsteps approach down the slope towards the witness box. All eyes in the court turn. Ronnie Hart, his face red and his dark hair neatly brushed back, approaches. He wears a suit and tie and looks almost as smart as the Kray twins themselves. Without looking at the men in the dock above him he marches to the witness box, climbs the two steps into it, and waits.

His appearance, clearly in civilian clothes and not produced from custody, causes a commotion in the dock, as if a hungry tomcat had been pitched suddenly into a box of pigeons. Ronnie and Reggie are each scribbling notes to be handed forward to their barristers. Two huddles of black-gowned barristers form in counsel's benches as the notes are read and absorbed.

Ronnie Kray's counsel is the first to speak. 'Would my learned friend for the Crown please confirm that this is, indeed, Mr Ronald Hart?'

Counsel for the Crown answers without standing. 'This is Hart.'

'Then, can it be explained to the Defence why this man is apparently at liberty, having been convicted last month for his part in McVitie's murder?'

That produces a set of puzzled expressions on the Crown's bench.

'This man has not been convicted of murder,' says prosecution counsel simply. 'He has turned Queen's Evidence and faces no charges.'

'He bloody well *was* convicted!' comes a woman's shout from the public gallery. All heads now turn to Violet Kray who has stood up. 'I was there,' she adds.

'You will be silent, madam, or you will be ejected from the court!' thunders Melford Stevenson.

'I repeat,' says leading counsel for the Crown, 'this man has never faced trial or been convicted of any part in McVitie's murder. He is a witness for the Crown. He was present at the party at Evering Road, and watched as Ronald and Reginald Kray tried to shoot McVitie and, when the gun failed to go off, stabbed him to death. And if my learned friends would settle down and let me get on with examining him, they will hear the evidence themselves.'

'I agree,' says Melford Stevenson. 'Unless you have any proper objection to this witness, you should sit down Mr Platts-Mills. Let the witness be sworn.'

Counsel resume their seats but Ronnie and Reggie Kray are still up in arms. Ronnie, his face suddenly drained of blood, is trying by facial expression alone to communicate something to his mother. She raises her hands helplessly. Charles leans sideways, out of Ronnie's line of sight. He so much wants to show himself, to reveal to the twins that he is, at least in part, responsible for their downfall, but common sense prevails. Better they are left with the conundrum and the belief that he is still behind bars.

Ronnie Hart proves to be an excellent witness. He describes, dispassionately, how he was ordered by the twins to go to the Regency Club and was relieved when Anthony Barry wouldn't allow any violence. He agrees that he was sent back to the club to order Barry to bring the gun to the party, and how he was told to wait, as a lookout, for McVitie's arrival. As McVitie descended the steps towards the front door it was his job to turn the record player up to drown the noise of the gunshot.

As to the murder itself, he describes how the gun didn't fire and Ronnie Bender tried to get it to work. When that failed, he said, Ronnie Kray pushed the carving knife into McVitie's back. Then he held McVitie by the arms while Reggie repeatedly stabbed him in the front, and finished him off by plunging the knife into his throat. His evidence is detailed, horrific and credible.

Charles watches as he is cross-examined. With each passing hour, the Krays' veneer of polished professionalism wears increasingly thin. The twins, particularly Ronnie, start shouting from the dock, spittle flying as they become wilder and angrier. Charles watches as the jury members start to regard them with distaste; then with horror. Throughout, Hart remains calm and his account consistent.

At the end, as counsel finally give up the attack, Charles decides it is safe to leave. There can be no doubt as to the verdict.

EPILOGUE

March 1969 is colder than average, with icy temperatures in London and frequent gales. Freezing fog closes Heathrow and leads to the loss of a French ship in the Channel.

However, inside the walls of Sunshine Court, with complete disregard for climatic conditions elsewhere, it remains a constant sweltering 75 degrees Fahrenheit. Charles has already divested himself of his coat and jacket and would remove another layer of clothing but for the embarrassment of sitting in the overheated dining area in his vest and suit trousers.

He has been reading the newspaper to his father. Harry wanted to hear, yet again, the report of the Krays' sentencing. Life imprisonment for the twins, with a recommendation for a minimum term of thirty years, the longest sentence ever handed down at the Old Bailey for murder. Four other Firm members also received life sentences for their roles in the Cornell and McVitie killings. Charles Kray, the older brother, got ten years for being an accessory after the fact, in other words, assisting with the cover-up and the disposal of McVitie's body.

The only defendant to be found not guilty was Anthony Barry, whose counsel managed to persuade the jury that his client was, indeed, acting under duress when forced to take the non-functioning pistol to Carol Skinner's flat. In Charles's opinion, it was a masterstroke by the Crown's legal team to have included Barry on the indictment. Many would have accepted his account and called him as a prosecution witness, but by prosecuting him with the Krays, his counsel was able to cross-examine the Crown's witnesses in a way that the Crown itself could not. By revealing the ruthlessness of the Krays and the terror they used to rule the East End, he certainly contributed to the Crown's victory.

The Krays and their Firm are finished. Like the Messina and Richardson brothers before them, they will fade into criminal history. A few associates remain at liberty and, of course, those former accomplices who collaborated with the prosecution. But no one is in any doubt: their reign of terror is over.

Harry listens intently as Charles reads, painstakingly feeding himself triangular sandwiches of smoked salmon, and occasionally gripping Charles's arm when Charles reaches sections of Melford Stevenson's sentencing remarks of which he particularly approves.

After a while Harry's hand slackens and his head drops. Charles looks at his sleeping father and folds up the newspaper. The concentration required to attend to Charles for a prolonged period is hard enough in itself, but that and the effort required of Harry to feed himself have combined to exhaust him.

Charles places the newspaper on the table before him and looks at his watch again. Sally is taking the baby to meet the clerks at Chancery Court before joining him here. David and Sonia will come by later, before the Sabbath starts.

Leia is now six weeks old, having been born two days after Sally's due date. The issue of her surname — Fisher or Holborne — is still slightly unclear, even to her parents. Now that the Firm is no more and the Krays are safely behind bars, Charles feels lighter and more optimistic than he has for years. He is surprised how much difference it has made. For the first time, he can plan without looking over his shoulder.

His first order of business is his relationship with Sally. He has been waiting for an appropriate moment to propose. Sally suspects that a proposal is imminent, and waits, with as much patience as she can muster. His more expansive ideas — a weekend trip to Paris was once a favourite — have been scotched by the arrival of their daughter, but he has confided in David and remains adamant that he can still come up with something special and romantic.

He looks up as Millie makes a noise. She too was asleep, in a dining room chair next to Harry's, and the carers have taken the opportunity of feeding other residents their lunches first.

She opens her eyes. Her gaze lands directly on Charles.

'Hello, Mum,' he says, standing briefly to plant a kiss on her cheek. 'I didn't like to wake you.'

Millie doesn't answer.

Andrea had been right. Millie's period in hospital did indeed result in a permanent downturn in her condition. It is impossible to tell if it was caused by the infections themselves or by the fact that, while in hospital, Millie ate little, remained unstimulated in her bed, or was traumatised by her separation from Harry and her familiar surroundings. Whatever the cause, by the time she rejoined Harry she was a different person, her cognition significantly worse than when she left.

Charles still finds the change in her shocking. She is now unable to focus for more than a few seconds before her attention and her gaze wander off. She speaks rarely and, when she does, she struggles to articulate her words. The last time Charles visited, she desperately wanted to convey something but only managed a series of sibilant proto-words. She sounded like a stylus trapped by a scratch on one of her old 78s. After several failed attempts she turned away, her eyes shut tight with failure and frustration.

Charles has even begun to find consolation in his mother's *refusal* to converse with him. On such occasions her frown and her deliberately averted gaze still say *"I'm not talking to you"* — an indication that *some* thought process is still at work. Maybe, he thinks, her animus towards me will be the last thing to disappear.

'Would you like a cup of tea?' he asks.

Millie looks towards him. She doesn't focus on him completely, but she nods briefly.

Charles stands and walks to the kitchen area.

A woman bustles up to him. 'You should be in the staff room. The meeting's about to start,' she says.

'No, Anne, it was cancelled,' reassures Charles. 'Why don't you go and put your feet up?'

Anne, a pencil-thin woman in her late eighties, was headteacher at a well-known girls' school. Despite retiring over twenty years earlier, she remains locked in a never-ending quest for a staff meeting. She has taken to addressing Charles as if he was her deputy head, and seems to find it soothing when he enters into her confused world. He reassures her that the meeting has been cancelled, or the supply teacher has arrived, or the field trip has returned from the coast, whichever particular concern is at that moment making her anxious. Sometimes he is even able to persuade her to stop her ceaseless pacing of the corridors. Usually, within a very few minutes, she will be up again, asking the next person she encounters where the staff meeting is being held.

He greets a couple of the carers while he waits for the kettle to boil. He carries over two mugs of tea, one with double handles to minimise the risk of Millie spilling hers. She will still only drink tea when it is scalding hot, hotter than the home will allow it to be served, which is probably why the few drinks brought to her by staff are ignored and remain, stewed and cold, beside her.

She reaches up for the mug and starts sipping, watching Charles over the rim. The intensity of her gaze is disconcerting. Andrea would say that she isn't thinking of anything in particular, or perhaps somewhere in the recesses of her broken memory she's trying to remember who Charles is. He disagrees. There is cool appraisal in that stare, and in it he thinks he detects frank dislike.

He reaches over and dabs a dribble of tea off her chin with the flannel he always carries whenever helping her to eat or drink.

'So, who's the series of leaking orifices now?' he says gently, smiling, wondering if she remembers how she once, memorably, characterised his early childhood.

She turns her head away, but whether it's to avoid the contact with her chin or in response to his comment is unclear.

Charles returns to the newspaper, but after reading for no more than two minutes he looks across at Millie. Her eyes are closed again and the mug is held loosely in her lap. He reaches over and removes it.

The lift door opens and Sally enters, Leia in her arms. Charles rises to greet her. They kiss, and Charles bends his head to touch the soft down on his daughter's scalp with his lips. He breathes in her sweet milky scent, looks up at Sally and smiles.

'Isn't that the most wonderful smell in the world?' he asks softly, an oft-repeated exclamation.

Sally smiles at him wanly. She is exhausted anyway, rising at least twice per night to breast-feed, but she looks out on her feet.

'Too much?' asks Charles.

'In retrospect, yes. They were all lovely with her, but yes, a bit too early.'

'Come and sit down,' says Charles, leading her to a vacant chair on the other side of his father.

'Do you think it would be all right to feed her here?' asks Sally, settling into the armchair. 'She's been grizzling on and off all the way back.'

'I can't see why not,' replies Charles.

As Sally gets Leia positioned to be fed, one of the carers approaches Charles. She has a tray in her hands on which there rests a single white plate and a dessert spoon. Since Millie's aspiration pneumonia and the realisation that she can no longer swallow reliably, all her food has been puréed. Forming a multi-coloured triangle on the plate are three equidistant half-spheres of purée: brown, orange and green. It could be an Andy Warhol painting. Food as pop art, thinks Charles.

'Your mother has not eaten yet, has she?' asks the carer.

She's new, or perhaps a supply carer, as Charles has not met her before. Her nametag says she is "Iris".

'Not yet.'

Iris leans over Millie. 'Hello, Millie?' she says.

Millie doesn't immediately respond, but Iris picks up the old woman's hand and squeezes it gently. 'Millie,' she repeats.

Millie opens her eyes.

'Are you hungry, dear?'

Millie makes no verbal response, but she sits herself a little more upright in her chair.

'Good.' Iris pulls up a chair and is about to sit when she turns to Charles. 'Would you like to do it?' she asks.

'Sure,' replies Charles.

He stands and takes the tabard that lay folded over the back of Millie's chair, pulling it carefully over her head. He pushes her chair closer to the table and sits beside her.

He raises the spoon and hesitates over the three coloured foods. The menu on the noticeboard announces that today's meal is veal cutlet, spaghetti in tomato sauce and peas. He looks again at the plate, lifts a spoon of brown and sniffs experimentally. It does, actually, smell of meat, but whether Charles would have known that had he not seen the menu he couldn't say. He offers it to Millie.

She's looking in his general direction, but her eyes are unfocused. He touches the spoon gently to her lower lip once, twice, and on the third attempt her mouth opens and she takes some food off the spoon. She makes a movement with her mouth — not quite chewing and not quite sucking — but most of the food disappears and she opens her mouth again without being prompted. Charles opts for orange this time, the smell of which is unmistakeably tomato sauce, and she accepts it.

Iris is waiting behind Millie's chair, watching how Charles is getting on. Satisfied, she says, 'That's good,' but the sound of her voice distracts Millie, whose head turns away from Charles.

Charles reaches with his free hand and strokes Millie's pale cheek to attract her attention. She turns her face, very slowly, back towards him.

'More veal?' he asks, lifting the spoon.

She raises the hand closest to him. For a second he thinks that she's about to mirror his gesture and stroke his face, but her hand lands on his and she pushes it and the spoon down gently towards the table. If that's all she's going to eat, thinks Charles, it's not enough, and he's about to try again when he looks into her eyes. This time it's undeniable: she recognises him.

'Well, hello there, Mrs Horowitz,' he says, lightly. 'How nice to see you again.'

Her mouth moves and she swallows. She looks directly into Charles's eyes. 'I used to hate you,' she says simply and with complete clarity.

Charles nods slowly. 'Yes,' he says. 'I know.'

He does know. He's always known, really. She's just never said it before. But to his surprise, it doesn't matter any longer. It seems such a very long time ago. He raises the spoon again to her mouth. 'Have a bit more, Mum.'

She opens her mouth and he moves the spoon towards her, but it seems she's not ready to take another mouthful; she has more to say. She repeats her earlier gesture, gently pushing his hand down to the table. 'But I love you now,' she says.

Charles's hand falters as he hears the words. She is looking straight at him and he knows she's entirely aware of what she's saying.

'Good,' he says finally. 'I love you too,' he adds and, rather to his surprise, he finds he means it.

The pressure on his hand ceases and she accepts a spoonful of brown.

The light of recognition fades from Millie's eyes as she disappears into whatever recesses of her being remain to her, but her mouth continues to open, suck and close automatically. Charles continues patiently to feed her. From behind him, Sally's hand touches the back of his neck. It remains there, soothing and loving, as Charles's tears form a small puddle on the shiny table surface.

HISTORICAL NOTE

As regular readers will know, I have been weaving Charles's story into that of the Kray twins for the whole of the 1960s. Less fictionalisation was required in this book than in many of the others, for the main strands of the police investigation, the charges faced by members of the Firm and the trial are all as set out here. Detective Superintendent Leonard "Nipper" Read managed what several senior police officers before him failed to do: he persuaded members of the public and members of the Firm to give evidence against the Kray twins. He did it by keeping his investigation separate from the rest of the corrupt Metropolitan Police, by choosing his team members with care, and by being completely straight with the people he interviewed. They knew they could trust him when he said that he would protect them from the Krays and when he offered them deals in return for giving evidence for the Crown.

As portrayed herein, the principal mistake made by Ronald Kray, and which led to the Firm's downfall, was his misplaced trust in McVitie to kill Leslie Payne. That hopelessly amateurish and botched assassination only succeeded in pushing Payne into Read's arms. The twins' second mistake was to try to force Ronnie Hart to accept responsibility for McVitie's murder. That too persuaded Hart that his only recourse was to tell Read the entire story and to turn Queen's Evidence. No one was more surprised than Superintendent Read when Ronnie Hart turned up in the wee small hours at Tintagel House, ready to hand himself in and give a statement. The Krays never believed for one minute that their own cousin would turn against them in this way, and the astonishment and fury portrayed in the book, albeit occurring at the magistrates' court, is exactly what occurred.

As for the mock trial, both I and barrister colleagues have pored over it to decide if it could possibly have occurred without breaking the criminal law. Our conclusion is that we can find no criminal offences in existence in 1968 that would render it impossible. As stated in the text, trespassing on a government building would have been tortious and could in theory attract civil damages, but absent any criminal damage thereto, would not have constituted a criminal offence. I therefore felt justified in allowing Charles to pull off the courtroom "sting" so as to divert the Krays' attention from Ronnie Hart. It was also handy to mislead them into believing that Charles was finished as a barrister and therefore could no longer be blackmailed. If any of my legally-trained readers disagree, and can find the authority which would have made Charles's mock trial a criminal offence, I'd be interested to hear chapter and verse (although I doubt it will prompt a revision of the text!).

A NOTE TO THE READER

Dear Reader,

Nowadays, reviews by knowledgeable readers are essential to authors' success, so if you enjoyed the novel I shall be in your debt if you would spare the few seconds required to post a review on **Amazon** and **Goodreads**. I love hearing from readers, and you can connect with me through my **Facebook page**, via **Twitter** or through my **website**, where you can sign up for my newsletter.

Simon

www.simonmichael.uk

Sapere Books is an exciting new publisher of brilliant fiction and popular history.

To find out more about our latest releases and our monthly bargain books visit our website:
saperebooks.com

Made in the USA
Las Vegas, NV
18 April 2023

70777862R00193